"Nancy Haddo..."

—Ali Brandon, *New York Times* bestselling author of
the Black Cat Bookshop Mysteries

"It doesn't get any better than this! Nancy Haddock's debut mystery is the perfect mix of intelligence and charm. The characters are varied and appealing, the setting is engaging and so vivid you can smell the flowers and taste the fried okra, and the plot is intricate and clever."

—Jennie Bentley, *New York Times* and *USA Today* bestselling author of the Do-It-Yourself Mysteries

"A slew of townsfolk I'd love to meet—as well as a few I wouldn't—all combined into a delightful and tasty mystery full of intrigue and twists . . . *Basket Case* is full of Southern charm, food . . . and mystery."

—Linda O. Johnston, author of
the Barkery & Biscuits Mysteries

"Ms. Haddock, a masterful writer, obviously has humor running through her DNA and mystery deep within her bones. You can't help but admire her 'silver' characters' energy, smarts, and loyalty. I wish I had that much oomph in my gas tank. Add a bright and funny niece along with a handsome detective, villains who deserve their comeuppance, and this book hooks you. I'm looking forward to many more Silver Six books."

—L. A. Sartor, author of *Viking Gold*

Berkley Prime Crime titles by Nancy Haddock

BASKET CASE
PAINT THE TOWN DEAD

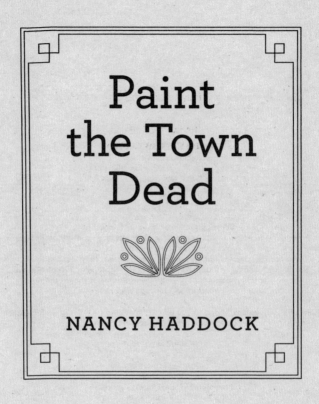

Paint the Town Dead

NANCY HADDOCK

BERKLEY PRIME CRIME
New York

BERKLEY PRIME CRIME
Published by Berkley
An imprint of Penguin Random House LLC
375 Hudson Street, New York, New York 10014

Copyright © 2016 by Nancy K. Haddock
Penguin Random House supports copyright. Copyright fuels creativity, encourages
diverse voices, promotes free speech, and creates a vibrant culture. Thank you for buying
an authorized edition of this book and for complying with copyright laws by not
reproducing, scanning, or distributing any part of it in any form without permission.
You are supporting writers and allowing Penguin Random House to continue to
publish books for every reader.

BERKLEY is a registered trademark and BERKLEY PRIME CRIME and the B colophon
are trademarks of Penguin Random House LLC.

ISBN: 9780425275733

First Edition: September 2016

Printed in the United States of America
1   3   5   7   9   10   8   6   4   2

Cover art by Ann Wertheim
Cover design by Diana Kolsky
Book design by Kristin del Rosario

*To Jerry for your support, your insights,
and the occasional kick in the pants.*

And for loving me.

Acknowledgments

I always risk leaving someone out of this section. If you aren't here, please know that you are appreciated and thanked!

I'm beyond grateful to Leis Pederson, my former editor, and to Allison Janice, my amazing new editor! Two awesome stars I'm blessed to have in my galaxy!

Heartfelt thanks to Roberta Brown, agent and soul sister. Words fail, but you know how I feel, Roberta!

Many thanks to the people of Magnolia, Arkansas, for welcoming me, answering my questions, and clarifying so very many points. Among my research angels are Dana Thornton, Columbia County Library; Megan, CID Secretary, and Heather, Sheriff's Secretary, both of the Columbia County Sheriff's Office; Brenda, Columbia County Prosecutor's Office; and Randy Reed, Columbia County Coroner. For this book in particular, I spoke with Jerri Lethiew of the Columbia County Co-op Extension Services, the Rev. Bruce T. Heyvaert, Vicar of the St. James Episcopal Church, and Donna Pittman King of Pittman's Nursery. Fantastic conversations! Thank you! Angela Flurry Lester and Deb Baker of Magnolia Cove™ also provided inspiration and information in and on Magnolia. Deb also created the most amazing soap for me to give as swag. Aster's Garden Soap rocks, Deb, and so do you!

I also extend my deep appreciation to artisans Bonnie Eastwood, Colleen Thompson, and Melissa Watson.

Big 'ole tubs of thanks to my critique buddies, my writing friends, and my writer retreat sisters. In no particular order, they are Katelin Maloney, Julie Benson, Sandy Blair, Lynne Smith, Nancy Quatrano, Lorraine Heath, Neringa Bryant, and L.A. Sartor. Y'all will never know how much you mean to me, but I'll keep trying to tell you.

Thanks also to Barbara Berry of Sapulpa, Oklahoma, and to the other unsung heroes in my life. Whether kin or neighbors, these folks were second parents, mentors, and friends to me and mine. Deepest gratitude to the families Allen, Berry, Bingman, Davis, Lindenberg, Livermore, Jones, Kidd, Masters, Maulding, Price, and so many more.

Abiding appreciation for the caffeine and support to my friends at Starbucks #8484, Barnes & Noble #2796, Second Read Books, and the Anastasia Island Branch of the St. Johns County Library system!

Last but never least, thanks to my children for their love and unwavering encouragement.

Oh, and hubby. If you haven't noticed, this one's for you!

Chapter One

"NIXY! NIXY, CHILD, WE'RE WAITING FOR YOU."

"On my way," I yelled down the stairs from my apartment.

I paused long enough to eye myself in the large oval mirror in the small entryway. Yep, I'd applied mascara to both sets of lashes. That should've been a given, but I'd been known to miss a set. Especially since I'd gone makeup-free for the past month. No point in primping when I'd spent my waking hours sanding, staining, and sealing nearly every surface of this old building. I'd even learned to wield a power sprayer to paint the twelve-foot-high walls and ceilings, and exposed ductwork. We'd installed three new fire-rated entry-exit doors, two roll-up service doors, and security cameras and alarms. We'd also made improvements to the kitchenette and bathroom in back of the store proper. Now the place shone, and we were ready for our grand opening.

By the way, I'm Leslee Stanton Nix, known to pretty much everyone as Nixy. The "we" who were waiting for me were my Aunt Sherry Mae Stanton Cutler and her five housemates, collectively known as the Silver Six. They lived together in Sherry's farmhouse and were closer than blood family. The Six were in their late sixties and early seventies, but they'd worked every bit as hard and long as I had to renovate the twenty-seven-hundred-square-foot building that housed my apartment, the storefront, and the workroom. They were every bit as invested in the success of our new folk art and crafts gallery as I was. Oops. Not a gallery. The Six thought "gallery" sounded too highfalutin, aka expensive, for Lily-vale. We'd settled on naming our enterprise The Handcraft Emporium.

"Nixy! Doralee will be here in twenty minutes!"

"Coming!"

I clambered down the interior staircase leading to the building's back room. This space was as wide as a three-car garage, though not as deep, and it served as Fix-It Fred's workshop. However, we'd decided to use it as an arts and crafts classroom as needed. This evening it was needed for our Gorgeous Gourds class.

Fred scowled at me. "You know you sounded like a thundering herd trompin' down them stairs, don't you, missy?"

"Thundering herd?" I echoed, grinning.

"You laugh, but steep as those steps are, you're gonna fall and break a bone someday when nobody's here to help you."

"Point taken, Fred. I'll slow down."

"Nixy, child, how do we look?" asked Sherry.

I realized the Six stood in a line, as if for inspection as our former U.S. Navy nurse Maise Holcomb—who stood beside the others with her shoulders proudly thrown back and her eyes front—would say. We'd decided on a kind of uniform for the store, and so had ordered both short-sleeved forest green polo shirts and aprons in the same color, each with *Handcraft Emporium* embroidered in white above the left breast. Tonight Dab, Maise, Fred, and I wore the shirts while Sherry, Aster, and Eleanor wore the aprons. Most of us paired the emporium wear with blue jeans and tennis shoes. Dapper Dab—Dwight Aloysius Baxter, to be precise—and Fix-It Fred Fishner had donned their typical gear with their shirts. For Dab, polyester pants and loafers, and overalls for Fred.

Elegant Eleanor Wainwright was the exception to casual. A beautiful black woman with an ageless complexion, her style ran to timeless, tailored outfits, much dressier than the rest of us usually wore. Tonight she'd paired blue linen slacks, a matching blouse, and low-heeled pumps with the emporium apron, and still looked like she belonged in a fashion magazine. I imagined she'd wear only the apron. Never the polo shirt. And that was fine by me.

In fact, to borrow a Fred-phrase, I'd bet my last nuts and bolts the shirts and aprons would fall by the wayside sooner than later. Probably even mine, but the Silver Six were rocking them tonight.

I smiled at them in turn. "Y'all look fantastic, but are you comfortable?"

"I am," Dab said.

"I do believe the aprons and shirts turned out quite well," Eleanor declared.

Aunt Sherry ran her hand down the front of her apron. "These are wonderfully soft, too."

"I'm so glad we went with the hemp fabric," Aster Parsons added. Aster was Maise's sister, our throwback hippie, and all-things-herbal expert. She carried lavender oil mixed with water, and sprayed at will. "Hemp is sustainable, you know."

"We know, and this color will hide dirt and dust smudges," Maise said.

"Considering how thoroughly y'all have cleaned, I don't think we'll get too dirty," I soothed. "Does the shirt work for you, Fred?"

"I ain't used to working with a collar around my neck, but it's okay."

Fix-It Fred was a walking hardware store in bib overalls. Tonight's dark denim pair partly covered the embroidery on the polo shirt, but he did look spiffy. The many tools he stuck into each of his dozen pockets stood soldier straight.

Maise clapped her hands. "Time's ticking. Is everything shipshape for the class?"

I looked over the room setup. Two four-foot folding tables were in place for Doralee Gordon, the gourd class instructor. She'd face the wall separating the workroom from the store. Two similar tables held refreshments at the back of the room. Four eight-foot solid wood tables, which Fred used for workbenches, were positioned in a semicircle to give all the students a good view of Doralee. The arrangement accommodated sixteen students, four per table, a roll of paper towels at each place.

We'd scrounged a variety of barstools to use for classes, and duct-taped green plastic dollar store tablecloths to catch paint spills. Fred's table surfaces were pretty much beyond harm, but Eleanor had insisted that the tablecloths gave them a clean, unmarred, less well-worn look.

"It's perfect, Maise. We only have eleven paid students, including you, Sherry, and Fred, but this gives us room for walk-ins." If we had any. I hoped we would.

Sherry patted my arm. "Even eleven is a good turnout for our first guest instructor. It will take time to build a following. Besides, it's June. People are taking vacations."

"I hadn't thought of that."

"Chin up, child. It's all good."

I blinked at Sherry's use of slang, then blinked again as all the seniors but Fred headed through the door into the emporium proper.

"Where are y'all going?"

Sherry gave me a wave. "I told Doralee to park out back, but we'll be mingling in the store, where I can watch for her in case she forgets."

"And we're still training Jasmine," Maise tossed over her

shoulder as she and Aster scooted out. "We'll send her back to help Doralee unload."

Eleanor followed. "I do believe that girl is a splendid addition to the business. She'll bring in the younger crowd."

"Maise assigned me to pass out name tags as the students arrive," Dab said as he strode out, his pants riding on his bony hips.

When the door closed behind the exodus, I chuckled, knowing that their true mission was to fuss over and re-arrange their individual art displays.

I cocked a brow at Fred. "You're not going out front?"

"Nope, out back. Got all my tools and projects locked up," he said, gesturing at the wall of richly patinated pine cabinets, some open-shelved, some with doors and padlocks. "I told Ida Bollings to park in the lot out there, so I'll go keep a lookout for her."

"You're seeing Ida, Fred?"

He winked. "What can I say? I got a weakness for dames with hot wheels."

"Wheels as in her big blue Buick or that new walker she's sporting?"

"Both. Besides, she's bringing her famous pear bread."

With that he clanked-clunked his walker, loaded tool belt fastened to the front of it, out the new door that led to the alley and the parking lot just beyond it. I didn't know how much Fred needed the walker to steady his steps versus how much he simply wanted to keep all his tools near to hand. I did know he lifted the walker more than he scooted it. He'd developed the arm muscles of a weightlifter to show for it. And it tickled me that he had a thing for Pear Bread Lady Ida.

When the door closed behind Fred with a solid *thunk*, I noticed I'd left the nearby door that led up to my apartment open. I crossed to shut it, then turned to gaze around the room. I took a deep breath, basking in the quiet for a moment.

The last month had been exhausting, and the next week would be another whirlwind. Thank goodness Jasmine

Young was doing a work-study program through the Business and Marketing Department at the technical college, and had chosen to do it with us. With skin the color of rich chocolate, she was enthusiastic about crafts and eager to learn the business, and all for minuscule pay, store discounts, and free classes if she wanted to take them. Since she had opted to take tonight's class from six thirty to eight thirty, Dab, Eleanor, and Aster would man the store.

Doralee Gordon should be here any old time now. I sure hoped she'd bring all the supplies she'd need. She'd seemed well organized when I confirmed the class details by phone, and what I'd seen of her art pieces lived up to her business's name: Hello, Gourdgeous. But if she'd forgotten anything key to teaching the class, we'd have a roomful of unhappy students.

Tomorrow we'd celebrate the first day of our grand opening and host a week of prize drawings, demonstrations, and discounts that we hoped would bring in buyers as well as lookers. Since three of the Silver Six, including Aunt Sherry, were folk artists themselves, they knew hundreds of other folk artists and craftspeople in our little part of southwest Arkansas and all over the state. A gratifying number of those artists had agreed to have their work sold in the emporium. In fact, we'd had such an overwhelming response, the store was well past full and verging toward cluttered territory.

Okay, so maybe only I found the space cluttered. I'd worked in a Houston fine art gallery where we carefully balanced featured pieces with negative, blank space, so being in the stuffed emporium made me feel claustrophobic early on. Now I was getting used to the shelves and display tables cheerily overflowing, Sherry's baskets hanging from the ceiling, quilts bursting with color hanging on racks, and several dress forms crowding the floor in a quirky formation. We even arranged some of the crafts on lipped benches out on the sidewalk. I'd worried about thefts, but Sherry had assured me the goods would be safe. And Aster spritzed me with her infamous lavender water to calm me. An outside security camera would've been more practical than lavender, but we'd had three installed inside. One provided a partial view of the sidewalk, which would have to do for now.

Still, with the crowded condition in the store, and artists counting on sales to boost their incomes, I sure hoped we sold a lot of merchandise during the grand opening. We needed to launch the store on Friday and Saturday with a super big bang because we'd be closed on Sunday. That's the day Sherry Mae had decided to rededicate the Stanton family cemetery. Aster had already smudged the graveyard to clear negativity by burning sage, cedar, lavender, and something else I couldn't recall now. Sherry, though, had wanted a formal blessing, and had sweet-talked her Episcopal priest into doing the honors. She'd also insisted on holding an outdoor reception following the short ceremony. Her farmhouse sat on half a city block, so she'd invited the whole town to attend.

I hoped for a much smaller turnout. I still shuddered, remembering why we were blessing the cemetery at all, and I didn't want to spend the afternoon rehashing those events of just eight weeks ago.

I glanced at the oversized wall clock hung near the stairway to my loft apartment. Dang, where was Doralee? I'd barely finished the thought when Jasmine flew through the store door wearing her emporium T-shirt and nearly bouncing with excitement.

"She's here, Miss Nixy. Just pulling around back."

"GOOD TO MEET YOU, NIXY, JASMINE," DORALEE SAID with a firm handshake when we met at her SUV. "This is my gentleman friend, Zach Dalton."

"Nice to meet you both," he said, meeting my gaze, then Jasmine's, his voice on the soft-spoken side, but pleasing.

"I hope you don't mind me bringing him to the class," Doralee continued. "He's going to act as my assistant, and then we're making a weekend of it in Lilyvale."

"Are you staying at the Inn on the Square?" I asked as her gentleman went to the back of the car to begin unloading. Jasmine joined him.

"Yes. We haven't checked in yet, but I understand we don't have to. Not in the usual way, I mean."

"You're right." I knew Clark and Lorna Tyler, the owners of the Lilies Café and Inn on the Square, so I knew the drill. "Just enter the code Lorna e-mailed you at the alley door and go up the stairs. A small jog to the left, and you'll be in the hall. Your name will be on the door of your room and the key will be inside."

"Good to know, thanks. I'd better help unload."

I followed, and took the handle of one rolling bin while Jasmine took the second one. Zach carried the large box of gourds. The box was awkward, but not heavy, Doralee said.

"Even a box of large gourds is fairly lightweight."

Sherry had told me Doralee Gordon was fifty-five, but her chin-length golden brown hair and her cheerful smile made her look younger. Zach was probably in his early to mid-fifties, too. Trim and handsome, he dressed as country-casual as Doralee, and had kind hazel eyes almost the same color as hers. As he helped us arrange class materials on the tables, he worked quietly, but was quick to smile. He exuded a Zen-like calm that balanced Doralee's high-energy chatter.

When all the bottles of paint, the brushes, and handouts were set on the tables, Doralee greeted not only Sherry and the gang, but also the students as they came in. We'd made stick-on name tags printed in large block letters so the students wouldn't be anonymous faces. Doralee took advantage of our efforts and began to call people by name.

The class filed into the workroom, friends chatting with

each other. I'd been a bit surprised when Maise, Sherry, and Fred had opted to take the class. I hadn't wanted them to pay at all, but when they protested the freebie, I insisted on giving them a discount rate. I was curious and a bit concerned about Sherry wanting to learn gourd art. She'd always crafted baskets. Perhaps she wanted to branch out or away from her basket weaving due to the macular degeneration, but I hadn't asked for her reasons. I did notice she'd let her hair fall over her left eye, and with her bangs blocking that eye, she could focus better using her right one.

Sherry, Maise, and Jasmine shared the table closest to the refreshments so they could hostess at the break. Ida Bollings also shared their table, taking a seat at the far end where she could park her new walker out of the way. Fred's walker was next to Ida's, and he sat beside her on the tractor-seat stool he'd brought from his old workshop at the farmhouse.

At Sherry's request, I introduced Doralee, and then stood in the back ready to assist if needed. Zach took an empty spot at the far table, but we still had room for four walk-ins. Not that I figured anyone else would come this late, but I shrugged that aside and snapped a few pictures to post on our in-the-works website pages.

"Welcome, everyone," Doralee began. "First, my thanks to Sherry and Aster for inviting me to teach you about gourd art, and to Nixy for her lovely introduction. Second, thank you for being here this evening. I hope you'll enjoy the class. Now, if you have questions as I go along, just holler. Let's begin with a quick history about the use of hard shell gourds."

And off she went, telling the class about the different kinds of gourds, how she came to work with them, and the ways to craft with gourds. She then passed around samples of her various gourd art, from simple birdhouses, to gourds with designs etched using a woodburning tool, to beautifully painted gourds. She said gourds had been called nature's pottery, and I could see why.

"Why is a thick gourd better?" Sherry asked.

"They're more durable, and easier to work with, too. The longer the growing season, and the drier the gourds are before they're cut from the vine, the better."

"Where do you get your gourds?" a lady in front asked.

"There are farms around the country you can order from, Ann. I get mine from an organic farm in California."

"Is it hard to grow your own gourds?"

Doralee tilted her head. "I can't really speak to that, Deena, because I've never tried growing my own. I'm sure the local nurseries, agricultural extension, or the technical college could help you find that information. Be aware that cleaning gourds is a messy process. Whether you're cleaning gourds or cutting, chiseling, or wood-burning them, rubber gloves are recommended, and wearing a dust mask or respirator is an absolute must. I also work in a smock. Generally, I'm not a sloppy painter, but I have my moments."

When the audience members muttered and glanced at their own clothing, Doralee held up a hand.

"Not to worry about getting spills or splats on yourselves tonight. I brought oversized T-shirts to wear if you want to protect your clothes. Any more questions?"

"Do gourds rot?"

"Not if they're properly dried, Jasmine. Gourd farms use all the correct drying procedures, so unless you plan to grow your own or you soak the ones you buy for any reason, rot won't be an issue."

"What do you use your decorated gourds for?" Ida asked. "What I mean is, are these used for flower vases, or anything practical?"

"Painted and carved gourds can be sculptures in and of themselves, purely ornamental. However, they can also be used as vases, pencil holders, card holders. Again, depending on the shape and size—and your vision—they can have a variety of uses. One artist I know turned a huge gourd into a cat bed. Birdhouses, as I mentioned earlier, can be made from a plain, unadorned gourd, or be painted or otherwise decorated."

"How many kinds of gourds did you say there are?"

"If I name them all, Ginger, I'll sound like Forrest Gump." The students chuckled and Doralee grinned. "Seriously, there are at least eight to ten kinds of shapes, and some lend themselves to a project better than others. I like to examine each gourd and let it spark my imagination as to what it will be."

Doralee glanced at her watch. "We're due to have refreshments, and I know you probably want to get to the fun part—painting your gourds. Does anyone have another question before we break? No? Let's go nosh, and then paint."

I snagged a piece of Ida's pear bread, but left the three kinds of cookies Maise, Aster, Eleanor, and Sherry had baked to the students. We'd opted to serve only bottled water to reduce spills, but no one seemed to mind.

When class resumed, Doralee asked me to pass out gourds. I grabbed stacks of tees, too, and placed them at the ends of the tables. Class members could snag one if they chose.

"Now these bottle gourds are all about the same shape," she said as she donned her smock. A white one with liberal drops and drips of paint colors from butter yellow to blue-black. "I brought a small size so you could finish tonight, and I removed the neck so they'd be easier to handle. You'll find a variety of acrylic paint colors on the table, and some summery and patriotic stencils and sponges if you want a design on your gourd but don't want to freehand. I'll circulate to give you help if you need it."

I stood at the back, ready to assist again, which I figured would be about the time students needed to rinse their paintbrushes. Doralee had brought clear plastic tubs that I'd put by the utility sink, and I started that way to fill them, when the emporium door banged open.

A scowling, burly man stomped into the workroom, and pointed at Doralee.

"Doralee Boudreaux, where do you get off teaching classes?" the man loudly demanded. "You learned everything you know from me. I should be the one up there."

Chapter Two

I MOVED WITHOUT THINKING, BLOCKING THE ANGRY man's path even as Dab charged behind the intruder, clearly outraged. Before either of us could so much as speak a stern word to the man, Doralee cleared her throat with an attention-grabbing "Ahem."

"My name is no longer Boudreaux, Ernie. It's Gordon again, as you well know," she said firmly. "Had you been here at the start of the class, you'd know I did mention you and your birdhouses. Class, this is Ernie Boudreaux, my ex-husband. Who didn't teach me quite everything I know."

She said the last bit with a twinkle in her eyes, but no one made a peep for a long moment. Then Jasmine piped up.

"I don't care who the flip he is. He made me mess up my gourd."

A few students snickered. Ernie flushed but didn't retreat.

"Not to worry, Jasmine, I'll help you fix it. Zach, would you be a dear and fill a few of those little tubs with water?"

I'd been so focused on Doralee, I'd forgotten her gentle-man friend had been sitting at the far table. He'd obviously risen when Ernie burst in because he was already on his feet. With a nod to Doralee, he went to the utility sink.

"Thank you. A wonderful reason to use acrylics, class, is that it's a forgiving medium on a hard surface like a gourd," Doralee continued, going right on with class, and, bless her, heading directly to Jasmine as she spoke.

She didn't spare Ernie another glance. I still stood directly in front of him, and took a step closer to really shift his attention away from Doralee. Dab flanked me.

"Time to leave, Mr. Boudreaux," I said quietly so as not to disturb the class further.

He straightened to his full height, which made him shorter than Dab but towering over my five-three.

"I understand this class is open to anyone."

"To anyone who pays the twenty dollars, although I should charge you double for causing a scene."

"Done," he said, a sly smile inching onto his lips.

I hadn't expected that response, but nodded. "Fine. Dab, will you please escort Mr. Boudreaux to the cash register?"

"What about his companions?" Dab asked. I raised a brow. "Two ladies came in with him. Aster's got them corralled in the store."

"They pay the fee, they can take what's left of the class." I gave Ernie the stink eye. "But you do anything to annoy me or interrupt the class, and you're out of here. I keep the class fee. Got it?"

He arched a bushy brow. "Ferocious little thing, aren't you?"

"Darn right." I didn't let being called "little thing" bother me. I *am* short, and I look younger than my almost thirty years. Especially since my hair is nearly always in a ponytail.

Staying focused on the matter at hand, I watched as the rude man turned smartly and headed for the door. This time he opened it quietly. Dab gave me an I-hope-you-know-what-you're-doing look and trailed after Ernie.

Me? I let out a long breath, willing my surge of adrenaline to subside. I gave a brief thought to snagging some calming lavender from Aster to sprinkle or spray around the room, but there wasn't time. I needed to join Zach at the utility sink to help dole out the water buckets. We'd completed the task when the door quietly opened again to admit Ernie and two women.

I did a double take at the woman clinging to Ernie's arm like a Texas sticker burr. The auburn-haired beauty had to be twenty years his junior. It also struck me that, except for having a more pampered, polished look, she resembled Doralee enough to be a sister. She even wore the same general outfit of jeans and a collared blouse. But while Doralee sported a simple, unadorned style, the younger woman was decked out in what looked like real silk and jewelry in silver settings. Dangly earrings, a pendant, three silver bracelets, and a diamond boulder on her left ring finger. Wowza! Sure seemed that Ernie had replaced Doralee with a younger, poutier, more expensive version.

The older woman who trailed behind Ernie and the redhead wore jeans with a simple flowered tunic blouse. I deduced she was his sister because she resembled Ernie in her facial features—same patrician nose and sharp chin. She was thinner, no bull neck like Ernie's. That was a blessing because her short salt-and-pepper hair didn't complement her face as it was, and neither did her sour expression. She didn't wear jewelry except for a rope chain necklace that looked like real gold.

The trio took their seats quietly. I noticed Zach back at the utility sink. His face expressed distaste, but he filled three more tubs for the newcomers. I reined in my ire and picked three gourds from the bin where Doralee had stashed the extras. As I set them before Ernie and his companions, I noticed their hastily handwritten name tags. KIM, the younger woman's read, and GEORGINE was printed on the elder woman's.

Doralee would've had every right to ignore the newcomers, in my opinion, but she didn't, and I admired her poise.

While most students carried on low conversations with one another, Doralee made the rounds, complimenting each student, including Ernie's and Georgine's gourds. Kim didn't participate. She didn't look like a woman who painted her own perfectly oval fingernails, never mind a gourd.

Ego-Ernie's response to Doralee's praise of his freehand design was an arrogant, "Of course. I'm a gourd master."

I rolled my eyes at that, and kept a wary watch on the three latecomers. Kim sat thigh to thigh with Ernie, speaking in a low, wheedling voice. The sole smile she spared for Doralee struck me as superior rather than friendly. Georgine completely ignored Kim's mumbling and shifting on the stool, but shot the occasional scowl at Ernie.

To my surprise, the older woman gave Doralee a cordial nod and murmured, "It's good to see you again."

Doralee smiled back. "You, too, Georgine. I hope you're well."

She aimed a look of loathing at Kim. "Things are tolerable."

Wow. I could hardly wait to buttonhole Sherry and Aster, the two who seemed to know Doralee the best, and get the scoop on these people.

A long forty minutes later, the class wrapped.

"Thank you again for coming tonight. If you've caught the gourd art bug, I encourage you to continue experimenting. Remember, your handout has information on where to buy cleaned and craft-ready gourds. My website URL and e-mail are there, too, if you want to contact me."

"We appreciate you making the trip to teach us about gorgeous gourds, Doralee," I said as I went to her table. "Ladies and gentlemen, you have a few minutes to finish up, but remember Doralee and The Handcraft Emporium's own Sherry Mae Cutler will demonstrate more gourd-decorating techniques tomorrow afternoon. If you can't be here, I hope you'll join us for our other grand opening events listed on the flyers out in the store."

Seven ladies from the class crowded around Doralee to ask more questions. Ernie hung back, too, as if he wanted a word with Doralee. This time she did ignore him. She chatted with the students as she packed her supplies in their case, including the extra painting tees. Sherry and Aster also stood nearby. I hadn't seen Aster come in from the store, but I was glad they kept Doralee busy.

Kim pulled at his arm. "Let's go, Ernie. You can ask her tomorrow."

His expression torn, Ernie finally ushered Kim and Georgine through to the store and, I hoped, straight out the front door.

None of them had taken their gourds with them, although I noticed Georgine's featured fireworks in red, white, and blue paint. Not as elaborate as Ernie's design, but it was surprisingly well done.

Zach had started gathering the paints, paintbrushes, and water tubs, so I joined in, working from the other side of the room. I made sure each paint bottle was capped tightly, and I then met Zach at the utility sink to empty and rinse water tubs. He spoke over the sound of the running tap.

"Thanks for the way you handled Ernie."

I flashed a smile. "You're welcome, but Doralee put him in his place just fine. I hope she doesn't have to deal with him often."

Zach shrugged. "A few times a year, especially from about May to October when they both travel to arts and craft festivals."

"No wonder she knows how to take him down a peg." I tilted my head. "He bothers you, doesn't he?"

"Yes, but so does that new fiancée of his. She's a piece of work."

"What about the other woman? Is she his sister?"

"Yes, she is. I haven't been around her enough to have an opinion. Hey, looks like the stragglers are leaving. I'll start packing the bins if you'll finish rinsing the tubs."

"Deal," I said. "Jasmine will be over to help me wash and dry in a minute." And she was.

I spotted Fred escorting Ida out the back door to her car. Jasmine saw where I was looking and nudged me. "That's so sweet."

"It is, isn't it?"

She and I made short work of cleanup duty, and I sent her into the store with her still-drying gourd. I carried the dried water tubs and a few more paintbrushes to Doralee.

"Here you go. I think that's the last of your supplies."

"Thanks, Nixy. I'm sorry about Ernie's appearance. I was just telling Sherry and Aster that I don't know what gets into him sometimes. Well, I never did."

"He wants you back," Zach said quietly.

Doralee reached for his hand. "Not going to happen. He has Kim, or he will. I think the wedding is a month or two away, but she was after him before our divorce was final." She paused for a second and laughed. "That sounded bitter, didn't it?"

"It can't be easy for you seeing that rock on her hand," Sherry said.

"It is ostentatious, isn't it? I can say that because I wore it. The Boudreaux family ring was so elegant. A large square-cut diamond in a gold art deco–style band. But Ernie insisted it was too old-fashioned, so he had the stone taken out and reset with slightly smaller diamonds flanking it. I never did care for the ring, so I was glad to give it back." Doralee shook her head. "Kim is spoiled and single-minded and self-absorbed, but she's not an evil person. In fact, I should probably warn her about Georgine's peccadillos, but Kim's former in-laws make Georgine look like a saint. Besides, I have the sense not to get in the middle of that dynamic."

I wanted to ask, "The middle of what," but bit my tongue so Sherry and the ladies wouldn't accuse me of being a nosy parker.

Instead, I steered the conversation more or less back on track. "Ernie aside, the class was amazing, Doralee. You have a gift for teaching as well as art."

"Nixy's right," Sherry said, beaming. "You made a wonderful impression on everyone."

Aster nodded. "We heard nothing but compliments as the students came out front. Oh, and Dab prepared your check. Here you go."

"Thank you. All of you. It was fun, and I look forward to doing the etching demonstration tomorrow afternoon while Sherry demonstrates vine weaving."

"Then you'll be showing how to attach the vines, right?" I asked. The demonstration programs all week were free, partly to get people in the door, but I wanted them to be every bit as professionally presented as they'd be for a paid class.

"Sherry and I will talk about that together, but yes. And here's to Ernie not showing up again."

I'm sure we all seconded that, but Fred clanked-clomped his way inside about then. Time to get the bins to Doralee's SUV. She and her gentleman had a long, romantic weekend to start, and I wanted to put my feet up.

THE FEET-UP THING DIDN'T HAPPEN BECAUSE THERE were still students and customers in the emporium. The wind chime Aster had insisted we use in lieu of a shopkeeper's bell tinkled merrily as people came and went. The chime hung from the ceiling on a long S hook. The plan was to remove it when we expected heavy traffic, or during the demonstrations that would be held in the store, but we'd forgotten to take it down this evening. It was fine, though. The cheerful sound spelled shoppers spending money. No complaints about that.

At nine fifteen, I showed the last person out. At nine thirty, I sent Jasmine home and locked the door behind her.

At nine thirty-five, Detective Eric Shoar of the Lilyvale Police Department knocked on the door. Eric Shoar. The man who had semi-strong-armed me into coming to Lilyvale just weeks ago in April, insisting that I ensure that Aunt Sherry and her gang weren't in danger of blowing up or burning down their farmhouse. They were not, of course, but Detective Shoar and I subsequently forged a budding relationship while solving a murder. Would the bud blossom? Too early to tell, because the man alternately miffed me and made me melt.

Which was saying a heck of a mouthful since I'd had dated a lot of men. Okay, a lot of first and second dates followed by a parting of ways entirely or becoming just friends. Still, Eric tripped my trigger in a way no guy had in a long time. We had a dance of attraction going, but I didn't seem to know the steps. I swung from feeling comfortable with him to a state of awkward hyperawareness. Of course, it didn't help that he made his usual "uniform" of jeans, collared shirts, and boots sexier than all get-out.

The wind chime sang as I let Eric inside and murmured hello. The Silver Six stood shoulder to shoulder behind the long glass-topped and fronted pine counter that had been original to the Stanton General Store. We displayed our most delicate items, or those that were most expensive, in the antique case, but no one gave a hoot about the goods at the moment. The Six avidly watched us, hanging on our every word.

I don't know why. They already knew we were friends and sort of dating. Okay, one real date.

"No more trouble tonight, Nixy?" Eric asked.

"How did you hear about that?"

"I called him when Ernie pushed his way into class," Eleanor said. I swear she had him on speed dial.

"Once he got here, the situation had changed," Dab added.

"But he said he'd check back," Aster offered.

"And here I am." Eric gave me one of those melting smiles, and my surroundings almost faded away.

Almost. I cleared my throat. "That's kind of you, Eric. The man who pushed his way in—Ernie—struck me as an egotistical jerk, but our gourd artist put him in his place. Doralee is his ex."

"Glad the situation resolved itself. Do you still want help hanging your grand opening banner tomorrow morning?"

Oh, geez, I'd forgotten I asked him that a week ago when we were on the dinner date. One of those recent times I hadn't managed to apply mascara to both sets of eyelashes. Aster had pointed it out before I'd gotten out of the store, but she hadn't caught the very stylish streak of white paint in my brown hair that shampooing had missed. Blame it on my embarrassment. His offer to hang the sign had slipped my mind.

But hey, I bluffed. "If you're available, that would be great."

"Eight o'clock?"

"Sure."

"Should I bring a ladder?"

"No, we've got a ten-footer in the workroom."

Eric glanced at the emporium's displays of art on the polished pine shelves and tables, and the hanging baskets. "We don't want to break anything, so I'll meet you at the back door, and we'll carry the ladder around the building."

"Of course. I should've thought of that. We can take it out the service door."

"Sounds good."

Neither of us spoke for a moment. For my part, I was lost in his warm brown eyes. Sue me.

A throat cleared.

"This ain't the most rivetin' conversation, missy," Fred barked. "Walk the man out, kiss him, and get back here so we can firm up tomorrow's schedule."

"Fred!" Sherry swatted his arm.

"What? I'm ready for bed."

"We all are," I said, then blushed when Eric slowly grinned. "Oh, for heaven's sake. Come on, Eric."

He chuckled. "No need to see me out. Just be sure to lock up tight. I'll see you at eight."

Eric strolled into the sultry night. I flipped the deadbolt on the door and turned to Fred. "Happy now?"

"Dang near delirious."

Maise clapped her hands for attention. "All right, you and Eric put the sign up early, but we open at ten, correct?"

"I do believe we decided to come in about nine," Eleanor said.

"Yes, but there's no need for all of you to be here the whole day."

"On the first day of our grand opening?" Sherry gasped. "There certainly is. We *want* to be here."

"Especially if the *Lilyvale Legend* sends a photographer," Aster chimed in.

"I hope the newspaper will run a photo," Sherry said wistfully. Our modestly sized daily newspaper was great about running all sorts of local items, so I figured at least one picture would make the cut. "I'm so proud of what we've accomplished."

Dab patted her arm. "We all are, Sherry. Now Fred's right. Time to go on home so we'll be fresh for the big day."

Dab's dark gray Caddy, Fred's old red pickup truck that he was now driving again, and Sherry's blue Corolla were parked in the lot behind the store. Because of the macular degeneration, Sherry didn't drive much anymore, and never at night. She shared her ride with the other women, all of whom had their own sets of car keys. Heck, Dab and Fred likely had keys, too. The women, though, pooled funds to pay for insurance, gas, and maintenance. The arrangement worked out perfectly for them all.

I hugged each of the Six as I ushered them through the workroom and out the back door. Deadbolt thrown, service door secure, I returned to the front room to turn off all but the security light. After double-checking that the front door was locked tight, I headed upstairs, flipping off the workroom lights as I went.

Upstairs, I toed off my shoes in the foyer, plodded to my spacious bedroom that overlooked the square, and faceplanted on my queen bed. The plain white, fluffy comforter puffed up to cover my nose, a smothering sensation that made me roll on my back. My thoughts drifted.

The ceiling looked good, and I was proud to have fixed it. I'd once dated a construction guy—Drywall Danny—who had shown me how to patch holes and cracks. With that knowledge, plus advice and supplies from Big George Heath at Heath's Hardware, the ceiling was pristine smooth and painted a bright white. Not blind-you bright, but a clean, crisp color. The same color we'd painted the emporium and workroom. White walls, too, except for the wall of Victorian-esque paneling in the dining room with its rich, dark patina. That woodwork was art, and far too exquisite to paint. Part of the paneling concealed storage and the other part hid a lift between the two floors. My Aunt Sissy from generations back had the woodwork crafted when she'd lived in this apartment and ran Sissy's Five & Dime downstairs.

I'd never thought much about my decorating style. When I'd shared an apartment with my Houston roomie Vicki, we had the post-college, hand-me-down, not-entirely-adults-yet vibe happening. I appreciated antique and vintage pieces, but my true taste ran to modern, monochromatic, and minimalistic. The minimalist part may have been a knee-jerk reaction to the happy chaos of the emporium. Of course, I might also be both boring *and* too lazy to want to dust intricate pieces of furniture and shelves of bric-a-brac, but I found peace in my uncluttered almost barren apartment.

Huff's Fine Furniture on the town square had run a big sale over Memorial Day, and I'd scored good deals on my bedroom and living room sets—or suites as store owner and city councilman B.G. Huff called them. The bedroom style was called "panel," and I love it for its matte white finish, clean lines, and no fussiness. The living room love seat and two overstuffed chairs upholstered in white twill were just as plain as the bedroom pieces, though I'd added graphic throw pillows in blues and greens. The additions did make the space less cavernous and more cozy. I hadn't bought any rugs yet. The pine floors had been sanded and restained a dark walnut color, and were too amazing to cover. Of course, by winter I'd want a couple of rugs to warm my feet.

Right now, the ceiling fan spun slowly, barely making a sound, yet the gentle breeze tempted me to fall asleep where I was. But no. I had to hang the grand opening banner with Eric at eight. If I showered tonight, I could sleep a little later tomorrow.

The only bathroom in the loft apartment was large, also mostly white, and had two doors. One door allowed access from the living area, and the other connected to the bedroom. There were no windows, but when Sherry had updated the bathroom for the previous tenants, they'd installed a powerful exhaust fan and great lighting. The previous renters, who'd also owned the antique store below, had put a refinished claw-footed tub in the room. They'd left the tub behind when they shut down their business and moved to Texas to be close to their daughter. The old-style tub didn't feed my modern taste, but it was great for a long soak when I took time for one.

My blah-brown hair was still in a ponytail, but I fixed it higher on my head and snapped on a shower cap. Hot water washed away the stress of the day's last-minute store and class preparations—and of the scene Ernie had made. I sure hoped he wasn't sticking around with the fiancée and the sister. Kim and Georgine. The Silver Six and I had enough going on without being referees, although Doralee hadn't really needed my intervention this evening. It still amazed me that she'd been so calm and cool. I'd have just slapped Ernie upside the head.

Then again, I'd been told my personality was much like my Aunt Sissy's. Technically my triple great-aunt, if I had the genealogy right. She'd been a mover and shaker in Lily-vale. A get-'er-done, get-out-of-my-way kind of woman. I wasn't sure about the mover-shaker aspect, and if I tried to shove anyone out of my way, Aunt Sherry would knock me upside the head.

My mother used to say when we see something that needs doing, we do it, and I'd heard Sherry say the same thing. I must've absorbed that attitude because, admittedly, I got things done. Most of all, I tended to go full bore after my goals, and I considered that a good thing.

Right now, my main goal was to make the emporium not only survive, but thrive. I'd do everything within my power to make that happen.

Chapter Three

ERIC KNOCKED AT THE ALLEY DOOR THAT LED TO Fred's workroom at eight sharp, just as I was flipping the deadbolt.

"Good morning," he said with a bright smile and an odd twinkle in his brown eyes.

"Good morning. Let me open the service door."

"Okay. Do you know you have visitors?"

"Besides you?"

He pointed down and to the side of the doorway. I stepped out and stopped short.

A dog and cat sat on their haunches, gazing at me with soulful eyes. The dog reminded me a bit of a Doberman a friend had owned except this one was much smaller. Not a miniature, but more the size of a beagle our neighbor in Tyler had when I was a kid. This dog was black with tan markings, and its coat gleamed with apparent health. Floppy ears framed its face as it blinked at me with intelligent golden eyes.

Uh-oh.

The cat made a sound between a meow and a chirp, its mesmerizing green eyes steady on my face. Its short-haired coat was tiger striped in browns and golds, and it had a white chin. They were both adorable, but—

"How did they get here?"

"Walked would be my guess."

His sarcasm untied my tongue. "I mean why are they *here* here? You think someone dumped them?"

"I doubt it." He hunkered down to pet them, first the dog, then the cat, who leaned in for a scratch under its chin. "They both seem to be in good shape. Their coats aren't matted, no cuts or skin abrasions except on their paws, and no sign of fleas."

"Gee, thanks for mentioning fleas."

"All part of the service."

I refrained from rolling my eyes. "So they can leave anytime they want?"

He slanted me a look. "You don't like animals?"

"No. Yes. I mean, I like animals. I played with my friends' dogs and cats when I was a kid. We just never had animals because my dad was allergic. After he died, well, I was in college, and I guess my mom never felt the urge to get a pet."

"These two are small, but they're out of the young puppy and kitten stage. They may have been the runts of their litters."

"Maybe they belong to one of the shop owners."

Eric shook his head as he stood. "I've never seen them, but I can ask around. The thing is, our county animal control will pick them up if they're running loose."

"You don't have a rescue shelter? I could take them there if they don't leave on their own."

"We have a small one, but last I heard, it was full. Tell you what. Let's get the banner up. Now that these two have had some attention, they may go on home."

"Except they don't have collars or tags." I murmured the comment more to myself than Eric. They could've slipped

out of their collars, but chances were just as good they were
strays. With super soulful eyes.

With a sigh, I caved and stooped to offer the back of my
hand for each of them to smell, first the dog, then the cat.
The dog sniffed my knuckles and gave them a shy lick. The
cat sniffed, then rubbed its cheek against my fingers. Okay,
I was charmed, and I scratched them behind their ears. Cute
and sweet as they were, though, I did not—repeat *not*—have
time for pets right now. Besides, the dog probably wouldn't
be happy in my apartment. My apartment with its freshly
stained floors and white furniture . . .

I went inside with Eric and helped him take down the
ladder from the hooks Fred and Dab had installed to store
it, then I grabbed the folded banner and tucked it under my
arm. When I opened the four-foot-wide service door, I had
a moment's concern that the animals would dart inside and
make themselves at home in the workroom. Or worse, make
a mess. I needn't have worried.

The dog and cat stood as we came outside, Eric holding
one end of the ladder, me the other. Then they pranced ahead
as we carted the ladder into the alley. Since the emporium
occupied the last space on the west side of the square, it
didn't take long to round the corner, pass the catty-corner-
facing shop door, and arrive where we'd hang the banner.

The critters parked themselves on the edge of the sidewalk beside a concrete planter overflowing with lilies and
ivy. Not in our way, not in the street, the dog and cat watched
intently as we strung the banner. We looped the ropes tied
in the corner grommets through eye bolts in the façade that
must have been there for years but still held. When the banner was tied off at the four corners, we stood back to admire
it flapping in the gentle morning breeze.

I glanced around the quaint, picturesque square in the
town I now called home. Bizarrely enough, Lilyvale didn't
have a Main Street. Nope. Magnolia Road was our north-
south two-lane highway that cut through town. It split to flow

around the limestone courthouse and a small white gazebo that sat elevated in the center of the square. Magnolia trees dotted the property, and lilies flourished in the flowerbeds.

On the south end of the square, Lee Street carried traffic east and west. On the north end, Stanton Drive, named for my ancestor and Lilyvale's founder, ran along the emporium's side wall. Every building on the square dated from the late 1800s to the 1960s, and each one was occupied, though most businesses didn't open until nine or ten Monday through Saturday.

"I hope this horizontal sign gives us enough visibility," I mused aloud. "I thought a vertical banner would be more eye catching, but the Silver Six vetoed the idea."

He glanced at the concrete sidewalk and street. "Where would you have put it?"

"In the planter."

"But those can be harder to keep secure when the wind kicks up," Eric said. "Which reminds me. We may get a storm on Monday. If we do, I'll help you take this down so it won't be a flying hazard."

I nodded. "Good thinking. Otherwise Maise will be ordering us to batten down the hatches. Ready to move the ladder back?"

I could've sworn as soon as I said "back," both animals stood, and sure enough, they trotted in front of us as we hauled the ladder to the alley.

Again, I feared they'd dash inside. They didn't. Not when we hung the ladder, not when I lowered the service door. And yes, I felt terrible about shutting them out.

Eric glanced around the workroom as if searching for something.

"What?" I asked.

"Do you have a small bucket or pan to fill with water?"

"Eric, the pup and cat are darling, but if I start taking care of them, they won't go home."

"Giving them water won't keep them here, Nixy. If they

do stick around, though, you don't want them to get dehy-drated. It's supposed to be close to ninety degrees today."

The alley was on the east side of the building, so the back of our space would be shaded until at least noon. Still, I didn't want the little critters to be thirsty.

I huffed a breath. "We keep a few bowls in the kitchen-ette."

He followed me into the small space that shrank more with him standing so near. I got soup bowls from the upper cabinet, filled one with water, and handed it to Eric before filling the other.

I opened the door to the alley, and there they were, curled up together. Both twitched their ears and lifted their heads when Eric and I put the bowls near them, then slowly rose to drink.

"There," I said. "Our fur friends are taken care of, and you, sir, are due at the station, I believe."

He glanced at his watch. "I'm overdue. See you later?"

"If you have time to stop by, yes."

He gave my arm a friendly squeeze. "Hope the grand opening is a smashing success."

Success, yes. Smashing, not so much. We had breakables in the emporium, and let's face it, we'd need every sale to make a go of this business.

I went into the store proper, fighting off a mild wave of claustrophobia at the sight of the overflowing displays. The Six hadn't rearranged their art and Aster's herb balms and such so much that they needed tweaking, so I grabbed a duster and gave every surface a swipe. Nervous energy, I knew. The life changes I'd made were a bit frightening, but they were also exhilarating.

When I'd proposed the idea of opening a folk art gallery, with me as manager, and Sherry and her friends supplying the art, I'd done it to be able to stay near my aunt and yet still use my art background. Sherry owned the building free and clear except for taxes and upkeep, and she and the housemates had artist contacts. The antique dealers who'd been renting the building were closing shop, and my roommate in Houston was marrying and moving out. Plus, our lease was expiring. In short, the timing to relocate and open the emporium seemed to fall into place—both on the Six's end and on mine.

True, my experience was in fine art. I'd given up my job at the prestigious Gates Gallery in Houston to move to Lilyvale. But art is art, whether it traced its origins to the primarily practical or the purely aesthetic.

We'd expanded from our initial concept of selling folk art only to carrying a variety of crafts from handmade jewelry, to stained glass, to mosaics and about everything in between. Art is supposed to evoke emotions, and I'd seen that happen in response to a skillfully crafted basket, or beautifully designed quilt, and even to certain aromas in Aster's collection of goodies. Seen it? I'd experienced emotional connections myself. Besides, we needed to offer a wider range of items with a wider range of prices. Affordable prices. Disposable incomes tended to be a closely guarded commodity here in Lilyvale as much as anywhere. No point in being too specialized.

Even Fred and Dab got in on the action. They'd taken to welding odds and ends in one of the farmhouse sheds to create whimsical metal art, and had already sold a few pieces to Jasmine's dad and to her boyfriend.

My cell phone alarm beeped. The Six would be arriving soon. I put the duster away, brushed off my emporium tee and twill capris. One hour until the official first day of our grand opening. Time to take down the wind chime, put out the wooden display benches, and fill them with goods.

"YOU KNOW THOSE ANIMALS ARE STILL IN THE alley, missy?"

I turned to Fred as he and Dab came into the emporium

from the workroom. We'd had steady traffic until the noon hour, but the store was virtually empty now. Thankfully Fred had removed the loaded tool belt from his walker to make navigating in the store easier. And quieter.

"You've mentioned it every half hour, Fred," I reminded him.

"Ain't you gonna do somethin' 'bout them?"

"I don't know what I *can* do right now. Doralee is due here to set up her demonstration with Sherry. Besides, you said you tried shooing them away. They went to the end of the alley and came right back."

"That dog is smaller, but reminds me of coon dogs we had when I was a boy," Dab said, hitching his slacks up to his waist. They fell right back to his hips.

"Uh-huh," I mumbled as I moved a few of Aster's Aromatics products to fill a hole. Thankfully we'd had buyers this morning, not just fellow shop owners and other well-wishers stopping for a look-see. Still, I needed to put out another couple of plates of cookies and refill the sweet tea pitchers.

"Or she could be," Dab continued, "some sort of Doberman mix."

"She?" That stopped me. I hadn't paid attention, and Eric hadn't mentioned the sex of the dog. "The dog is female?"

"Yep," Fred confirmed. "Both'a them animals is female. Dab and me think they've been spayed, too. Saw faint scars on their bellies."

I considered that a moment as Eleanor approached. She'd waved Sherry, Aster, and Maise off to lunch, and would take hers when they got back.

"Are you still talking about those animals?" she asked.

"Fred and Dab think they've been fixed. And if someone went to that expense, they must have owners. We just have to find them."

"I do believe you could take pictures with your tablet and set up a slide show so customers can see them."

"Brilliant, Eleanor," I said with a grin.

"You wanna get a shot of that little cat's paws," Fred instructed. "She's got three forward claws on her front paws 'stead of four. Might could be a clue to find the owner."

I'd heard of the polydactyl cats at the Hemingway Home and Museum in Key West, but had no idea how common or rare a three-toed cat might be. Still, Fred might be right about it being a clue.

I didn't have a ton of time before Doralee showed up and Sherry returned from lunch at the Lilies Café. The metal folding chairs we'd borrowed from various churches to keep for the week were set into neat rows and the small folding table for the demonstration was up and ready. I could make time to take photos.

I grabbed my tablet and strode out the workroom to the alley. Dab and Fred came along to help me pose the critters.

The men had put a cardboard box out to give the animals shade. Big softies. The critters came right out and sat when we appeared, their eyes—the dog's golden and the cat's green—gazing at me with trust. They darned near posed as I took photos, staying side by side. They allowed Dab and Fred to separate them enough for me to get pictures of them from their sides—the better to see their markings. The cat let Dab hold her for a close-up of her three toes, but wriggled to get down when I'd finished. As soon as her paws hit the pavement, she returned to her canine friend's side. They had full water bowls, I saw, and it was no stretch to figure who had seen to that.

I'd just set up the slide show and set my tablet by the cash register when Doralee and Sherry, Aster, and Maise came in laughing. Zach trailed behind with a rolling bin of Doralee's supplies. He greeted me with a soft-spoken, "Good afternoon, Nixy," and then began unloading what Doralee needed for the demonstration on the table near the workshop door.

I tingled with anticipation when people began trickling in. Some cruised the displays, others claimed a seat. Cindy

Price, the peppy forty-something reporter-photographer from the *Lilyvale Legend*, began taking pictures as soon as she entered the store. Sherry as our official emporium spokeswoman gave Cindy an informal interview as they toured the space. Eleanor had volunteered to take photos for our website today, so I circulated. I also checked to be sure Aster had bowls of loose lavender and lavender sachets strategically stashed on the shelves. In April I'd learned firsthand that the herb really did have a calming effect. Not that I expected trouble, but hey, liberal use of the lavender couldn't hurt.

With ten minutes until demo time, a group from the technical college where the Six volunteered came in the store. The students were noisy but not unruly, and the affection the students held for the seniors was obvious and touching. The photographer even snapped a few shots of the two generations posing together.

Not so touching was seeing Ernie saunter through the front door, Kim gripping his arm and Georgine trailing behind. Ernie looked comfortable in faded black jeans and a green polo shirt and tennis shoes while Kim wore a short black skirt, a figure-hugging blue blouse, chunky-heeled sandals, and almost as much jewelry as she'd been draped in the night before. In contrast, Georgine was dressed rather like her brother in plain blue jeans, a collared shirt open at her throat, and loafers.

Ernie's gaze swept the gathering and he scowled when he spotted Sherry, Doralee, and Zach chatting with a group of students near the door to the workshop. When Ernie moved toward the group, Kim still clinging to his arm, I moved to forestall another scene. I intercepted the couple before they reached the demonstration table.

"Mr. Boudreaux, you might want to find a seat before they're all taken."

He drew himself up, looked down his nose at me. "I don't

intend to cause a problem—Nixy, isn't it? I just want to see the tools Doralee intends to use."

He edged past me, not quite pushing me out of the way, but nearly so. I caught up at the demo table.

"Hmm. I wonder why she's not using a rotary tool. It would be faster. Personally, I'd use a wood burner."

"Then you'd set off our smoke alarms, Mr. Boudreaux. And the power tool creates too much dust," I said, arms folded.

"Ah, then I understand her choice of hand tools. Looks like a new set, too." He peered at the tool kit, each tool nestled in a thin plastic molded space that fit its shape. He poked at a few, making the plastic crackle, then faced me. "Of course, one can do more with power tools. I'd be happy to demonstrate carving and burning methods outside. Give these people more gourd art ideas. "

I bit off what I was tempted to say and forced a smile. "Our craft demo schedule is full, Mr. Boudreaux. For the entire week. Now, please take your seats."

"Some people would jump at that offer," Kim huffed. "Come on, Ernie. Let's go shopping."

They moved off, and I followed about five feet behind, blending with the crowd, but staying close enough to eavesdrop. Rude? The Six would say so, but I wanted to know if Ernie was plotting trouble.

"You go on if you want," Ernie said. "Find Georgine and shop with her. I'm staying."

Kim heaved a sigh. "This was supposed to be a romantic weekend. First, you let your sister tag along with us, and now you want to be around Doralee."

Ernie stopped at Aster's display of balms and soaps. "I told you. I need to know if she's stealing my designs."

"I don't see how she could be if you haven't seen her for months and months. Not even at an art fair." Kim gave Ernie the stink eye. "Besides, you're supposed to ask her about the opal. You promised."

"I will, I will. After she finishes."

"For cripes sake, Ernie, her room is next to ours. You could knock on the door anytime."

I nearly choked. They were all staying at Inn on the Square? Awkward.

"She's with Zach. Would you appreciate her knocking on our door?"

She heaved an exaggerated you're-right-but-I-won't-admit-it sigh. "Fine, we'll stay, but you ask her about the opal, and then we do what I want."

Ernie didn't respond but escorted Kim to the only empty seats in the middle row. I pivoted away and came face to scowling face with Georgine.

"So sorry. I didn't know you were behind me."

"You should watch where you're going," she snapped and brushed past me. I had to wonder if she'd heard Ernie's and Kim's exchange. Double awkward.

At the demo table, I checked to be sure Doralee and Sherry had all they needed at hand. They did, and our gourd artist donned her smock, while my aunt wore an emporium apron. After I made the introduction, I stood at the far side of the sales floor, halfway to the front windows near Eleanor's display of carved figurines. Georgine, I saw, had found a chair near the front but not that far from where Ernie and Kim sat.

Doralee began by describing the various tools used both in wood and gourd carving, throwing out terms like veiners, gouges, and skews or chisels. She held each up in turn, and the audience was quiet enough that I could hear the flimsy plastic crackle as she removed each item. I didn't notice that much difference in most of the implements, but I was also distracted by watching Georgine. She alternately ran her fingers around her rope necklace, and hooked her arm over the back of the folding chair to turn and glare at Ernie and Kim. They either didn't notice or flat ignored her. Hard to do since I could almost see cartoon steam come out her ears.

I idly wondered what Georgine would do if I spritzed her with Aster's lavender water. For that matter, how would Kim react? I almost chuckled aloud imagining their outrage even as I noted latecomers quietly slip in the door. Two middle-aged women hovered behind the rows of chairs and watched the demonstration. A guy in his thirties wearing a royal blue scrubs shirt with jeans and a black and gold New Orleans Saints ball cap stood near the ladies, but didn't appear to be with them. He wore dark sunglasses, and tugged the cap bill low as if shielding his eyes. Hmm. If the scrubs meant this guy worked in health care, I sure didn't recognize him as a local nurse or lab tech. At least not from any of the medical offices I'd been in for Sherry's checkups. Maybe he worked in Magnolia, not Lilyvale.

The door opened again to admit two teens, a man, and a woman, but I sensed they weren't all together. For one thing, the teens sat on the floor up by Doralee and Sherry without a backward glance. In contrast, the adults darn near hugged the wall by the door. The woman was a platinum blonde with perfectly coifed hair dressed in a pale green linen skirt suit, ecru pumps, and oversized retro round cat eye sunglasses. She linked arms with a man who looked a good bit younger, maybe in his thirties. He wore mirrored shades, navy slacks, and high-end burgundy slip-on shoes. Not penny loafers, thank you very much. No tassels either. Those were costly shoes.

With their noses in the air, I wondered why they'd come into the store in the first place. Did they have a similar business and were checking out the competition? If so, I'd not heard the emporium had a rival. Or they could be art snobs slumming in our pedestrian shop. I'd met their type in Houston. Thankfully, most folk artists and crafters were down to earth almost as much as Doralee.

I turned my attention back to her demonstration.

"You can see I've sketched feathers on the gourd and I've begun carving them," she said as she raised it above her head to show the audience. "Instead of using clamps or vises, I'm securing my gourd in this box. It has a partially open front and a nonslip pad inside to hold the gourd steady while I work. My friend Zach"—she gestured to where he sat in the front—"designed and constructed this for me, and he's working on an adjustable box to accommodate the different sizes and shapes of gourds."

Zach merely smiled. I liked that he didn't make a show of modesty. The idea really was ingenious. With or without an adjustable model.

"I'm an advocate of using masks when cutting, carving, or burning gourds, but I don't want to wear a mask for the program. And I certainly don't want to expose anyone to dust. So I'll be carving just enough for you to see the process."

She launched into the next part of her presentation to a rapt audience, mentioning the various tools to make cuts deep or shallow, wide or narrow, as she went along.

"While I finish," she said, "Sherry Mae will show you how to weave the grapevine we'll use to top off the gourd."

Sherry wore her bangs over her bad eye again. I hoped she'd be able to see well enough to weave.

"I presoaked these vines," she said, "and began the initial weaving to get the size right, and to save time. You can use single strands of vine, or you can twist or braid them. As you see, I've braided some for more visual interest."

I let out a breath I hadn't been aware of holding as Sherry wove the vine in a circle maybe two inches in diameter. Each layer of vine added to the height of the piece until it was as tall as wide, and all the while, she described her technique without a stumble or even a pause. She finished with a flourish, and held the vine top high for all to see.

"See the tendrils hanging here?" She pointed to five hanging bits of vine. "I curved them to more or less conform to the inside of the gourd and worked them in as I wove.

These tendrils will hold the woven vine in place, so long as you don't jerk on it. Or you can secure your vine topper by drilling holes along the rim and tying off your vine with twine. Doralee?"

"If you want more decoration, embellish with beads, charms, or whatever you fancy. Use raffia to tie your decoration to the vine."

She picked up a silver-colored sun charm tied to raffia, attached it to Sherry's vine work, then she and Sherry both gently squeezed the tendrils to fit them inside the gourd.

"I still need to do some finish work. A few strokes with my tools, and a little sanding, but this is a fair example of the finished product."

Doralee again held the gourd high with one hand. With the other, she took Sherry's hand and they stood together to take a bow. Not every artist would be willing to share the spotlight, and I was grateful Doralee had given my aunt's talent time to shine.

A rousing applause, a few questions, and the audience rose. Some crowded around Doralee and Sherry while others shopped, meandering from display to display. I spotted Ernie and Georgine on Doralee's side of the demo table, then lost sight of them and Kim. Which was more than fine by me. We'd made it through the demo without any ugly outbursts, and I sure didn't want a commotion disturbing shoppers.

The only hitch came when Doralee and Zach were packing her supplies and she discovered a missing tool.

"It's a scratch awl." At my apparently blank look, she added, "It looks like an ice pick."

"The handle is wood and round," Zach added. "Someone talking to Doralee probably jostled the table and it rolled off."

"But Zach," she protested, "each tool was in its mold in the kit."

"Honey, you held up the tools to show the class, and you may not have seated the awl securely when you put it back.

Besides, that plastic isn't the least bit sturdy. We've popped
tools out just by hitting the kit wrong. The awl is here somewhere."

"You're probably right," Doralee said as she unsnapped
her smock and dropped it in the bin. "I'd stay and look for
my tool, but we have massages scheduled in fifteen minutes."

"We'll search," I assured her. "With so many people in
here, it could've been kicked under a display."

"Or even a shelf," my aunt added.

Doralee cast a dubious glance around the store. "Your
shelves are floor to ceiling, Sherry."

My aunt patted Doralee's arm. "You'd be surprised what
we found hiding under these old shelves and that glass counter."

"Don't worry about your tool," I told Doralee. "If we
don't find it, we'll get you a new one."

She waved that offer away. "It's not that valuable. I just
hate to think there was a petty thief in the audience."

Right there with you, I thought as they left. I also thought
of the three oddballs who'd come to the demo—the snooty
duo and Ball Cap Guy. I didn't recall seeing any of them
after the presentation, much less seeing them near Doralee.

The rest of the afternoon passed quickly. The Six and I
took turns helping customers, ringing up sales, and rearranging shelves. When Jasmine came in at four, she
rehung the wind chime over the door, then helped me search
in earnest for Doralee's tool. We struck out, and I dreaded
breaking the news to Doralee.

Fred spent most of his afternoon in his workroom repairing a toaster.

And, I imagined, checking on the animals. Which made
me smile.

Unfortunately, though our patrons looked at the slide show
of the dog and cat, no one recognized them. And no one
offered to take them off my hands.

* * *

THE SILVER SIX HEADED HOME AT FIVE. JUST BEFORE closing at six, Jasmine was straightening displays and I was cleaning the kitchenette and bathroom when the wind chime signaled someone entering or leaving the shop. I didn't hear Jasmine greet anyone, so figured she'd gone to check for any stock still outside.

A few minutes later, I heard the chime again. And giggling.

"Good evening, Detective Shoar," Jasmine sang in greeting.

I smiled as I dried my hands. Eric had stopped by after all. Okay, I did have it kind of bad for him.

Until I saw what he'd set on our antique counter.

Small bags of puppy and kitten chow. Small boxes of puppy and kitten treats. Stainless steel bowls. A plastic pan. Kitty litter. A scooper.

"Subtle, Shoar. Real subtle." I planted my fists on my hips, glanced at Jasmine. "Did you help him haul this stuff inside?"

She shrugged innocently. "He is the law, Miss Nixy."

I rounded on Eric, but he held up a hand. "I swung by the alley a while ago. Fred told me your visiting critters were still out back."

"And he thought I'd let them go hungry?"

"He didn't think you'd have time to get food for them."

"So you volunteered."

"The Silver Six were going to do it, but they looked bushed, Nixy."

"I told you I don't have experience with pets, but I know this. If I feed them, they'll stay."

"We'll take them to the vet tomorrow. Fred said they've been fixed, so Dr. Sally might recognize them. If not, she'll scan them for microchips."

Jasmine, who had been avidly watching us, spoke up suddenly.

"I told you I can't take them, but I'll put out the word."
She snapped her fingers. "I know a teacher at the college
who lost her cat and dog. Well, not lost them. They died.
She might be ready to have pets again."

I arched a brow at Eric. "Why don't you take them
home?"

"My schedule is too erratic, you know that. It wouldn't
be fair to leave them alone so much."

"I'm busy here, so what's the difference?"

"They're just upstairs. You can look in on them easily."

I had a feeling the critters would be in Fred's workroom
rather than confined to my apartment. I gazed at Jasmine,
then Eric.

"I'm not getting out of this, am I?"

"Nope."

Chapter Four

JASMINE WENT HOME, AND ERIC AND I TOTED THE pet paraphernalia to the workroom.

"You're going to make them stay down here?"

"This floor is linoleum. The rest of the place has original wood floors that you know we've just refinished."

"I'm sure the cat is litter box–trained if it had an owner, plus I saw both of them do their business in the strip of grass by the parking lot. I cleaned it up, by the way. Dropped the bag in the Dumpster out back."

"Thanks, but I really don't want these original floors ruined."

"Tell you what," he said reasonably. "Let's see if they'll come inside at all. Then I can guilt you into taking them upstairs."

I gave that remark the answer it deserved: none. But I went out the alley door with Eric to find the cat and dog curled up together in the cardboard box. They immediately came out, stretched in perfect unison, and looked up at us with those sweet expressions.

"You sure seem well behaved. Time to prove that. Come on." Eric snapped his fingers and went to the doorway.

The critters didn't move. Their gazes shifted from Eric to me. I sighed, made a sweeping gesture at the door.

"Okay, okay. Come on in, you two."

The cat and dog rose as one and trotted inside, the cat rubbing along the doorframe as she entered.

"See? They waited for you to invite them in. You're their pack alpha."

"Even I know cats don't do packs. Is it odd that they aren't sniffing around? That would be normal, right?"

He shrugged. "Could be they're more than just well behaved. Could be they've been trained."

"It's kinda creepy. I mean, shouldn't they be more play-ful? Inquisitive?"

"They might be both when they feel more secure. For now, they'll be perfect ladies, won't you?" He knelt to scratch each of them under their chins. "Look at it this way. If the doc knows them from her practice, they'll be gone tomorrow. Houseguests for just one night."

Who was I kidding? Even if I left them alone in the workroom, I'd be up checking on them all night.

"All right, but you're helping me clean any messes," I said, looking down at all three of their pleading, adorable faces.

"Done," he said as he rose and crossed the few steps to open my stairwell door. "Come on, critters."

The preternaturally quiet animals stayed seated.

"Oh, for heaven's sake." I stood on the first step, bent down, and clapped my hands. "Let's go."

The cat emitted a gravelly *mreow*, the dog bayed a *bark-aroo*, and both bounded up the stairs.

I threw Eric a frantic, "Oh, no," and charged up behind them, but they weren't tearing up my apartment. I found them sitting beside the kitchen peninsula, the dog softly panting, the cat with her tail curled around her. I could've sworn they smiled.

Eric entered with a food bag under each arm, a food dish in each hand. I took the bowls, rinsed them, and opened the bags while he went back down for the next load.

Not sure how much to feed the critters, I read the directions on the bag, estimated their weights, and scooped the food with a measuring cup. The dog and cat perked their ears as soon as the nuggets hit the bowls, but they waited until I put the dishes on the floor under the window to calmly walk over. One sniff, though, and they dug in.

Eric caught me smiling at them as he filled the water bowls that had been outside and set them near their food.

"Told you it wouldn't be so bad."

"They've been here five minutes."

"Five good minutes. I like your place. I didn't realize the kitchen would be so big. What's your square footage?"

"Twelve hundred, give or take. I feel like I'm rattling around in here compared to sharing an apartment."

"The place is more modern than I thought it would be, too. Did you update it?"

"Sherry did when Vonnie and her husband leased the building. She did the bathroom, too. You've never been up here?"

"Never had the occasion to be, and that's a good thing considering my line of work."

"True. Well, the Vances took good care of the place," I said, absently caressing the rounded edge of the stone-look countertop on the peninsula. The darker browns in the fake vein complemented the dark hardwood floor.

"Will you show me around? You need to decide where you want the litter box."

"Definitely not in the kitchen. Where do you suggest?"

"Bathroom?"

"I don't know. The stacking washer and dryer are in there,

and that takes up floor space." Plus I wasn't keen on facing a litter box every morning and night.

I opened the door that accessed the bath from the living room, and immediately noticed I'd left the other door open. The one that led to my bedroom. At least I'd picked up my clothes and made my bed.

I knew the minute Eric spotted the bed because he stilled, and I was thrown deep in one of those awkward moments.

I heard a snuffling rustle and the dog trotted in via the bedroom, plopping down near the claw foot tub. An instant later, she was followed by the cat, who hopped up onto the sink and broke my too-aware-of-him spell.

"Looks like they're taking the tour with us, doesn't it?" He turned back to the living room. I followed. So did Cat and Dog.

"Anywhere else that will work for the cat box?" he asked, talking a mile a minute, "How about over there." He pointed at my would-be dining room. "Whoa, that is some amazing craftsmanship."

He strode past the boxes I still hadn't unpacked to the paneled back wall of the dining room, and almost reverently ran his hand over the wood. "This can't be original to the building."

"The story is that my several times Great-Aunt Sissy had it built when she lived here in the early 1900s," I said, grateful for the subject change. "And it's not just ornamental. Watch."

I pushed on a section and it sprang open to reveal deep shelves.

"Great storage. There are shelves down in the store, too, aren't there? Behind where y'all set up the antique counter with the glass front and top."

"Yes, that's where the downstairs lift access is."

He blinked. "The what?"

"These two panels hide a lift." I gave the two middle panels a quick push, and doors popped open to reveal an ornate iron door. "I don't know exactly how old the lift is, but it's in perfect condition."

"And this is how you get furniture up here. Through the store, up the lift, and through this dining room. That Aunt Sissy of yours was one forward thinker."

I grinned at his enthusiasm.

A squeaky *meow* interrupted us. We both looked down into green eyes.

"Uh-oh, do you think she needs to go?"

"I don't speak cat, but let's set up her litter in here for now. You can always move the box."

He went to the kitchen peninsula, where he'd left the critter supplies, and I followed. He added the box liner, opened the litter bag, and poured slowly to minimize the dust. I carried the pan to the dining room, set it down near a wall, and backed away as the cat came to inspect her toilet. When it looked like she was going to do her thing, I turned and found the pup sitting a foot away, big golden brown eyes pinned on me.

"I suppose she should go out, huh?"

"I bought a collar and leash."

"Of course you did."

"And a halter and leash for the cat."

I sighed. "Of course you did."

Eric used his pocketknife to first cut the tags off the turquoise collar and coordinating leash. I snapped my fingers and the pup trotted right to me. No squirming when I fastened the collar, although the cat came over to sniff and then rub her cheek against it. Then, when Eric handed me the now tagless halter that matched the dog's collar, Cat stood on her hind legs for a better look.

"Yes, this is for you," I told her. "I'm not sure how to get you in it, but we'll figure it out."

With a little coaching from Eric, I held the halter

correctly, and then knelt hoping I wouldn't have to wrestle Cat into the contraption. I didn't. She daintily stepped right into the thing and stood still as I snapped it closed. Maybe this pet deal wouldn't be so bad after all. In the short term, that is.

"Uh, Nixy, do you have any plastic bags?"

"Under the sink. Why?" Then I got it. Dog poop. Oh, joy.

ERIC AND I WALKED THE DOG AROUND A BLOCK away from the square where there were more houses, and where grass grew between the sidewalk and the street. The dog could do her business without being in someone's yard proper. It was nice, walking through the town at dusk. With Eric. Even if he was carrying a bag of dog poop.

The cat trotted right beside of her canine BFF, both seemingly proud of their new accessories. Striding next to them as we strolled, I realized the dog's shoulders came about to my knee. The cat was shorter by about six inches, but she kept up with her taller friend.

Eric offered to pick up some takeout and then help me unload some boxes. I took him up on the burgers and fries, but turned down unpacking the boxes. I was too worn out to make sorting and stashing decisions.

After he left, I got on the floor to play with the critters. Just for a few minutes. Not like I was getting attached, although calling them Dog and Cat was wearing thin. Naming them? That seemed permanent, but hey, it was practical.

"All right, you two, listen up," I said as the critters lounged, bellies up on either side of my outstretched legs. "I feel stupid talking to you, but I'd feel more stupid not talking. I mean you're right here, and it's not your fault I've never had a pet."

They flipped over and cocked their heads at me like they were really listening. It was adorable, and talking to them suddenly seemed more natural. I forged ahead.

"I also feel lame calling you Dog and Cat. You need names. Just temporary ones, of course."

The animals looked at each other, then back at me, cocking their heads in the other direction. A little whine burst from the dog. I could swear their eyes twinkled.

"So I found you two in the alley, but Alley and Cat? Clichéd, don't you think?" The dog sniffed and I swear she shook her head. "Okay, how about Amber for your golden eyes?" The dog barked and licked my hand. "Amber works for you?"

She barked again, wagged her tail. Not to be outdone, the cat crawled into my lap and put her paws on my chest. Her three little claws caught on my emporium shirt and her purring rumbled pleasantly.

"Yes, yes, I'm getting to you, and watch those claws." I caught one of her paws in my fingers and her three little toes splayed. "You're a tri-claw cat. How about T.C. for tri-claw?"

The cat rumbled even more deeply and licked my chin with her rough tongue.

"Okay, Amber and T.C. it is."

As I scratched my newly named companions, a hand on each furry head, a wave of both calm and sleepiness came over me. Time to crash.

I forgot to close the bedroom door, and emerged from the shower to find the animals curled up together on the foot of my bed, Amber spooned around T.C.'s smaller body. I started to move them to the living room, but figured my comforter was easy enough to dry clean. Hopefully, there'd be no accidents. There was plenty of room for all three of us in the bed.

Besides, they'd be forever gone if the vet knew them and their owner.

I IMMEDIATELY LIKED DR. SALLY BARKLAY WHEN I met her early the following morning. Yep, her real name.

About my age, she was slender in her animal print scrubs, her short ash blonde hair giving her an impish look. She ran her one-doctor office with a receptionist, an assistant, and students interning in veterinary medicine.

On the downside, Sally didn't recognize Amber or T.C. from her practice, and a scan showed they hadn't been chipped. On the upside, she confirmed that both critters had been fixed, and pronounced them in excellent health except for minor cracks in their paw pads. This condition, she told Eric and me, was likely because they had wandered for a week or more, walking on hot road surfaces. If a surface was too hot for bare human feet, it was too hot for paws. She applied a balm to their pads and gave me a sample to continue applying several times a day.

"Did you groom them?" At my blank stare, she added, "Did you brush their coats, pick out burrs, anything like that?"

"Nope. They showed up looking like they'd walked down the block, not walked for days."

"They've done a good job of grooming themselves, then. Or each other. There is no sign of them having been mistreated, either. Certainly not in the recent past," she said, stroking Amber's back. Amber gave her an adoring gaze. "Your dog is probably a German pinscher. That's an unusual breed for around here, but she may have a dash of coonhound or something else. I don't think she'll get much larger, especially if she was the litter runt."

"What does much larger mean, Sally?"

"She should stay medium sized, maybe get to twenty-five pounds, maybe not. I'm not an expert on German pinschers, but I believe they need a fair amount of exercise."

Since I didn't know "Come here" from "Sic 'em" about dog breeds, I vowed to do some Internet research. Right. Soon as I had the time.

"Your cat is a domestic short-hair," she said, scratching T.C.'s chin to a rumbling purr. "Some would call her a tiger stripe. I don't think she'll grow that much more either. Both animals are about a year old." Sally scratched each animal behind their ears. "They both sure have calm dispositions, don't they? Are you keeping them?"

"I don't know yet."

"I understand, but they need rabies shots today. If you do keep them, they'll need other vaccinations and tests for conditions like heartworm and feline HIV."

"Should I get them chipped?"

"It's recommended, but by no means required. Whoever had these two originally may not have been able to afford all the shots, surgeries, and chipping on top of that."

"Vets don't do pro bono work?"

"Not like you're thinking, Nixy. We'll take vouchers from humane societies, or we might give discounts, but that's it. We can't vaccinate, spay, neuter, or chip animals for free. It's a liability issue."

I paid the shockingly hefty bill, and got more information about chipping the critters. Then, with Sally's advice about how to advertise the found pets and her promise to stop in at The Handcraft Emporium, Eric and I loaded T.C. and Amber in the extended cab of his pickup to swing by the rescue shelter.

Miranda Huston, the shelter director, came off as caring but frenzied. She confirmed she couldn't take one more animal, much less two, and agreed to let us post photos of my temporary pets on her lost and found board. She also said she'd let me know if places opened in the shelter, but left me with a don't-call-us-we'll-call-you vibe.

Eric dropped the critters and me at the alley door. I'd spotted Sherry's and Dab's cars and Fred's truck in the parking lot. I hadn't realized it was after nine, but was certain the Six had everything under control.

I planned to get Amber and T.C. settled in my apartment, but Fred wouldn't have it.

"Get the cat's litter box—"

"T.C."

"What?"

"I'm calling the cat T.C. and dog Amber."

"You named them?" One corner of his mouth tipped upward, then he cleared his throat. "I take it the vet didn't know their owner."

"No, and they weren't chipped either, so I'm planning to put their pictures around town and on Facebook."

"Well then, missy, bring the litter box on down. T.C. and Amber can keep me company while I finish a mess of fix-it jobs."

The day flew by with Fred fixing, and the rest of us setting up the chairs and a six-foot folding table for the craft demonstrations. We'd thought about using Fred's workroom for the free-of-charge grand opening programs as well as the occasional paid evening classes like Doralee's—the workroom was roughly the size of a three-car garage, for heaven's sake—but decided against it in the end. Fred frequently worked on more than one repair project at a time, and the man had a ton of tools that took up space in spades. Besides, although floor space was at a premium in the emporium proper, it boasted a touch more square footage than the workshop. We had room for fifteen to twenty chairs when we moved display tables to the back wall of the store. That was the only wall without floor-to-ceiling shelves. For the time being anyway.

We hosted a local needlepoint artist for the morning demonstration. In the afternoon, Eleanor showed off her whittling skills. Since it was a perfect summer Saturday, I figured people would be busy with outdoor work or play activities, but we had a good crowd for the demos, and decent enough sales to give me encouragement. Oh, we'd have slow times, no doubt about that. However, if we got the emporium website up sooner than later, I hoped Internet sales would take up the slack. Since Jasmine's boyfriend was designing the website as a class project, aka a freebie for us, I hated to push him. I'd drop a hint instead. Mention the photos we needed to upload to the site. A totally legit hint, because Dab had taken more shots of the needlepointer's and of Eleanor's presentations.

Admittedly I braced for another round of trauma-drama when Ernie, Kim, and Georgine came into the store. Thankfully, the three browsed, then sat together peaceably for Eleanor's demo. I'd have liked to think the calming lavender did its thing, but maybe the trio behaved because Doralee wasn't there to be a target.

Afterward I caught sight of Ernie chatting with Eleanor, with Georgine at his elbow. She fingered her necklace even as her gaze roved the room tracking Kim. I tensed for trouble, but it didn't come. Kim bought earrings, Ernie bought one of Sherry's handwoven egg baskets, and Georgine bought one of Eleanor's less expensive animal carvings. Then they left peacefully.

Only one event marred the day. One of Eleanor's whittling tools went missing.

"It's a chip carving knife with a contoured handle. I don't know how it could've rolled off the table."

We searched thoroughly—the seniors, Jasmine, and I— but didn't find the knife.

"First Doralee's awl, now Eleanor's knife," my aunt said with a huff. "Someone must be starting a craft tools collection."

Or we'd attracted a kleptomaniac to the demos. Dang it, we'd prepared for the possibility of shoplifting by having video cameras installed. Head smack.

"Wait a minute. I should've remembered this yesterday."

"What?" Aster asked with her usual calm.

"We have security cameras. I'll look at the recordings."

"We also have photos of the events on Eleanor's digital camera," Sherry said and waved a hand toward Dab.

"That's right," he said, holding the camera up. "We've taken turns snapping pictures, and I'll bet we have some dandies."

"Great," I said. "Maybe they'll show something none of us saw at the time."

I sat behind the antique glass-fronted checkout counter with Eleanor, Sherry, Aster, and Maise crowded around me as Dab read the instructions Greg Masters, the security system guy, had left for us. After exiting the T.C.-and-Amber slide show running on my tablet, I pulled up the store surveillance footage. Split screens let me replay video from each camera simultaneously to cut overall viewing time, plus the system let me fast-forward, rewind, and pause. Each screen was small on my tablet but adequate, and I could enlarge a screen if we wanted to more closely examine footage.

My hopes of catching the culprit crumbled, though, when I realized where the cameras were trained. Camera one was aimed at the wall of display shelves, especially those holding the smaller or more fragile crafts. Camera two provided a view of the checkout counter and the front door, and a peek of the sidewalk outside. The third camera caught part of the center of the store, but the area around the demonstration table was a big ole blank. It was close enough to the work-room door that I hadn't seen the need to aim a camera there.

For fifteen minutes, we skimmed the recordings to watch the general movements of the audience members. First I ran the loops at normal speed, then fast-forwarded when I realized I could conclude little to nothing from the footage. No one appeared to behave furtively. No one appeared to have concealed a tool or anything else on his or her person. No one appeared to scream "suspect here."

I put my tablet aside and pored over the still photos on Eleanor's digital camera. Again, no one struck me or the Six as being obviously "off." Well, except the man and woman who'd huddled by the front door during the gourd demo on Friday afternoon. We had both video and still shots of them.

I might recognize the woman's helmet of blonde hair if I saw her again, but the oversized dark glasses she wore and the man's mirrored pair obscured more of their features than I remembered.

In a few frames, they appeared to scan the room as if looking for someone. They never gave any indication that they'd spotted who—or what—they were looking for, and they never left the front of the store. They also hadn't attended today's demo. Conclusion: squirrelly for sure, but not necessarily suspicious.

The other oddball from Friday afternoon's gourd presentation, the thirty-something guy in the blue scrubs, dark shades, and New Orleans Saints cap, had his head down in the one photo we had of him. The video camera had caught him drifting among displays, pausing now and then, but never looking at the goods as if he'd buy something. Once the presentation started, he stood behind the last row of chairs, his gaze glued to his cell phone more often than not. The phone was pointed toward the floor, so I doubted he was sneaking photos. He certainly didn't appear to be interested in the demonstration, so why had he come?

Huh. Come to think on it, I had sensitive eyes, and unless the skies were seriously overcast, I put on my shades as soon as I stepped outside. However, I took them off inside buildings. Why hadn't these people? And why hadn't I spotted any of the sunglasses squad in today's video feeds? Was it happenstance that they'd only attended the Doralee and Sherry Show?

I glanced at the ring of seniors. "Do any of you recognize these three people?"

"I don't," my aunt said as she passed the camera to the others. "Do you think they're important?"

"Not really. None of them appears to have approached the demo table yesterday, and they didn't show up today."

That's what I said, but then I wondered if those three

people had been together, perhaps casing the store. The likelihood was slim, but I'd be extra careful to lock up and set the alarms. Bottom line was that we'd struck out identifying a possible tool thief.

"I'm sorry, Eleanor. Maybe we'll see something if you upload these pictures to y'all's laptop at the farmhouse. That will blow them up a bit."

"I do believe that's worth a try," she said. "I'll e-mail any pictures that merit another look."

"Done, and I'll call Greg on Monday to order another camera to cover the blind spot. Until he can come, though, one of us should stand guard over artist's supplies."

"Roger that," Maise said. "I'll make a duty roster."

"Put me on it, too," Jasmine said, leaning on the opposite side of the counter, her braids dancing. "I can take afternoon shifts, and I'll keep guarding even if you get another camera."

Maise gave her a decisive nod. "We'll be squared away in no time."

THAT NIGHT PLAYING WITH THE CRITTERS TOOK MY mind off the puzzle of the missing tools. Dab had gone off to buy toys at some point, and he and Fred proudly announced they'd taught Amber to sit, turn in a circle, and lie down on command. I had to wonder how many dog treats they'd fed her to accomplish all that, yet she dug into her food.

From all I'd heard, you can't train cats; they train you. But T.C. must've hung out with Amber long enough to think she was part dog. She, too, sat on command. Okay, close to it. She lowered her hindquarters halfway to the floor, and then snapped up the cat treats as fast as Amber did hers.

Eric didn't call to check on the animals Saturday night, but he did text that he'd be at the rededication party the next morning. I hoped his job didn't get in the way of his coming. We'd both been busy since I moved to town, me with refurbishing the building, him with detecting. When all the dust settled, I hoped we'd be able to spend more time together, but at least I'd learned some things about him on our one-and-so-far-only dinner date.

I knew he'd been a military policeman in the U.S. Army, and had been deployed to the Middle East. He'd bought a house a few years back and fixed it up with help from friends. He fished when the mood struck, but didn't hunt. Not animals anyway. He liked football, soccer, and baseball more than basketball. He watched the History Channel and movies when he had the chance, but his job demanded more than a nine-to-five commitment. Especially since the other detective, who'd been out sick in April, had experienced complications and was still out of commission. The police and sheriff's departments fully cooperated with each other, so there was usually someone to take up the slack, but Eric took his work seriously, and it was a part of him I appreciated. When he'd mentioned the department was looking to hire more personnel soon, I'd nearly done backflips. Yes, we'd first been drawn together by a murder case, but I sure didn't want to continue *that* trend.

I sighed and looked at my furry companions, their small warm bodies curled at my side. A relaxing end to a hectic day.

It was not so relaxing to awake to paws on my chest the next morning. Amber licked my cheek, T.C. gave me a gentle head bump. At least they'd let me sleep until nine. Perfect since the cemetery rededication wouldn't start until one.

Should I be going to church? Probably, especially since I now lived in Small Town USA in Aunt Sherry's shadow. Not to mention the rest of the Six. I put that little guilt trip aside and dealt with the morning feeding and exercising of Amber and T.C. Yes, the cat refused to be left behind during Amber's amble. Did the leash law extend to cats? If so, I was covered, but I held hope someone would claim the critters soon.

As I strolled the square with the critters, a leash in each

hand, it hit me that I'd learned the rhythm of Lilyvale. Or at least my corner of it. I'd absorbed the routine sights and sounds of the neighborhood, and become part of its beat. Not that I knew every resident by name, but I recognized people's faces, or simply their voices when they called greetings to one another. Now that I walked T.C. and Amber, I was learning to pair people with their pets, too. This morning I stopped on a street just off the square to chat with teenager Louie while Amber and Louie's beagle, Harley, did their business.

"Nice car," Louie said of a silver Audi that glided around the corner and headed toward the Lilies Café.

"I thought you were into motorcycles," I teased because I knew that's why he'd named his dog Harley.

"Hey, a sweet ride is a sweet ride. Have you seen that black pickup with monster tires? Don't know who drives it, but I could do some serious off-roading in that sucker." He paused, cocked his head. "Although that truck needs a tune-up soon."

Louie had an eye for cars, but also had an ear for engines. He could identify the big-as-a-boat blue Buick Ida Bollings drove by the growl of its motor, and Eric's dark gray extended-cab truck made a deep hum.

Harley tugged at his leash, and Louie waved as he shuffled down the sidewalk. My cell phone alarm played from my pocket. Time to get home, do my chores, and get on with the day.

I'd promised the Silver Six to come early and help with the table, food, and games setup. After a bowl of frosted wheat cereal, I gave the apartment a light dusting and then a once-over with the vacuum. Amber and T.C. might be short-haired, but they had to be shedding, right? I'm not a total neat freak, but I didn't want my new furniture covered in a thick blanket of fur.

A shower later, I did the makeup and hair thing, and dressed in a simple denim skirt paired with a blue scoop neck T-shirt and blue flats. Subdued for the blessing ceremony, and appropriate for the rest of the festivities.

Aunt Sherry assured me the critters were welcome, so I loaded them in the white Camry I'd inherited from my mother, and we were off.

WHAT REMAINED OF THE STANTON ANCESTRAL land occupied a full half of a city block near the edge of the city limits. A rustic split-rail fence separated the wide front yard from the street, with the gravel driveway running to the back of the house. The south and east sides of the property were neatly hemmed by pines trees, red buds, and dogwoods in a mini-forest. Aster's herb and veggie garden was on the south side of the house, but it hardly took up any of the huge south and east lawn space with neatly cut native grasses.

The farmhouse itself sat on a slight rise. Wood construction and painted white, the two-story structure boasted a porch that wrapped all around the home, and spilled onto a deck in back. A barn and two buildings a bit larger than one-car garages stood behind the house, all painted barn red. Fred stored the tractor with its riding mower attachment in the barn, and Dab distilled Aster's herbs in one of the outbuildings. In real stills, but redesigned for safety and efficiency by Fred and Eleanor. Yes, Eleanor. She looked like a fashion model, and held an advanced degree in mechanical engineering.

The family cemetery was tucked a short walk behind the barn, bordered by both low fencing and azalea hedges on three sides. In April, the bushes had been a wall of pink flowers. Now, on the first official day of summer, the flowers were long gone, but the bushes still made a nice border of greenery.

My aunt had invited a select group of people to the rededication—Mayor Patrick Paulson, the Lilyvale city councilpersons, Police Chief Gene Randall, and Fire Chief Dan Throckmorton and their spouses. Only the sheriff of Hendrix County had declined because he was out of town.

The Silver Six and I made up the rest of the group.

The blessing ceremony was short and very sweet. Sherry got misty eyed, and she wasn't the only one. When Father Bruce had finished, Aster sprinkled lavender flowers and rosemary leaves at the cemetery gate. Lavender for tranquility, rosemary for remembrance.

That bit raised a few eyebrows. It did mine when I'd first met Aster. Now I'm used to her sprinkling or spraying lavender at the drop of a hat.

The party was in full swing by two o'clock. Half the town seemed to be there at one point or another, and many were strangers. Jasmine showed up with friends from the technical college. Neighbors, church friends, and local artist friends came as well. Although most of the adults simply visited with one another, some entertained the children by playing with toys Dab and Eleanor had bought—a football, soccer ball, and a young child's foam T-ball set. Teenaged boys played with the Frisbee, and the girls took photos I'm sure were instantly posted online.

I circulated along with the Six, meeting new people and reconnecting with those neighbors I'd met in April but hadn't seen much since I moved to Lilyvale. I was surprised that Lorna and Clark Tyler, owners of the Inn on the Square and the Lilies Café, weren't at the party. I wasn't wild about Clark, but Lorna, Sherry, Aster, Maise, and Eleanor were fairly good friends. Then again, the Tylers had an almost full house at the inn with Doralee and Zach, Ernie, Kim, and Georgine there.

I'd just introduced Eric to Doralee and Zach when I spotted my aunt's ninety-three-year-old neighbor, Bernice

Gilroy, standing on her back stoop next door. The woman who pretty much never came out of her small house had taken a liking to me in April, and now she waved at me.

Not a mere friendly wave. I was being summoned for a command appearance.

Chapter Five

I EXCUSED MYSELF FROM THE GROUP, HEAPED TWO paper plates full of finger sandwiches, cookies, and brownies, and went down the front gravel drive to get to Old Lady Gilroy's house.

I'd met Bernice in April when the Silver Six had loaded a box of food for me to deliver to her. Taking meals over wasn't new for them, but they'd warned me she wouldn't so much as crack her front door. So my instructions that day had been to leave the box on her porch.

I don't know why she'd broken her pattern that first day, but as soon as I'd raised my hand to knock, the old woman had thrown open the door, grabbed my wrist, and pulled me inside with such force I'd almost dropped the box of food. The Six had been agog that I'd forged a sort of friendship with Mrs. Gilroy, but the woman had been helpful in solving a murder, and I was grateful. Besides, the lady was a hoot. She'd taken to calling me Sissy, and at first I feared she was confusing me with my ancestress. But no. Though Aunt Sissy had been much older, Bernice had known and admired my aunt, and had been the first person to liken me to her. Miscalling me was her way of teasing, and I was flattered. Bernice didn't take to just anyone, and I made a point of visiting each time I was at the farmhouse.

I stepped onto the wooden porch and raised my hand to knock. As usual, the door flew open, then she snagged my wrist and tugged me inside. Good thing I'd quickly learned to keep a vise grip on everything I brought to her.

"Come in the kitchen with those," she said, and I followed her through the dim living room, which held only two wingback chairs upholstered in a hideous, faded plaid, a scarred wood coffee table, and a massive flat screen TV. Did I mention the woman was an enigma?

For a change, the kitchen was flooded with light. Mrs. Gilroy had parted the dull brown curtains at both the back and the side windows that looked onto Sherry's property. The brighter light didn't completely dispel the sadness of the age-dulled paint and yellowed appliances. I'd never asked if the stove-oven combo and fridge were supposed to be harvest gold rather than simply dingy. I'm not that rude, and this woman flat intimidated me half the time.

I eyed the pair of black binoculars on the 1950s kitchen table, a lone chair facing the window. That single chair always tugged at my heart, and today I noticed Bernice's hair looked thinner. I could see her pink scalp.

She clapped her hands in front of my face. "Pay attention, girl. I talk to air enough without you acting like an airhead."

I chuckled and waved toward the binoculars. "Been spying again?"

"Living vicariously sounds better, don't you think? That big party must've set Sherry Mae back a wad of money."

I shrugged and placed the paper plates on the table.

Mrs. Gilroy cackled. "Never discuss money, politics, or religion with people you don't know well, am I right?"

"So I was taught, ma'am."

"I'm not surprised, your mother, Sue Anne, having been Sherry's sister. Well, how was the rededication?"

"Very nice. How have you been? Are you feeling well?"

She cocked her head at me. "It's not nearly as exciting over yonder since you moved to the square, and most of the other neighbors are boring."

"You mean they aren't worth spying on?"

"Don't be fresh."

"Yes, ma'am."

"Did you bring those pictures of the emporium you promised?"

I smacked my forehead. "Shoot, I'm sorry, Bernice, I forgot. I'll bring them next time, and I'll have photos we've taken of the craft presentations, too."

"You know I'm not getting any younger."

"Yes, ma'am."

"But I'm not ready to kick off yet." She cocked her head at me. "I saw that dog and cat you took in running free earlier over yonder in the yard. Fred sure gets a kick out of them, doesn't he?"

"Yes. They'd probably be better off here, but Aunt Sherry hasn't offered to take them."

"She won't. Last pet she had died shortly after her husband, Bill, did. Got her heart broken twice in about as many days."

I stared openmouthed. "I didn't know that."

"No reason you would. How's that handsome detective fella? I hear you had a date with him a few weeks back. Is he a good kisser?"

I blushed. "He's excellent, and he's waiting for me at the party. How about I come back and visit another time?"

"So long as you bring food. And don't come when my programs are on the TV. And don't stay too long like you're doing now." She shooed me out to the porch, but paused before she closed the door. "There's a storm brewing yonder, Nixy. You be careful."

I frowned as I walked back to Sherry's. Bernice seemed healthy, but she hadn't once called me Sissy. Was the lack of teasing a sign that Bernice's memory was slipping? I sincerely hoped not.

And that storm brewing bit? I looked up to fluffy clouds dotting an almost painfully blue summer sky. Had she been giving me tomorrow's forecast? Why the warning to be careful? I shook off the skitter of unease that shot up my spine. Mrs. Gilroy was a cagey old gal, but she wasn't a seer.

ERNIE AND KIM HAD SHOWN UP WHILE I WAS GONE. I'd say they'd crashed the party, but my aunt had invited one and all. I'd rescind the invite if they made trouble, though, and it appeared they were doing just that since Doralee was backed against the double barn doors with Ernie and Kim standing close. Standing far too close, in my opinion.

I hustled nearer as Kim stomped a high-heeled foot and shook her finger at Doralee. When Kim waved her hands, Ernie caught them.

"Stop it," he said loud enough for me to hear.

"I want that opal, Ernie. Make her give it to you."

"I can't make her, I don't want to make her, and I'm about done with your harping, Kim. You already have enough jewelry to open your own store."

"Is there a problem?" I asked.

Ernie and Kim spun toward me, and I had to give Kim credit for not getting her heel snagged in the grass. In addition to the usual bling, she wore skin-tight jeans, a marginally modest camisole, and a beaded denim vest. None of which were appropriate for a small town, casual, family-oriented event. Doralee looked like she might die of embarrassment.

Ernie, dressed pretty much as I'd seen him before, now shook his head.

"No, uh, Nixy," he said, clearly uncomfortable and barely remembering my name. "No problem here."

"Nothing you can help with," Kim snipped.

"Good, that's one less thing on my plate. Y'all enjoy the party now," I said dismissively. "Doralee, where's Zach? Fred wants to ask him about that gourd box he designed, and Aster wants to see you."

Doralee appeared more bemused than cowed by Kim, and her attitude toward Ernie came off as long-suffering. Not angry, certainly not frightened. She did, however, look relieved to be rescued.

"Zach had a call from his office, but he should be off the phone by now. Let's find him."

She walked smack between a fuming Kim and shame-faced Ernie, and linked her arm in mine as we strolled toward the large back deck that linked the house's full wrap-around porch.

"Thanks for coming when you did. I knew Kim was single-minded, but I didn't realize she was obsessive. I swear, I have half a mind to sell Ernie the stone just to get them to go away."

"It must be amazing," I said mildly, not wanting to pry, but itching with the curiosity bug.

"It is. It's a five-carat black opal from Australia although that's a misnomer if you haven't seen one. The stones actually glimmer with color on a dark background. Mine is red and it appraised as extra fine in quality."

I didn't know squat about opals, and not much more about any other kind of gemstone, but I heard a touch of awe in Doralee's tone. "I take it that means the gem is pricey."

"Very. I bought the oval cabochon on a whim at an estate sale years ago. I didn't pay nearly what it was worth—not that I intended to cheat the seller, you understand. I simply didn't know the true value, and obviously he didn't either." She paused, a faraway look in her eyes. "I meant to have it set in a ring for Ernie, but never got around to it. Kim heard about it, and thinks the stone should be his. Or rather hers."

From the corner of my eye, I spotted Kim marching along the north side of the house. Doralee must've seen her, too. She leaned nearer.

"She wants the gem for her wedding ring."

"Why? She already wears that huge diamond. Besides, I thought opals were unlucky."

"Not black ones, and not if the opal is in a setting with diamonds."

"I never heard that. How fascinating."

Doralee shrugged. "I suppose if you're into folklore and superstition, it is. As for why she wants the stone so desperately, I don't know. She might not like wearing the ring he had remade for me, but how is having the opal going to be so different?"

"Because she'll believe she bested you?"

"It's as good a theory as any, but I wish Ernie had never opened his big mouth about it. Look, here's Zach."

He strode toward us from the south side of the yard. "Doralee, honey, I'm sorry about that, and sorrier that I need to leave. The office messed up my expense report, and I have to go to Texarkana to fix it."

"On a Sunday?" she asked, touching his arm. "You sure that new girl in the office isn't just angling for you?"

He covered her hand with his. "She wouldn't stand a chance, but yes. If I don't resubmit today, I don't get paid this week. You can go with me, or I can borrow the car and be back in three or four hours, tops. I'll bring wine, and we can finish our weekend."

"I'll stay, and that wine sounds like a plan. Aster put my purse in the foyer. I'll get the car keys. Do you need to stop at the inn for anything?"

"Nope, I'm heading straight out."

Zach and I followed Doralee into the farmhouse through the back door, waving to Aster as we passed the kitchen, and heading on to the foyer and Doralee's purse. Down the hall, I thought I heard the front door close softly, but that couldn't be so. I remembered Maise bolting the door to keep people from wandering around the house.

"Oh, shoot, Doralee," Zach said as she fished her keys from her purse and handed them over, "how will you get back to the inn?"

"I'll take her when I go home," I volunteered.

"Perfect," Doralee said. "I have a gift for you, and I forgot to bring it with me today. You can run up to our room with me and I'll give it to you there."

There was no point in demurring. "That's fine, but do you mind riding with a cat and dog in the car? Are you allergic?"

"Are you talking about those precious pets I saw playing with the children? Heavens, no, I don't mind. I have fur babies of my own."

I cocked a brow. "I don't suppose you want two more?"

Doralee laughed. "I've got all I can handle. Two dogs, two cats, and a goat."

"Worth a shot."

I crossed to open the front door and usher them onto the porch. There they'd have privacy for their good-byes.

The door wasn't closed, though. It stood slightly ajar when it should've been locked up tight.

Shoot. Had Maise forgotten to throw the deadbolt? Even if she had, the door was made of solid, heavy wood. It didn't just blow open. Had someone merely peeked in, or prowled though the house? What with those tools gone missing at the emporium, and now the farmhouse front door unlocked, the Six needed to do a sweep to see if everything was in its place. I sure hoped we didn't have a petty thief roaming Lilyvale.

ABOUT THREE O'CLOCK WHEN ZACH LEFT, I SAW Ernie and Kim headed down the farmhouse's gravel drive toward the street. I didn't see Georgine with them, but then I didn't recall seeing her at all today. Hallelujah.

I lost track of Doralee for a while, but spotted Lorna Clark chatting with Aunt Sherry. Lorna owned the Lilies Café and the Inn on the Square. The same inn where Doralee and Zack, Ernie, Kim, and Georgine were staying. Why was all of this suddenly starting to sound like a bad French farce?

I started to go greet Lorna, but Eleanor asked me to restock the ice tea. When I brought fresh, chilled pitchers from the house, I saw Doralee again. She stood on the far side of the deck with Ernie. No Kim in sight. As I watched, she put her hand on his chest and kissed him on the cheek. Her expression carried regret. His was just profoundly sad.

He trudged away, shoulders sagging. Doralee turned and was startled when she spied me. Then she met my gaze, and shrugged. "Old habits die hard," she said cryptically before she gathered two empty food platters and went into the house.

I shoved the scene to the back of my mind. These people would be gone tomorrow. Their troubles were not mine.

My only problem might be missing critters because I didn't see them bounding around the yard as I expected. Then I spotted Amber and T.C. cuddled in an Adirondack chair with a little girl whose leg was swathed in a neon yellow cast. The three of them watched my favorite detective play blindman's bluff with a dozen children.

"I'm Randa," she said when I knelt beside her and gave the critters a pat each. "I like your dog and kitty."

"They must like you, too, Randa."

"They do," she replied with blithe confidence. "I bet you think your doggie's markings are tan, but my daddy would call it fawn. Like right here on her head. See?"

She pointed at the broad slashes of fawn on Amber's face that I'd supposed were eyebrows. The dog turned her golden gaze on me, and I swear she waggled those brows.

"So, Randa, is your dad an expert on dogs?"

"Some, but I'm a 'spert on cats. Did you know your kitty's got orange mixed with her gold stripes?"

I leaned in for a closer look as Randa ran her little hand

backward on T.C.'s side. I'd heard cats didn't like that, but T.C. didn't flinch. And sure enough, Randa was right. A few places were pale orange.

"You're very observant, Randa."

"I know. I want to keep 'serving now, so you can go away."

Summarily dismissed by a preschooler, I turned my attention to the game. Eric didn't wear a blindfold, just squeezed his eyes closed. The kids jeered him when he peeked, and giggled when they eluded him. I laughed and he swung toward me.

"Look out, lady, he's gonna get ya," a boy of about seven hollered.

I'd never played with children because I'd never been around them. Growing up, my friends had been the youngest in their families. Instead of babysitting to earn money, I'd done chores for my parents and our neighbors.

But when that boy shouted his warning, I dove into the spirit of the game without a thought.

"He won't get us. Let's confuse him."

The children and I called to Eric, and then darted away again and again until Eric threw up his hands and dramatically collapsed on the grass. I didn't follow suit, but I was more out of breath than I should have been.

"Hey," said the boy who'd told me to look out for Eric. "You play good."

"Thank you, so do you."

"I know. I'm Brandon." He said that like his name explained his prowess. I grinned.

A much younger girl tugged my skirt. "What's your name?"

I squatted to be at her eye level. "My name is Nixy. What's yours?"

She flashed a grin. "My name is Wendy Lynette Murphy, and I'm four and a half years old, and I have a loose tooth."

"Nice to meet you, Wendy Lynette."

The child nodded, then whirled and ran off.

"Nixy," Eric said from beside me, "I think the party's wrapping up."

"Aw, I thought we was playing again," Brandon said.

"Not today. A storm is building."

I looked up and saw gray-tinged clouds racing northeastward. Ah, Mrs. Gilroy's brewing storm. I'd been so distracted playing, I hadn't noticed the wind had kicked up considerably.

"Oh, gosh, Eric, the banner at the store."

"According to the weather service, we have time. Let's start moving things in the house while the Six see their guests off."

The yard emptied quickly, although several guests, including Doralee, pitched in to help clean.

Amber and T.C. curled up under a chair on the deck, safely out of the way as we ferried food inside, and separated the recycling from the trash. Eric and I folded the small tables we'd used at the emporium and stashed them in the barn. The kitchen was a mess, but the Six assured me they could clean up by themselves. Maise insisted I take food home.

"You don't have two crumbs to rub together at your place," she scolded. An exaggeration, but not far off. I rather desperately needed to grocery shop.

After hugs all around, Eric hopped in his truck, and Doralee and I carried Amber and T.C. to the car. I stowed the paper bag of food-filled containers on the back floorboard.

"Do you mind a detour to the emporium?" I asked Doralee. "I need to help Eric take down the grand opening banner."

"I don't mind at all. Do you want to drop off your fur friends?"

I considered that, but shook my head. "I don't know if they freak out in thunderstorms, and what they might tear up in the apartment if they do. I won't be staying long at the inn, so they should be fine in the car with the windows cracked."

Eric and I parked in the alley and made short work of getting the banner down, and the ladder stowed away again. He gave T.C. and Amber a pat and told Doralee good-bye before he drove off.

The coming storm had sucked more light from the day, and the tinge of greenish-black signaled possible tornados. I drove the short distance to the Inn on the Square with lights on, and hoped Lilyvale had tornado sirens.

As I approached the alley, a dark mud-splatted pickup shot out in front of me, one fitted with huge tires. I slammed on the brakes and earned a warning yip and a ticked-off *yreow* from the critters in the backseat.

"Sorry, girls," I said over my shoulder, then glanced at Doralee. "You okay?"

"Fine. I hope that fella slows down before he causes an accident."

"Amen." I accelerated slowly toward the stop sign at the corner. "People in Lilyvale generally don't drive crazy."

"Unlike in Houston?" she teased.

"You know it."

A right turn took me to the concrete parking lot behind the inn, but as I wheeled into the drive, I had to hit the brakes again for a silver Audi barreling toward us. I had a split second to recognize the four rings on the front grill, and another eye blink to see a woman driving the car, a man in the passenger seat, before the car swerved hard to the right, bumped over the curb, and disappeared down a back street.

"Geez," I breathed, hands shaking. "This storm front must be making people nuts."

"And it's not even raining yet," Doralee said. "Well, we're here now, and there's a space next to Ernie's car."

I pulled alongside the Honda Accord that looked purple but was probably supposed to be blue. Was this an older car? Is that how Doralee knew it belonged to Ernie? Or perhaps she and Zach had seen Ernie driving it. Whatever. I wasn't about to judge Doralee's relationship with Ernie, even after the quiet moment I had observed between them at the farm-house.

Thicker clouds roiled overhead, and the June day turned cooler by the minute. Cool enough to make me shiver. If it weren't for the gift Doralee wanted me to have, I'd have watched her get in safely and gone home. But hey, it wasn't raining yet. Surely I could get up to Doralee's room and back before a downpour.

As I set the emergency brake, Amber let out a long, mournful howl. T.C. meowed like she was in distress. I shot a startled glance at Doralee, then unbuckled my seat belt and turned toward the back.

"What on earth is the matter, you two? Did you get hurt when I slammed on the brakes?"

Amber and T.C. paced circles on the fabric seat, first one direction, then the other. Neither of them limped or other-wise appeared physically injured, but both were obviously shaken. Amber finally flopped on her belly, and T.C. licked her friend's head as if to calm her.

"They probably hear thunder we can't hear yet. My ani-mals get restless in storms. Maybe you were right not to leave them alone at your place."

"I suppose. Okay, girls," I said, giving them a reassuring pat, then rolling the windows down a good six inches. Not enough to allow them to escape, but enough to keep the car cool for a short time, and give the pets plenty of ventilation. "You're safe, and I'll have you back home in no time. Have a quick nap."

"Oh, a nap sounds good," Doralee said, heading for the back door of the inn while I sent a last glance at Amber and T.C., paws on the dashboard, looking out the windshield. "I'm going to take one before Zach comes back tonight."

By day, guests could get to the inn by going up the stair-case inside the Lilies Café. Otherwise, they used the alley entrance. The back stairs didn't have the old character, but they were enclosed and safe from the elements.

Doralee entered her passcode, and I followed her up. I sure hoped Ernie had taken Kim and Georgine to dinner somewhere. I was not in the mood to run into them again.

The hallway upstairs had a high ceiling and was wide enough for three to stand abreast, but there were no windows to provide direct light. Two period fixtures from the 1930s hung on rods like a ceiling fan, but one light had a burned-out bulb, and the working one didn't chase the gloom and shadows from the hall. Lorna and Clark Tyler needed to spring for higher wattage, long-life bulbs.

"I know the key is in here," Doralee said, digging through her purse as we walked the few steps toward her room.

I took my cell out of my skirt pocket and turned on the flashlight app. "Here. Shed some light on the subject."

She flashed a grin. "You sound like Sherry."

"I'm picking up a right lot of phrases from the Silver Six."

"That you are," Doralee said on a chuckle.

She balanced her purse on one arm, leaned against the jam as she felt for the key, and the door suddenly swung open.

"Huh, that's weird," she said. "I'm sure Zach and I locked the door securely."

It was more than weird. Something was off. The air was so still.

My flashlight beam fell on a form lying on the floor at the foot of the bed just as Doralee flipped the light switch.

"Oh my God," Doralee cried. "Is that Kim?"

Chapter Six

SHE LUNGED FORWARD BEFORE I COULD REACT.

"Doralee, stop!"

Her steps faltered, and she glanced over her shoulder. "What? We have to help her."

Kim lay on her left side, blessedly facing away from the door. Her head rested on her outstretched left arm. Blood pooled around her torso, and though I was frozen in place some ten feet away, I saw no sign of breathing. No rise and fall of her right arm where it draped over her rib cage. If my gut was right, Kim was beyond help. I didn't say that.

"She doesn't look like she's breathing."

"She might have a pulse. We have to help her," Doralee said impatiently, continuing into the room.

"Then be careful where you're stepping."

She stopped short and looked down at the blood pool near, but not touching, her right shoe. "Oh." Pause. "Oh!"

She backpedaled until she stood at my side, and I hoped she wasn't going to be sick. I felt queasy enough for both of us.

"Please, Nixy, you check on her. We have to do *some*thing."

I steeled myself to cross the room, eyes firmly locked on the denim vest Kim still wore. I didn't see an obvious injury, but whatever had happened and when, she hadn't changed clothing.

I hunkered next to her head and, with my eyes closed, pressed my fingers to her neck. In three places, in case I wasn't doing it right. No pulse, and not a whisper of breath. Not even a twitch.

I opened my eyes, stood, and backed away, fumbling the phone that I'd forgotten I held in my hand. The flashlight function was still turned on.

"She's dead," I confirmed when I met Doralee's shocked stare. "We need to go out to the hall now."

I cupped her elbow and led her to the hallway, where she sagged against the wall then immediately straightened.

"Nixy, wait. What about Ernie? He has to be here somewhere. His car is in the lot. And Georgine should be here, unless . . ." She paused, her already widened eyes taking on an edge of panic. "Unless they've been attacked, too."

I gripped her forearms to keep her from flying down the hall. "Doralee, try to be calm. I don't know where Ernie and Georgine are, but we can't look for them now. We need to wait right here for help."

She darted a glance at Kim again, swallowed, and nodded.

I disabled the flashlight app, and then punched Eric's phone number, breathing a relieved sigh when he answered on the second ring.

"Nixy, you okay?"

"Yes and no. I need you to come to the inn." I paused. Gulped. "Kim is dead."

"What? Who's Kim? Never mind. Be there shortly. Call—"

"The emergency number. I know and I will. Hurry, Eric."

I keyed in 911, stayed on the line while both Doralee and I leaned against the wall opposite her guest room. My knees threatened to buckle, but she seemed to completely wilt before my eyes, shoulders hunching, her expression turned slack. And though she tried not to stare at Kim's body, her gaze returned to it again and again.

I couldn't blame her. I looked, too.

Maybe it was silly to have shut my eyes when I checked for her pulse, but I hadn't wanted to see her up close. I didn't want to see where all of that blood was coming from. I'd been through that drill in April when I found a murdered woman, and the nightmares had lasted over a month. But now, observing from this distance, I noticed a few strange things.

Kim was barefoot. I could see she had high arches. Her body was sort of curled in on itself, and the blood looked ominously dark as it spread on the aged pine floor. On her left hand, that huge diamond she'd worn all weekend didn't sparkle. I blinked. Was she even wearing it? Hard to tell. Even with the overhead fixture on, the light in the room wasn't exactly bright, and Kim's body lay in the shadow of the bed. I squinted. Thought I did see a band on her finger. Had the ring simply slipped sideways so the diamond wasn't visible? Whatever the reason, the ring looked dull to me. Perhaps it had lost its sparkle when its wearer died. A thought that made my chest hurt.

I glanced at the rest of the messy guest room. A black suitcase with pink polka dots yawned open on the unmade queen bed. Clothing, shoes, and toiletries littered the bedroom and what I could see of the bathroom. Even the pillows had been tossed to the floor. Sure, Zach might be a super slob, but he struck me as the things-in-their-place type. For that matter, so did Doralee.

Conclusion? Kim must've been madly searching for something. Perhaps the black opal? She either hadn't cared about stealth, or she'd been attacked before she could straighten the room.

"Do you think someone mistook her for me?" Doralee whispered. "We do look a bit alike, and she is in my room."

"You have an enemy vicious enough to kill you?" I countered.

She blinked at my bluntness. "I wouldn't have thought so. Ernie is going to be devastated."

I had my doubts about that, especially considering Ernie's conspicuous absence. No point in voicing my opinion. For all I knew, the guy could be in his room injured or dead. Georgine could be a victim, too, though a triple homicide of tourists in sleepy Lilyvale was farfetched. Instinct told me Kim was the sole victim.

A crack of thunder punctuated the scream of sirens pulling into the parking lot behind the inn.

Amber and T.C. were in the car. I knew they'd be fine physically, but I hoped they weren't too frightened by the storm. Or maybe the storm hadn't bothered them at all. Maybe their odd behavior when we first parked the car was due to them sensing death, and trying to tell us something was wrong.

Whatever the case, I needed to roll up the windows before the rain hit. Soaked seats in the Camry was a small thing by comparison, but a big deal to me. Maybe I could run and check on the critters. Better yet, run the animals home right quick.

"Ma'am," the emergency operator said, pulling me back to the moment, "we haven't reached the inn's owners yet."

"Shoot. I saw Lorna earlier. I hope she and Clark didn't go out of town for dinner."

"I don't know about that, ma'am, but the responders will need a code to get inside."

"Oh, right, of course. Just a sec. Doralee?" I jostled her arm. "Doralee, you with me?"

She turned her head slowly, as if it hurt her to move. "What?"

"I need your entry code."

"Sixteen twenty."

I repeated the numbers, heard steps on the staircase moments later, and then first responders swarmed the hallway. I recognized one of the young paramedics as Ben Berryhill, but didn't know the woman who carried a black box, probably filled with equipment. Middle-aged officer Doug Bryant—Dougie to some of the oldsters in town—followed Ben, and female Hendrix County Deputy Megan Paulson had responded to the call, too.

"You okay?" Ben asked, his gaze touching both Doralee and me.

"Shocked, but not hurt," I said.

He nodded and joined his female partner who knelt beside Kim's body. Officer Bryant watched them until Ben looked up and slightly shook his head.

"Let's move away," Officer Bryant said. He cupped Doralee's elbow and ushered us a few steps down the hall from both her room and the stairs.

Bryant asked some initial questions and, with her permission, had just finished searching Doralee's purse in hopes of finding the elusive room key, when footsteps pounded up the stairs.

Eric strode into the hall, seeming to take in everything in a glance, including Kim's body in the guest room. He nodded at Officer Bryant, spared Doralee a look, then gave me his cop stare.

"Are you all right?"

"Fine, Detective Shoar," I said, reverting to his title under the official circumstances. "We just gave Officer Bryant the short version of finding Kim."

"And I let him search my purse," Doralee added.

"Thank you for your cooperation. Now who is Kim? I don't believe I met her."

"Remember the disturbance we had on Thursday night at the gourd class?" He nodded. "The man was Ernie Boudreaux. The woman in there is his bride-to-be, Kim Thomason."

"And where is Mr. Boudreaux?"

I opened my mouth to answer him, but a commotion erupted in the stairwell.

"I'm a guest here, I tell you," Ernie shouted. "My sister and fiancée are upstairs. Are they okay? What's going on?"

Eric cocked a brow at me. "Mr. Boudreaux?"

"That's him."

My detective issued a quick, "Stay here," before the real chaos began.

I'd been on the periphery of the crime scene investigation in April, but hadn't experienced one this up close and in an enclosed space. Voices grew louder, more strident. Ernie's was at the top of that list.

"I wish that policeman would let me calm him," Doralee fretted beside me as Ernie barreled into the hall proper.

"Detective," I automatically corrected, as Eric stopped Ernie's charge. I didn't point out to Doralee how odd that might sound. Ernie's fiancée dead in his ex-wife's room, and said ex providing comfort. Suspicious only scratched the surface.

Torn between being antsy to get the critters home and plain old being nosy, I avidly eavesdropped on Shoar's rapid-fire questioning of Ernie. Not hard since they weren't but steps away. Where had he been? Walking, sitting in the courthouse gazebo. How long? An hour or more. What was he doing? Thinking. Checking e-mail on his cell. When had he last seen Kim? About three fifteen when he'd dropped her at the inn. Next of kin?

"She has a brother in Louisiana. Caleb Collier. I've never met him, but the contact information should be in Kim's phone." He paused to swallow hard, and visibly regrouped. "Now what about my sister? Georgine could've been attacked, too." He turned to Doralee. "Have you checked on her?"

Eric cut his gaze to me. I shook my head to tell him I hadn't seen or heard her.

"Ernie," Doralee said soothingly, "she's probably sleeping. You told me Georgine took migraine medicine before you and—" She broke off, cleared her throat. "Before y'all came over to the party. If I recall, that stuff knocks her flat for hours."

"Detective Shoar," I said, "can you check on Ernie's sister right now?"

"Of course."

He led Ernie to Georgine's guest room door, and after a good minute of knocking, she stepped into the hall, pale and hollow-eyed, wearing yellow pajamas, the top buttoned to her throat.

Her speech slurred a little when she asked, "What is the commotion?"

"I'm Detective Eric Shoar with the Lilyvale Police, ma'am."

"The name," she said in all her disheveled dignity, "is Miss Boudreaux."

"I understand you took headache medicine today, but did you see or hear anything unusual?"

"What are you talking about?" She faced her brother. "Ernie, what's happened?"

"It's Kim," he said, anguish obvious in his voice. "She's dead, Georgine. Someone killed her."

"Kim killed?" she whispered before her eyes rolled back and she fainted, collapsing between the two men. They got her back into the room.

Eric called for a paramedic even as he and Ernie supported Georgine back inside her room. When he returned to the hall, he called to Officer Bryant.

"Stand guard over those two," he said.

Doralee had overheard, judging by her worried expression.

"Detective Shoar," I said with a little wave. "A moment, please?"

"What's up?" he asked as he closed the scant distance between us.

"Is it all right if I go home? It's getting awfully crowded up here, and I'm just feeling in the way. Besides, I've got T.C. and Amber in the car."

He frowned as the lanky coroner, Terry Long, stepped into the hall, adding to the number of officials in the space. "Officer Bryant took your initial statement, right?"

"He did."

"And Ms. Gordon's, too?"

"Yes, why?"

"Nixy, Ms. Nix, would you mind taking Ms. Gordon to your apartment? Just until I can get there to complete your interviews. Officer Benton is guarding the door downstairs. Tell him I okayed you leaving."

"I don't mind, but do you need anything else from us first?"

"Don't discuss the case, okay?" he said. Then he moved in close enough to whisper in my ear, "No questions. No snooping. I mean it."

I PARKED BEHIND THE EMPORIUM BEFORE THE storm broke, and with time to spare. While Doralee phoned Zach, who was still in Texarkana, I let Amber do her business on a strip of grass in the parking lot. I led the now-calm critters and the still-shaken Doralee inside just as thunder rattled the door and the first fat raindrops splattered in the alley.

Doralee freshened up when we got upstairs. I fed T.C. and Amber, stashed my care package in the fridge, and made a quick call to Sherry and company.

The Lilyvale grapevine had already spread the news of Kim's death, a fairly accurate version at that.

"Do you want us to come over?"

"No, Aunt Sherry Mae," I said as my electric kettle—the one kitchen appliance I actually used more than once a week—began heating water for the tea I'd offered Doralee. "Y'all stay safe and dry at the house. I'm not sure how long it will take Detective Shoar to get here, but I'll update you when I can."

"All right then. Give Doralee our best, and call if you need any old thing. Come to think on it, she and Zach will probably need a place to stay tonight. Tell her I'll have a room ready."

I knew that meant my aunt would give up her room for the night or as long as needed. She'd done the same for me in April. "I'll mention it to her, Sherry."

"Mention what?" Doralee asked when I disconnected.

I relayed my aunt's message, pouring the boiled water over a bag of a soothing herbal tea Aster had given me as a housewarming gift as I spoke to Doralee. She added two teaspoons of sugar from an old cut-glass sugar bowl the antique dealers had left in the cabinet.

"Your aunt and her friends are the sweetest, and bless her, I may have to take her up on her offer. When I filled Zach in on what happened, he had the foresight to realize we'll need at least one change of clothing and some toiletries. He'll stop at his house and mine to pick up some things before he comes back."

Cradling her mug of tea, she crossed to my living room and sank onto the couch with a sigh. "Although after seeing my clothes strewn around that room, I'm not sure I ever want them back. In fact, I'm not wild about going back to the inn at all, and that's a shame because it's a lovely place."

"If you can't face being in that room, I imagine Sherry would be happy to gather your things when the time comes."

I sat in an armchair, but Amber and T.C. jumped up on either side of Doralee and snuggled in with their heads on her lap as if to offer comfort. She looked off into space, absently stroking Amber, then the purring T.C., and I realized the critters just might be more calming to Doralee than a whole jar of Aster's lavender. They didn't even flinch when lightning flashed at the windows and cracks of thunder shook the building. My apartment might be short on furnishings, but it was a cozy port in the storm.

I had intended to sit quietly with Doralee and wait for

Eric to arrive, but there's a saying about good intentions. Keeping them soon proved impossible, because as Doralee overcame her shock, she talked nearly nonstop. Questions arose that absolutely begged to be asked, and I obliged.

"I just feel so horrible for Ernie," Doralee mused aloud. "In spite of Kim's flaws, I really thought the third time could be the charm for him."

I rested my mug on my knee and leaned forward. "The third time?"

"Kim was to be Ernie's third shot at marriage," Doralee said with a wave of her hand, "although his first engagement ended before he could get married. The poor girl, Margaret, died in a car accident. In fact, she died in a car accident along with her brother, Walter, who was Georgine's fiancé."

"When was this?"

"Oh, gosh, years ago. Ernie and Georgine were in their mid and late twenties when they lost their sweethearts, and worse, Georgine was pregnant. She'd kept it a secret. Her mother had died, but her father was a stern, cold man and would have cut her out of the will if he found out. I don't know if you're aware, but Ernie comes from old oil money, although much of it was gone by the time we got married."

I wasn't aware of Ernie's money troubles or lack thereof, and didn't really care. I wanted to hear the rest of Georgine's story. Before I could prompt Doralee, she spoke again.

"I don't know how Ernie isn't flat broke what with the property taxes and insurance and upkeep on that old house. But I suppose he must have something in the bank or Kim probably would've left for greener pastures."

"Go back, Doralee," I said before she went off on another tangent. "What happened to Georgine's baby?"

"Georgine miscarried a few weeks after her fiancé's death. The stress was just too much."

"That's so sad."

"Ernie helped her through the miscarriage, and he was fairly sure their father never knew about the baby. When his dad died six months later, Ernie inherited the house and most of what family money was left. Of course, he said his father was a severe, old-fashioned man, and Ernie was the elder sibling."

"He's older than Georgine?"

"By four years. Her dour personality makes her seem older, and bless her heart, I always thought she looked older, too. I think the ordeal with her fiancé and miscarriage prematurely aged her. Anyway, old Mr. Boudreaux only bequeathed some family jewelry and a modest amount of money to Georgine. A dowry of sorts. After all, he'd have expected her to get married someday."

"But she never did?" I asked.

"No, and they both stayed on in the family home. Georgine kept house for her brother and looked after him for over a decade before I ever met him."

"She didn't seem to like Kim. Did she like you?"

Doralee sipped her tea, which was probably cold by now, but she didn't so much as wrinkle her nose. She seemed deep in thought, paying no notice to the rain lashing the windows or the whistling wind.

"I'm not really sure the issue was liking me or not as a person. You have to realize she was very protective of Ernie. She still is. I didn't meet and marry him until we were both in our forties, so except for Ernie's forays into dating, Georgine had him to herself. Ernie was a player for a while, never serious about anyone. When he got serious with me, I could see that she was jealous of him having another woman in his life, and in her home."

"So how did you handle that? Did Georgine move out?"

"Heavenly days, no. Their family home north of Shreveport isn't quite a mansion, but it's plenty large. Georgine and Ernie lived in separate wings with the main public rooms in the middle of the house. I insisted we keep that arrangement. I also insisted that Georgine keep running the house the way she wished. I'd help or stay out of her way."

"I take it you stayed out of her way."

"Yes, but I paid attention to how she did things. That came in handy when she got sick a couple of years into my marriage. I was able to take over for about three months until she was well."

I thought about Georgine's personality, or what little I'd seen of it. "Was she grateful or did she resent you?"

Doralee rested her head on the sofa cushion. "She resented me. She swung between being aloof with me or passive-aggressive, but we shared the occasional moment of harmony. During her recovery she nitpicked, and I expected that. I didn't let it bother me much. After she recovered, though, I either got the cold shoulder or the snide comments."

I sipped at my own cool tea. "That must've been extremely difficult."

"Yes. I never thought she was quite right, you know? Whether that was from her fiancé and baby dying, I don't know. She seemed more fragile after her illness. She stopped driving, too. Wouldn't even take herself to the grocery store, although that could've been a control issue, not a medical one."

"So you or Ernie or Georgine's friends drove her places?"

"She didn't have friends, Nixy. No social life, even before she got sick. She became touchier, too. Small things upset her, and she got migraines more often. I suggested to Ernie that we move and give Georgine her own space. He house-hunted with me a few times, but nothing came of it. I kept as busy as I could with my art and volunteering, but when you live with a sister-in-law who is subtly cutting you at every turn—" She broke off with a shrug.

."Georgine destroyed your marriage?"

"Her jealousy and possessiveness of her brother and her home were tipping points, but I can't hold a grudge. Ernie and I were responsible, too. Looking back on it, I don't know how much we loved each other versus how tired we were of being alone. I cared for Ernie. I still do. But neither of us fought for each other. We didn't try hard enough to stay together. You know what I mean?"

I nodded and Doralee went on. "When I left, I urged Ernie to restore the family engagement ring and give it to Georgine, but of course he never did. The flashy ring isn't something she'd want to wear, but she was partial to the original. I always wondered if that was part of the reason she resented me."

"From what little I saw, Georgine was set to make Kim's life with Ernie a challenge, too."

Doralee shook her head. "I don't know. Georgine doesn't confront, she undermines. I worked to make peace with her, whereas Kim simply ignored her. Besides, Ernie gave me the impression he and Kim were moving into the home Kim inherited from her last husband."

I sputtered a sip of tea. "Her last husband?"

A twinkle lit Doralee's eyes. "Kim came from humble beginnings and married up, as they say. Twice, and both times to wealthy men who were some twenty years older. Her first husband, Craig Franks, had a stroke on the golf course. Her second, D.B. Thomason, had a heart attack after a board of directors meeting."

I blinked. "That's some marriage history. I hope she wasn't expecting Ernie to keel over."

Doralee's expression sobered. "One thing is certain. None of us expected Kim would die so young. Not even her former in-laws. Dennis, D.B.'s son, will be relieved, and D.B.'s sister, Margot, will be ecstatic."

"Why? Just because they didn't like Kim?"

"No, although that's a big part of it. Heck, Margot once attempted to kill Kim. Maybe more than once."

"What?"

Doralee nodded. "The incident I heard about was that Margot drove a golf cart straight at Kim. The woman claimed the accelerator stuck. As if."

"What happened?"

"The cart just clipped Kim's hip, but had she fallen and hit her head on the paved cart path, she could've been seriously hurt or even died."

I snapped my gaping mouth closed. "How do you know this?"

"A friend of mine, Buffy Phillips, runs in Margot's social circle. Buffy never met a morsel of gossip she didn't pass along, but the point I meant to make is something she told me. She heard that the portion of the estate D.B. left to Kim in the trust passes on to his family upon Kim's death. If that's so, I wouldn't put anything past those snooty folks."

Would this sister-in-law from Kim's past arrange to meet her, then kill her? Snooty was a far cry from murderous.

I startled when my cell buzzed in my pocket. It was Eric calling.

"Come down and let me in," he said without a normal hello.

Okay, not Eric. Detective Shoar. Because even his sexy voice was firmly in cop mode.

Chapter Seven

ALTHOUGH THE RAIN HAD LET UP A BIT, THE WIND still whistled through the mature trees surrounding the square, and around the buildings. When I opened the alley door to admit my stone-faced detective, I saw Zach wheel Doralee's SUV into the parking lot. I held the door for him to enter, too.

Inside Fred's shop area, both men brushed raindrops from their lightweight jackets as I reintroduced them. They cordially shook hands, made noises about remembering each other from the lawn party, but tension crackled in the air like lightning waiting to strike.

Upstairs, Zach and Doralee immediately embraced. She teared up; he comforted her. They didn't say much to each other. I'm sure they were very aware of having an audience, one of them in law enforcement.

Amber and T.C. had leaped off the couch, but didn't seek attention from Zach. Instead they looked adoringly at Eric, and he squatted to greet them and scratch them behind the ears.

I quickly did the hostess thing, making more tea for Doralee, and handing the requested glasses of ice water to the men.

"Ms. Gordon, Mr. Dalton, please have a seat," Eric said. "I'll try to make this brief."

He took the chair I'd sat in earlier, and Doralee and Zach sat on the couch. I thought the pets would sit with me in the second comfy chair, but they scooted under the coffee table and watched the humans. I swore they felt the gravity in the room. Amber's floppy ears swung as she looked from one person to another. T.C. swished her tail anxiously.

"First walk me through what happened after we all left the emporium this afternoon. Ms. Gordon, you start."

With her hand linked with Zach's, she gave Eric the highlights, and he made notes in a small spiral notebook. He let her talk without interruption until she got to the part about not being able to find her room key.

"You still haven't found the key?"

"I haven't looked since I emptied my purse for the officer," she answered, grabbing her bag from where she'd dropped it on the floor. She opened the flap to show him the single compartment. "I had the key right here in this zippered pocket."

"If I may, Detective," Zach said, "Doralee always keeps her room keys there when she travels, although the key is usually a card type. It's so she won't accidentally put her cell phone near the card and deactivate it."

"Zach's right. I change purses, of course, but they all have outside pockets for my phone, and inside zipper slots where I put my hotel keys. I established that habit even before I was married to Ernie."

"Do you mind if I look again?"

Doralee gave him an impatient glance, but plunked the purse on the coffee table. In under two minutes, he'd emptied the contents, then sorted and repacked them while we looked on in silence.

"Thank you, Ms. Gordon." He closed the purse flap and handed it back. "Now I know this part may be more difficult, so bear with me. Ms. Nix drove you to the inn. Since you had something to give her, she went upstairs with you. You both found Ms. Thomason when you opened your door?"

"No, the door fell open when I leaned on it."

"She didn't touch the doorknob," I interjected. "Neither of us did. It was so dim in the hall that I aimed my phone's flashlight into Doralee's purse so she could see better. She backed up, leaned against the hinged side of the doorjamb for just a second, and the door swung open. We never noticed the door was ajar."

"And," Doralee added, "we didn't see Kim until I flipped the light switch."

Shoar raised a brow. "Why didn't you see her?"

"It was a dark and stormy afternoon, Detective," I said. "Darker inside the room than in the hall."

He gave me a flat stare. I threw up my hands. "Hey, I'm just offering some clarity."

If he hadn't been on duty, I think he'd have rolled his eyes at me. Instead, he refocused on Doralee.

"What time was this?"

Doralee glanced at me. "A little after five thirty? Did you notice, Nixy?"

"No, but that's a good estimate."

"Fine. What did you do after you turned on the light, Ms. Gordon?"

"I went into the room to see about Kim but Nixy told me to stop." She went on to recount what had happened before the police arrived. "Then Nixy led me into the hallway, and we waited for the authorities to come."

My detective cut his gaze to me, one brow lifted as if asking me to confirm Doralee's account. Since she'd been true to the general facts, I nodded. He turned back to Doralee.

"You didn't touch anything?"

"No, but it's our room," she said, glancing at Zach.

"You had to notice it had been searched. Did you attempt to straighten anything? Retrieve clothing? Anything like that."

"I noticed the mess, of course, but I didn't touch a thing. I was too stunned."

He made another note in his spiral. "Assuming it was Ms. Thomason who searched, do you know what she was looking for?"

"No, I don't."

Doralee answered him without hesitation, and it was all I could do not to either gape like a fish or contradict her.

Truly, did Doralee not have a clue why Kim was in her room, or was she simply not thinking about the opal? Not connecting it to Kim's search?

Or was she holding back that information for a reason. Perhaps to protect Ernie?

I glanced at Zach. He watched Doralee with loving concern, but made no attempt to butt in. He'd said that Ernie wanted Doralee back. I'd seen Doralee kiss Ernie this afternoon. Sure, it was nothing but a chaste peck on the cheek, but would she have kissed Ernie with Zach looking on?

Not unless she was out of her gourd.

NEARLY THREE HOURS AFTER WE'D GONE TO THE inn and found Kim dead, Detective Shoar finished questioning Doralee and Zach and cut them loose. Well, for the evening and with restrictions. They were to go to the station the next day to sign their statements, and they were not to leave town.

The couple politely argued that they lived only about an hour and a half away, Zach in Texarkana, Doralee on a little acreage outside of the city, and they'd gladly return to Lilyvale if needed. That didn't fly, although Shoar conceded that

Zach could leave town for his job as a security alarm technician. Apparently Zach had a healthy security clearance, and Shoar decided he was trustworthy.

I thought about asking Zach to look at the emporium's security measures. Then again, no. I didn't want to make waves with the security consultant and installation guy we already had. Greg Masters was, after all, a buddy of the Silver Six—Dab and Aster in particular. And he'd done a good job, thankfully. In a small town, it had to be a touchy thing to fire a friend—or a friend's company—without igniting a feud.

I made a quick call to Sherry to confirm that Doralee and Zach were welcome and flat out expected at the farmhouse. If they wanted a full meal, it was minutes from the table. If they wanted a snack, that'd be ready in two shakes of a lamb's tail.

Rain pelted the couple as they dashed for Doralee's SUV. I'd given Doralee an umbrella, one of several spares we kept in Fred's workshop space. I'd also brought the critters downstairs with us to see if they wanted to go out. They showed zip interest in getting soaked, so the three of us watched Zach and Doralee drive away.

Detective Shoar had stayed upstairs to make a call, and now I heard his footsteps descending the staircase.

"Do you know how Kim died?" I asked as he joined me.

"I have to hand it to you, Nixy," he said on a tired chuckle. "You don't soft-peddle your curiosity."

"Hey, no law against asking."

"But you know I can't tell you."

"I know, I know. The state medical examiner in Little Rock does the autopsy to determine cause of death, all the evidence goes to the state lab in Little Rock. You won't have any reports or results for at least several days if not several weeks."

"You've got it. Listen, I need to get back to talk with the Tylers. They're fit to be tied that someone died at their inn."

"I can only imagine," I said, feeling sorrier for Lorna Tyler than I did for her husband, Clark. Mr. Personality he was not. "I hope this mess convinces them to install security cameras."

"We can hope. Before I go, I need a couple of things from you. Can we sit?"

"Sure." I led him to a workbench with the mismatched barstools from Doralee's class, and plopped on one. "Shoot."

Moving in his usual unhurried gait, he sat facing me, one boot heel hooked on a rung. Then he opened his spiral again, laid it on the worktable, uncapped his pen. I couldn't read what he'd written, but noticed double question marks here and there.

"First, can you confirm what Ms. Gordon told me? You both went into the guest room, but only you touched Ms. Thomason?"

"On her neck, in three places."

He did a double take. "Three?"

"I had my eyes closed when I felt for her pulse." I shrugged at his disbelieving expression. "I didn't want to see any more than I already had."

"And then you both went to the hallway and stayed there?"

"We did. Scout's honor."

He arched a brow. "Were you ever a Scout?"

"No, but I dated one. Scott the Scout."

"Naturally." He grinned. My past dating life had been active yet painfully platonic, and had become a source of his teasing me. "Now, what about that room key? I tend to believe Ms. Gordon is telling the truth, but if it was secure in her purse, how did it turn up missing?"

I flashed on that afternoon. Thinking I'd heard the front door close when I entered the farmhouse with Doralee and Zach. Finding the front door ajar when it should've been dead-bolted.

I relayed that to Shoar, and added, "I know it's thin, but

you know how security conscious Sherry and the gang have been since April. And before you say it, no, they didn't have the back door locked most of the day. One of them was supposed to be in the kitchen or on the deck at all times to keep guests out of the house."

"You're thinking someone slipped in? Ms. Thomason?"

"Unless she swiped the key at some other point and made a copy, how did she get into Doralee's room?"

"How indeed?" He tapped his pen on the paper. "Okay, did you see anyone else in the alley before you went inside?"

I started to say no, but then remembered. "Oh, my gosh, yes, Eric. In the drama, I forgot. I almost hit a dark pickup with oversized tires when it sped out of the alley right in front of me. Not monster truck huge, but big enough. I think they're called mudders. For off-roading, you know?"

"I do, but how did you conclude that?"

"Matt the Mechanic, a guy I dated, loved the things. And I'm pretty sure the truck from the alley was splattered with mud, too."

"You see the driver?"

"Not the truck's driver. I didn't have a good angle, and the storm closing in made it pretty dark by then. But when I turned into the lot behind the inn, a woman driving a silver Audi nearly clipped me. A man was in the passenger seat. My headlights picked them out."

"Can you give me descriptions? License plates?"

"Sorry, both near-misses happened too fast."

He dragged his free hand through his dark brown hair, his frustration obvious. "One last thing for now. Do you know anything about these people that can help me? Are the ex-spouses enemies? Are the parties jealous of each other? Did you notice anyone harboring hard feelings?"

I drew a circle on the pockmarked surface of the table, debating what to say for a moment. When I looked up, his steady brown eyes bored into me.

"First, you need to understand I don't know any of them

well. What I tell you I've drawn from observation, and what Doralee has said in conversation." I shrugged. "She talks a lot."

"In other words, you got an earful tonight while you were waiting for me."

I nodded. He didn't seem upset, but I launched into speech before he could lecture me. "To start with, Doralee and Ernie are more or less cordial to each other. Ernie and Zach pretty much ignored each other the only time I saw them together. I believe Kim—Ms. Thomason—was jealous of Doralee, but not necessarily in the way you would assume."

"Explain."

"Kim wasn't jealous of Doralee's previous relationship with Ernie or anything. She wanted an opal that Doralee has. Ernie was impatient with Kim nagging him about it, but in a put-his-foot-down kind of way."

"Is this an opal Mr. Boudreaux gave his ex?"

"Actually, no. Doralee bought it, had planned to put it in a ring or something, and then give it to Ernie. They divorced before that happened. Technically it never belonged to Ernie, but from what I overheard, Kim thought it should, and she wanted the stone."

"Assuming Ms. Thomason was the one who ransacked the guest room, do you think she was searching for this opal?"

"Makes sense to me."

"Then why didn't Ms. Gordon tell me about the opal?"

"I have no idea, but the stone isn't the big deal to her that it was to Kim. The idea that Kim was searching for that one thing might not have occurred to Doralee."

He flipped a few pages in the spiral, frowned at his notes. "All right, let me recap. Ms. Gordon and Mr. Boudreaux are divorced."

"And Zach Dalton is Doralee's current gentleman friend."

"Kim Thomason was engaged to Mr. Boudreaux, and Georgine is his sister."

"Right."

"None of them live around here, yet they converged in Lilyvale and now the fiancée is dead. I know Ms. Gordon came for your grand opening events, and I understand why Mr. Dalton would accompany her, but why did the ex-husband show up? To make his own fiancée jealous? To get his ex-wife back? To get this opal Ms. Thomason wanted?"

I shrugged. "I honestly can't say. Maybe a little of all three. You'll have to ask the players, and you might want to ask Doralee about Kim's former in-laws, too."

"Why?"

"Because Doralee indicated that at least one of them hated Kim."

"Enough to kill her?"

"Enough to run her down with a golf cart. To kill her up close? That's for you to discover. I'm on the sidelines."

He stared at me, one corner of his mouth quirked. "You stumbled across another body, but you're not playing Nixy Drew this time? You're staying out of my investigation?"

I wrinkled my nose at him. "I'll only get repeated lectures if I snoop, right?"

"Somehow I don't think my lectures will deter you. They didn't last time."

"Last time was different. Last time Aunt Sherry's neck was on the line. This time I have no vested interest in your case. Besides, Detective," I said with a bright smile, "once burned, twice smart. I'm limiting my adventures to running a new business."

"I hope so." He bent to give Amber and T.C. quick scratches under their chins, then eyed me again. "I certainly hope so."

AMBER AND T.C. DID A MORNING STRETCH ROUTINE that reminded me of the yoga my old roommate had practiced, and the position called downward dog. My personal yoga experience was limited to exactly two classes, but watching the critters made me follow along with them. More or less. Arms over my head, then touch my toes, then arms over head again and reach for the sky. Obviously I wasn't ready to run out and join a gym. I didn't think there *was* one in Lilyvale. Whatever. The stretch felt great, and I hit the ground running that gorgeous Monday morning.

Okay, walking. Specifically, walking the critters. We hoofed it—pawed it?—past the businesses on and just off the square, and then meandered through several blocks in the adjoining neighborhood. Amber sniffed at everything, occasionally pawing at the ground hard enough to pull up grass. Then she'd sniff again and give me a triumphant look with those golden eyes. I felt the need to be impressed, so I praised her each time with a "Good girl." T.C. did her share of sniffing, then batted at bugs she'd dislodged. When a grasshopper suddenly leaped high in front of her, she launched herself to catch it, but was thwarted by my hold on her leash. She shot me a disgusted look, but didn't try to Houdini out of her harness.

I'd had an ulterior motive to the long stroll. I'd hoped to see Louie out with Harley. Louie might be able to describe the truck and Audi drivers from last night. They might not be relevant to Kim's murder, but more information couldn't hurt. I didn't run into the boy and his dog, but I'd ask him another day.

Back at home, I breakfasted somewhat resentfully on my last PowerBar and promised myself a trip to the grocery store. Today. Without fail. The critters weren't low on food, treats, or litter, but it couldn't hurt to stock up.

Yes, I still hoped their owner would turn up. I'd simply hand over all the extra supplies, or donate them to the shelter. Although I had to admit I'd miss seeing their sweet faces and the comfort of stroking their sleek fur baby bodies.

The Silver Six convoy of the Corolla, the Caddy, and Fred's truck rolled into the parking lot behind the emporium before nine. From the collective gleam in their eyes as I greeted them, I figured they wanted to pump me for information, but before we confabbed, Dab helped me put the grand opening sign back up out front. He carried one end of the ladder, then steadied it for me as I climbed up and down to tie off the banner's four corners. Fred, Amber, and T.C. supervised, Fred and Amber voicing and woofing advice from the sidewalk, and T.C. chirping from the concrete planter, where she had jumped for a better view. I feared she'd dig up the lilies or ivy, but she didn't even nibble a leaf. Good thing. It hadn't occurred to me until that moment that I had no clue which plants were harmful to animals.

Then again, Amber and T.C. had trekked who knows how far away from their home. They had to be smart enough to steer clear of poisonous flora.

With the stools we'd used for Doralee's gourd class pulled up to a worktable, the seven of us sat down to share cups of coffee Eleanor and Sherry had brewed, and the exquisitely sticky cinnamon buns Maise had baked that morning.

"So tell us," Aster said, "what is your take on Kim's death?"

I choked on an overambitious bite of bun and grabbed my coffee cup. "I don't have a take, Aster," I said as I swallowed.

"Well for heaven's sake, child," my aunt huffed, "you must have some opinion. You were right there, and you've talked to our Detective Shoar. What did he have to say?"

"Eric didn't confide a single detail," I reported honestly. "He asked me some questions, but I couldn't tell him much. I mean, that was the last thing Doralee or I expected to see yesterday. I'm still stunned."

"I do believe Doralee feels the same," Eleanor offered.

Aster nodded her agreement. "I doubt she slept at all well. Poor thing had dark circles under her eyes when she and Zach left the farmhouse this morning."

"They were going to the police station after they reconnoitered another place to stay," Maise added.

I blinked at that news. "There's another hotel in town?"

"Motel on the road goin' east, but it ain't much." Fred pinched two pieces of bread from his bun and casually dropped them on the floor. Amber and T.C. skittered over and quickly slurped up the people food. "Heck, I ain't sure it's open no more."

"It is," Dab put in. "Rather it might be. Some people from Florida bought it long about February, remember? I heard from Big George that the owners have been sprucing it up."

Since Big George Heath owned the hardware store, he'd definitely have the scoop on who was repairing, renovating, and refurbishing properties.

"Have we met these people?" Maise asked. "If not, we should."

I fought a smile at this new reminder I was now living the small town life. If everyone didn't know absolutely everyone else, it wasn't for lack of trying. I could almost see Maise flipping through her mental recipe files looking for the perfect Welcome Wagon offering.

And since they'd veered away from talking about the murder, I jumped in to get us on our business track.

"Let's review this week's schedule before we go open the store."

ACCOMPLISHED KNITTER SHIRLEY HINES, WHO CRE-ated her own designs and who'd independently published a book of her patterns, presented the morning's featured craft workshop. A legion of ladies showed up to support her, and with the addition of a Girl Scout troop on a field trip and run-of-the-mill shoppers, we stayed slammed for the first three hours of the day. Even Fred had visitors—aside from his loyal assistants, Amber and T.C., hanging out with him. A few students from the technical college learning auto repair came in to pick his brain.

As I watched Fred answer questions, I had an idea: He

could do a workshop on the care and maintenance of small household appliances. The topic should draw a decently wide audience. Couldn't hurt to ask him.

And no, I didn't think for a minute teaching such a class would hurt his fix-it business. Gadgets would still break, and Fred had a way with them. I swore he could lay hands on a machine and know what ailed it.

Jasmine arrived at one that afternoon to begin her shift. We briefed her on the morning's events, and on the crafts for the Fourth of July demo happening at three o'clock. The Silver Six ladies were about to pop home for lunch, and then bring Fred and Dab their sandwiches, when Zach ushered a sniffling, red-eyed Doralee through the emporium door.

"Gracious, Doralee!" Sherry exclaimed. "What on earth is wrong?"

"Your detective thinks I killed Kim," she said baldly. "I need an attorney fast."

Chapter Eight

JAWS DROPPED, INCLUDING JASMINE'S. THE POOR girl didn't expect her work-study program would include having a murder suspect stroll into the store. Never mind that the suspect was innocent.

She had to be, didn't she?

As Maise hustled Doralee, Zach, and the Silver Six to Fred's workshop space, I gave thanks no customers had been in the store. I reassured Jasmine that we'd go on with business as usual, and to holler if she needed us. Then I dashed to the back to hear what had happened at the police station with Detective Shoar.

As we had this morning, we sat around one of Fred's large workbenches, Zach and Doralee side by side at one end.

"He separated us and then questioned us for hours," she said, her voice breaking. "I must've told him the same thing dozens of times. I didn't kill Kim. I didn't care about her enough to kill her."

Now *that* didn't sound like a statement you'd want a cop to hear.

Aster, bless her, had her trusty bottle of water-diluted lavender oil in hand. "Doralee, now stop and breathe. You, too, Zach. This is my special essential oil and water. I'm spritzing it over your heads, and it will calm you. Then we can talk."

Aster sprayed them, then the room at large. Amber and T.C. sneezed, and retreated to the beds Fred and Dab had set out for them. They exchanged a look that I could only interpret as, "Humans are weird."

"There now. We know a crackerjack attorney, Dinah Souse, but tell us why you think you need her."

"I told you. Detective Shoar believes I killed Kim."

"Did he say why?" I asked. "I mean, did he give you a motive?"

"First he mentioned me being jealous of her, but then"— she shot me a scorching stare—"he started pelting me with questions about the opal. I guess you told him about it?"

"I mentioned it last night when he asked if I knew why Kim would be in your room. It was the only reason I could imagine."

Doralee's glare melted. "You're right, of course. The problem is I didn't think about the stupid stone last night when Detective Shoar questioned me. For heaven's sake, it's in my safe-deposit box. It wasn't on my mind. Now the detective thinks I was holding back information if not outright lying."

"Shoar is paid to be suspicious," I said soothingly. "I promise you he's a fair, thorough investigator."

"I hope so because he also asked me about my presentations here, and if I'd had any problems."

Maise frowned. "What sort of problems?"

"If I'd lost anything or had something stolen. I told him that my awl went missing on Friday afternoon, and that all of you knew about it. He showed me about a dozen photos of various tools and asked me to identify my awl."

My heart sank even as the senior ladies murmured a chorus of "Oh dear."

"The thing was, I could point out the picture of the kind of awl I had, but I couldn't say that particular one was mine. I told him my awl was in a new set of gourd-crafting tools, and that I hadn't put my initials or any markings on them yet." She vise-gripped my hand. "You know I'm telling the truth, Nixy. Will you talk to the detective?"

Before I could answer, Sherry pinned me with her blue-eyed teacher gaze. "Do you think the awl was the murder weapon, Nixy?"

"I do believe it must be," Eleanor said. "Otherwise, why would he query Doralee about it so closely?"

"Ladies, ladies, hold it. You know Detective Shoar doesn't show his hand. All I get out of him is that the evidence goes to the state crime lab. However," I added, turning to Doralee, "I will confirm with him that your awl disappeared just as you told him." I paused. "Did Shoar say anything more about the room key?"

"Only that Kim likely didn't have a copy made—at least not in the two places in town with a key-cutting machine."

"So he believes Kim used your key."

"Or he thinks I let Kim in and then killed her."

"When does he think you managed that? You were at Sherry's."

She cut her gaze to Zach then looked back at me. "Shoar says he has a witness who saw me on the square, but I didn't come back to town until I came with you."

Huh. Why had she evaded my eyes when I mentioned her being at the party? Why the glance at Zach that seemed a touch guilty? She was lying about something, and that bugged me.

Still, I again promised to talk with Shoar.

"And I'll get you that attorney's number," Maise said. "It's after one, so Ms. Souse should be in the office if she isn't in court."

"Thank you," Zach said quietly. "Doralee, you didn't tell them about the missing item."

"It's a tiny detail compared to everything else," she began. "But the detective also had me look at the inventory of my clothes, jewelry, and toiletries to see if my belongings were all there. Everything was there but my smock."

"The one you wore during your class?" I asked.

"And the program with Sherry. I took it and some paint to our room so I could put some finishing touches on your gift—a gourd pencil holder for your office. I'd left it on the sweet little vintage desk in the guest room."

I didn't have an office except for the box of files I'd amassed and kept in the apartment, but I appreciated the thought.

"Where did you last see your smock?" my aunt asked.

"On the chair back where I'd tossed it. Why someone would take that one item, I can't imagine."

I could. The killer had likely wiped off his bloody hands with the smock, but then I'd watched more crime shows than were probably good for me. Then I had another thought.

"What about all your other crafting tools? Were they on the inventory?"

"No, but they wouldn't be. We left them locked in the car all weekend along with my other supplies. That's why I think the detective found my missing awl at the crime scene. Why else would the subject come up?"

"Good point." Even though all of us except perhaps Fred could corroborate her account of the vanished awl, that the presumed murder weapon belonged to Doralee was damning.

"Will you be able to get your personal things back?" Sherry asked.

"The police are holding them for now," Zach said. "However, we found a place to stay until the detective allows us to go home. The Pines Motor Court."

"It's not as spacious as the Inn on the Square," Doralee put in, "but it's a cute little retro sort of place, and it'll do fine for a few days. We can't impose on you all anymore," she said, nodding at the Six.

Zach nodded, too. "I thought I'd take Doralee to buy a few necessities, then go back there to rest."

"An excellent idea," Aster said. "I'll send along some lavender to help you relax."

"And we'll have you out for dinner tonight," Maise offered. "That is, if you feel like being in company."

Doralee exchanged a small smile with Zach. "That's very sweet, but we got permission from the detective to go to Magnolia for dinner."

"The Backyard Bar-B-Q?" Eleanor asked. I couldn't imagine pristine and proper Eleanor chowing down on ribs but, I realized, there was so much I still didn't know about each of the Six.

"The same, but we appreciate your invitation." She caught Aster's hand, and her gaze touched each of us. "Truly, thank you. All of you. I don't know what I'd do without your help."

"We'll get this sorted out," Aster assured her.

"We certainly will," Aunt Sherry vowed with a gleam in her eye that told me this was not the end of this conversation. I wondered absently if it would be rude to invite myself along to the barbeque joint. I'd heard the pie alone was worth the trip, and it would delay having to deal with whatever amateur sleuthing my dear aunt was certain to propose.

THERE ARE TIMES THAT BEING RIGHT SUCKS, AND this was shaping up to be one of those times.

Sherry and Aster, Maise, and Eleanor had been home, eaten, and brought lunch back for the rest of us. They dropped off snacks for Jasmine, too, then joined me, Dab, and Fred at the worktable, where we'd talked with Doralee and Zach.

But the ladies had brought back more than sandwiches and sweet tea. As I feared, they'd cooked up the cockeyed idea that we should investigate Kim Thomason's death. I was having none of it, even though I was likely partly to blame for their wheedling ways. When I arrived a few months back, they thought snooping was rude and now I was going to have to rein them in.

"No, and no again, Aunt Sherry. Absolutely not."

"But we must investigate. You know the Stanton family dictum: When we see something that needs doing, we do it."

"But that's the point. Investigating a murder is not something we can do."

"Of course we can. Now let's start with a description of the crime scene. Doralee wouldn't tell us a single detail. Did you take photos with your cell phone?"

"No cell pictures, and I am *not* describing the crime scene," I said, but the image of Kim on her side, arm outstretched, her ring looking so odd on her limp finger, made me shudder. I shook off the mental picture. "Let the police investigate, Sherry. We have to stay out of Eric's way."

"Poo. We know Doralee is innocent. We'll solve this case just like we solved the last murder."

I choked on my tea and carefully set the glass on Fred's worktable. "Aunt Sherry, we did not solve that murder. We blundered into the killer, and you were put in mortal danger."

"We came out of it fine and dandy."

"You were injured, and the whole episode took years off my life."

"It also got you to move here," Fred put in.

"Yes it did. So?"

"Just sayin'. It weren't all bad."

"And we'll help, just like we did before," Aster said.

"Right. We'll mobilize to ask questions around town," Maise declared. "See who could have had it in for Kim."

"I do believe we ought to discover if anyone saw Kim and Ernie bickering," Eleanor said. "He's my top suspect."

"Of course," Dab offered thoughtfully, "it could be someone else entirely. By all accounts, Ms. Thomason was not the most pleasant of women. She could have had a number of enemies."

"Enemies who followed Kim to Lilyvale?" I challenged.

"An enemy Kim would let into the inn? An enemy who'd wait while Kim searched the room, and then whack her?"

Admittedly, the snooty sister-in-law Doralee had mentioned, Margot, sprang to mind as I ranted, but would a society maven like that stab Kim? Risk ruining her manicure? Actually, she might with a strong enough motive.

"Here now, Nixy. You got no call to be sarcastic," Fred scolded. "No call whatsomever."

I refocused and blew out a breath. "You're right, Fred. Dab, I'm sorry for snapping. But truly, I think sticking our noses in this is a really bad idea. If you'll recall, the only reason we snooped around in April was because Aunt Sherry was the prime suspect, and we were on the list right after her."

"What's your point?" Maise demanded.

"The last time was personal. This time it isn't."

"I beg to disagree," Aster huffed.

"As do I," Sherry snipped. "Doralee is a friend. She wouldn't have been here had we not invited her to teach the gourd-painting class and stay for the demonstration. I feel somewhat responsible for the fix she's in here."

"Exactly," Aster said. "And you of all people know we don't abandon our friends. Besides, you told Shoar about that opal. Whether you realize it or not, you're already on the case."

I dropped my head in my hands with a groan. "The superstitions are true. Opals *are* bad luck."

Fred chuckled. "Might as well give in, missy. If you don't agree, we'll just do it on our own."

"And perhaps ask some of our other friends for help," Eleanor added.

"Like Big George at the hardware store, and Bog Turner at the barbershop, and Duke Richards at the Dairy Queen," Dab said with mock solemnity.

I gave Dab a wary look. I knew they were manipulating me six ways from Sunday, but invite Duke Richards and his shotgun into the middle of this situation? Not on my watch.

The thought of any of the Silver Six being in harm's way made me queasy, but I had to pick my battles. If I went along with them investigating the murder, I'd get their reports and more or less be able ride herd on their snooping. That in turn would hopefully keep them out of too much trouble, especially with Detective Shoar.

"Okay, tell you what. I'll let Shoar know about Doralee's awl, and Eleanor's missing whittling tool, too."

"Excellent, child," Sherry said. "We'll check with downtown merchants and clerks. If Kim visited any shops, I'm sure she made an impression."

"If she ate at the Lilies Café," Maise added, "Lorna will know how she and Ernie behaved together."

"We can search for her on the Internet, too," Aster said. "Eleanor and I have been getting lessons in computer research from Jasmine."

"Great, and I have a search task for you," I said, Kim's sister-in-law popping to mind again. "Look up Kim's last set of in-laws. D.B. Thomason was the husband's name. Look in Louisiana. The Shreveport area."

"We're on it," Aster said, she and Eleanor beaming.

"Time to move out, Nixy," Maise commanded. "Go see Eric and hurry back. Sandy Brown will be here in forty minutes for her Crafting for July Fourth demonstration, and that group of Scouts is coming back for it. We'll need all hands on deck."

THE LILYVALE POLICE STATION WAS ONLY TWO AND a half blocks from the emporium. I needed the exercise and decided Amber and T.C. could use the walk, too. And yes, I figured seeing the critters might soften the good detective.

Turned out that only service animals were allowed in the station, so I told the young black officer at the desk, Taylor Benton, that I had information vital to the murder case. Within minutes, Eric met me in the parking lot behind the building. Circles under his eyes betrayed his exhaustion, and though he gave our furry friends attention, he didn't look all that happy to see me.

"What's up, Nixy?"

"Doralee told us you questioned her about an awl."

His mouth tightened, and I held up a hand.

"I'm not going to ask you about it. I just want to tell you that Doralee had an awl on Friday afternoon for the demonstration she did with Aunt Sherry. Afterward, when she and Zach were packing up, the awl was missing."

"Did you actually see the awl yourself?"

Uh-oh. I didn't want to lie, but I only saw Doralee's tools in passing. I compromised.

"I know the awl was in a kit with her other tools, and every tool was in its own molded slot thingy when Doralee and Sherry started the presentation."

"But you didn't see the awl yourself."

"Not so I could say, 'Aha! There's Doralee's awl.'"

He quirked a brow. "Aha?"

"Will you please listen to my part two of this?"

"Proceed."

"On Saturday we had another incident. One of Eleanor's tools went missing after her demo. Doralee wasn't at the store that day. We searched the store for the awl on Friday, and for both tools on Saturday, but they didn't turn up."

"What about the feed on your security cameras?"

I flushed. "I didn't remember we had them until Saturday, and unfortunately, there's a big honking blind spot where we set up the demo tables."

"Do you think a customer swiped the tools?"

"Since we've thoroughly searched, it's a darn strong possibility."

"Okay, I'll keep this information in mind."

"Great. Aren't you going to ask what Eleanor's tool looked like?"

"Why should I?"

"No reason if you've determined the awl was the murder weapon."

He blinked. "I didn't say that."

"Nope, and I won't repeat it, but something is bothering me."

"I thought you weren't investigating."

"I'm not. Not exactly. I'm collecting information to keep the Silver Six happy. If I think something is important, I'll come to you. But here's the thing," I rushed on. "I saw the blood pooling around Kim's torso. If she was shot, and if the shooter didn't use a silencer—"

"Suppressor."

"Okay, suppressor. Anyway, wouldn't Georgine have heard the shots? Are her migraine meds so strong that they'd knock her into oblivion?"

I paused, but Shoar held his passive expression. Which didn't deter me.

"If Kim was stabbed, wouldn't the killer be covered with enough blood to leave a trail?"

Again, I got the stone face.

"Can you at least acknowledge my logic?"

His eyes softened. "I acknowledge your logic, but I'm not discussing the details of the case."

"Fine. I have a couple more questions, and I don't see why you can't answer them."

He huffed a breath. "Okay, shoot."

"First, who is the witness that saw Doralee in the square?"

"I'm not saying."

"Did you remember to ask Doralee about Kim's former in-laws?"

"Gee, no, Nixy. I had more pertinent, pressing questions."

"Sarcasm, Eric?" And a taste of my own medicine. No wonder Fred had called me on my snarkiness earlier. "You're under the gun on this thing, aren't you?"

"Having two deaths in two months isn't making the chief or anyone else happy."

"Understood, but about the in-laws—"

He raised his hand in the universal sign for stop, eyes narrowed. "Tell me why I should question Ms. Gordon about Ms. Thomason's in-laws."

"I told you last night after you talked with Doralee. She told me Kim's sister-in-law, Margot, attempted to run Kim down with a golf cart."

He blinked. "All right, give me the scoop."

I relayed only what Doralee had reported to me, not embellishing the story, or making suppositions. Much.

"This is gossip, pure and simple. You know that. Ms. Gordon had the story from a friend, and the friend didn't witness the incident. This is probably fifth-hand information at best."

I tapped my foot. "Gossip or not, it could be true. You could check it out."

He only said, "What's your second question?"

"What is Kim's brother's name? I overheard Ernie tell you last night, but I'm drawing a blank."

"Caleb Collier. Why?"

"The seniors want to know. Is Caleb in town yet, or is he coming?"

"Are the Six planning a condolence call, or is this part of your information collecting?"

"A condolence call might be in order, but mostly they're curious."

"They're gossiping."

"Let's call it a desire to be in the know."

"No comment," he said, but a smile played on his mouth. He did have a soft spot for the Silver Six.

"You're no fun."

"Nixy," he drawled as he stepped closer and leaned toward me, "you have no clue how much fun I can be. I haven't had the chance to show you. Yet."

I nearly swallowed my tongue. Wow. He certainly knew how to change the subject.

"I've got to get back inside for another round of interviews," he said, putting space between us again. I realized that I had been holding my breath.

"That is unless you have more insights for me," he added. "What did you tell Officer Benton to get me out here? Information vital to the case?"

"It worked, didn't it?" He shook his head. "Good luck this afternoon. I'll let you know if I stumble over anything new."

On the walk back, I realized my dear detective hadn't told me a thing about this Caleb Collier except his name. At least I had that before Eric suddenly and blatantly flirted with me. Dang, the man was good at distraction. And I lapped it up.

And okay, I readily admitted I was curious about the murder. A perfectly natural response to finding the body, right? I also conceded that I didn't want to see Doralee accused of said murder. As for me truly investigating? No. I flat didn't have time much less the expertise. I could ask a few questions, and would let Eric know if I learned anything important. Between managing the emporium so we'd make a profit and being a novice foster pet mom, I had my hands full. I didn't need or want a distraction.

I would, however, give Aster and Eleanor the name "Caleb Collier" to help them research Kim. Maybe they'd find her first husband with the extra information. Maybe they'd find a whole list of suspects we could turn over to Shoar.

SANDY BROWN'S PRESENTATION ON CRAFTS TO celebrate the Fourth of July was a hands-on mini-nightmare, but it could've been worse. It could've put red and blue paint into the hands of four-year-olds.

None of us realized that Sandy meant to bring supplies for both adult and children's craft projects. None of us expected so many tykes to come in with their parents. None of us thought to have card tables in the store at all times and ready to snag just in case this sort of thing cropped up.

None of us would ever forget it again.

Perhaps I should've reconsidered all the free programs.

Aster was quick to whip out her lavender spray, and it all worked out in the end. The audience was game to sit on the floor or kneel at the old metal folding chairs while they crafted in a patriotic theme. The young 'uns, as Sandy called them, decorated empty and scrubbed-clean plastic mayonnaise jars with star stickers and ribbon in red, white, and blue. Somehow, a group of Boy Scouts had already painted jars in the requisite colors and began making small door wreaths out of embroidery hoops, ribbon, and wooden clothes pins. That's when I realized that Sandy had jump-started their project, and must be in cahoots with the Scout master. Scout mistress?

The adults helped the children, but most had time for their own projects, decorating blue, white, or red plastic buckets with coordinating precut foam stars. Sandy emphasized that the day's activities were chosen for their simplicity with relatively few supplies required. The crafts could take as little or as much time as one liked, were great for entertaining guests of varied ages, and could be adapted for any season or party theme.

She plugged the dollar store as her source of supplies more than once, but she also plugged the emporium's wares to the adults. Some who hadn't brought children stayed to browse and shop, and I was grateful.

When the customers left, the entire emporium staff jumped in to clean. Dab, Jasmine, and I wiped off the table and metal chairs, folded them, and stored them in the workroom. I'd given thought to leaving the chairs out so we didn't have to rearrange them each day, but I didn't want the store space to be more overcrowded than it already was. I sure didn't want to risk a customer tripping, but with all the setting up and taking down, I might change my mind and simply leave the chairs in neat rows.

With the center of the store cleared, Aster and Maise swept and lightly mopped the floor while Jasmine and Sherry went over the day's sales receipts and Eleanor then put the deposit money in a bag. We must've done much better than I thought because the bag looked pleasantly plump.

Just before closing, I realized I'd forgotten to call our security camera guy, Greg Masters. Ah, well. I'd do it tomorrow. Of course, as soon as we installed another camera, we'd never be in a position to need it again. Fortunately, Aunt Sissy had left money that had been very wisely invested over the years. I don't know if it was in a formal trust fund, but we'd already used some of that money for the security system and to buy a few boatloads of paint to spiff up the building in and out. Sherry was still insisting that I stay in my apartment rent-free, and that my utilities come out of Sissy's trust, which Sherry managed. For now, I went along with her wishes, but I didn't want to deplete those monies that were used for things like upkeep to the family cemetery. The monetary padding was great, but I didn't want to be dependent on it or Sherry. It was a driving reason I was determined to see the emporium thrive.

I shooed Jasmine and the Silver Six off. I'd see the seniors shortly for dinner at the farmhouse, but first I needed to feed Amber and T.C., and put my feet up for a few minutes.

As I crossed the sales floor to flip the deadbolt, Ernie Boudreaux burst through the front door like a rampaging bull. He snorted and stomped his way straight to me.

"I'm suing you for slander, Ms. Nix. I'm taking you for everything you're worth."

Chapter Nine

AFTER A STUNNED SECOND, I DID SOMETHING I'D never imagined doing. I jabbed my index finger into Ernie's polo-shirted chest.

"Back off, Mr. Boudreaux," I snapped. "Threaten me again, and I'll call the police. Got it?"

He backed up.

"Now, you can tell me what's wrong in a calm, civilized manner, or you can hit the road. I don't care which you choose."

It had been a long day.

He growled, alternately clenching and unclenching his fists. Meanwhile, I noticed Georgine standing just inside the store, eyes huge, face pale. Her pastel-striped blouse was buttoned to her chin, and her short salt-and-pepper hair stuck up as if she'd repeatedly pulled on it. She'd twisted a white handkerchief into a soggy knot. Today she didn't look angry or sour. She looked ill and scared.

I put my focus back on Ernie. "All right, what is your problem?"

"You're the problem," he snarled. "You've caused extreme mental duress to both me and my sister."

"How did I manage that?"

"You told Detective Shoar that Kim was obsessed with Doralee's opal. He thinks that's why Kim was in Doralee's room."

"Why else would she have been there?"

He gave me a blistering glare. "What do you mean?"

"If Kim wasn't looking for the gemstone, why did she ransack Doralee's room?"

"There's no proof she did. She could've interrupted a thief. Why, the thief might've searched our suite next."

"You honestly think a random thief got into a secure building, into a locked guest room, and then killed Kim when she caught him? If it was a thief, why not steal her diamond ring?"

He blustered, "Well—she, well—but." Then his shoulders sagged.

Georgine abandoned her distressed damsel pose, hurried to pat Ernie's shoulder, and stood by his side. I almost suggested sitting in the workroom to talk, but I didn't want them sticking around. I'd make my point, maybe gather information to help Doralee, and usher the Bourdreauxs out the door for good.

"Listen, Mr. Boudreaux, I overheard Kim nag you about that gem. I heard you be short with her over her nagging. I told Detective Shoar that Kim might've been looking for the opal, not that she definitely was."

"Any idiot would know Doralee wouldn't travel with that thing. It was too valuable."

"How valuable?"

He huffed. "It's a unique stone, but I haven't researched how much it's worth."

"Did you straight up tell Kim that Doralee didn't have the black opal with her?"

"Yes, of course." He paused, frowned, glanced at Georgine as if seeking her input. Then he returned his attention to me. "I know I was clear about it. Kim traveled with her good jewelry, but Doralee didn't. I told Kim that. The point is, you should have kept your opinions to yourself."

"I found your fiancée dead," I said baldly, hoping to break through his self-absorption. "I'm a witness, and I'm not about to apologize for cooperating with the police."

"I didn't kill her!" he bellowed.

"Then why does Detective Shoar think you did?"

"Only because my car was in the parking lot but I wasn't upstairs."

"Tell me what happened after I broke up Kim's rant at the lawn party. I might be able to help you."

Georgine gasped and stepped forward protectively. "You don't have to explain yourself to this woman, Ernie."

"You're right, Georgine," I said.

"That's Miss Boudreaux to you," she sniffed.

"Your brother doesn't have to explain a thing to me. Only to the police."

Amber suddenly bayed an *aroo* in the workroom. Agreeing with me, or just reminding me she and T.C. needed attention?

"Mr. Boudreaux, Ernie, tell me what you did or don't. It is past closing time, and I have things to do."

He frowned. "What did you say about helping me? You know the detective personally, don't you?"

"She's probably sleeping with him," Georgine sneered.

I pointed at the door. "Get out now."

"No, wait." Ernie threw a hand up, paced away, then back. "Yes, I was angry that Kim cornered Doralee at the party about the damned opal. After you steered Doralee away, Kim wanted to come back to the inn. I dropped her off, and headed back to the party to find Doralee and apologize."

"Did you drop Kim in front at the café door or at the back entrance?"

"The back."

"Did you watch her go inside?"

"No, I drove on out of the alley."

"Did you see anyone else outside?" When he shook his head, I plowed on. Hey, I was on a roll on this interviewing thing. "Did you stop anywhere on the way back?"

"I—" His gaze faltered, slid to Georgine again before he stood taller. "I stopped at a convenience store for a pack of cigarettes."

Georgine's mouth tightened, and Ernie waved a hand at her.

"I have quit," he said, "for the most part. I just needed half a smoke to calm down."

"Then what?"

"I was headed back to the party and saw Doralee, uh, walking."

Uh-oh. I could tell from his chagrined expression that he hadn't meant to let that slip. "Walking where?"

"About half between the square and your aunt's farmhouse. I gave her a lift back."

The distance between Sherry's place and the square was roughly a mile. "Did you tell Shoar you saw Doralee near the square?"

Ernie straightened, lifted his chin. "I did not. There was no point in bringing it to his attention. It was an innocent encounter between us, and she certainly would *not* have killed my fiancée."

Hmm. Interesting that Ernie was protecting Doralee. I pressed on with questions while he was in an answering mood—and before Georgine interfered.

"So you took Doralee back to the party. When did you leave again?"

His shoulders slumped. "I don't know. Near four o'clock?

I wasn't ready to talk to Kim yet, so I left my car in the parking lot and took a long walk."

"Did you tell Shoar where you went?"

"I didn't *go* anywhere. I passed the hospital, the laundromat, a couple of closed stores. I didn't talk to a soul."

"Which doesn't mean someone didn't see you. The detective will ask around." If a citizen had reported seeing Doralee, someone should've seen Ernie.

"How hard will he look when he thinks I killed Kim? I sat in that little gazebo by the courthouse for close to an hour, and I shouldn't have."

"Why did you?" I couldn't help but ask.

"I wanted more time alone. I knew I'd have to take her out for dinner, but I dreaded dealing with another of her tantrums."

"Perfectly understandable," Georgine huffed.

"Yet if I'd gone back, Kim might be alive now," he said helplessly. I could see that under his anger was true, deep sadness.

I half expected Georgine to say something snide, but she only set her mouth in a tight line.

"Will you talk to the detective for me, Ms. Nix?"

"I'll do what I can, but you should know that Detective Shoar is an honest, fair, careful investigator. He's interested in the truth, not merely making an arrest."

"I hope so because I don't know how I'll get out of this."

"I won't let anything happen to you." Georgine shot me a fierce glare as she gripped her brother's arm. "I never do."

I WANTED TO IMMEDIATELY TRACK DOWN DORALEE and ask some pointed questions about leaving the party on Sunday and where she'd gone. Not to mention what had passed between her and Ernie. Heck, for all I knew, Doralee and Ernie had conspired to kill Kim.

Yes, that theory was a stretch about as wide as Arkansas

and halfway through Oklahoma. Still, I'd have to talk with Doralee at some point. I wasn't about to take potentially damning information about her to Eric without checking it out first.

Interesting that Doralee thought she was Eric's main suspect, and Ernie thought he was the one in Eric's sights. It made sense that my dear detective was looking at both the fiancé and the ex-wife, though.

I'd mull on that more later. For now I needed to keep my dinner date with the Silver Six.

The farmhouse dining room took up nearly a fourth of Sherry's downstairs. Early evening light spilled through large windows, two facing west and two south, making the old farm table's age-darkened patina glow with warmth. The west windows looked onto the deep front porch while the south windows featured a view of the narrower side porch, a peek at Aster's garden, the big oak tree, and the yard beyond.

I overlooked the fact that Fred and Dab allowed T.C. and Amber to scoot under the table, probably conspiring to get their paws on more contraband people food. Instead I moved the candlesticks and decorative bowls, one of them filled with lavender, to the long sideboard and finished setting the table.

Maise, Aster, Sherry, and Eleanor bustled through the swinging door from the kitchen carrying bowls and platters. I could make a meal of Maise's famous fried okra alone, but tonight's menu included pork loin, cauliflower, and a tossed salad. Oh, and sweet tea. What else?

"I sure wish we'd been in the store when Ernie and Georgine came by," Sherry Mae said as we all began passing the serving dishes around the table.

Yes, I'd filled them in on the highlights of why I'd run late for dinner.

"Busted in, you mean," Fred growled from his seat on my right. "Man's got no manners a'tall."

"I'm simply relieved he didn't have more mischief on his

mind," Maise declared. "Do you think we need to keep a weapon of some kind in the store for protection?"

"No," I nearly shouted as I rose halfway out of my designated chair at the foot of the table.

Six pairs of eyes regarded me as if I'd lost my tiny mind. Maybe I had because what leaped to memory was that Fred owned a Colt .45. Though he could fix about anything on the planet, I didn't know when he'd last cleaned that pistol, or if it even fired. I sure didn't want to find out by having it in the emporium.

"What's wrong with keeping a little insurance policy handy?" Maise demanded.

"We have Jasmine there," I said, striving for calm. "Young children coming in, too. And we might need a permit to keep a weapon on a business premise."

"Not for a baseball bat," Dab offered reasonably.

"No," I ground out. "No bats. No weapons of any kind."

Sherry gave me a speculative stare. "I suppose it wouldn't hurt for you to have something like pepper spray, child. After all, you're walking the animals at night. However, I agree we don't need a weapon in the store. Besides, Detective Shoar will solve this case in no time flat, Doralee will be cleared of suspicion, and it'll be business as usual."

From her seat on my left, Eleanor gave my hands a pointed look. Hands I realized were trembling slightly. She arched a brow. "I do believe Ernie Boudreaux unnerved you more than you want to admit."

"Which isn't surprising, I suppose," Aster added, "since he's still our number one suspect."

"Did you uncover anything about him or Kim?" I asked, happy to redirect the conversation. "Did you have time to visit with any of the merchants today?"

"With most of them," Sherry said proudly. "Kim visited the shoe store and tried on twenty pairs of sandals without buying a one. Twenty pairs. Brooke was annoyed."

"And she went to both the clothing stores on the square,

and the beauty supply," Aster added. "She bought a red blouse at Clarra's Closet and red nail polish, both on Friday afternoon."

"Ernie and Georgine weren't with her during any of these shopping expeditions," Maise put in, "but Miss Anna and Hope both said all three were in the pharmacy on Saturday. She didn't recall what they bought. Dab, you went to Virginia's. What did you find out?"

I'd been in our upscale jewelry store, and could see why Kim would be drawn there. They carried exquisite—and expensive—pieces. Too pricey for my pocketbook, as Sherry would say.

"Virginia Hale wasn't there, but I talked to Pearce. Kim was definitely in there, and without Ernie. She pulled the shoe store stunt. She tried on rings, bracelets, and necklaces. She also looked at men's watches she told Pearce were for her fiancé, but didn't buy anything."

"I doubt what she bought or didn't is critical to the case," I said, "but it's good information. What about your computer searches? Anything there?"

"Disappointingly little," Eleanor said. "He has a business website called *The Gourdian Knot*. There's only a short bio, a list of the fairs and festivals where he sets up, and a lot of photos of his birdhouse gourds."

I patted Eleanor's arm. "I know he was your front runner, but let's face it. He couldn't be that bad if Doralee married him."

"True."

"We moved on," Sherry said, "to Kim and uncovered a bit of information about her first marriages, and her stepfamilies."

Fred snorted. "Information with a liberal sprinklin' of gossip."

I speared several chunks of my rapidly cooling okra. "Tell me all."

I got to eat while the Six—Dab and Fred included—took

turns regaling me with what they'd gleaned about Kimberly Rebecca Collier Franks Thomason. As Doralee had told me, Kim had humble beginnings in a rural area north of Minden, Louisiana. Other highlights were Kim's local beauty pageant wins as a teen, and her wedding announcements, first to Craig W. Franks, and later to D.B. Thomason.

"Franks was a fifty-year-old widower, a successful businessman from Alexandria," Eleanor said. "She was twenty-three. We saw photos of them attending charity functions."

"They appeared happy enough," Aster added, "and they were married for almost eight years before Craig Franks died."

"Granted she waited a few years after Craig Franks's death to remarry again," Maise said, "but it's interesting that she hooked another wealthy man who left her a chunk of change and a passel of slot machines."

I cocked my head at Maise. "Come again?"

"D.B. Thomason and his family own a resort hotel and casino in Shreveport."

"Have for years," Dab piped in, "and had oil money before that. They're upper-crust folks in the Shreveport area."

"And the family must be riled somethin' fierce about what she inherited 'cause they were suin' Kim," Fred put in.

"Don't tell me she got the casino."

"Only some minor interest in it," Eleanor said, "but Kim got the family mansion and more money than the rest of them thought she should have. We found a notice of the suit in the public records."

"There are a few photos of Kim and D.B. Thomason online at yet more charity events," Aster said. "They were married for just over nine years."

"Great work! You found much more information than I thought you might."

"I do believe the Internet can be a glorious place," Eleanor quipped.

Sherry nodded. "Except that we didn't find much on the two sets of in-laws. The younger Franks relatives have Facebook pages, but they didn't tell us anything interesting. The Thomason son, Dennis, also has a page, and the posts indicate he's engaged to someone from Dallas."

"I don't suppose he put any rants about Kim on Facebook."

"No, but he posted about his plans to live with his bride in his childhood home. He says maybe it will happen sooner than later."

"Hmm. What about Margot Thomason?"

"One listing and it's from the woman's debutante days," Maise said. "The photo online was scanned from an old newspaper article. It's so grainy, I'm not sure I could identify the person pictured if it was my own sister."

"She's right," Aster confirmed. "And we couldn't find a record of Margot's married name."

"We can ask Doralee, or I'll bug Eric about getting it." I paused, drummed my fingers on the table. "You know, Doralee told me that when Kim died, her part of the Thomason estate goes back to her in-laws. It's a rumor, of course, but if it's true, it sounds like a motive for murder. Were Kim's first set of in-laws—who were they again?"

"The Franks family. Craig was Kim's husband."

"Was that family okay with whatever Kim inherited?"

"Personal details are sketchy," Sherry jumped in. "However, the Franks heirs—a son and twin daughters—didn't seem to actively hate Kim. They didn't file any lawsuits that we could find."

"How about prenuptial agreements? Did she have one with either husband?"

"Nothing firm on that score, but we can dig more. Jasmine's boyfriend has access to some sites we can't get to."

Eeks, I thought. "No hacking, y'all," I said. "Promise me."

From the halfhearted agreement, I figured I'd be bailing one or more of them out of jail in the near future.

"You thinkin' we should follow the money, missy?"

"Fred, I really don't know. Killing someone for money is a time-honored motive."

"We're certain that Doralee didn't have motive," Sherry said firmly.

"I tend to agree. She didn't want Ernie back, and that's all she could gain from Kim's death." Although I wanted to hear from her lips why she was near the square on foot Sunday afternoon. "As for Ernie," I continued, "I can't see what he'd gain by killing Kim. If he'd changed his mind about marrying her, he'd have just broken it off."

"That's logical," Eleanor said.

"So we've cleared Doralee and Ernie," Maise said.

I didn't so much as twitch at that statement.

"And Zach," Sherry added. "He has no motive whatsoever."

"So who did?" Aster asked.

"I don't have a clue," I said. "If the Thomason clan was suing Kim, why bother to kill her?"

"Afraid they'll lose the lawsuit?" Dab suggested.

"Possibly, but it takes us back to Fred's question. Who inherits Kim's money and property now? Is the brother her only relative? What if the Thomason family doesn't get a thing? And what if her murder has nothing to do with inheriting?"

We'd finished supper by then, and mulled that question over our empty plates and full stomachs.

"You know," I said slowly, "Doralee also told me that Georgine broke up her marriage."

After I related the gist of that conversation, Maise tapped her chin. "Even assuming Georgine was as jealous of Kim as she was of Doralee, would Georgine kill Kim?"

"If she did, she'd get her brother back," Aster offered. "There was no love lost between the two women."

"True, but would she kill Kim to keep her from marrying

Ernie?" Sherry asked. "If so, why not kill Doralee before *she* married Ernie?"

"I don't know," I said, shaking my head. "Doralee said Georgine's modus operandi was subversion. She didn't confront Doralee about anything. She was a passive-aggressive underminer. Besides, she looked drugged to her eyeballs on migraine meds yesterday."

"Nevertheless," Sherry said, "we'll see what we can learn about Georgine, and keep asking questions about Ernie."

"I still say follow the money," Fred declared as he rose and grabbed his tool-belt-laden walker. "You help with the dishes, missy. I'll take the critters out."

BEFORE I LEFT THE FARMHOUSE, I TEASED FRED about adopting T.C. and Amber himself. He said he'd be happy as a pig in slop to help me with them, but refused to take them permanently.

"'Cause they didn't come to the farmhouse for me to find, missy. They come to the store for you. A'sides, you're still lookin' for their proper owner, ain't you?"

I murmured my agreement. Naturally I wanted to reunite the pets with their owner. Just the ticket to make everyone happy, right? For now, the critters were relatively undemanding company, and they had done a wonderful job of calming Doralee. I admitted I loved stroking their soft fur, and watching them play together. They had even begun vocalizing more, perhaps because I'd found myself talking to them. And the more we got to know each other, the more their little personalities shone through. Okay, I had avoided playing with them too much, or looking too deeply into their precious faces and huge, trusting eyes. Some instinct told me if I did that, I'd be a goner.

And it would be rotten if, just when I well and truly fell for Amber and T.C., their rightful owner showed up.

On the way home, they sat side by side in the passenger seat, heads swiveled toward me, ears perked and expressions expectant. They looked like that a lot, and I figured the consistent expectation was to eat. Tonight I countered their "what's next" looks with brainstorming. Specifically, I bounced investigation ideas off them. Yes, I still felt odd talking to animals, but it was a step up from talking to myself.

"I didn't want to remind the Six of this, but I'm pretty sure Detective Shoar will be all over the inheritance question, and he has the resources to get answers."

T.C. curled her tail around her paws and *murped*, a sound I took as agreement. Amber thumped her tail on the seat, cocked her head, and emitted a short, sharp whine that sounded like, "*Uh.*"

"Not that it can hurt for Sherry and company to poke around on the computer or ask questions around town." I worried my lip. "Can it get them into trouble? I don't want a repeat of April."

Amber sneezed and shook her head. T.C. almost toppled over from the force of the unexpected blast, looking aghast at her companion.

"No, you're right. I won't worry. I'll be happy they're occupied with the mystery and not fretting about the business. I'm doing that enough for all of us."

A few blocks from home I came to a stop sign. The crossroad ran east toward the Pines Motor Court, where Doralee and Zach were staying. I didn't have Doralee's cell number, but I could pop in on her. The summer sun had set, and the temperature had cooled enough that it wouldn't sound too odd to ask her to take a walk with me. I'd be able to question her about Sunday's private encounter with Ernie without risking that Zach would overhear. No point in making trouble for the couple.

On the other hand, I was tired, and had another long day tomorrow. And critters to walk first thing. Cute as they were, caring for Amber and T.C. demanded time. However, as Fred had pointed out, they had come to the emporium to find me. They were mine to deal with until I found their owner.

I felt something wet and looked down to see T.C. delicately sniffing my elbow. I sighed.

I REMEMBERED I HADN'T BEEN TO THE GROCERY store when I opened the bare cupboard on Tuesday morning. Great. Time to give in and jog down the block to the Great Buns Bakery—a pleasure I'd indulged in several times a week since moving to Lilyvale. Until lately.

Grant and Judy Armistead owned Great Buns and were in their early thirties. I didn't know if he was a descendant of the Confederate general named Armistead, but Grant ran the place with military precision. Maise, with her Navy background, loved Grant. I didn't know him well enough to have much of an opinion, but I was becoming friends with the five-foot fireball Judy.

She had a cordless phone wedged between her ear and shoulder when I entered the shop, but gave me a wave and the universal just-a-minute sign.

I approached the old-fashioned lunch counter with the grill behind it, and a glass case down on the right for breads and pastries. Tall bistro chairs lined the length of the counter rather than stools. The dark espresso wood stain matched the seat and back cushions. Both tall and normal-height bistro tables and chairs dotted the floor space, and the wall art was a mixed bag of blown-up photos showcasing moments in Lilyvale's history and vintage signs.

I took a seat at the counter just as Judy ended her call.

"Hey, girl. About time you came to see me."

"Sorry, but I've been busy, and I'm rationing my visits to watch the waistline."

"*Pfht*. You do *not* need to sweat gaining weight yet. Now, give me your order, then tell me about finding that dead woman."

"Way to ruin my appetite."

She snorted. "Impossible. I've seen you snarf down my biscuit sandwiches. Is that what you want today?"

"Yes, thanks."

Judy was the most masterful of multitaskers I'd ever seen. She unwrapped and slapped a sausage patty on the grill, made and set my usual vanilla latte in front of me, then whirled again to flip the sausage. All in what seemed like the blink of an eye.

"Okay, I know the victim's name was Kim from the gossip flying around town. Now spill the rest. Curiosity is about to wear me thin."

I talked while she made my favorite hard-poached egg, sausage, and American cheese on one of her fabulous buttermilk biscuits. I glossed over the more disturbing details, of course, but Judy uttered commiserating noises now and then. When she plunked my plate on the counter, she gave me a measuring stare.

"What?"

"Are you snooping into this the way you did with that other murder?"

I choked on a bite of biscuit. "No."

She held my gaze.

"Okay, I'm asking a few questions here and there, but only because Aunt Sherry insisted we help Doralee. If I'm not involved—"

"The Silver Six will run amok. I figured as much. I'll say this. I don't think y'all's friend Doralee did the deed."

"Why is that?" I asked after a swallow of my latte.

"She was in here once with that handsome guy, and they were both nice as could be. That Kim woman, on the other hand—"

"Wait. Kim was in here?"

"That's what I'm telling you. She was in here with a

woman whose hair was more platinum blonde than mine is. The blonde was dressed to the nines, and she and Kim were *not* having a friendly visit."

I put down my sandwich. "What happened? And when was this?"

"It was Saturday late morning after the early rush. I overheard the women arguing. In low voices, but there was no mistaking the tone and body language."

"Did you overhear anything in particular? Did Kim call the other woman by name?"

"No, but the blonde told Kim she wanted the ring, and Kim told her she'd have it over Kim's dead body." Judy paused and shuddered. "I know that's something people say but don't necessarily mean in a literal sense, but still."

"Yeah, it sounds more ominous now than it probably did then."

"Exactly."

"How did the blonde woman respond?"

"She said, 'If that's what it takes.' It clearly sounds like a threat now, but it didn't at the time."

"I know. It's another one of those things people say. Did you tell Detective Shoar about this squabble?"

She blinked. "No. He didn't question us, and I didn't think to go to him. You think I should?"

"Actually, I do. Have you seen the blonde since Saturday morning?"

"No, I'd remember if I had."

"Do you think Grant might've seen her while he was covering the counter?"

"Doubtful. He's been back in the kitchen baking or in the office most of the time since Friday."

Great Buns didn't serve full meals like the Lilies Café did, but they made a few specialty sandwiches on thick slices of heavenly fresh-baked bread.

I wolfed down the rest of my sandwich and latte and slipped a ten-dollar bill on the counter by my plate. "I need to get back to walk the dog and cat, but call Shoar, will you? It could help Doralee."

"Which would get your Aunt Sherry Mae off your back, I know. By the way, since when did you adopt pets?"

"How did you know about them?" I asked, sliding off the tall chair.

"I saw you with them a few mornings ago, but I was too busy to pop out and say hi. Where did you find them?"

"Actually, they found me."

"They sure are cuties," she sang out as I hustled to the door. "Bring them by some morning. Or maybe I'll meet them if I can cut out of here and get to one of your grand opening events."

A BRISK WALK LATER AND I WAS BACK AT THE EMPO-rium. Mindful of Dr. Barklay's warning about giving Amber lots of exercise, I tossed a tennis ball in the parking lot for her a dozen times. She loped back immediately each time she fetched while T.C. stretched out on the blacktop and became absorbed in licking her entire silky coat. Neither seemed interested in wandering off. Good deal. Not worrying about them gave me the time to think more about my conversation with Judy.

And to think back to the video and still photos of the strangers in sunglasses who'd been in the store last week. Specifically, on Friday afternoon. Eleanor, who was becoming more and more tech savvy by the day, was to have downloaded the stills to the communal farmhouse laptop so she and the others of the Silver Six could see the photos on a larger screen. She was supposed to send me any pictures that might be worth a closer look. Had she sent them? I didn't remember getting an e-mail from her, but then I hadn't checked my mail in days and she hadn't mentioned sending anything.

Okay, so Doralee's class was held Thursday evening, and

the in-store demo with Aunt Sherry on Friday afternoon. Judy witnessed an argument between Kim and a blonde on Saturday late morning. About a ring. Maybe she was talking about the opal Kim wanted Doralee to fork over? That seemed odd since the opal was a loose stone.

The key point was that Judy could verify if my Friday shade-wearing blonde was her Saturday confronting-Kim blonde. If so, and adding the overheard threat, Eric would have another suspect to pursue. I had a strong suspicion that suspect would turn out to be Margot, Kim's former sister-in-law.

Okay, so stabbing someone was a long stretch from a body clip with a golf cart. And I couldn't picture how Margot would've come to have the supposed murder weapon, Doralee's awl. But hey, the blonde had threatened Kim, and sometimes threats weren't so idle.

Not that I didn't trust Judy to follow through, but I'd call Eric later and nudge him to pay a visit to Great Buns. Now, though, it was time to start getting the store ready to open.

I allowed both T.C. and Amber into the retail area while I set up chairs for the day's demos. Still energized from their outing, they darted around my feet talking to each other. Or that's what it sounded like this morning.

I happily endured the trip hazard and critter chatter. They'd initially been so quiet, it tickled me to see them being playful. Yes, the activity might lead them to shed more, but hopefully not enough to trigger a customer's allergies. I'd do a quick swipe with the dusters after I took them back to Fred's space.

Twenty minutes before we were to open, sharp rapping summoned me to answer the emporium's glass front door. Eleanor had texted me that the Silver Six would be late, so I was alone in the store, and for a second, I feared it was Ernie showing up to harangue me again, but no.

An elderly woman with elegantly styled gray hair rapped again, this time on the door frame with the curved handle of her cane. Tall with just the barest stoop, she wore a simple tailored blue pantsuit with sensible flats. Her heavily powdered face lit with a smile when she saw me.

"We aren't open yet," I hollered through the door even as I opened it a crack.

"My name is Ruth Kreider, dear, and I surely am sorry to intrude," the lady said in a soft but firm voice, "but I must see you before I get back on the road to Little Rock."

"Um, all right, then," I said, swinging the door wide to admit her. "What can I do for you, Mrs. Kreider?"

"Call me Ruth. I've come to see the animals you found."

Chapter Ten

"OH MY GOODNESS, HERE THEY ARE!" RUTH CRIED as Amber and T.C. scampered to greet her, Amber's nails clicking like crazy on the hardwood floor. For a second, I feared they might jump on her, but they sat quivering at Ruth's feet talking to her.

Yes, talking. I'd heard the T.C. meow, *murp*, and chirp more frequently in the last few days, but nothing like she was doing for Ruth. Now she went through that repertoire and added more. Amber, who was normally the quieter of the two except for the occasional *bark-aroo*, voiced excited whines while wagging her whole body. My heart sank a little in my chest.

"Hello, darlings, hello," Ruth cooed. Clearly she wanted to pet them, but just as clearly had difficulty bending to reach them.

"Come sit, Ruth," I said as I cupped her elbow to guide her to a folding chair.

The animals backed up to get out of the way of both her feet and her cane. I swore they understood that she needed more space to move than I did. They parked themselves square in front of her as soon as she hooked her cane on the upright stave and was settled.

"Let me look at you, you sweet things!" She patted her lap, and T.C. leaped lightly into it while Amber stood next to the chair, paws on the edge of the seat, panting at Ruth with an adoring look on her puppyish face.

Ruth's visit, and especially the reaction of the critters, caught me off guard, and I fumbled to find my equilibrium.

"Are these your pets?"

I'd be happy if she were their rightful owner. Of course I would. They were deliriously happy to see her. I could feel some sadness creeping in, too, but I shoved that emotion away, and waited for her to fend off enthusiastic licks before she answered.

"No, dear, they aren't mine. These little ones lived with my neighbor down near Minden."

I blinked. "Minden, Louisiana?" That's where Doralee said Kim had been raised.

Ruth nodded, one hand on each critter. "We lived in the country, well, I still do. But my neighbor, Doris Roche, bless her soul, is the one who took in Blackie and Tiger."

"Blackie and Tiger?" I echoed, still reeling.

"Not terribly original, I grant you, but we don't much cotton to fancy names for pets in the county. Doris was the salt of the earth."

I lowered myself to a chair beside Ruth. "You said Doris took in these animals. Were they strays?"

"Indeed. They showed up at her back door one day—they were even smaller then—and simply stayed. Well, Doris had been feeling poorly and wasn't getting around so good, but these babies perked her right up. Didn't you?" she asked T.C. and Amber. Or should I be calling them Tiger and Blackie?

"Um, Ruth, we noticed that both animals had been spayed. Did Doris take care of that?"

"She surely did. My grandson and his friend got some vouchers from a humane society, then drove Doris and her new pets to the vet. She had their shots done first. Two rounds of them. Then she got more vouchers and had the veterinarian fix them. Didn't she, sweeties?"

Ruth paused to lavish attention on the critters. T.C. made a *meep* sound as if meowing while she purred. Amber panted happily and gave Ruth's arm a lick now and then.

"How old were they when Doris took them in?"

"The doctor figured they were already a good five months old, so it was the right time to have them fixed. He wanted to put those identity chips in them, too, but Doris couldn't afford it. Those vouchers didn't pay for everything, you know. They only defrayed some of the costs. But Tiger and Blackie gave her so much love and attention, she was happy to spend the money she could spare."

I nodded absently. I couldn't call the critters by their old names. Those didn't seem to fit any longer, but I wanted to know a bit more about their history.

"How long were they with Doris?"

Ruth met my gaze with a sheen of tears in her green eyes. "Until the end, dear. About four months after these two showed up, Doris died at home. In fact, Blackie here got out the screen door and ran to my house over a mile away to fetch me. I'm embarrassed to say that in all the confusion of calling out the paramedics and deputies and the chaos, I lost track of Blackie and Tiger. I didn't even remember them until two days later, and by then they had gone."

"If Doris was ill, I'm surprised she kept the animals. They never got underfoot?"

Ruth tilted her head at me. "You know, I worried about that and mentioned it to Doris. She said her furry angels— that's what she called them—were as calm and well behaved as could be. I saw it for myself, too." Ruth sighed. "They could be playful and distracted her from her pain with their antics, and then they'd curl up with her when she rested.

They gave Doris so much happiness before she passed on. It may be whimsy, but I always thought they came to Doris for that reason—to lighten her load those last months."

"I wonder where they've been since Doris passed."

Ruth chuckled. "Doris and I used to speculate where they'd been before they came to her. We laughed about them having one of those adventures out of a Disney movie. The kind where the animals travel to reunite with their owners, except these two were looking for a new owner. Or owners, I suppose, now that they've found you."

"I can see that," I agreed with a smile, watching her continue to lavish attention on the critters.

"Well, dear, wherever they've been, they've found you now. They deserve another good home."

I avoided her pointed comment. "Ruth, how did you find out about them being here?"

"Why, dear, my grandson's friend saw them on a computer. The two boys—well, they aren't boys, they're grown men—helped me around my place, and helped Doris, too."

I frowned. "And your grandson's friend told you?"

"Well, no, Rusty called Ray, my grandson, and Ray called me. He knew I was coming this way, and that I'd been worried about these two. He suggested I stop by and hopefully put my mind at rest. And now I have."

"So Ray and Rusty knew T.C. and Amber?"

"Is that what you call them, dear? I like those names. Yes, they knew these babies. They'd take the animals out for a romp when they worked over at Doris's. Fact is, they knew the animals better than I did, and I visited Doris several times a week." She paused, and seemed to shake herself. "Now then, I must be going. My daughter's driving me all the way to Little Rock for a little reunion with some old friends. She went to top off the gas tank after she dropped me off, but she's likely to be circling the block by now."

As if sensing Ruth's intent, T.C. jumped down from her

lap, and Amber backed up as if she knew to give the woman room to move. I unhooked Ruth's cane and then held her elbow to stabilize her as she stood.

"You two be good now," Ruth said to the critters as I escorted her out of the store. "Maybe I'll come visit again on my way back home."

Amber barked, her tail wagging. T.C. meowed and rubbed her cheek on Ruth's leg before padding away to sit with her canine bud.

"You're most welcome to stop in any time," I said.

I helped Ruth to her daughter's car, said a quick hello to Marilyn, a fiftyish woman with a slightly harried smile, and returned to the store deep in thought.

I found myself at the checkout counter absently gazing at the cash register. More or less the same spot I'd placed my tablet to run the slide show of the pets beginning on Friday around noon.

Amber and T.C. had lived with Doris outside Minden. The town Kim had lived in. Odd, but coincidences did happen, even whoppers. I never thought the six degrees of separation theory would connect animals to humans, but what did I know? The how and why of the critters showing up on my doorstep was as much a puzzle as Bernice Gilroy was.

Odder still, Ruth said the family friend had seen photos of Amber and T.C. on a computer, but where could he have seen them? I hadn't had time to put their pictures on social media, or to e-mail them to Dr. Barklay the vet, or to Miranda Huston at the shelter. I felt sure Eleanor would've told me if she had posted them elsewhere.

All of which meant that the friend, Rusty, had to have seen photos of the critters on my tablet in the store on Friday or Saturday because, in all the chaos, I'd forgotten to run the slide show on Monday.

So why didn't this Rusty guy tell us on the spot that he knew the animals?

"Maybe, maybe not, but I *have* been meeting people. Grant and Judy at Great Buns Bakery. Carter and Kay at Gaskin's Business Center. Greg Masters, our tech guy. Plus, I belong to the Chamber of Commerce. We all do. We volunteered for the holiday lights committee."

Fred humphed. "You volunteered us."

"Because you want to move the folk art festival from the farmhouse grounds into town this fall," Sherry added.

"Y'all agreed it would be a good idea to get Lilyvale businesses involved."

"Not to mention," Dab piped up, "Chamber sponsorship is smoothing the way to get permits and whatnot."

"Which reminds me," Sherry said, "we need to follow up on that. I'll send out an e-mail. Meantime, Nixy, it wouldn't hurt you to find your own organizations and connect with more people your age."

"Not that you wouldn't be welcome anywhere, including the garden club," Aster assured me. "The club does more than hold meetings. Last year they organized a group tour to Eureka Springs to see the fall color."

"I went, too," Sherry said. "We should all do that together now that you live here, Nixy. I'll bet you've never gone leaf-peeping."

"Sounds fun," I said, and I meant it, but I didn't ask who would run the emporium if we all took off to see the fall foliage.

I wandered to the front windows, glad to leave the subject of clubs behind. I'd been a joiner in my school days on a limited basis, and I'd put myself out there to meet people and make friends. After college, I'd left joining behind. When I worked in the art gallery in Houston, I was too busy, and I didn't want to fight traffic to attend meetings. Here in Lilyvale, traffic jams were more or less nonexistent, and the time it took to get from one end of town to another averaged fifteen minutes, tops. I might have a harder time holding out if the Silver Six pressed the club-joining thing.

But for now, I was concerned that Rose wasn't in the store yet. We were fifteen minutes short of her session starting.

As I headed over to round her up, I spotted her pulling a laden wagon along the sidewalk. I jogged out to help, and we soon had her paraphernalia arranged on two folding tables. Just in time for the ladies of the Lilyvale Garden Club to inspect her wares—vases of various heights and widths, wonderfully fragrant real flowers and vibrantly colored silk ones, and supplies like wires, picks, and floral tape.

Aster gave Rose the perfect introduction with an extra few plugs for the Happy Garden, and the presentation flowed beautifully. Except for Rose's occasional sniffling. Talk about irony. The poor woman who adored flowers suffered from allergies to them, and her medications hadn't kicked in enough to cancel her symptoms. Still, her demonstration of floral designs was a hit, and she allowed us to keep the silk flower arrangement for the big giveaway drawing on Saturday.

Shortly after Rose left, Doralee came by, and we all—even Dab and Fred—gathered around her.

"How are you?" I asked. "Any more word from Detective Shoar?"

"Not a peep, but we're well, thanks. Our room at the Pines Motor Court is small, but cute as it can be. Fifties decor with a flat screen TV, Wi-Fi, and a private sitting area out back with a retro table and chairs. And the owners, Winne and Woody Needham, are the sweetest people."

"I'm glad it's working out, but you and Zach come back to the farmhouse if you need to. You're always welcome."

"I know, Sherry Mae, and thanks. I came to town to grab lunch for Zach. I left him checking in with his office, and setting up appointments for later in the week."

"Do you have time for us to eat together?" Aster asked. "It won't take more than half an hour longer."

Doralee's eyes twinkled. "I imagine Zach expects me to do just that. Let's go."

While the ladies took lunch orders from Dab and Fred, who were not coming to lunch, I seized the chance to pull Doralee aside and steered her out the front door.

"What is it, Nixy?" she eagerly asked. "Do you know who killed Kim?"

I snorted. "Not by a long shot. But I had a conversation with Ernie last night. He barged into the store as I was closing."

Her eyes rounded. "Why did he come to you? Because we found Kim together?"

"Because I told Detective Shoar about the opal Kim wanted. Shoar suspects him of the murder, too, but he didn't throw you under the bus."

She blinked. "What do you mean?"

"He didn't tell Shoar that he saw you walking near the square."

She closed her eyes and absorbed that for moment. "I didn't realize Ernie didn't mention my walk, but someone else did see me. I'm still a suspect in your detective's book."

"So why *did* you leave the party, Doralee?"

Her gaze slid away from me, then back. "After Zach left, I thought about how much grief Kim was giving Ernie about the damned stone. I started walking back toward the inn thinking I'd find him and offer to sell him the opal. I was debating about how much to charge him. On the retail market, it's worth a lot."

"And?" I prompted when she paused.

"And I was a block away when I turned around. I decided I'd wait to talk with him. I didn't want to make an emotional decision and then regret it."

"So you didn't mention your thoughts to him during the ride back to Sherry's?"

Her gaze turned flinty. "I almost did, but no."

"You weren't sealing a deal when I caught you kissing him?"

"A peck on the cheek, Nixy," she said with a chill in her

voice. "That's all it was. I didn't kill Kim, and for the record, I don't believe Ernie did it either."

"Who do you think did do it?"

She sighed. "I wish I knew."

The door chimes sang, and the Silver Six ladies spilled outside. Sherry hooked her arm through Doralee's and they headed across the square to the Lilies Café chattering a mile a minute.

I felt good about my talk with Doralee, but did I believe she'd come completely clean? No. For one thing, why not simply call his cell phone to offer him the opal? Maybe she wasn't as over Ernie as she thought.

I NEEDED TO GET TO THE GROCERY STORE BEFORE our afternoon got busy, and my chance came after the ladies headed out for lunch and Jasmine arrived for her shift. I ducked to the workroom to gather the animals for a walk, but Fred and Dab already had them outside. When I told them I was headed for Mac's Fresh Market, the grocery closest to downtown, they gave me a short list of supplies to buy for the emporium. Coffee, tea, and fancy crackers because Dab had eaten the last of them this morning.

As I pulled into the parking lot, I realized I hadn't been food shopping above three times in the five weeks I'd been in town. The Six had fed me nearly nightly, *and* sent me home with leftovers. Embarrassing to think I'd mooched off of them that long. Well, not exactly mooched. I had been invited to dinners at the farmhouse after all.

At least I knew where Mac's and the other grocery stores were located. Bold red letters spelled out the store name on an older building that had housed another chain in the past. Inside, though, the space was spotless, the aisles clear, and the goods well organized so I could zip in and out without getting sidetracked too much.

I grabbed a red plastic hand basket, counting on the

smaller container to help keep me from impulse buying, and dashed through the aisles. Coffee and tea for the emporium. Two boxes of protein bars, a jar of almond butter, couple of frozen ready-to-stir-fry dinners, two plums, an apple, and three peaches. I avoided the deli with divine-smelling fried chicken. Maise would have a fit if I bought so much as a drumstick. The bread aisle, though, was safe enough.

Until I spotted Eric Shoar in the aisle with a shopping cart.

I might have made a noise because just as he lifted a loaf of whole wheat, he looked up and our gazes locked.

"Hey, Nixy, how are you?"

I smiled at him, moved nearer. It would be rude not to, right? Besides, his deep, dreamy voice always drew me. He looked fine in what I thought of as his uniform, too. Boots, blue jeans, and a collared short-sleeve khaki shirt that set off his early-summer tan.

I gestured at his cart, and yes, inhaled the aroma of fried chicken rising from it. "Is this for lunch?"

"Maybe a snack, but I'll save most of it for dinner. I expect to work late again tonight."

"Is there anything new on the case?"

"Nice try, but nothing I can share."

"It was worth a shot," I said with a grin, then peered up and down the aisle where we stood. We were alone, so I stepped closer and lowered my voice. "I might have something of interest to you. Did Judy Armistead call you yet?"

"Great Buns Judy?"

My lips twitched. "That's the one, but I wouldn't call her that around Grant."

Now he grinned. "I haven't heard from her. What's up?"

"Kim Thomason was arguing with a blonde woman in the bakery on Saturday morning."

He frowned. "Did she get this blonde's name?"

"No, but I think we have at least one photo of the woman, and video, too."

His eyebrows shot higher as I explained taking pictures of our grand opening events for the website. I reminded him, too, that we'd reviewed the security footage after Eleanor's whittling tool had vanished on Saturday.

"And you think the blonde arguing with Ms. Thomason is the same woman who was in your store?"

"I think it's possible. I sure didn't recognize her, or the man she was with, and none of the Six did either. Do you know who she is?"

"I just may." He glanced at his watch. "Can you get Eleanor's camera and meet me at Great Buns?"

"I can after our afternoon artist's presentation."

"What time will that end?"

"About three fifteen. Maybe three thirty."

"I'll phone Judy to see if she can spare us some time then. You can show her the photo."

"Works for me."

"Don't mention this to the Silver Six, Nixy. I don't want idle speculation turning into full-fledged gossip."

I DIDN'T KNOW IF THE LADIES STILL HAD DORALEE out for lunch, but Fred wasn't in the workroom when I returned from the grocery store. Neither was Dab, and Amber and T.C. were MIA, too. Maybe they were all minding the store.

I sprinted up the stairs, tossed the frozen dinners in the freezer, and the rest of my food into cabinets, then raced back down to get ready for Melissa Osborne's folk painting demonstration. We'd arranged to have her teach a full-fledged class like Doralee had done, but not until next week. I had to admit, I was looking forward to having fewer events after the grand opening wound down.

I remembered to grab the coffee, tea, and fancy crackers for the emporium and take them downstairs. Should I have picked up extra cookies, too? Head slap. No way. Nothing but homemade passed muster with Maise, and Sherry, Elea-nor, and Aster would be insulted, too. Plus, they always made more than enough.

Fred was manning the checkout counter when I entered the emporium through the workshop door. I spotted Dab through the front windows talking with Bog Turner. Bog owned the barbershop just off the town square proper, and though he and Dapper Dab had similar taste in clothes, Bog was bald to Dab's full head of thick white hair.

"I see you remembered the supplies," Fred observed. "Put 'em back in the kitchenette, and then take over for me."

I hustled to do as Fred asked even as he clack-clomped his walker toward his workshop.

"Are the ladies still out with Doralee?" I asked.

"Yep, and Dab's got your critters with him, if you're won-derin' where they are, though I ain't thinkin' he's walked 'em yet. Been jawin' with Bog upward of ten minutes. Heat prob'ly ain't good for either of 'em."

"Dab and Bog, you mean?

"The heat ain't doin' Dab and Bog no favors, but I meant T.C. and Amber. You're still puttin' that salve on their paws, ain't you?"

"Faithfully."

"That's good, but those animals shouldn't ought to be standin' on the hot concrete for long."

Fred was right. I hadn't given the sidewalk the barefoot test Dr. Sally the vet had mentioned, but if a surface burned human feet, she'd said, it could easily burn paws.

"Thanks, Fred. I'll send Dab inside and then go walk the critters."

"Take 'em walkin' by the café, find the women, and tell 'em to hurry up with our food."

I smiled at Fred's grumbling as I opened the front door. Dab and Bog turned at the sound. T.C. and Amber looked up from under a display bench where they rested in the shade.

"Hey, Nixy," Bog said. "Dab here says your grand opening is going great."

I grinned. "We're pleased with the response we've had. You need to come by for refreshments."

"Is Maise baking old-fashioned peanut butter cookies with the crosshatches and powdered sugar on top?"

"Is there any other kind?" Dab said on a laugh. "Maise and the other gals made sugar cookies, too."

"For people who don't like peanut butter?" Bog asked.

"For those who have nut allergies," I corrected. "In fact, they made and wrapped the sugar cookies first so nothing peanutty would contaminate them. We don't want any health emergencies if we can help it."

"Ah, of course. Well, save me a few of those peanut butter cookies. I'll see about stopping by after I close."

Dab and I watched a moment as Bog walked off toward his shop, then I took both leashes.

"Why don't you go inside and cool off. I'll wander over to the café and see if the ladies and Doralee are about ready to come back."

Dab patted his belly. "Good deal. I'm hungry."

The wind chimes sang again as he entered the store. I reminded myself to take them down before Melissa's presentation and headed straight to the courthouse grounds, where Amber and T.C. could cool their paws on grass. In fact, I could tie off the leashes on the old stone hitching post. The critters would be fine under the shade of one of the numerous magnolia trees on the courthouse grounds long enough for me to pop into the Lilies Café. I'd just begun to tie the leashes when I heard Sherry's laughter ring in the square.

All five of the friends—Doralee, Sherry, Eleanor, Aster, and Maise—looked to be bursting with news as they crossed the street to meet me. Amber's floppy ears lifted, and T.C.'s swiveled as if they, too, were eager to hear what kept the ladies so long. I'm sure they also smelled the food in the take-out bags Doralee and Aster carried for Fred and Dab. My stomach growled as well.

"These two are so cute," Doralee said, avoiding eye contact with me as she bent to scratch each animal under the chin. Embarrassed that I'd called her on her lie? Maybe.

"Are you on your way back to the emporium?" Sherry asked me.

"Not yet." When she frowned, I said, "Why? What's up?"

"We got some interesting intel at lunch," Maise said.

"And I do believe," Eleanor added mischievously, "we have clues to follow."

"Great," I said with more caution than enthusiasm. "Let me finish walking these two, and I'll be all ears."

"Fine," Aster said with a decisive nod. "We'll get the store ready for Melissa's painting presentation so we'll have time to fill you in later."

The ladies hurried off toward the store, and I hustled the critters on their walk, heading to the neighborhood behind the café and Inn on the Square. The June heat and lack of rain had already taken a toll on the lawns, but Amber sniffed each bush and tree along the sidewalks. T.C. seemed more interested in batting at unsuspecting insects that crossed her path.

When Amber had done her business, we cut across the parking lot behind the Inn on the Square to take advantage of the bit of shade cast by the building. Yes, I felt the weight of having discovered Kim's body upstairs, but shoved the discomfort aside.

I'd just dropped the poop bag in the Dumpster when I noticed Georgine standing at the inn's back door. The woman looked right at me, probably because the Dumpster lid had banged shut. No point in hiding, so I nodded at Georgine, and started walking toward the end of the alley with the critters.

"Ms. Nix, wait," Georgine called.

I debated about being rude and ignoring her, but my mama had raised me better. I straightened my shoulders and turned. Georgine approached me cautiously, eyes on the pets and especially on Amber. Both animals sat quietly at my feet, but Georgine kept her distance. Perhaps she'd been bitten by a dog at some time in her life.

"They won't hurt you," I assured her. Her capris and the three-quarter sleeve blouse buttoned to cover her neck weren't the least rumpled, but the woman herself gave off a disordered vibe. She looked thinner to me, her salt and pepper hair seemed lank and dull, and she had dark circles under her eyes.

"I'm not afraid. I'm allergic," Georgine said, sticking out her sharp chin. "I need to speak with you. Please, will you hear me out?"

Wow, a please from her? "Speak with me about what?"

"Ernie, of course." She paused, and grasped her hands at her waist until her knuckles whitened. "Did you talk with your detective friend on Ernie's behalf?"

"I haven't had the opportunity yet," I said with only a twinge of guilt. We could've discussed Ernie at the grocery store, but I'd flat forgotten to mention him.

Her lips thinned. "Will you arrange time to do so? We'd consider it a kindness."

Not another please, but I was being asked not ordered. "Has Detective Shoar talked with Ernie again?"

"Yes, and all this stress is taking a toll on both of us, but especially on Ernie. We're not allowed to go home, you know."

Yes, and staying in the room next to the one where Kim was killed had to be stressful on steroids. Although, bad as Ernie had it, could he look more haggard than Georgine did? And, okay, her tone of voice and body language swung between demanding and pleading, but she was making the effort to be civil. I cut her some slack. After all, I knew the anxiety of having a relative be a murder suspect.

"I'm positive Ernie is innocent, Ms. Nix, but Kim's brother Caleb is telling the police that Ernie and Kim fought.

Which is ridiculous. For one thing, Kim herself told us she and her brother weren't close. We certainly never met the man."

I frowned. "How do you know what Kim's brother is saying?"

"By the questions that detective asked Ernie."

"You sat in on your brother's interview?" I asked, puzzled.

"Of course not. I wasn't allowed to accompany him." She massaged her temples. "Will you please stay on the subject?"

"The subject being how could Kim's brother know if she and Ernie squabbled?"

"Exactly. He could not. He's lying. Ms. Nix, Ernie wouldn't have killed Kim. He loved her."

Georgine looked away and visibly swallowed, as if she were choked up. Maybe she was, and maybe she wasn't.

"But you didn't."

Georgine looked up, surprised. "I didn't what, Ms. Nix?"

"You didn't like Kim one bit."

Georgine glared at me, her hands fisted. "You're right, I didn't care for her. I'm not even particularly sorry she's dead, except for Ernie's sake. She was his choice."

"If Ernie knows Kim's brother is lying, why doesn't he call Caleb on it?"

"My brother," she said with dignity, "is a gentleman. He will not call the man out on his lies. Besides that, this Caleb person isn't here."

"But you'd confront him if you had the chance, wouldn't you?"

"I would, and whether you talk to the detective on Ernie's behalf or not, I'll stand up for my brother at any cost."

I gave her a long look, then shrugged. "I'll talk to Shoar, but I can't promise you it will do a lick of good."

Spine stiff, shoulders back, Georgine gave me a regal nod. "Thank you, Ms. Nix."

She'd already turned on her heel when I thought to ask about the money. "Georgine," I called, "one question."

"Yes?" she said, giving me narrowed eyes.

I forged on. "Did Kim have a will?"

Georgine's brow furrowed in thought. "The deaths of two wealthy husbands left her with a large amount of money, and possibly property. So, yes, I think she had a will. Why do you ask?"

"Do you know who inherits her money and property?"

Her mouth twisted. "She never mentioned it in my hearing, but if you think Ernie stands to get it, you're wrong. First, Ernie is quite comfortable. He didn't need her money. Second, he wouldn't have allowed her to make him an heir until after they married."

"What about the Thomason family. Do they get back any of the estate Kim inherited?"

"I've no idea, Ms. Nix. And I doubt Ernie does either."

She turned on her heel as sharply as she'd snapped her reply to my question.

"Thanks," I called after her, just to see if she'd acknowledge me. She didn't.

As I headed back to the emporium, I ran the conversation through my head. Georgine was definitely protective of Ernie. If push came to shove, I could see her killing for him.

What she wouldn't do was let Ernie take the fall for murder.

Chapter Eleven

BY THE TIME I RETURNED WITH THE CRITTERS AND put them in the workroom with Fred, Doralee had gone on back to the Pines Motor Court with Zach's food. Which was fine. As Maise said, they didn't need Doralee present to fill me, Dab, and Fred in on the scuttlebutt. They also didn't have the time to talk with me before our folk painting artist, Melissa Osborne, swept into the emporium like a diva taking the stage. I swear, if it had been the 1940s, she'd have waved a sterling silver cigarette holder in one hand.

Melissa had been an actress in various local theatre companies, including in Atlanta, Dallas, Kansas City, and Little Rock. For all her flamboyance, she wasn't haughty or diva-difficult. She brought a fun sense of the dramatic with her simply by entering a room, never mind by donning the bright colors she favored. Today she sported a hot pink sleeveless blouse, dark blue jeans, and banana yellow flats. Her fire-red hair was piled atop her head in a loose bun. Over her clothes she wore an apron so huge it swallowed her, and so paint-splotched, you could barely see that it was once a solid light blue.

"Hello, hello," she sang and moved to embrace each of us—Dab included. She'd have nailed Fred, too, but he'd hidden in his workroom.

"So good to see you, Melissa," Maise said.

"It's good to be seen! I have all the supplies in my car." She paused and gazed at the arrangements of the demo table and chairs. "Oh, but this won't do."

"Fifteen chairs aren't enough?" I asked.

"It's not the number of seats, Nixy, darling, it's the arrangement. I'll be painting a large wooden tray as the main part of my program. The table needs to be in the center, and the chairs in a semicircle around it with plenty of space for people to stand around me so they can better see what I'm doing."

I went to work rearranging the furniture, and a few early bird attendees helped. By the time we'd reorganized, Melissa had set up an easel and a 16 x 20 inch canvas board showing some of the basic brush strokes she'd be using. She launched into her presentation right on the hour.

"Decorative folk art painting is as old as man and paint, and as versatile," she began. "Classic patterns include Pennsylvania Dutch symbols, florals, animals, and nursery figures. Modern patterns can be accented with scraps of metal or wood if you like mixed-media effect. I believe that whimsy plays a large part in folk art painting, but folk painting is also as fresh as the artist is inventive."

She pointed at the canvas board. "These are some of the simple brush strokes I'll be using today. If you know anything about Penn Dutch symbols, you'll probably be able to spot the ones used in those patterns."

Melissa continued her lesson on types of brushes, stroke work, varying strokes to get different looks. Three fourths of the audience nodded their heads as she threw out terms like the comma, crescent, and dots, then touched on brush loading techniques. The remaining fourth looked overwhelmed, but still interested. If I hadn't studied art, Melissa's rapid fire primer in painting techniques would've had me completely befuddled. It was a win that no one's eyes had glazed over into a blank stare. With luck even the overwhelmed attendees would enroll in the course Melissa would teach for us next week.

"All right, time for the fun." Melissa rubbed her hands together, then picked up a large wooden tray. "In the interest of time, I've applied a white base coat, although you could certainly use another base color if you like. I'm going to decorate this with a stylized lily in honor of Lilyvale! Now since I need to lay the tray flat to paint it, y'all come stand around the table so you can see what I'm doing."

Melissa kept up a lively narration, talking her group through her own painting process, and managing to make eye contact with those gathered around her as she wielded her brushes. She fielded questions as she worked, and gave next week's painting class a plug.

During a short show and tell on mixing paints, one of the open bottles of acrylic fell and splashed on the floor. The audience members jumped back and avoided being paint splatted, but the spill of red on our wood floor made me picture Kim as I'd last seen her. Forever still and lying in a pool of blood. For a moment I couldn't move except to convulsively swallow. Then Eleanor shoved a wad of paper towels in my hands. I shuddered, and pulled myself together to clean the mess.

MELISSA LEFT IN A FLURRY OF HUGS WITH THE promise to bring the newly painted tray back to the emporium as soon as the paint had dried thoroughly and was sealed. This was one of the prizes we'd be drawing for at the end of the week, along with the other crafts our demonstrators had completed.

Now beyond impatient to tell me what they'd learned during lunch at the café, Maise and Aster, Eleanor, and

Sherry dragged me into Fred's workroom. They didn't let Dab escape either, insisting that Jasmine could handle customers for a while without any of us.

I went along because Eric had texted to meet up at three forty-five. That gave me plenty of time with the Six. However, I kept mum about what I'd learned from Judy this morning, and about my appointment with her and Eric. My hunch about the blonde's identity might be a bust, and besides, there was no point in me stealing their gossip thunder.

Fred stood at one workbench dismantling a blender and carefully arranging each part on white butcher paper. The rest of us gathered around an adjoining table.

"Do you want to join us for the conference?" Maise asked him.

He waved a screwdriver at us. "I can hear just fine from here while I'm workin'."

"All right, then," Aster said. "Now first, Doralee told us about the opal and what it's worth."

I felt my eyes bug. "She did?"

"We didn't ask about private financial business, of course," Sherry insisted with a tug on her apron.

"Of course not," I said. "That's the code of the South."

"We were quite shocked she shared so many details with us," Eleanor put in.

"But here's the kicker," Maise said. "We found out that Ernie could've bought Doralee's opal several times over, and that sucker is expensive."

"Wait. Doralee told me that most of Ernie's family money was gone when she was with him."

"I think it was," Sherry confirmed, "although he—or they—were far from destitute during the marriage. Anyway, she said you got her to thinking about why Kim would be with Ernie."

"Because she'd already married two very wealthy men," Maise interjected, "and why break the pattern?"

"So Zach did some nosing around about Ernie's finances,

thinking that he might have motive to kill Kim if he was in her will," Aster said. "I don't know who his connections are, but Zach called Doralee while we were eating and told her Ernie scored big in the stock market shortly after he and Doralee divorced."

"As in the high six figures big," Eleanor added.

I whistled. Guess that's what Georgine had meant about Ernie being quite comfortable. Maybe Doralee should've sold him that stone on Sunday. Or did she get money when she and Ernie split?

"Did Doralee get a divorce settlement of any kind?" I asked. "I'm wondering how contentious the breakup might have been."

"We only skirted that subject," Sherry said, "but Doralee said she left the marriage pretty much with what she brought to it. She had her own money from sound investments over the years. She had her personal property—her computer and other electronics, plus her books, knickknacks, clothes, and jewelry pieces like the opal."

"She also," Aster said, "had her own set of gourd tools, and some gourd art designs she'd created. They didn't have a pre-nup, so Doralee could have asked for a settlement, but she chose not to take one."

"Wow, she really was forthcoming about her finances."

"Only because she knows we're investigating on her behalf."

I wanted to remind them we were only gathering information, but who was I kidding? In as much as we had the resources, we were investigating. I might be a take-charge sort of person, but I generally did not confront and fire questions at murder suspects like I had lately with Doralee and Ernie, and even Georgine.

"Listen up, though," Maise said, pulling me back to the conversation. "The bigger news is that Kim's brother Caleb is supposedly coming to town tomorrow. He called Lorna about staying at the inn."

Eleanor shook her head. "Poor Lorna. I do believe she's about to have a meltdown over having a murder at the inn."

"She has to be worried it will be bad for business," I said. I wasn't best buddies with Lorna Tyler, and I didn't much like her husband, Clark, but I should stop by for a neighborly visit.

"The point," Maise said, "is the brother is Kim's only relative so he probably inherits his sister's estate. Remember, the money Kim inherited from her first husband was a considerable amount. What if the brother killed her?"

Dab straightened, rubbed his chin. We all turned toward him, waiting. Dab wasn't a particularly taciturn kind of man, but when he spoke, we paid attention. "It seems to me that we don't know enough about who gains from Kim's death."

"Dab's right," Fred called from his workbench. "We're long on rumors and supp'sition, but short on facts."

"You're both correct, of course," Sherry said, fussing with her bangs. "We're getting carried away with gossip."

I checked the time on the shop clock and realized I needed to be at Great Buns in just a few minutes.

"Can y'all watch the emporium without me for a bit?"

Fred humphed. "Jasmine's running the place right now. You going snoopin'?"

"I need to run down to the bakery."

"Why?" Maise challenged, narrow eyed. "We have plenty of cookies left."

She might like Grant Armistead, but she wouldn't serve the bakery's cookies if they were the last ones in town. She's just a bit jealous that way.

"It's not about food, Maise. It's about Kim."

"Judy knows something about the murder?" Aster asked incredulously. "She didn't breathe a word to us when we canvassed the square asking questions yesterday."

"If you'll recall, Aster," Maise said, "we talked to Grant, not Judy. She was out running errands."

"Oh, you're right." Aster gave me the eye. "Well then, get cracking, Nixy."

"Yes, ma'am. Eleanor, did you send any of those photos from Friday's gourd demo to my e-mail?"

"The ones from the presentation Doralee and Sherry did? No, I didn't see the need."

"Are they still on the camera?"

"I do believe they are. I recall downloading them to the laptop at home, but not deleting them."

"Fantastic. I need to take the camera with me."

"I'M POSITIVE THAT'S THE SAME BLONDE," JUDY said, head bobbing in a decisive nod. The bakery was empty at the moment, and bless her heart, she was having a blast answering questions. She'd be part of the Silver Six's posse before long.

Eric looked from the camera's digital display to Judy. "Her sunglasses cover half of her face. How can you be sure?"

"The helmet-head hairstyle, and the way she holds her mouth. Like she's bracing herself to smell something awful at any moment. And, look," she added, finger swiping at the screen. "Her nose is in the air in that picture. I remember that haughty tilt of her head."

"All right," he said slowly. "So the woman in the emporium Friday afternoon is the same one you overheard threatening Ms. Thomason on Saturday morning. And a ring was mentioned. You're certain of that."

"I'll swear to it if you want. Have I identified a suspect?"

"'Suspect' might be too a strong word," he hedged.

"But this *is* a photo of Kim's sister-in-law, isn't it?" I said, turning the camera in my hands to swipe between the two good photos of the blonde and her companion.

"Margot Thomason Vail, yes. D.B. Thomason's only sibling."

"So you followed up on my tip about her?"

He dragged his hand over the back of his neck. "Not

exactly. I'll say this much because I don't want either of you confronting her. But if this gets on the grapevine, I'll ticket your cars for unlawful parking for a week. Deal?"

Judy mimed locking her lips. I crossed my heart.

"I ran a check on Ms. Vail after she called the station this morning to demand that I release Ms. Thomason's effects to her."

Wide-eyed Judy whistled. "Wow, that woman has brass. Bet you told her to take a hike."

"More or less," my darling detective confirmed. "I need to know who rightfully owns what. I called Ms. Vail's attorney, who also drew up the Thomason family trust. He wrote Ms. Kim Thomason's will, too."

"I don't suppose you know all the terms yet," I said, "but at least you have proof that Margot was in town on Friday and Saturday. *Before* Kim was killed. She had motive for sure."

"What about the guy who's with this Margot woman?" Judy asked as she reached across me to point at the camera screen.

"That's Dennis Michael Thomason, D.B.'s son."

"Is he a suspect, too?"

"We're looking at everyone who might be connected, so don't confront him, got it?"

We solemnly nodded.

"I need to get back to the station, but thanks for your help." He met my gaze. "Nixy, walk with me?"

I told my friend I'd catch her later and followed him into the gentle afternoon heat. As we strolled toward the courthouse, I aimed for patience. I failed.

"Where are we going?"

"I need to talk with Clark and Lorna about releasing the guest room."

I stumbled on a curb, and must've looked pained because Eric asked, "What's wrong?"

I decided to be candid. "Every now and then I picture Kim's body. Do you get used to that?"

"No."

I met the understanding in his gaze, nodded, and took a deep breath. "How did you locate Margot? Aster and Eleanor struck out on their Internet search."

"Besides having better resources," he said with a grin, "I had her married name. She's only listed on Google once under her maiden name, and that's an ancient listing."

"That's it? You don't know people who know people?"

"You watch too much TV, but yeah, I talked to a guy in Shreveport who knows the casino scene in general and the Thomason's in particular."

"So what's Margot's story?"

"She's a widow, is big on family pride if not family feeling. She won an award for heading up about ten different committees in the last few years. She made a point of telling me she should be addressed as 'Missus Vail,' not Ms."

"She likes to be in control. Do you think she could be the killer?"

"Knowing that she was in town near the time of the murder is suspicious. My source indicated she's ruthless about getting what she wants, and she hated Ms. Thomason. Considered her a gold digger."

"But Kim was married to D.B. for nearly ten years."

"And there wasn't a hint of foul play in his death, but Mrs. Vail can hold a grudge. She was furious with her brother for the way he treated his son, her nephew. Dennis Thomason had a playboy reputation and Daddy disapproved," Eric elaborated. "The two had been estranged for years when D.B. died. I don't know yet if or how the split affected the son's inheritance, but Dennis is recently engaged."

"And he wants to live in the family manse again."

"How do you know that?"

"Eleanor found a Facebook post. It's astounding what people will put out there on social media."

"But sometimes it works in our favor."

I inclined my head and we walked in silence for a moment.

"Are you certain Margot called you from Shreveport?"

"Now that I know she and Dennis were here last week, no. I suspect they've been in the neighborhood all along."

"Well then, that makes me less suspicious of Ernie. That and his alibi."

Eric gave me a questioning look. "Ernie doesn't *have* an alibi."

"He has a partial one. I saw him leave the party with Kim a bit after three, but he was back at the farmhouse about three thirty. He was talking with Doralee, and he wore the same clothes he had on earlier. Not a red speck or stain on them. Besides, I find it hard to believe he'd kill his fiancée and then calmly return to the party."

"Murderers aren't predictable, Nixy."

"Yes, but if he'd killed Kim, wouldn't he have made the effort to establish a real alibi? Like watching a baseball game at the Dairy Queen? Hanging out in the ER. Running naked through the laundromat."

He flashed me a full-on grin. "Naked, huh? Yeah, I think we'd have found witnesses to that."

"A witness who'd need therapy the rest of his or her life."

Eric chuckled. "Tell me, did Ernie ask you to convince me of his innocence?"

"More like put in a good word. His sister did the same. She says Caleb is lying about Ernie and Kim fighting all the time."

"Mr. Collier mentioned a few recent conflicts, and that's all I'm saying."

"How can you share some details with me, but not others?"

He stopped and turned to me. "I trust you to come to me if information happens your way. I also trust you to keep certain things I tell you to yourself, but there are aspects of the case I won't divulge. I'm also sharing so you won't run around confronting potential killers."

"I don't do that."

"Forewarned is forearmed. You've been warned."

"Gotcha, but about those recent conflicts between Kim and Ernie? I'll bet those were all about the opal." We dodged parked cars and continued to the café. "I do have to wonder where Margot Vail and her nephew have been staying."

"Not at the Pines Motor Court. Doralee and Zach are the only guests."

I nodded, not surprised he'd checked out the place. "They could be in Magnolia or Camden."

"One of the many details I need to follow up on."

"And you're following the money, right?"

"If Mrs. Vail and her attorney continue to cooperate without making me jump through hoops, I should have answers on that score in a day or two."

"Will you have the scoop on Kim's will, too? Who inherits from her?"

He arched a brow. "I will, and if I learn that Caleb Collier is the sole beneficiary, I'll look into him. When I called to inform him of his sister's death, he was on the road doing maintenance on oil rigs."

"Or not. You didn't know Margot and Dennis had been in town until an hour ago. Caleb could've been here, too. Heck, everyone Kim ever ticked off could have been in town."

"Touché," he said, tipping his head as he opened the Lilies Café door.

Lorna and Clark Tyler, a couple in their fifties, owned the café, and the Inn on the Square—which was simply a different name for the upstairs part of the building. Originally the Lilyvale saloon and boardinghouse, the property had passed down from generation to generation until Lorna inherited. My forefather (and mother), Samuel Allan Stanton and his wife, Yvonne Ritter Stanton, had founded Lilyvale, and been contemporaries of Lorna's ancestors.

Both the café and the inn spaces had been updated from time to time, of course. I knew from having been upstairs that the inn now featured a 1930s ambiance from the furniture to the light fixtures suspended from the high ceilings. The bathrooms were modern, but with showers, pedestal sinks, and fixtures with a vintage edge.

In contrast, the café's decor didn't scream a particular era, yet it wasn't hard to picture cowboys climbing the staircase on the back wall—either alone or escorting a lady of the evening. The wide plank pine floors were original, as was the long oak bar with its dark patina. An eclectic collection of round and square tables, and mismatched bentwood-style chairs, dotted the dining area.

As my eyes adjusted, I saw that the lunch crowd had cleared. Full-bearded and barrel-built Clark Tyler bussed a table in the empty café while Lorna was at the long bar pouring two cups of coffee. She didn't look nearly as care-worn as when I'd last seen her, though there were wisps of gray in her brown hair I didn't recall seeing before today.

"Hi, Nixy, Eric," Lorna greeted us. "How's the case going?"

"Slower than I'd like, but going." Eric used his aw-shucks small town cop tone. "I came to tell you we're releasing the room. Here's the number of the cleaning service I promised to bring by."

Lorna took the white business card with black printing with one hand, held the coffee carafe up with the other. "Y'all want a cup?"

"No thanks," I said as Clark set the mound of dirty dishes, glasses, and cutlery on the bar, and topped the mess with the cloth napkins Lorna insisted they use to kick up the ambiance factor.

"Thank you for this information," Lorna said. "I sure hope the crew can come quickly. That dead woman's brother made a reservation, although it doesn't seem right to give him the room, uh . . ."

"That Kim died in?" I supplied.

Lorna lips pinched. "Exactly. Of course, I could give him the other room, but then he'd have to share a bathroom with Georgine Boudreaux. That would not do."

"Maybe Georgine will move," I said. "It can't hurt to ask her."

Lorna tapped the card on the bar. "I doubt she'll want that room either."

"Yes," I agreed, "but the worst she can say is no."

Clark snorted. "You sticking your nose in this murder like you did the last one?"

"Don't start, Clark," Lorna warned.

He glared, first at her, then at me, his bushy beard making him look even more menacing. "That's why you're hanging out with Shoar. I know it is."

See why I don't much care for Lorna's hubby? I plastered a smile on my face and stared him down.

"Detective Shoar," I said, deliberately using Eric's title and willfully stretching the truth, "does not discuss cases with me."

Clark looked away. "Yeah? At least I'm a witness this time, instead of one of your suspects."

"Witness?" I added two and two with blinding speed. "You're the person who saw Doralee Gordon in the square on Sunday?"

"Saw her a block from here when I was coming back from my golf game."

"That's why I was late getting to the lawn party Sunday," Lorna said. "I held down the fort while Clark played his round."

"Of course," I murmured. I remembered now. Lorna with Sherry. Me getting sweet tea from the fridge, and then seeing Doralee with Ernie when I came back outside.

"It was a nice get-together," Lorna commented, and she might have said more, but Eric's cell rang.

Yep, rang. He'd programmed a plain ring tone into his cell.

"Shoar," he said and turned away to listen. "What? Where?" Another pause. "Secure the scene. I'll be there in ten."

"It's not another death, is it?" Lorna asked, her eyes huge.

"No," he said with a glance at me. "It's new evidence."

Chapter Twelve

I WASN'T CRAZED WITH IMPATIENCE WAITING TO FIND out what kind of evidence Eric had run off to see. Nope, not me. I kept busy.

First, I dropped back by Great Buns. Yes, an éclair had been calling my name earlier, but I also wanted to be sure I hadn't offended Judy by basically bringing Eric to her instead of waiting for her to contact him. Not that I thought she'd hold a grudge, but then I hadn't known her long. But Judy was slammed sorting out an order for a baby shower, and serving other customers, so I merely waved and mouthed, "Later."

Second, I took Eleanor's camera to Gaskin's Business Center right next door to the emporium to have prints made of some of the photos. Carter and Kay Gaskin operated the store, which specialized in printing but provided other services. They also sold office supplies and some Arkansas kitsch like key chains and shot glasses.

Kay extracted the memory card from the camera, inserted it in the magic machine, and helped me select which shots

I wanted in hard copy. I got the hang of editing them—just for the sake of clarity, you understand. Then I selected the sizes I wanted, from 4 x 6 to 8 x 10 inches. Last, I pushed the button conveniently marked PRINT. Voilà! I soon left with physical copies of Margot and Dennis in case Eric needed them for the case, and with more than a dozen shots of the emporium for Mrs. Gilroy. And all right, I made some select copies for myself, too.

By the time I got back to the emporium, the day was winding down, but gossip had spiked. Word on the Lilyvale grapevine was that the police had found a bloody smock a few miles out of town in the countryside filled with a pine forest, a few farms, and fewer houses. The garment had apparently been stuffed in a large garbage can that animals had tipped over. The owners of said garbage had been out of town for a wedding.

A few minutes before we closed the store, Doralee called. She had talked to the police and she had news. Sherry invited her to bring Zach to dinner. Thankfully an early dinner because, come on, we all wanted the scoop.

The big reveal had to wait until we'd eaten and moved outside to the farmhouse's front veranda. A white porch swing and various white and natural-colored wicker, willow, and reclaimed wood chairs outfitted with cushions provided plenty of seating. Some seats were more rustic than others, but they were comfy enough for us to relax awhile and enjoy the sunset.

I'd claimed a seat on the top porch step. T.C. and Amber had been fed, and had stayed in the parlor while we ate, but now lay at my hip. T.C. batted at Amber's ear halfheartedly, but it looked like playtime was over, both of them sleepy from their busy day and full bellies. Puppy tummy, as Aunt Sherry called it.

When Maise declared it was time to hear the story, not just the scuttlebutt, Doralee complied with Zach inserting a detail here and there. No shock to learn the smock belonged to our gourd artist. But its condition had been grossly and gorily exaggerated. Rather than being blood-soaked, it was merely blood-smeared—along with the paint and wood stain spills that had already been there.

"I'm still glad," Doralee concluded, "I didn't have to see my smock in person. The photos of those rusty-colored places were bad enough."

Zach reached over to pat her hand. "If there are any usable prints in those stains, they won't be yours," he assured her.

"Prints?" the rest of us exclaimed in unison.

"Goodness, are you really worried about fingerprints, Doralee?" Aster asked. "After all, you've never hidden the fact that you owned the thing."

She shrugged. "No, I haven't, and I *am* relieved the darn thing turned up. I have to trust the detective will decide once and for all that I'm innocent."

"As long as you've been candid with him," Sherry declared, "I'm positive Detective Shoar will clear you. Now how about dessert and decaf?"

Guilt skittered in Doralee's eyes when Sherry mentioned being truthful with Eric. Shoot. Was she protecting herself or someone else?

KNOWING I WOULDN'T BE ABLE TO GRILL DORALEE until the next day, and then only if I was lucky, I opted to box up leftovers and take them to Mrs. Gilroy.

"Did you bring the photographs this time?" she demanded as she towed me through the typically gloomy living room and into the dim kitchen.

"I tucked them in the box."

Tonight the drab brown curtains at the back and side kitchen windows were open, and the setting sun offered a bit of light. Bernice didn't bother to turn on the overhead fixture, and the room always looked sadder to me at night. Her binoculars rested on the table again tonight, and the chair faced the side window where she could see Sherry's veranda. I sighed. Much as I'd like to freshen up the house with paint and new curtains, I knew Bernice wouldn't hear of it. She liked her simple, reclusive, no-frills life.

Of course, the no-frills thing didn't include her large flat screen, or the state-of-the-art computer I swore she had stashed in the second bedroom. How had she bought her smart phone and all the other electronics? How had she managed to get the devices up and running? She wouldn't say, but I hadn't ruled out fairies.

"Sissy!" Bernice said, snapping her fingers an inch from my face.

Reflex made me jerk back. "What? Wait, did you call me Sissy?"

"It gets your attention. I'll swan, for a woman so young, you sure drift into space a great deal. Now hand me those containers and be quick about it. My show comes on at seven."

"What show is that?" I said as I passed food and she loaded the fridge.

"*NCIS*. It's gonna be a good one."

"Isn't the series in summer reruns?"

She slammed the fridge door and glared. "I like reruns. You have a problem with that?"

"No, ma'am."

"You should watch yourself if you're getting involved with this murder case."

"You know about that?"

"I've told you before, I'm old, not stupid or senile."

"No, ma'am," I said, not daring to grin. "You're far from either."

She gave me a brisk nod. "Show me those pictures now."

I hadn't thought much about how Bernice would react to

the photos, but her response surprised me. She murmured "Oh, my" a few times as she flipped through the dozen photos, then raised her face to the ceiling before she looked at me with a hint of tears in her eyes.

"These remind me of when Sissy ran the store as a five and dime. She always had a kind word and a piece of hard candy for us children."

"What was your favorite kind?"

"Butterscotch and root beer barrels."

"I'm glad you approve of what we've done, Bernice."

"Yes, well, time for you to leave. Come see me another time."

As she bustled out of the room ahead of me, she handed back the pictures. I placed them on the table next to her binoculars.

THE SUN HAD SET BY THE TIME I GOT BACK TO THE apartment with Amber and T.C. They'd romped with Fred and Dab at the farmhouse awhile, but I decided we'd have a last walk of the day before we wound down for the night.

The critters sniffed and did their things while I thought about that flash of guilt in Doralee's expression. It bugged me that she was still holding back. Was it something to incriminate Ernie?

And what about Ernie? He hadn't meant to tell me he'd seen Doralee out walking alone near the square on Sunday. Once he'd let it slip, he'd been more cautious giving me the rest of his account. Did he have doubts about Doralee's innocence?

I considered how I could get the two to come clean. No, not my job, but they'd asked for my help in the first place. Time for them to step up. Besides, Eric was busy investigating in ways and with means I couldn't. I'd talk with Doralee and Ernie—and anyone else I could think of. Whatever information I gleaned, I'd pass on.

* * *

THE CLOCK READ EIGHT TWENTY WHEN I CRACKED
my eyes open on Wednesday. Hump Day. Middle of the
workweek. Two days short of the end of our grand opening.
The day we were to host a petting zoo.

That thought made me want to hide in bed all day.

Yep, Lilyvale 4-H Club teens were providing the animals,
and their parents and one or two sponsors were in charge of
staging the parking lot behind the emporium. Snap-together
fences would create covered enclosures and open pens.

Of course, since all the businesses on the block shared
the parking lot, I'd needed their okays as well as a city
permit. Fortunately, the merchants and city hall approved,
and I laid odds that a selling factor was that the kids would
also be on cleanup duty.

How did I get us roped into Project Petting Zoo? It began
when Maise and Aster proposed a presentation on nutrition,
one that featured recipes using local produce. I agreed it
was a great idea, and a program Maise and Aster could give
in their sleep. But no. They insisted I call Robin Cooper, the
director at the county extension agricultural office, to get a
speaker. Next thing I knew, the cheerful woman had talked
me into holding the zoo event in the late morning and then
the nutrition lecture at noon.

Okay, more than a lecture.

"Wouldn't it be wonderful to make summer fruit smoothies for the attendees?" she'd gushed. "Everyone will be
thirsty after being outside with the animals, plus you'd get
the parents inside to see the emporium."

I had a hard time picturing a group of children who were
either overstimulated or overtired from the zoo experience
being anything but cranky. Then again, the most contact I'd
had with children in eons had been at the lawn party.
Besides, Robin assured me that she and her cohort, Jerri
Yarrow, coordinated these kinds of events all the time and

would supply everything including the berries, yogurt, ice, and blenders.

After rolling out of bed at last, I did my version of the Amber and T.C. stretchercize, and then went through the rest of my morning routine. The critters ate their kibble while I munched on a protein bar from my newly replenished stash. Maybe I'd fix myself a balanced breakfast sometime next week. Hope springs eternal, right?

I dressed in green cargo shorts and a plain white sleeveless tee because I needed to launder my emporium tees. Wearing sandals around farm animals didn't seem like a bright idea, so I laced up my tennis shoes. My emporium logo apron might look weird with shorts, but today I didn't care. I needed to get a move on.

When I opened the back door that led to the alley, four teens and three men were already at work. Some unloaded white fence panels from the bed of a dark blue pickup. One teen and a rugged-looking guy in a cowboy hat plunked traffic cones around the perimeter of the parking lot. When Cowboy Hat noticed me, he waved and loped to meet me and my critters.

"Hey, I'm Clifton Drover. Cliff," he said, extending his hand. "You're Nixy, right?"

"That's me," I said, smiling as I gripped his calloused hand. "And these two are Amber and T.C. You're already setting up for the zoo?"

"Just prepping right now," Cliff answered after submitting to a thorough sniffing inspection by my pets. "We don't want to have to track people down later to move their cars."

"Like mine." The Camry sat front and center in the lot. "I'll move it when I get back."

"No problem. If we're not here, we've gone to Great Buns for a bite. Just move the cones out of your way, and put 'em back soon as you can. The bulk of the 4-H kids will be here to get the animals settled about ten."

I called Sherry to remind everyone to park on the street.

"We remembered, child. Fred's leaving his truck at home, and Dab will drop him off in the back."

"I don't need no droppin' off. I walk just fine," Fred groused in the background before Sherry disconnected.

I set a brisk pace with Amber and T.C., taking them along the streets a block off the square, where they'd have more grass to sniff. I thought about stopping at the police station to see if Eric was in yet, but decided against it. If he had any new information, he probably wouldn't tell me anyway.

Sometimes he really was no fun.

PARENTS TOWING CHILDREN ALL THE WAY FROM toddler to elementary school aged began showing up just before eleven. The 4-H Clubbers had the animals ready, and most of the visitors seemed enchanted. Walk-in pens held baby ducks, chicks, and rabbits, and the children could enter a few at a time to hold them. Larger animals—calves, pigs, goats, and even a miniature horse—were housed in corral sections. Or that's what Cliff called them. These animals ambled up to the portable fences to be petted, and if I'd harbored any concern that they'd bite or simply break out of the fencing, their placidity put those fears to rest. The miniature horse, a gorgeous palomino with a golden coat and near-white mane and tail, was particularly sweet.

Word must've spread more than I'd imagined because a caravan of SUVs deposited children and teachers from two day care centers at the curb beside the emporium. Soon more cries of wonder rang out and echoed in the square.

Dab took our pets out back to see the show, sure that they'd behave and that the visiting animals wouldn't have a problem with two more. I stood at the back door just in case, but he was correct. Amber stayed on her leash, of course, and T.C. in her harness, but they blended right in and garnered attention of their own.

Back inside, I met the county extension ladies when they

came in the store to set up. Both women wore jeans, tennis shoes, and white-collared shirts with the Hendrix County logo embroidered over the left breast. Robin Cooper's dark blonde hair curled around her face, her blue eyes twinkling as if she knew a secret. The secret of getting me to approve the petting zoo, I bet.

Jerri Yarrow specialized in family and consumer-oriented programs. She was about my height of five foot three, but she looked tiny. With hazel eyes and a gentle smile, she projected a calm I figured she'd need later during the smoothie tasting.

Fred ran a grounded extension cord from the kitchenette to the demonstration tables, then plugged in a power strip with enough outlets for all the blenders. After he duct-taped the cords to the floor to mitigate a tripping hazard, he went back to his workshop.

Dab ducked in a few minutes later to ask me to come outside, so the ladies helped our guest speakers get the rest of their supplies ready to roll.

"What's up, Dab?" I asked when I found him near the miniature horse's corral.

"Cindy Price wants to get pictures of you," he said, pointing to the *Lilyvale Legend* reporter-photographer snapping photos of toddlers holding rabbits.

She'd done a great job covering our first grand opening day, but I shook my head. "She should be shooting Cliff and the teens."

"Already has. She also got photos of all of us last week. Even Fred. She never got you, so go get your little piece of the limelight."

Good thing I'd worn makeup today. I took my ponytail down and fluffed my brown hair as I approached Cindy.

"Nixy," she said, beaming. "I need several shots, so let's start right here."

She took pictures of me with Cliff, me with the teens, and then me with several children who looked worn out and on the verge of whiny. I hoped they got a second wind when they went inside the store. Maybe the smoothies would perk them up.

The last shot Cindy insisted on was with my arm draped over the beautiful miniature palomino, and then she set me free. Since it was nearly noon, I moved from group to group reminding them the smoothies would be served shortly. I figured that was a bigger draw than the nutrition program, even for the moms.

As I turned to go back inside, I spotted a woman hovering on the sidewalk at the edge of the parking lot. Dressed in a pink skirt suit and pumps, she had blonde hair. Holy helmet hair! Kim's ex-sister-in-law. It had to be. Every instinct confirmed I was right, and screamed for me to seize my chance to meet and question her.

Can a body stride stealthily? If so, I did, hustling through the crowd to come up behind her.

"Margot Vail, I presume?"

I expected her to whirl around. To be at least a little bit startled. That would have been a normal reaction, right?

Instead, the woman squared her shoulders and stood tall enough to look down her straight nose at me when she turned. She held a designer handbag, but wasn't hiding behind sunglasses today. Cold gray eyes met mine.

"I want the ring."

I blinked. "Excuse me?"

"I said I want the ring." She spoke with such command, I expected her to hold out her hand so I could drop it in her palm. "I will not press charges if you turn it over without a fuss."

"What are you talking about?"

"You *are* the person who found the body of my now delightfully dead sister-in-law."

It wasn't a question, so she knew of me somehow. "I was with someone else when we discovered Kim, but yes."

"Of course. The gourd artist."

Even in her cultured Southern accent, she made "gourd artist" sound like "petting zoo poop." However, that confirmed she knew of Doralee, too. How? The newspaper hadn't identified us as the citizens who stumbled upon Kim's body, so Margot had to have heard town gossip. Which meant she must've been drifting around here for days.

"Listen, Miss Whatever—"

"Nix," I interrupted. "It's Ms. Nix."

"You may address me as Mrs. Vail. Now, I no longer care that you took the ring as long as you return it. Today. Otherwise, I shall press charges."

"Hold it," I said, my temper rising. "You think we took something from the room where Kim died? That's obscene."

Margot shrugged. "It happens."

"Since when? Did you forget to take it yourself when you murdered Kim?"

She sniffed. "I did nothing of the sort. I met with her, but I would never be so crass as to kill her."

"So you had your nephew do it? Where is he, by the way?"

She gave me a pitying shake of her head. One that didn't jostle a single hair on her head. "Turn over the ring, Ms. Nix."

"The opal?"

She blinked at me, the tiniest bit of uncertainty in her cold eyes. "What opal?"

"The opal that Kim wanted, but it's not set in a ring. It's a loose stone. Isn't that what you're talking about?"

"I am referring," she enunciated slowly, "to the Thomason family engagement ring. An old mine cut solitaire diamond in a gold setting. It is a priceless heirloom, and I want it back."

She said the last bit with enough implied threat to make me shudder. I wasn't sure she'd soil her hands to commit a crime, but I wouldn't put much else past her. Then, from the corner of my eye, I saw the nephew, Dennis. He emerged from the men's clothing store across the street, then strode to a silver Audi parked at the curb. I'd seen that car on the night Kim was killed.

"You said you met with Kim. When did you last see her?"

Margot waved a hand. "Oh, I believe it was on Saturday."

"Not on Sunday?"

"No, and I am not interested in answering your questions."

"That's too bad. The detective on the case will love knowing you were seen behind the Inn on the Square on Sunday."

Her gaze never wavered, even as she released the latch on her handbag. "You are mistaken."

"I think not. You were driving the Audi that rocketed out of the parking lot that evening. You almost hit me head-on."

"Which is apropos of nothing. Now, Ms. Nix, have we come to an agreement?"

"Not by a long shot, lady." Yes, it was rude, but Sherry wasn't here to censor me. "Why are you suddenly asking me about this ring? It's been days since Kim was killed."

She shot me a superior smirk. "I had planned to speak to you in your little store, but in this case, you accosted me. I am merely taking advantage of the opportunity, as I always do."

"But why on earth accuse me of theft?"

She narrowed those gray eyes. "That backwoods detective evaded my demand to return the ring in such a way that I do not believe the police have it. For a mere shop girl, the ring would have been impossible to resist. Understandable, but nevertheless criminal."

Little store? Shop girl? I opened my mouth, but what could I say to this crazy lady? She didn't listen.

She glanced down, pulled a card from her purse, and extended it to me. "Contact me when you are ready to deliver my property."

With that, she turned and crossed the street without checking for oncoming traffic. Probably used to the world stopping for her.

Not all rich folks carried a sense of entitlement, but Margot Vail toted enough for half a social registry. How humiliating to have her only brother marry a much younger woman, one she considered a gold digger and a social climber to boot. Margot had tried to kill Kim by golf cart, and now that I'd met her, it wasn't a leap to imagine she'd taken other shots at her sister-in-law over the years. And if she wanted this one ring so badly, what would she do to get back other pieces of the estate Kim had inherited?

Chapter Thirteen

"REMEMBER, BRIGHTLY COLORED FRUITS AND VEG-gies contain antioxidants," Jerri told the audience of moms, teachers, and surprisingly quiet children all sipping on sample smoothies, "and here's another fun flashback to high school chemistry."

The adults chuckled. I think a child snored.

"Blackberries and blueberries contain anthocyanins, compounds also known as flavonoids. Eating these and other blue, purple, and red-colored fruits can reduce the risk of cancer, stroke, and heart disease. Both wild and cultivated blackberries also contain vitamin C, potassium, and, of course, fiber."

"But picking wild berries can be a thorny prospect," Robin chimed in, "so dress accordingly. Also be aware that poison ivy can grow near wild blackberry brambles. Protect yourselves and your kiddos if you take them picking. Any questions? No? Then thank you for coming, and remember we at the county extension offices love to hear from you."

"And," Jerri said, "if you didn't get the handout with

* * *

THE SILVER SIX WERE AS PUZZLED ABOUT THE MYS-
terious Rusty as I was, but delighted that Ruth had visited
and been able to give me background on the critters. I admit
it was a good thing to have the question of ownership
settled.

Was I ready for T.C. and Amber to truly be mine?

I put that question and Ruth aside to get on with my real
job of managing the emporium.

Rose Eden from the Happy Garden Florist catty-corner
across the square from the emporium was slated as the
morning's craft presenter. Aster knew Rose better than the
other ladies of the Silver Six did, so had issued the invitation
to demonstrate her art. Aster knew the garden club ladies,
too. We expected a good turnout from that quarter, and I
hoped we'd get it.

"I don't attend the garden club meetings as much as I did
a few years ago," Aster confided as we all gathered around
the counter waiting for Rose. Even Dab and Fred had lingered with cups of coffee. "I just didn't have as much time
after Maise and I moved in with Sherry Mae."

"Do you still pay dues?" I asked.

"The club never charged dues. No one wanted to deal
with all that formal, legal stuff, but I'm still on the roster,
and I get meeting notices. You know," she said, tapping her
chin and giving me a piercing look, "you should think about
joining some local organizations."

"I can't agree more," Maise chimed in. "They're great
for meeting people and networking."

"If the garden club isn't your style," Eleanor said, "I do
believe there is a book club."

I cringed. "The book club meets at the library, and I'm
still a persona non grata with the head librarian."

"Over that murder business this spring?" Aster asked.
"Don't worry. Debbie Nicole will come around."

nutritional facts and recipes, the extras are over on the counter."

Women began herding children out the door, most thanking Sherry and company on the way out, and promising to come back for a leisurely look around.

I'd missed the smoothie-making portion of the program while confronting Margot. Since I could use those antioxidants, I made my way to Robin and Jerri as Maise and Aster joined them.

Robin spotted me first. "There you are! I hope you didn't have to help with any animal wrangling out back."

I grinned. "No, the 4-H crew has the zoo covered."

Jerri touched my arm. "We saved you a sample of smoothie. Here you are."

She removed a small plastic cup from an ice bucket on the demo table and passed it to me. "It's better when it's right out of the blender and frothy, but it'll wet your whistle."

The first sweet sip sold me. "Save me a handout, Aunt Sherry. I've got to try this at home."

Maise snorted. "You'd have to buy a blender first, and you don't even have a toaster."

"But now I have motivation," I teased back.

"A better motive to buy appliances would be to fix a meal for Eric Shoar. The way to a man's heart and all that."

The way to my detective's heart might be his investigation, and I needed to tell him about Margot before I got sidetracked by anything else.

I GAVE T.C. AND AMBER A PAT, LEFT THEM IN FRED'S company, and excited through the back to jog over to the police station. The parking lot was already animal-free, and Cliff was directing a teen to spray down the cement using the hose we kept out back. The nozzle didn't produce a power-wash jet of water, but between the scooping and rinsing, the lot looked great and didn't smell of eau d'animal.

On the way back, I'd stop to move my car to its normal slot. For now, I trotted to the police station and greeted the desk officer, young black cutie Taylor Benton.

"Hey, Ms. Nix. Do you have more information vital to the murder case?" he teased.

"Matter of fact, I might. Is he in?"

"I'll let him know you're here."

He waved me to the few molded plastic chairs along the wall, but I didn't want to sit. I pulled Margot's card from my shorts pocket to reread it. More an old-fashioned calling card than a business card, it was hand-letter-pressed, printed with only her name and a phone number. Why go to the expense of having these made? My mother used to tell me the rich were different, and I'd known some ultra-wealthy folks in the world of art collecting, but Margot was flat weird.

"Come on back," Officer Benton said, and I heard a buzz. "Just push the door over there, then go straight to the bull pen."

Wow, my first time in the inner sanctum. Not that there was much to see in the short hallway aside from some wall plaques and cheaply framed group photos of Lilyvale's finest. The hall opened onto a room of seven desks and four times as many mismatched filing cabinets lining the perimeter. Rolling chairs for the officers, and stationary chairs for visitors were in orderly positions at each desk, and most of the furnishings looked less than a decade old. I spotted two restroom signs near a battered counter accessorized with a coffeemaker and a single sink. A smattering of closed doors on either side of the main area probably led to private offices, or to interview or conference rooms.

Surprisingly, Eric was the only soul in sight. "Where is everyone?"

"On patrol, on calls, and on vacation," he said, motioning me to a metal chair in front of his uncluttered desk. One manila file folder sat at his left elbow. Closed, of course. No chance for me to see anything but the pale yellow sticky note on the folder. I didn't have the vantage point—or the binoculars—to read the few words on it. The print was tiny.

"What's up?"

I jerked my gaze to his and sat.

"Margot Vail is delighted that her former sister-in-law is dead. I know this," I continued as I set her card on his desk and pushed it toward him, "because I talked with her about an hour ago."

He gave me his cop stare. "You aren't supposed to talk to suspects."

"This time, a suspect was looking to talk to me, although according to her, I did the 'accosting.'"

"Should I expect her to file charges?"

I huffed. "Do you want to hear the rest?"

"Might as well," he said as he leaned back in his desk chair.

I walked him through my exchange, leaving nothing out. His expressions ranged from puzzled to amused to outraged.

"You accused her of killing Ms. Thomason?" he growled. "What were you thinking?"

"I wanted to get a reaction from her. That woman isn't just cold. She's permafrost."

"Which doesn't make her a killer."

"No, but she didn't deny nearly hitting me head-on on Sunday. And she drives a silver Audi."

"I know. I pulled her registration yesterday. I also confirmed she and the nephew are staying in Magnolia." He paused, then clasped his hands of his desk. "I can't believe I'm asking you this, but how viable a suspect do you think she is?"

My shoulders slumped. "She had motive in spades, and she was in the area on Sunday late afternoon, but I can't see her doing the deed herself."

"And the nephew?"

"I don't get a hands-on killer vibe from him either, but what's bugging me is this ring business. Will you answer some questions if the answers won't compromise the case?"

"Try me."

"First, are Kim's personal effects just the items she had on her, um, person when she died, or are they all her other belongings?"

"Both. Mr. Boudreaux put up token resistance to us taking everything that belonged to his fiancée, but I think he knows now it was for the best."

I agreed. It was difficult enough cleaning out my mother's house when she died a few weeks after suffering a stroke. Packing up a murdered loved one's things had to be beyond-words wrenching.

"Okay, so you have photos and a written inventory of the stuff at the crime scene and her other things, right?"

"I do."

"Can you look for this engagement ring Margot is so hot to have? Just see if there are two diamond rings on the property list?"

"Why?"

"After the first time you questioned Ernie, he came to the store to unload on me."

"He what?" Eric said and came halfway out of his chair.

"I handled it," I said as I waved him down. "The short of the story is Kim thought Doralee would have that opal lying around her room. When I asked Ernie why she'd believe that, he said Kim traveled with her good jewelry and was convinced everyone else did."

"But isn't this elusive opal a loose stone?"

"Yes, but that distinction must've been lost on Kim. However, Kim was married to Margot's brother for nearly ten years. She'd probably know about Kim's penchant to take her jewelry on trips."

"Which is why she accused you of swiping the ring." He

drummed his fingers on the desk. Once. Twice. "Explain why I should look for two rings instead of one."

"Because if there is only one ring when there should be two, Kim's killer might have stolen the other."

He gave me a considering look and nodded. "Okay, what do these rings look like?"

"The one Ernie gave Kim had big diamonds. Super sparkly. Probably in a platinum setting. Before Ernie married Doralee, he had the family ring redone. A large square diamond was remounted and other stones were added to the setting. I can't give you an exact description but Doralee or Ernie can, I'm sure. Even Georgine."

"Did Mrs. Vail describe her heirloom?"

"She said the setting is gold, with a solitaire diamond she called a mine cut. I don't know exactly what that means, or how different those diamonds look from any other kind."

"I can have someone at Virginia's Jewelers evaluate anything we need examined."

"That's good," I said, though I planned to see what the Internet could tell me. I was too impatient to wait on him to enlighten me when I could research the question myself. "By the way, did you find out what Kim's brother drives?"

He flashed an indulgent smile. "Caleb Collier owns a late model Chevy Silverado. Dark blue."

"With oversized tires?"

"That I don't know, but there are over a hundred dark-colored Chevy trucks registered in northwest Louisiana and southwest Arkansas. And before you ask, he isn't in town yet that I know of."

"But didn't he make reservations at the inn starting today?"

"Yes, but Lorna let me know that he called with a change in plans. He said he probably wouldn't make it until tomorrow, but asked her to hold the room for him."

I heaved an exasperated breath. "His sister was killed on Sunday. Doesn't it seem odd that the sole relative of a murder victim hasn't shown up yet? It'll be four days tomorrow. Wouldn't most people at least ask about claiming the body to arrange for a service? I know and you know the body is in Little Rock, but would her brother know that?"

Eric held up a hand. "Yes, he would because I told him when I notified him of her death. I also assured him I'd call when his sister's body was released. That might be today."

"Why didn't you tell me all this?"

"You're not a cop," he said dryly.

"Well, still it would be more normal to show up sooner, right?"

He shook his head. "Nixy, I gave up on what's normal in these circumstances years ago. Let's change the subject. How are Amber and T.C. doing?"

I knew I wasn't getting another morsel of information from him, and had no choice but to take it in stride. "They're good. I'm getting comfortable with them, but I think Amber needs more exercise than I've been able to give her."

"Are you planning to keep them both?"

"I guess I have to. I found out their former owner died. Didn't I tell you?"

He shook his head. "How did you learn that?"

I gave him the highlights of Ruth Kreider's Tuesday morning visit, including how wildly happy the pets had been to see her.

"I still think it's odd that this Rusty character, the grandson's friend, wouldn't simply tell me he recognized them."

"Probably didn't want to get your hopes up in case he was wrong. Listen, you said Amber needs more activity. Will you be home tonight?"

"Um, I'm not sure," I fumbled. "I don't usually eat with the Silver Six on Wednesdays, but I'll have to check. Why? Do you want to take the dog for a run?"

"Better. Some friends of mine are creating a dog park over by the technical college. It's not officially open yet, but I could get us in. Throw the ball around for Amber. Then take the pets home and go to Adam Daniel's for dinner?"

' He named the new restaurant on the highway running north to McNeil. Not the most posh or romantic place, but then there weren't many posh dining opportunities around here. Since he'd taken me there for our official first date, I counted it as romantic enough.

I didn't do the evening-with-Eric happy dance, but I broke into a wide smile. "I'd love to have dinner after we check out the park, as long as T.C. can come, too."

"That can be arranged. Here's another idea to exercise Amber. Have you seen Taylor Benton riding his bike? He trained his terrier to run alongside and the dog loves it. You could try that on the days you can't get to the dog park. With a basket on the bike, T.C. could cruise with you if she doesn't want to run."

"Something to consider," I said, not about to mention that I hadn't ridden a bike in years. And the last time I had, I'd fallen off three times in the space of four blocks.

IT WAS THREE FIFTEEN WHEN I GOT BACK TO THE emporium. Dab's Caddy and Sherry's Camry were still parked on the street, I noticed, but there was plenty of space in the lot.

I entered through the alley door, but didn't see Fred or the fur babies. Maybe he'd taken them for a stroll. If nothing else, he'd walk them to prove he "didn't need no droppin' off."

Jasmine had come in early to help with Petting Zoo Day, so she'd left at three o'clock. Only a couple of middle-aged women I recognized as Lilyvale residents were in the store, so I didn't bother to keep my voice down. "Aunt Sherry, I want to move your car. Dab's, too. Who has the keys?"

Every last one of my ladies bee-lined to the shelves in back of the counter, every one of them pulled out a purse, and in another twenty seconds, every one of them dangled keys from their fingers.

"Take your pick," Maise said.

I chuckled and crossed to accept her set. "Thanks. What about Dab's keys?"

"I'll move my own car," he said as he emerged from the kitchenette. "Thanks for offering, but I have the seat in exactly the right position."

Dab was tall. I was short. Long legs, short legs. I got it. My taller-than-me roommate used to borrow my car and never got the seat back in position.

"Okay, then. I'll be right back."

"No, rush, child," Sherry said. "In fact, you need to go by the bakery. Judy dropped in to see you an hour ago."

"Will do, but I'll be quick."

And I was quick because I felt guilty for disappearing earlier with only a wave and a "running an errand" excuse. Sometimes—most of the time—I forgot that the Silver Six weren't used to eight-hour workdays. They had all retired, and though they all volunteered at the technical college and had other activities, they'd had plenty of time to rest and relax.

Okay, so none of them were exactly basking in their retirements. They tended to be busy every waking moment, and that was *before* we'd begun making the emporium a reality. Still, I needed to pull my weight, do the jobs I'd signed on for in this venture. I hoped that, once the grand opening was over and the newness of the emporium wore off, the seniors would take shifts instead of all of them being here every single day. For one thing, they needed to keep producing woven baskets, whittled wooden figures, and herbal potions and lotions or we'd have nothing of theirs to sell. Of course, Fred might be here every workday. He'd moved the vast majority of his tools from the barn and sheds at the farmhouse to his new fix-it space. And if nothing else, I knew the Six planned to continue volunteering at the technical college once the fall semester began. That would cut their emporium hours at least by half. I had no doubt I could handle the store with Jasmine and additional help only now and then.

Of course, I'd have tons more time if I could steer clear of mysteries.

At Great Buns, Judy wanted to know the latest murder case scoop. She especially wanted to know if Eric had caught the victim's "shifty sister-in-law." I responded that I didn't think he was exactly ready to drag Margot into the station. My friend would not be happy with me if she learned that I'd met the suspect a block from here, but I'd take my chances that our new friendship would survive. I could always say I'd been sworn to secrecy. He wasn't likely to contradict me because the subject wasn't likely to come up.

THE SUBJECT *DID* ARISE AT THE EMPORIUM, THOUGH. Since the store was customer-free, I was hit with a frontal attack.

"So how is our favorite detective today?" Sherry paused wielding her duster when I walked in the emporium's front door and jammed her free hand on her hip. "Did you two discuss anything new about the case?"

I opened my mouth but nothing came out. Aster, who stood by her potions and lotions display, shook a finger at me.

"We have eyes everywhere."

"You should know that by now," Maise said, chuckling from behind the counter.

Eleanor winked.

I sighed. "I didn't have a chance to tell y'all, but I ran into Kim's ex-sister-in-law out back."

They exploded in chatter, and Eleanor hollered at Dab and Fred to come out front. In a flash, the Silver Six gathered around the antique checkout counter, one blocking my way to the front door, another barring my way to the back. Oh, and Amber and T.C. joined us because Fred wouldn't hear of leaving them in the workroom. I fully admit, I ate up their ecstatic, noisy greetings. Amber wagged her entire backside while she danced around my feet, and T.C. shocked me by leaping into my arms. The first time she'd done that, and I felt special. Paying attention to my pets gave me a moment to gather my thoughts.

Of course, they settled down as I related my encounter with Margot. The critters, that is. T.C. slinked out of my arms to lie on the counter. Amber sat at my feet, head cocked. They didn't make a peep, but the Six exclaimed over the story.

"Goodness, child, you never said a word before you took off."

"I didn't have time, Aunt Sherry. I wanted to talk to Eric before I forgot any details. Which reminds me. Do any of you know about mine cut diamonds? Are they any less shiny than a run-of-the-mill stone?"

"I do believe that might depend on the setting," Eleanor replied. "The one I inherited isn't large in terms of carats, but it sparkles in the light."

"I don't think the cut of a diamond is crucial here," Aster said. "We need to hold a team meeting."

"We can do it after dinner tonight," Maise said. "You in?"

"Uh, well, actually," I stammered, feeling a blush heat my cheeks, "I'm seeing Eric later."

Maise gave me the stink eye. "Is this a date or are you snooping without us?"

"It must be a date," Sherry nearly chortled. "Our dear detective doesn't condone any of us snooping."

"So where is he taking you?" Aster asked.

"We're taking Amber and T.C. to a new dog park."

Fred snorted. "In my day, a date meant dinner and a movie."

"Or dinner and dancing," Dab added.

"Or dinner and miniature golf," Eleanor said.

"We're going to the Adam Daniel's for dinner afterward," I said with a grin I didn't bother to contain.

Sherry shook her head, then pushed her bangs out of the way. "You won't be dining there tonight. Not unless they got the roof fixed."

"That's right," Maise said. "That storm Sunday was worse north of here. It took off part of the restaurant's roof and soaked the kitchen. Or so I hear."

"I'm sure Eric would know if the place was closed."

"Don't know 'bout that," Fred said, stroking his chin. "Boy's been awful busy with this murder. You may end up at the Dairy Queen."

I arched a brow at him. "Will that still count as a dinner date?"

"Will if you order somethin' expensive," Fred advised. "Boy's gotta understand you know your worth."

I grinned. "I love you, Fred."

"Bet your nuts and bolts you do. Is that all we're discussin' for now? I got work to finish."

Fred pushed out of his chair, gripped his walker, and clank-clunked to his workroom.

Aster shook her head at me. "I can't believe you're taking a cat to a dog park. What if the other dogs frighten her?"

"She can hold her own," Dab declared.

"They're inseparable, Aster, and besides, Fred and Dab taught T.C. to chase a ball. She doesn't like to be left out."

Sherry rose and patted my arm. "You have a good time tonight, child. You deserve a break."

What I really wanted was a break in the case. But then, I imagined our dear Detective Shoar wanted the same thing.

SHOPPERS CAME IN A STEADY STREAM IN THE LATE afternoon, and a few became buyers, too. Dab retreated to the workroom to make notes on a new herb distilling project.

Aster, Eleanor, and Sherry manned the sales floor while
Maise and I retreated to the tiny space in the kitchenette to
do paperwork. Although nursing had been her primary
career, she had taken accounting classes to help her husband
in his insurance business. She lent those skills to the emporium, teaching me bookkeeping, and helping with inventory
control. If we needed more merchandise from an artist, I
was the one to make the call, but Maise had a knack for
knowing what would sell.

We were wrapping up the day when the wind chimes
played and Ruth Kreider came in, her cane smartly striking
the floor. The elderly woman looked much the way she had
when I met her on Tuesday morning. Gray hair styled just
so. Heavily powdered face wreathed in a smile. Tailored
pale pink pants with tunic-style blouse.

"Nixy, hello, again!" she called gaily.

"Ruth, I didn't expect to see you this soon but welcome.
Come meet my aunt and her friends."

I hurried to shake the papery hand she extended, then I
took her elbow to lead her to a chair. After I introduced Ruth
to the ladies, I sat beside her.

"Did you have a good time at your reunion? Is your daughter outside?"

"She's gone to get gas, and yes, dear, I did have fun in
Little Rock. Thank you for asking. We used to make a few
days of it, but we're old enough now that we want our own
beds. Or I do. I simply had to stop back by to visit—what
did you name the pets?"

"The cat is T.C. and the dog is Amber," I answered. "And
I think they hear your voice, Ruth."

She cocked her head, listening to the excited yaps and
loud meows coming from the workroom. "I think you're
right."

Before I could get them, Fred jerked open the door, and
my critters raced to Ruth.

"What in tarnation?" he exclaimed.

"Fred, you and Dab come meet the lady I told y'all about. The one who knew Amber's and T.C.'s last owner."

Ruth welcomed the critters just as she had the first time. Amber stood with front paws on the chair seat wagging so hard, she kept slipping, knocking herself off the smooth surface. T.C. jumped into Ruth's lap, gently head-butted her chest and *meeped*, with excitement. The Silver Six circled chairs around Ruth and the animals, and I made the introductions.

"I see these little fur babies are faring just fine," she said. "I hope you don't mind me coming by again."

I smiled at her, and at the animals. "Absolutely not. I love seeing how crazy they are about you."

"I can't tell you how much that means to me. I felt better after meeting you, of course, but I'll always regret letting them run off when Doris died. Things do happen for a reason, though, don't they? Rusty seeing these two on the computer, and then telling my grandson so he could tell me. To know these two are safe and happy, it's a weight off my shoulders, I tell you."

"I hope I can thank Rusty in person someday."

She blinked. "But you can. He's here in town. I just saw him driving that truck of his."

The hair on the back of my neck tingled. "Pardon me, but what kind of truck does he drive?"

"I'm not sure of the model, dear, but it's dark blue. Why he put those monstrous tires on it, I'll never know." She paused and flicked a glance at Fred and Dab. "No offense to you gentlemen, but I never understood why a man's ego was tied up in the size or sportiness of his vehicle, especially trucks. In my day, those were strictly utilitarian."

Except for the pets, the room had gone quiet. Then Sherry breathed, "Goodness, can it be?"

Ruth flicked her gaze to each of us and frowned. "Be what? Have I misspoken somehow?"

"No, no, not at all," I said. "It's just that we're interested in finding Rusty to thank him. And we have been looking for someone who owns a truck like that. What's his last name?"

Ruth fluttered a hand. "My stars, I knew I should have asked Ray again. My memory isn't as sharp for some things as it used to be, and I'm so accustomed to simply calling him Rusty. Let me think." She paused, then brightened. "The name reminds me of a man's shirt. I'll think of it eventually."

I patted the hand that rested on Amber's head. "It's okay, Ruth. What does Rusty look like?"

My question must've been too sharp because she shot me a suspicious look. "He's a good boy."

"Well, of course he is," Sherry soothed. "But we'd like to be able to recognize him if we see him on the square."

I nodded. "I wouldn't want to chase after every dark-colored pickup I see in town," I said. "I'd probably frighten the poor guy off."

Ruth's expression cleared. "You never want a man to think you're chasing him," she said on a chuckle.

"Amen," Eleanor said.

"Well, then, Rusty is about six feet tall, neither fat nor thin. Red hair, but I don't recall the color of his eyes. He's handsome enough in an average way, and he's as nice as can be. He travels some for his job, but he's always willing to lend a hand when he's home."

Redheaded Rusty. Was Rusty a nickname? Maybe, maybe just a good-ole-boy named by some good-ole-boy parents. Hippies had saddled their children with worse. Plus Ruth struck me as a person to be precise whenever possible. I'd think she'd mention the guy's real name if she knew it. Or remembered it.

I tried a different tack. "Does he live in Minden, too?"

"Not anymore, but he comes to visit Ray, and they both help me around the house."

"They sound like wonderful young men," Sherry said. "Now tell us about this reunion."

And with that, my dear seniors directed the rest of Ruth's

visit, chatting like they'd known each other forever. Fred and Dab even wedged in a few questions about the life Amber and T.C. had lived with Doris. I appreciated their Southern social skills in situations like this because I couldn't hold my end of a light conversation at the moment.

I itched oh-so-desperately to find the extra copies of the surveillance photos from last week and show them to Ruth, but I didn't want to upset her. Even if she recognized our Ball Cap Guy as Rusty, what would that tell us?

That Rusty drove a truck generally like the one I'd seen tearing from the alley on Sunday.

That Rusty drove a truck similar to the one registered to Caleb Collier.

That Rusty and Caleb might be the same guy.

And if all that was true, then we'd know Kim's brother had been in Lilyvale before she was murdered.

No clear motive, murky means, but being in town gave Rusty/Caleb the opportunity to kill his sister.

Chapter Fourteen

I TOLD ERIC ABOUT THE CHANCE THAT ADAM DAN-
iel's was closed as soon as he picked us up. He immediately
called, put the cell on speaker, and his face fell as we lis-
tened to the recorded message.

In spite of having dressed up for our dog park/dinner date
in my best navy capris, coordinating sleeveless scoop-neck
blouse, and rhinestone-studded navy sandals, I flashed a
sunny smile. "It's okay, Eric. I don't care if we end up at the
Dairy Queen as long as you feed me."

He gave me a doubtful frown. "You'd be okay with
the DQ?"

I shrugged. "We've been there before together. Besides,
I feel the need for a banana shake coming on."

"Not one of those frozen latte drinks you like?"

Aww, he remembered.

"Maybe I'll have one of those, too," I said, giving a mental nod to Fred's order-expensive advice.

Eric started to put his shiny-clean extended cab pickup
in gear, but stopped and gave me one of those long brown-

eyed gazes before turning his attention to the road. The kind that made my bones liquefy and butterflies take flight in my tummy.

The bonelessness and butterflies subsided, and I lapsed into my own thoughts during the short drive. I wasn't sure when to tell him about Ruth's latest visit. Or ask if he'd gotten a description of Caleb while running the search for his truck. Maybe a driver's license photo? And why was I obsessing about the case during my date, for heaven's sake?

Eric noticed my distraction. He didn't say anything, but I caught his assessing glances from the corner of my eye. I had to stop fretting and enjoy the moment.

Near the technical college, Eric turned onto a side street, and there was the dog-park-in-progress. It appeared more completed than not, and was far more elaborate than I'd expected. I chuckled when T.C. and Amber crowded in the console space for a windshield view. Before we let the critters out, he grasped my hand and squeezed.

Touched by his concern, I gave him a bright smile, then gathered a fidgeting T.C. in my arms while he took Amber's leash. The evening was unusually cool, and I vowed to have a good time.

Eric introduced Dottie and Donnie Hawthorne. The couple in their mid-thirties had spearheaded the dog park project and guided it every step of the way. Rightfully proud of their efforts, they tag-teamed telling us about the park as their golden retriever, Samson, got acquainted with Amber and T.C. Yes, the cat and her new canine acquaintance bonded at first sniff.

The acre and a half of land, partially shaded by old trees, was covered in native grasses except for thick mulch lining the fences and circling the trees. Adjacent to a small city park with a children's playground, the dog park was divided by another fence to accommodate and separate large and small breeds. Brand-new agility equipment, each piece in bright colors and made from heavy-duty recycled plastic, dotted the area. Amber and Samson romped through hoops and over hurdles. They dashed up ramps leading into and out of a tunnel, and up and down more ramps without tunnels. T.C. watched a few minutes, then raced to the tunnel, and leaped. In short order, she draped herself over one end. Every time pups trotted through, she swiped a paw at them, and they tore off again with big doggie grins. Their antics weren't as funny as some of the cute-cat-cute-dog videos I'd seen, but I got a kick watching them play. Maybe because they were mine.

Eeks. Was I taking full ownership of the critters? The thought rattled me, so I refocused on Eric's friends.

"That's why we aren't officially open yet," Dottie was saying as she pointed to the small dogs area. "The last of the small dog agility equipment should be here by Saturday, and we plan to be open by the Fourth of July."

I looked around to check on the animals. Samson was prancing in a kiddie pool trying to catch sprays of water in his mouth. T.C. sat well to the side, out of the splash zone, eyeing her new friend like the dog had lost his mind. Amber was investigating the mulch around a nearby tree. I knew that circling thing she was doing, and headed for the nearest poop-scoop station.

"We wanted a doggie splash park," I heard Donnie say while I dealt with Amber's business, "but we decided to put money into installing surveillance cameras in the trees."

"Any special reason why?" Eric asked, his tone only a touch sharp.

Dottie waved a hand as I rejoined them. "We want to be proactive. People get up to all sorts of things they shouldn't and we want to ensure Wags and Woofs Park is safe as much as humanly possible."

I trusted they'd place their cameras more carefully than we had at the emporium, but her comment reminded me I needed to talk to Eric about Ruth sooner or later. Later still worked.

"I hope you'll bring Amber back," Dottie said kindly.

"I'm not sure I can. She and T.C. are all but joined at the hip, and I don't think other dogs or owners will be happy to see a cat here."

"As long as the park is empty, let her play," Donnie said. "You get any flak, you say I okayed it."

"Thanks, both of you," Eric said and casually draped an arm over my shoulders. "We may just take you up on that offer."

"We need to get Samson home," Dottie said, "but you're welcome to stay longer. Just secure the padlock when you leave."

AMBER LOOKED SAD TO SEE SAMSON GO, BUT SHE soon raced around a tree T.C. had climbed, barking and leaping on the trunk. When T.C. came back down, she launched her body at Amber, and the dog took off. The chase was on.

As the sun sank lower, Eric and I sat on a bench with a bone-shaped back to watch the critters play. He threw his arm over the bench back, his fingers just brushing my shoulder. Though we weren't sitting thigh-to-thigh, we were close enough for his body heat to curl around me.

"So, Nixy," he said casually, so much so it put me on alert. "How many guys from your past am I competing with?"

"Huh?" I jerked to face him, my gaze meeting his lazy smile.

"You know. All the guys you dated. Mick the Mechanic."

"Matt," I corrected automatically.

"And Skip the Scout."

"Scott."

"Right, and there was an ER doctor, a couple of attorneys, and a private investigator as I recall."

I leaned back, narrowed my eyes. "You don't honestly see any of them as competition, do you?"

"A man's ego is a fragile thing," he said, straight-faced.

I rolled my eyes. "I've told you, every time I thought there was a spark, it sputtered after two or three dates, tops. What about you? You have to be one of the most eligible men in Lilyvale. Do you have hordes of women in your black book?"

"My book is blue." I saw the twinkle in his eye and playfully punched his shoulder. "Okay, straight answer. Even if there were hordes of names in my blue book, I'm only interested in one of them. And, Nixy."

I held my breath, then let it out slowly. "Yes?"

He leaned closer. "I hope we don't sput—Oof!"

He jerked and I jumped because Amber and T.C. had launched themselves onto the bench and ran across our laps. Had Amber been barking all this time? I'd been too wrapped up in Eric to notice, but now the animals circled back. Amber put her paws on Eric's knees and panted. T.C. sat on me and head-bumped my chest.

"Does this mean they're ready to go?" I asked.

"Imagine so," he replied with a sigh.

He patted Amber's head, rose, and offered his hand. Being no fool, I took it, and savored the thrill that raced through me when he laced our fingers together.

"Let's all go have dinner."

WHEN ERIC SAID WE'D ALL HAVE DINNER, HE MEANT the critters, too. He insisted we dine outside at one of the patio tables in front of the Dairy Queen, and ordered large waters for each of them even though I knew Amber had slurped half a bowlful at the park. He also ordered a large burger for himself, the perfect medium one for me, and the kiddie-menu chicken strips for the critters. The server didn't bat an eye over the kiddie meal, or when she handed over two sundae-sized cups for Eric to use as water bowls.

"Dr. Sally said not to feed them people food," I protested when we had our food in front of us and began to dig in. I didn't mention my own lapse in sticking to that rule.

"I know they ate before I picked you up, but they played hard since then. I've give them three bites, max. And see? I'm stripping off the fried batter."

"Are you slipping them fries?" I pointed to the one he'd scooted to the edge of the table.

"I'm not planning to."

"Uh-huh, but you might accidentally drop a few?"

"What can I say? Sometimes I'm a sloppy eater."

"Who will be nowhere in sight if they get sick in my apartment."

"I'm a phone call away. So what did you think of the park?"

I finished another bite and chased it with the DQ version of an iced latte. Yes, I'd decided to save the banana shake for another time.

"It's terrific. A bit far for me to walk in the morning unless I get up extra early, but I can drive over to see if the coast is clear for T.C."

"Or try taking them about this time of night. The park won't close until sunset."

"I'll keep it in mind."

"What did you think of Dottie and Donnie?"

"I like them. Have you been friends long?"

"Donnie and I went to the academy together, but he dropped out. Decided being a cop wasn't for him, so he went to welding school. Sometimes I wonder if I should've done the same thing."

I blinked. "You don't like being a detective?"

"I love what I do, but it has its drawbacks. Chief Randall is on another rampage about making an arrest."

"I can't blame him." I paused for another sip of cold latte, fidgeted, and finally spit it out. "Eric, I have some more info about the case and I am about to burst."

"I can tell that. What's up?"

"Remember the elderly woman who came in earlier this week? The one who recognized Amber and T.C.?"

"Sure. They were her neighbor's pets before they showed up here. Does she want to adopt them?"

"No, Ruth can't take the pets, but she knew I had them because her grandson's friend saw them on the computer."

He put down his all-but-eaten burger. "Why is that significant?"

Abandoning the rest of my meal, too, I thought about how I wanted to lay out the information. "First, let me ask you this. Did you put Amber's and T.C.'s photos online anywhere?"

"No. You didn't e-mail them to me. Why?"

"Because I didn't e-mail them to anyone. Not to Dr. Sally, or Miranda at the shelter, or you. I flat out forgot, and I didn't put them on social media either. The only place those pictures appeared was on my tablet screen in the store. That's the only place this Rusty guy could've seen them."

"Ruth came to see you Tuesday morning, correct?"

"Yes, but this man had to have seen the photos on Friday or Saturday. The emporium was closed Sunday, and I forgot to run the slide show on Monday."

"Why does it matter when he saw the photos? What are you getting at?"

"Ruth came to see me again this afternoon, and the Silver Six were there this time. I happened to say that I hoped to someday thank Rusty for telling her about the critters, and she told me he was in town. She'd just seen him driving his dark blue truck, Eric, and she called the truck tires 'monstrous.'"

His whole body went on alert. "Caleb Collier's truck matches the same general description."

"Which also matches the description of the truck that nearly hit me on Sunday."

"Did Ruth describe Rusty?"

"Average looking, average height and weight, I think, though she didn't specifically say. The only detail she mentioned is that he has red hair. Kim had auburn hair."

"Which means nothing," he said, but I saw his mental wheels churning.

"Agreed, but here's another oddity. On Friday, three people I didn't recognize as being from around here came for Doralee's and Sherry's demonstration. I noticed them in particular because they never took off their sunglasses."

"Granted, removing them would be the more usual thing to do."

"Exactly. We now know two of those people were Margot Vail and Dennis Thomason. The third was a guy in a blue medical scrubs shirt, jeans, mirrored shades, and a baseball cap. I don't recall seeing his hair period. He kept the brim pulled low, and he looked at his phone instead of following along with the program. The camera caught more of the top of his head than his face."

"Was the same man there on Saturday any time?"

"If he was, I didn't notice. He may have been dressed differently. Or he may have been in the store when I wasn't. If Ball Cap Guy is Rusty and Rusty is Caleb, he was in town before Kim was killed."

Eric glanced at his watch, and I checked the time on my cell. Just after eight. "You still have that surveillance video, right?"

"And some of the still shots we took for the website. Eleanor has more on her camera."

"Feel like helping me investigate?"

I blinked. "Really?"

"Hey, your video, your lead. Just don't let this get back to a soul in the department."

"Be still, my heart."

THE CRITTERS CURLED UP TOGETHER NEAR THE door from the store to Fred's workshop. I turned on just one bank of store lights, hoping for less glare on my tablet screen.

With Eric and me seated on stools side by side at the

emporium's antique counter, the partially lit room made the space feel just a bit romantic. I firmly ignored that, and pulled up the video footage. Yes, there was a way to access the feed from my apartment, but I didn't want to take the time to figure it out. And surprisingly, I learned that Eric wasn't super tech savvy so he was no help on that score.

Heads close together, we watched Friday's footage first. Eric might lack tech skills, but he was a master at watching the action of all three camera angles, and of manipulating the play and pause functions.

We saw townspeople trickle into the store, then the students. Then Ernie, Kim, and Georgine entered. It was difficult to watch the images of the then-living Kim, but not quite as much as it had been last time I'd seen them.

"There. There's Ball Cap Guy," I said, pointing to the man entering the front door.

Eric immediately changed the speed to slow motion, and we watched in rapt silence. I noticed details I hadn't noticed when the Six and I looked for a tool thief.

"We can't see his eyes for those mirrored sunglasses, but does it look to you like he scans the crowd? Watch the way his head moves."

"I see it. And right there he seemed to be looking across the room." I pointed at the feed from a different camera. "Look, that's Ernie sitting down next to Kim."

"And there goes Georgine out of this shot and into the angle covering the front of the store. They didn't sit together?"

"Not on Friday. They may have on Saturday. I don't recall."

"What's Ball Cap doing? Look, he turns away as Georgine gets closer."

"And when she passes, he walks over to stand behind the chairs."

Eric played the feed at normal speed until the end of the gourd program. I pointed at camera one's screen.

"Here's Ernie getting up. And you can see part of Georgine over here in the camera two shot as she stands."

Eric leaned in closer, then paused the screens. "They both move out of range. Where'd they go?"

I closed my eyes to replay what I'd seen. "I remember Ernie and Georgine standing at Doralee's side of the demonstration table, but I'm not sure they ever spoke with her."

He nodded and we turned back to follow Kim as she stood and turned toward the front of the store. In another angle Ball Cap Guy headed for the counter at more or less the same time.

"Okay," I said when we'd finished viewing that section of footage. "Is it just me or did Ball Cap seem like he was watching Ernie and company, but then dodged them?"

"I thought the same thing. I know it's getting late, Nixy, but are you game to watch Saturday's surveillance?"

I wasn't about to turn him down, especially when his big brown eyes held mine. He leaned closer to me. I swayed toward him. My stomach did flips anticipating his kiss.

Then I nearly flopped off the stool when Amber shot to her paws, barking madly, just as someone pounded on the emporium's front door.

"Nixy, child," my aunt called loud enough to easily hear through the glass. "Duke saw the lights on and called us. What are you and Eric doing here of all places?"

Eric steadied me and squeezed my shoulder before he went to open the door. Sherry and the rest of the Silver Six spilled inside.

"This here's a dang odd place to be considerin' you're supposed to be on a date," Fred growled as he clank-clunked to the counter. "What in the Sam Hill *are* you doing here, missy?"

I looked to Eric for help, but he was busy holding back laughter.

I'd get him for that. "Actually, we're investigating."

"Without including us?" Sherry exclaimed, her expression a mixture of hurt and disappointment.

Maise slapped a palm on the counter. "That's next door to mutiny."

"Are you hacking a website?" Aster asked.

"We're reviewing your surveillance video," Eric informed them, obviously having composed himself. "In fact, we were just going to fire up the footage from Saturday."

"The day of your program, Eleanor. The day your whittling tool went missing."

"If we can all crowd around the tablet," he added, "I'd appreciate the extra sets of eyes."

Fred humphed. "I ain't got time for this. Dab and me wanted to catch part of the double header. You girls mind if we skedaddle?"

"Go ahead," Maise said. "We've got the Camry."

"And I'll follow you ladies home to be sure you get there safely," Eric said.

There went any more alone time with him.

WITH ERIC MANIPULATING THE SPEED OF THE PLAY-back, Sherry, Eleanor, Maise, Aster, and I watched the Saturday security feed. A few minutes in, Aunt Sherry excused herself in order to make tea for us all in the kitchenette. She used her macular degeneration as the excuse, yet I knew she was still smarting at being left out, and I'd have to make it up to her.

Heck, make it up to all the Six. They were a little sensitive sometimes about being vital and useful. Yes, in spite the fact they knew darn well they could work rings around me.

Ball Cap Guy didn't show up on the cameras, but another man caught our attention. Dressed in jeans with boots, a plain tan work shirt, and a battered straw cowboy hat, he wore black-framed sunglasses with amber lenses. And he moved a lot like Ball Cap.

"Hit pause," Eleanor suddenly said.

Eric did, and she leaned closer to the tablet.

"I do believe this man came to the table after my demonstration. I don't recall what we chatted about, but I remember he spoke softly."

"Softly as in he was hoarse?" Maise asked.

"No, although his voice might've been a little raspy."

"Let's see what else he does on the tape."

Straw Hat, whom I was all but convinced was Ball Cap Guy, again scanned the room, and seemed to watch Ernie and company. When the presentation ended, he pulled the brim of the hat down, and slid away as Kim started his way. We lost camera contact with Ernie and Georgine, but Eleanor remembered speaking with them. She also remembered that Straw Hat approached her after Ernie and moved on.

When we finished watching, I closed the feed while Eric stood and stretched.

"All right, Detective Shoar," Sherry began, "it's time to at least give us some crumbs. Why are you looking at this man?"

"Right on," Aster said. "We thought it was that blonde woman you were interested in finding."

He sighed. "Did you get that from Nixy or Judy?"

"Judy," they all sang.

He gave me the eye, and I shrugged. "You didn't ask either of us to keep quiet about Margot Vail."

"Then I slipped up, but please listen. All of you. Keep tonight's activities to yourself. I don't want anything to compromise the case."

"Loose lips sink ships," Maise declared. "You can count on us."

Chapter Fifteen

THE LADIES SAID THEY WANTED TO CHECK ON something or other and shooed me outside to wait with Eric. I saw the twinkle in Sherry's eyes and knew they were giving us a few moments alone before he followed them home.

Whatever bit of romantic buzz we'd had was pretty much long gone, but hey, I'd take another private moment no matter what we talked about. And yes, I wanted to know Eric's thoughts about the security feeds.

We drifted to the huge concrete planter out front. I sat on the edge and looked up.

"Now that you've seen the footage, what do you think? Are Rusty and Caleb the same person?"

"What makes you think I can answer that?"

"Didn't you pull up a driver's license picture when you ran the truck registration?"

"Yes, but I can't make a positive ID."

"Oh. Bummer."

"Buck up. I'll enlarge the license photo tomorrow. Nixy, did Ruth give you Rusty's last name?"

"I'm not a hundred percent positive that Rusty is his real first name, and she didn't remember his last one. She did say it reminded her of a man's shirt."

He tipped his head. "Polo? Button down?"

"For all I know, it could be a designer's name. Armani, Calvin Klein, Ralph Lauren, Brooks Brothers, Abercrombie & Fitch."

"The way those brands rolled off your tongue, you must've dated some fashion-obsessed guy."

"Nope, just a clothing salesman. Men's Wear Wally."

He snorted. I grinned. The wind chimes alerted us that Sherry and the ladies were coming.

"One more thing," I said as I stood and moved closer so the women wouldn't hear. "Did you look at Kim's property list for those diamond rings?"

"Not yet. I mentioned Chief Randall is chomping for an arrest. He called a meeting after you left. I'll do it tomorrow when I pull Caleb's license up again."

"I don't suppose you'll fill me in on what you find."

"We'll see."

I TRIED TO GET AMBER TO GO OUT FOR A LAST walk, but she and T.C. wouldn't budge from the foot of my bed. I could've used the exercise to burn off some adrenalin, but I changed into my sleep shirt, and started a load of laundry instead.

And began drafting a murder board, like on cop shows, too. Feel the burn, right?

Okay, I didn't make a board per se. I propped myself against my headboard with the spiral notebook I'd kept for making renovation notes and began my list of things to do and people to see. Tops on the list were Doralee and Ernie.

It was odd not to have seen Ernie since Monday late afternoon. I'd expected him to storm my castle again, demanding to know what I was doing to help him. Not that

I wanted him in my face. It just seemed odd for him to disappear. Heck, if I hadn't happened on Georgine in the alley, I wouldn't have seen her either.

But Ernie and Doralee both needed to tell me the whole truth of seeing each other near the square. Neither of them felt like a killer, but who knew what evil lurked in the hearts of men?

What else did I need to chart? A timeline might be helpful. That was another cop show thing. I began sketching out who did what when, but found myself yawning and let my head clunk softly on the headboard. Tomorrow I'd finish the time chart and make more notes. Maybe I'd recruit the Silver Six to help. Fred acted like he didn't give a rip, but his mantra was, "Follow the money." Which was another thing to ask Eric.

MOST WOMEN WOULD'VE DREAMED OF ERIC AND THE two almost-kisses.

I dreamed about motive, means, and opportunity, which turned out to be both exhausting and productive. By eight thirty Thursday, I'd showered and prepped for a day of case solving—and for hosting jewelry maker Lexie Gibson. Hers was the only program slated, and we'd set the time for one thirty. I'd have the morning to track down Doralee and Ernie, have a confab with the Silver Six, and follow up with Eric.

Oh, and find out if Caleb Collier kept his reservation at the inn this time.

While Amber and T.C. munched their dog and cat chows, I grabbed my spiral from the bedroom and a protein bar from the cabinet. A page of notes later, we took a brisk morning walk. I didn't see my teen friend Louie and his dog, Harley, but greeted several people I knew in passing. They weren't inclined to visit, so I stayed on schedule.

Back at the emporium, I began setting out the lipped

wooden benches for the outdoor display of baskets, pillows, and gourds. Then, before the Silver Six arrived, I ducked into Gaskin's Business Center for a few murder case–busting supplies.

"What in tarnation is that?" Fred demanded.

I'd taken down his large sports calendar in the workroom and hung something of my own. The hefty-sized nail held it just fine.

"It's a flip chart. For us to make notes on the case."

"Oooh, like a murder board?" Aster asked.

"More or less."

"If this is about last night, child," Sherry said, "we understand that sometimes you have to do things your way and do them alone. Just like we do."

I tried not to shudder. They'd stayed out of trouble for months, but before that there had been booms in the basement and smoke bombs in the kitchen.

"That doesn't mean I don't want your input. Besides," I said, playing a trump card, "y'all got me into this investigation. I need you to help me sort the facts. We need to open the store in a few minutes, but isn't Jasmine coming in at eleven?"

"She is," Eleanor said, "and I do believe we'll have time to hold our meeting before the craft demonstration."

"I'm counting on it."

"Have you cracked the case?" Dab asked.

"No, but we just might do that together. I just have a few more questions to ask a few more people."

"Humph. All you need to do is follow the money."

"I'm working on it, Fred."

I REALIZED I'D NEVER ASKED DORALEE FOR HER cell number, but Aster had it and gave it to me without batting an eyelash.

She answered on the fourth ring, and said she was

painting gourds in the little sitting area behind their room at the Pines Motor Court. "I really don't want to put every-thing up and come to town. Do you mind coming out here?"

I agreed, and this time told the Six where I'd be. Sherry asked me to take a few pictures of the place with my cell camera, but didn't ask to come along.

I'd hoped to set up a meeting with Ernie before eleven, too, but none of us had his cell number. I'd either have to go over to the inn or see if Doralee had his number.

The businesses and homes on the highway thinned as I drove to the little motel. As Dab had said, it wasn't that far out of town, but groves of pine trees grew right up to the two-lane road.

I found the place where two country roads intersected. I couldn't miss the three-sided wooden sign elevated on what looked like pine tree poles. Line drawings of pine trees were etched in the signs, and the words "Pines Motor Court" were spelled out in white paint. The motel rooms were actually tiny cabins, arranged in a horseshoe shape, and connected only by the parking lot and pathways. The first cabin I passed on the left had a neon OFFICE sign in the window. I didn't see Doralee's car as I rolled to a stop at number 7 on the far end. Zach must have taken it, which meant he wasn't here, and that was a good thing. Doralee was more likely to tell me the whole truth without an audience. I didn't bother to knock, but walked around the side of the cabin to the back.

"Hey," Doralee said, looking up from the gourd resting on a drop cloth. "Have a seat."

She pointed to a metal retro patio chair painted in a warm cream color. Not original, but a great copy.

"Don't you love the vintage style? I've covered the table to protect it, but it's metal, too, with the old mesh top."

I let her chat a moment about how cute the cabin was inside and out. Much as I wanted to cut to the chase, if I pushed my agenda, she might close up on me.

She sighed. "I don't like the reason we're still here, but it is a darling place. And so affordable. It would be the perfect place for my author friend to come write. So, Nixy, what do you need to talk about?"

"I need to know exactly what happened between you and Ernie when he found you out walking."

She looked down at her gourd. "I told you what happened."

"Yes, but you've left out something. You've sidestepped a detail every time I've asked you about that afternoon. Are you protecting yourself or Ernie?"

Yeah, that was a spur-of-the-moment shot in the dark question, but it startled a reaction from her. Immediately, she paled and her hands trembled.

"If I tell you, do you have to tell that detective?"

"It depends. I won't know until you fess up."

She nodded and reached for a rag to wipe her hands. "I've probably blown this out of proportion, but here goes. I told you I left the party just to have some quiet time for a bit. I was seriously considering selling the opal to Ernie, but I didn't know what to charge him. I didn't want him to feel financially embarrassed."

"Right, so you changed your mind about offering the gem to him at all, and you headed back toward Sherry's."

"And that's where I left out something. When Ernie picked me up, I said I'd sell him the stone and he could pay me in installments. He refused but not because of money. He said Kim was going to learn she couldn't have everything she wanted no matter what it took to teach her."

I frowned. "No matter what it took?"

"See, that's why I wasn't completely open. It almost sounds like a threat, but I know he didn't mean it that way. If he got fed up, he'd break off the engagement, not kill her."

"I agree." I thought for a moment. Did I still need to talk with Ernie? Yes, I needed validation.

"Doralee, do you think Ernie will support this part of

your conversation with him? That is, without you coaching him?"

"Maybe if you promise not to tell the detective."

"Do you have his cell phone number?"

She jutted out her chin. "What makes you think I'd have it?"

"If he has the same number he did when y'all were married, why wouldn't you have it? I still have numbers of guys I dated five years ago. I just haven't bothered to delete them."

My it's-all-perfectly-innocent rationale won her over. She gave me the number, and I visited a few minutes more before I left.

IT WAS JUST AFTER TEN FORTY. I REALLY WANTED to talk to Ernie before I went back to the emporium, so I pulled over and called his cell.

"How'd you get my number?" he barked.

"Doralee gave it to me. You're the one who came to me ranting about being a suspect, and wanting my help. I've seen Georgine, but I haven't seen you since you barged into our shop."

"Between being called in for questioning over and over, and taking care of my sister and business concerns, I've been busy."

"Taking care of Georgine? Is she ill?"

"She's having more migraines, especially the last few days. It's the stress of being away from home."

"Not to mention in the middle of a murder investigation," I drawled.

"What do you want, Ms. Nix?"

"To ask you a few questions. Face to face. Preferably in the next hour."

Silence on the line except for an odd thumping in the background. "I'm at the laundromat if you want to come here."

"You're washing clothes?" I blurted.

"I'm not useless, Ms. Nix."

"That's not what I meant, Mr. Boudreaux. I'll be there in a few minutes."

IT WAS TRUE THAT I HADN'T THOUGHT OF ERNIE AS useless. I wouldn't have used that word. Seeing him fold clothes, though, was plain odd. He looked entirely too domestic. Like a square peg temporarily crammed into a round hole.

The place was empty but for us, and I decided to get right to the point.

"I talked to Doralee a bit ago. She told me she offered to sell you the opal."

He stopped folding and held my gaze. "I refuse to play a game of she-said, he-said."

"That's not my intent and this isn't a game. Doralee said she'd sell you the opal. Kim was driving you crazy about getting it, but you refused Doralee. Why, Ernie?"

Defiance drained from him, and his eyes held sadness. "I turned down the opal because Kim needed to know I wouldn't give her every little thing she wanted."

"And there it is."

"Excuse me?"

"Doralee held that back to protect you. She feared Detective Shoar would hear that as a threat."

He snorted. "It was no threat. It was a simple statement of fact."

"I agree."

"You do?" I nodded, and he looked out the wall of plate glass window. "Does that mean you will or won't be sharing this with the detective?"

"Unless it needs to come out, I won't."

"Fair enough."

* * *

HERE'S A FUN FACT FOR FUTURE REFERENCE. THE pages of a flip chart don't flip if the chart is hanging on a wall. Duh!

I learned this in short order because the Silver Six insisted that we skip a few pages before starting our official murder board. Turn the blank pages back over to cover our work, and voilà! Our notes and charts would remain our secret if anyone wandered into the workroom.

I would've bought an easel, but Sherry talked Carter Gaskin at the business center into loaning her one. With Jasmine minding the store, I placed the easel at the end of a workbench, set the flip chart on the easel, and we gathered around it. Except for Fred, who continued working, this time on an old electric can opener.

"So where do we start, child? With motive, means, or opportunity?"

"Means," I answered Sherry. "Since our favorite detective questioned Doralee about an awl, we can presume that was the murder weapon." I saw the protests forming and held up my hand. "Whether the awl in question belonged to Doralee, or someone else."

Heads nodded.

"Okay, I think Kim was stabbed in the stomach."

"Why?" Dab asked.

"Um, because of what I witnessed at the crime scene."

"Was there spatter?" Maise asked, her tone matter of fact as I'd expect of a former nurse.

"Not that I saw."

"If the killer didn't pull the weapon out right away, the wound would seep, not gush."

"Maise," Fred barked, "could you be less graphic? You're like to ruin my appetite for the whole dang day."

She rolled her eyes. "I'm just stating medical facts for the case."

"And we confirmed the scenario with Doc Thorson," Sherry said. "You remember my family doctor, don't you, Nixy? He came by the see the emporium this morning."

I did remember the darling man who was older than Sherry, still spry and sharp, and practicing medicine. "Didn't he think it was weird for you to ask about stabbing someone?"

"Oh, no. He's known me for donkey's years."

"Back to the subject," Maise said. "Remember that once the heart stops beating, blood stops pumping. And while the killer might not have pulled out the weapon, Kim could have done it if she was conscious."

"Maise, dear, I do believe Fred is turning a bit green. Perhaps we could move on."

"You're right, Eleanor," Aster said. "Let's consider motive."

"We've already eliminated Doralee and Zach," Sherry said.

I glanced at each team member. "Do you all agree to keep those two off the list?"

They looked at each other, exchanged nods.

"Okay, moving on. Ernie was getting fed up with Kim's harping about the opal. Georgine didn't like her, and didn't want Ernie to marry her. So sibling jealousy as a motive?"

"And to heed Fred's follow-the-money advice," Maise put in, "Georgine is Ernie's only relative. She's the logical choice to inherit everything if he never remarries."

"Good thinking," Aster said, beaming at her sister.

Eleanor cleared her throat. "I do believe Kim's former sister-in-law hated her."

"Margot Vail, yes, and Margot wants that heirloom solitaire ring back."

"Not to mention the family mansion and them shares in the casino," Fred chimed in.

"The money aspects give her a strong motive for sure. She could hire someone to steal the ring or force Kim to turn it over. Maybe she would even order a full-on hit, but she wouldn't do the deed herself."

"She could get D.B.'s son to do the dirty work," Sherry said.

"I don't know about that," Maise mused aloud. "From seeing the posts on his Facebook page, Dennis Thomason comes off as too self-absorbed to do much of anything for anyone else. I'm still surprised he bestirred himself to propose to a woman. I've never seen so many selfies."

Aster snorted. "From seeing him in the surveillance video, he does seem to have less personality than the snails in my garden, and I wouldn't trust him to buy bread at the market, much less kill someone."

"Nice image," Dab said with a grin. "So who's left to suspect?"

"Kim's brother. If he's been in town all along, he could've done it."

"His reason?"

"Maybe he's in Kim's will, and killed her for the money."

Fred grunted. "S'what I'm sayin'."

"Are there any other possible killers other than person or persons unknown?"

"What cop shows have you been watching, Maise?" Sherry asked.

"The same ones you've watched."

I glanced at the workroom clock. "Y'all, we have twenty more minutes until Lexie gets here to teach her class. You want to talk about our suspects' opportunity? I've narrowed the time frame to between three thirty when Ernie says he dropped Kim at the alley door and maybe five fifteen. We found her at five thirty, give or take a few minutes."

"That's a narrow window," Dab said. "Who had access to the inn during that time?"

"The five people staying there. Ernie, Kim, Georgine, Doralee, and Zach."

"And remember the truck and the Audi that came tearing out of the parking lot as Doralee and I got to the inn. The truck might be Caleb's and I'm sure Margot was driving the

Audi. She sidestepped the accusation, but didn't deny it. That puts three more people in the immediate area near Kim's time of death."

"Georgine was in her room knocked out on migraine meds," Maise said. "To be thorough, we have to include her as having access."

"True, but Ernie has the most nonexistent alibi," Aster pointed out. "He parked and locked his car, then wandered around Lilyvale for over an hour? Please."

"What if," Sherry mused, "Ernie is the one who hired a killer. If Kim was already nagging him about that stone, he could have hired a hit before he and Kim ever showed up here."

"I don't see it," Dab said. "A hired gun would use, well, a gun. A pistol, a rifle. A weapon that would kill from a distance."

"Agreed, and I do believe there's one matter that throws a different light on this," Eleanor declared. "Doralee's smock was found out in the country. The killer had to take it there, which means the killer needed transportation."

"You're absolutely right, Eleanor. Have y'all heard any scoop about who found the smock?"

"Lorna said it was in the Greens' garbage. They live, oh, about five miles out of town."

"Out of town proper, or from the square?"

"Reckon it's from the square," Fred piped up. "I went to Herb's place a while back to fix his tractor."

"Wait a moment," Dab protested. "The killer didn't have to drive away from the scene of the crime. He could've been on foot."

"Yes, but an average person walks a mile in fifteen to twenty minutes," Maise said. "Even with the smock hidden in a sack or such, you'd have to be awfully bold to hike that far into the county to dispose of evidence."

"Talk about being caught holding the bag," Sherry quipped. Moans greeted that pun, and we broke up to greet Lexie and those patrons who'd be attending her jewelry-craft program.

But brainstorming with the Silver Six drove home to me how critical time had been. If Ernie didn't kill Kim, and hadn't chosen to avoid her that afternoon, he might've found her much sooner. That would've narrowed the window of opportunity even more. Of course, his presence at the right time could've saved Kim, too.

Whether he had squat to do with her death or not, he did seem to feel remorse now. Or he was a darned good actor.

LEXIE GIBSON HAD ONE OF THE MOST INFECTIOUS laughs I'd ever heard, and she proved to be another excellent choice in artists for our grand opening. She'd come so pre-pared that she quickly crafted a half-dozen pairs of earrings from beads of pearl and semiprecious gems. At the end of her hour-plus program, she held on-the-spot giveaways for three pairs, and donated the other two to the emporium for our big end-of-the-week drawings.

And yikes, the end of the week was Friday. Tomorrow. Less than twenty-four hours from now. We planned to stay open until seven to host a thank-you reception for everyone who supported us during our grand opening week, and we expected the party to spill out onto the sidewalk. Attendees at the vari-ous programs had left their names and phone numbers on slips of paper. We'd been stashing those in a large hatbox Aster had bought at a craft store in Texarkana. No one had to be present to win, but most had said they wouldn't miss it.

Which reminded me I needed to call Melissa about the tray she was donating. The tray she'd painted during her demonstration. A trip to the grocery store for reception sup-plies was in order, too, unless Maise had already rallied the troops. Which she very likely had done.

Still, keeping up with these tasks was part of my job as

the manager. And again, I'd been doing far more investigating than investing time in the store. That had to change.

I DIDN'T HAVE TO CALL MELISSA BECAUSE SHE waltzed into the emporium shortly after Lexie had departed. We all exclaimed over the tray, and then firmed up plans for next week's painting class.

I didn't need to make a supply run either. Sherry and the ladies had indeed already taken care of it, but the goods were still in the trunk of Sherry's car.

"Who's got the Corolla keys?" I asked.

Sherry was the first to find hers, but held them out of reach. "Don't give me that disapproving look, child. I can still drive, you know. Especially in the daylight."

I put up both hands. "I didn't say one word."

"You made a face."

"It's my regular face, Aunt Sherry. Really. Drive all you like. After all, I'm not paying your insurance."

Aster giggled, and Sherry tossed me the set of keys. "Go on with you."

I unloaded everything from the trunk in short order. What I could stash in the kitchenette, I did. The rest—mostly paper products like napkins and paper plates—I stored in the workroom.

Jasmine left as I finished hauling supplies. Dab, who had a full, thick head of hair, had gone to Bog's Barber Shop across the square for a trim. Sherry and the ladies busily tweaked the displays, replacing stock as needed. Since Sherry's baskets, Eleanor's carvings, and Aster's line of aromatherapy lotions and potions had sold briskly during the week, there was a good bit of replenishing to do.

Fred had taken T.C. and Amber out and wasn't back yet. I found myself in the workroom alone, staring at our notes on the flip chart. Half-formed thoughts and fuzzy images flitted through my brain. I knew I was missing pieces of the puzzle, but what were they?

The awl was a weapon to wield up close. Was the killing premeditated or a spur-of-the-moment act? Perhaps a striking out in rage or fear or jealousy?

I remembered hearing that murders were committed for a handful of reasons. Passion was one. Kim had been hell-bent on having Doralee's opal. Margot was equally determined to get the family diamond ring back. Dennis? I had to agree with Aster about him. He hadn't demonstrated a nanosecond of emotion, and even assassins and serial killers smiled now and then.

Shifting suspects, Georgine didn't hide her dislike of Kim, but then no woman on earth would be good enough for her brother. And Ernie? The man was long on ego, and he never for a second behaved like a man in love. He'd been a man annoyed with his demanding fiancée. In a moment frustration and anger, could he have stabbed her?

I liked the possibility of Kim's brother being the killer. I easily pictured a scenario wherein he needed money, he asked her for a loan, and she said get lost. He still hadn't arrived in town. I'd know if he had because Lorna would've told the Silver Six about her new guest.

On the other hand, if Caleb and Rusty were the same man, then he'd demonstrated kindness to animals by telling his friend about Amber and T.C. so the news would get to Ruth. And Ruth had mentioned his kindness to her and to her deceased friend, Doris. Did a man like that kill his own sister for money?

And what about the disposing of the smock? Did the killer drive out of town and cram it in the first convenient place he found? Did he know the highways and byways around Lilyvale, and deliberately stuff the garment in the Greens' garbage can? Heck, I didn't know if the Greens lived on the highway or off it.

"Off it," Fred said behind me.

I jumped a foot and spun around in midair. An amazingly catlike move. T.C. looked downright impressed. Amber looked confused.

"I didn't hear you come in, Fred."

"I could tell. You were mutterin' to yourself about the Greens' property."

"And it's off the highway?"

"'Long 'bout a quarter of a mile back from the main road and around a bend. Hidden by trees."

"Got it."

"Why you want to know where Herb and Sarah live?"

"I was wondering if the murderer had dumped the smock in the first out-of-the-way place, or knew where to go."

"Or just drove a spell and stumbled on a house that looked like nobody was there. Storm was a'blowin' in that day. The Greens don't leave on lights when they ain't home. Waste of electricity."

I blinked. "Do the Greens have close neighbors? Are there nearby houses?"

"Ain't a one. Mark me, wouldn't take more'n about twenty, thirty minutes to get to the Greens, dump that smock, and get back to town. That is, if the killer was comin' back a'tall. Coulda been leaving town."

"Leaving town? Fred, you're kind of brilliant."

"A'course I am. Now skedaddle. I got me another toaster to fix."

Chapter Sixteen

I'D HAD A PRODUCTIVE DAY. I'D EXTRACTED THE final details of what happened between Doralee and Ernie regarding the opal. I'd brainstormed the murder with the Silver Six. I'd finalized plans for Melissa's painting class next week, and completed a few store duties. However, I still hadn't heard from Eric, and the waiting, to borrow a Judy-ism, was about to wear me thin.

Time to track him down.

I told Sherry where I was headed, promising to be back before five. After last night's video review, the Six had been up late. I wanted them to get home early for an evening of rest and relaxation.

T.C. and Amber looked up as I crossed the workroom on my way out, so I stopped to give their ears a scratch. They really were sweethearts.

"I'll spend more time with you soon," I said. "We'll go to the dog park when it officially opens, okay?"

Amber woofed, and T.C. chirped. I smiled and headed out the back to power walk to the police station.

Officer Benton was on front desk duty when I went in, and shook his head before I could ask for Eric.

"Detective Shoar is on a call," he said. "I'm not sure how long he'll be."

"Is it related to the murder?"

"I can't comment, ma'am, but I'll tell him you came by."

Uh-oh. Being called "ma'am" before I had my thirtieth birthday? I needed to give Aster's special skin cream a try.

I thanked Officer Benton, and stepped into the afternoon sunshine. Go back to the emporium, or go by the Lilies Café? Lorna wasn't usually open for dinner, but she might be there waiting on Caleb Collier to show up.

I wondered how she'd solved the dilemma of which room to give him.

Lorna was still at the café, but outside digging in the concrete planter near the front door. She'd pull a weed or three, and drop them in a plastic bucket. I started to ask why, then remembered. Each store owner took turns weeding and generally tidying the planters. My turn was coming up in July. Hmm. I'd shoved that to the back of my mind.

She waved the forked weeding tool she held when she saw me. I'd have to ask Aster if she had extra garden diggers I could borrow.

"That woman's brother hasn't come yet," Lorna said when I'd barely said hello. "Eric's called twice to check. I don't know why he's so all fired to see this guy."

She paused and shot me an inquiring glance. "Unless the autopsy's done, and the body's ready to be claimed up in Little Rock."

I shook my head. "Sorry, I haven't heard anything about that. I was wondering: how did you decide on which room to give your new guest?"

She stabbed at another weed. "I talked Mr. Boudreaux into taking the suite where his fiancée died once we got everything cleaned up, and moved the sister to his."

"I'm surprised he went for that."

She shrugged. "He didn't turn cartwheels, but the arrangement gives the both of them private baths. The sister needs it. She's been flat on her back for two days."

I suspected I knew, but asked anyway. "What's wrong with her?"

"Mr. Boudreaux says it's the migraine medications. He's been paying extra for me to take food trays up to her, but she barely makes a dent in them."

"She's that ill?" I asked. "Have you seen her?"

"She looks worse every day, and acts loopy. She buttons her PJs all the way to her neck, which looks horribly uncomfortable, especially being sick. I tell you, I just hope I never have those kinds of headaches."

"Where are you putting Caleb Collier when he comes?"

"He'll have the room nearest the shared bath. No one has stayed there in several weeks."

"I hope he doesn't postpone on you again."

"So do I. I'm determined to wait for him to arrive."

"Why? You usually have guests let themselves in with their codes."

She dropped the gardening tool in the plastic bucket, and the weeds inside it muffled the *thunk*. "Let's just say I'm curious why a man wouldn't come running when his sister is murdered. Something is just not right about that."

I wholeheartedly agreed.

ERIC HADN'T CALLED BY THE TIME THE SILVER SIX went home for the night. T.C. and Amber raced me up to my apartment (T.C won easily) where I fed them their kibble, and then fixed myself a stir-fry dinner. I even sat at the counter to relax while I ate. Taking my time, practicing patience.

No call. *Grrr.*

I washed, dried, and put away my pan, stirring spoon, bowl, fork, and glass by hand. I didn't rush.

Still no call. *Argh!*

Okay, time for me to call him. My mother had always said girls shouldn't call boys. Let the guys come to you, Mom had advised. But this wasn't about a date. This was about a murder, and I'd asked questions Eric had promised to answer.

He didn't answer his cell. Shoot. What kind of crime wave in little Lilyvale could possibly be monopolizing his time? With all the people the Silver Six knew, someone would've spread the word if there had been another murder. Or serious accident. Or huge brawl. Or any other situation that would keep my detective out of touch.

Was he ducking my calls? Could be. If Caleb hadn't made it to town, Eric wouldn't have any more information on that score. However, I still wanted to know how many rings were in Kim's personal effects, and who benefitted from her death. Scanning the inventory list shouldn't have taken Eric five minutes, but lawyers could be incredibly slow. An attorney in a different state, and one representing several interests? News from that quarter could be delayed a good while longer.

I hadn't bought a television yet, so to keep myself busily distracted, I tackled mundane chores. Having a washing machine in the bathroom was more a European than an American home thing, but I loved my stackable unit right where it was. Easy to toss my clothes right into the washer tub when I undressed, and it would be wonderful to wrap myself in warm towels straight from the dryer come the winter.

Yes, Fred would call towel warming a waste of electricity. Fluffing clothes I'd forgotten to take out of the dryer fell into the same wasteful category, but I did it anyway. My bills were so low, I barely supported my local energy company. Correction, Sissy's trust barely supported the company since the trust paid the utilities. I'd take over those and pay Sherry rent one of these days. If I could ever get her to agree.

While the dryer ran, I gave the bathroom a quick once-over. Just in case a certain detective happened to come by with news about the case. Even with Amber on my heels with a what-are-you-doing tilt of her head and T.C. batting a wadded paper towel I'd dropped on the floor, the bath spiff-up took all of fifteen minutes. Next task, cleaning up for a certain feline.

I snagged the plastic bag I used as a trash can liner and went to scoop the litter box. Amber had jumped to the couch and parked herself on the armrest, as perfectly balanced as a cat. T.C. sat patiently waiting for me to finish with her box, then promptly sniffed, scratched, and used the facilities.

I considered emptying one of the moving boxes still in the dining room area, but quickly rejected that idea. I'd already unpacked the essentials. What was left were items to consider letting go of. Right now I had too much on my mind to make those decisions.

Geez, I really needed to get a TV to watch at times like these.

Hands on my hips, I looked down at the critters. "Reruns would be better than twiddling my thumbs, right, girls?"

Amber barked, leaped off the couch, and ran to the basket by the door, where I'd begun dropping her leash. She nosed around, fished it out, and sat, first eyeing the door, then me.

"That's a new trick. Did Fred and Dab teach you that?"

She sniffed and shook her head so hard her ears flopped.

"You taught yourself, huh? All right, I'm in. Let's go, girls."

WE SAW MY TEEN FRIEND LOUIE WITH HARLEY, HIS beagle, a few blocks from the emporium.

"Hey, Ms. Nix, I heard you got to take Amber and T.C. to the dog park. It's not open yet, is it? It's not supposed to be open until July."

"Early in the month, yes, but how'd you know I was there?"

"I got accepted into some summer classes at the tech

school, and my welding teacher is Mr. Hawthorne. We've all been helping with things like installing the chain-link fences, and he mentioned a cat that went everywhere with her dog friend." He paused and scratched the side of his neck. "Not many of those around."

"Probably not. You've all done an amazing job with the park. You'll be taking Harley over, won't you?"

He nodded, rubbed his neck again. "Harley may spend more time sniffing for squirrels than playing on the equipment, but he'll love the freedom to run."

"Maybe Harley and Amber can play there together," I said, then got distracted by the teen's continued scraping at his skin. "Louie, do you have allergies?"

He gave me a puzzled look.

"You're scratching your neck."

"Sorry, my mom's using a new detergent, I guess. I usually wear T-shirts, but she made me put this one on to help her at church after we had dinner." He heaved a put-upon sigh. "I know I'll have to get used to wearing these when I'm a man, but I really don't like collared shirts."

I stared at Louie, but I suddenly wasn't seeing him. I was remembering Ruth Kreider tell me Rusty's last name reminded her of a man's shirt.

Men's shirts. Collar. Collier.

Was it a stretch from "collar" to Collier? I didn't think so. Sure, Ruth forgot Caleb's last name anyway, but she said her memory wasn't sharp for some things. Names could become notoriously challenging to remember as people aged. I'd read that in a magazine in Sherry's eye doctor's office.

Now I *really* wanted to talk to Eric.

I said good-bye to Louie just as Amber began madly barking and pulling on the leash. What the heck?

A dark truck rolled down the street toward us. A dark blue truck fitted with monstrous tires. The elusive Rusty Caleb Collier. I had to do something!

Acting on pure instinct, I quickly looped both of the leashes around the leg of a bench and flew from the sidewalk into the street waving my arms. The driver's brakes screeched, and the truck rocked to a stop.

In the next moment, T.C. wriggled out of her harness and leaped to the hood of the truck, and Amber began baying like she'd treed a raccoon, tugging on her leash.

The driver cursed a blue streak as he jumped down from the cab.

"What the hell, lady? Why did you run out in front of me? You could be dead right now."

At easily six feet, with a chiseled chest visible under his white tee, and muscled arms, the guy who stormed at me wasn't wrestler-brawny, but he could snap me in half if he wanted. With adrenaline flooding my body, I wasn't backing down.

"Lady, did you hear me? I could've killed you."

I held my ground and raised my chin at the red-haired man. "Like you could've killed your sister?"

His mouth hung open. "What?"

"Caleb Rusty Collier," I said, channeling Eleanor, "I do believe the dog you knew as Blackie is trying to get your attention."

SOME OF CALEB'S HOSTILITY SUBSIDED WITH A last muttered cuss word. I untied Amber and brought her over to the truck. Caleb bent to greet her, then turned to pet T.C., who still stood on the hood of his truck. Both critters lapped up his attention, and that seemed to calm him more. Whew! Having an angry murder suspect yelling in my face wasn't my idea of a good time.

Within minutes, middle-aged Officer Doug Bryant parked his patrol car behind Caleb's truck, blocking him in from that direction. Officer Bryant had responded because

Louie had called 911. After I explained why I'd flagged down the truck in the first place, Officer Bryant called Detective Shoar. The look Bryant gave me said, "You're in trouble now."

I didn't care. Yes, the brakes could've failed and I'd be road kill at this moment. Or the driver might've run me down on purpose. I'd taken a risk. I got that. But sometimes you have to listen to your gut.

When Eric pulled up, I went on the offensive.

"Detective Shoar," I said, clamping a hand on his arm, "meet Rusty Collier. Mr. Collier, this is Detective Eric Shoar of the Lilyvale Police Department. He's handling your sister's murder case."

Caleb shot me an irritated look. "I know who he is. I've talked to him on the phone."

Eric scanned the sidewalks where citizens had come outside to see what was happening. "Let's go have this chat at the station."

"Am I under arrest?" Caleb asked.

"As of now, no."

"Have you been to the Inn on the Square yet?" I asked.

Eric gave me an inquiring glance, and I shrugged. "Lorna was planning to wait for him at the café."

"I'll give her a call." He turned to Caleb. "I'm going to let you to drive on over to the station. You know where it is?"

Caleb nodded.

"Officer Bryant," he said, nodding to the man at Caleb's side, "will follow you. I'll be along shortly."

When Caleb was far enough away, I looked up at Eric. "I'd prefer it if you didn't rip into me in front of all these people. The Six Silver probably know about this adventure by now. I'd rather not compound the gossip."

"Agreed. Why don't you take T.C. and Amber home and join me at the station?"

I held his bland gaze. "What for?"

"I thought you might want to observe the interview."

I blinked. "You did? I mean, yes, I do. But why are you inviting me? What about compromising the case?"

"You're my witness. You're the one who first mentioned Rusty to me and connected Rusty to Caleb Collier. Besides, you caught the guy. You should hear what he has to say firsthand."

He didn't have to ask me twice.

OKAY, HE DIDN'T LET ME CHARGE INTO THE INNER sanctum bold as brass, much less into the interview room.

Since the emergency phone lines were manned by the sheriff's office, no one sat at the reception desk at night. I cooled my heels in the front foyer alone. I hope it stayed that way.

I'd taken the critters to my apartment, and was relieved they didn't seem to mind being left alone. At least Amber didn't whine, and neither of them scratched at the door when I closed it behind me. As I hit the back door to go to my car, I called Sherry. She had heard I'd been involved in some "hubbub." I told her it was nothing, but that I would be hanging out with Eric for a while. From the lilt in her voice, she assumed I meant we were having an impromptu date, and I didn't correct her. If a little white lie kept Sherry and crew at home tonight, it was worth the penance I'd have to do later.

At last Eric came for me.

"Officer Bryant is back on patrol for the rest of the night shift, but that could change if he makes an arrest. Just be quiet and wait for me."

I nodded, and slipped into a space the size of my apartment's small walk-in closet. Being short, I decided sitting in the single chair would cut my view of the interview room. I elected to stand, and watched through the one-way glass, where I had a side view of Caleb. In the bright fluorescent lights, and with his New Orleans Saints ball cap off, he looked haggard. From being on the run, or was he distressed that his sister was dead?

Eric entered the interview room, sat across the metal table, and placed a tape recorder and a manila folder on its smooth surface.

Recorder running, Eric stated the date, time, and the names of those present in the room.

"Do you understand this is an interview, Mr. Collier?" Eric was every inch Detective Shoar at the moment, but not coming on strong. Put Suspect at Ease 101. "You are not under arrest."

"I understand, Detective." He touched the cap on the table.

"I know you've been in Lilyvale since Friday. Did you arrive that day or earlier?"

"Just to be clear, I haven't been in the area all the time. I told you I maintain pumpers. I've been working near here, but also in north Texas."

Eric opened the folder, clicked his pen twice, but reminded silent. Oldest cop trick in the books, and Caleb caved.

"Friday morning." His shoulders slumped and his hands stilled. "I was in town Friday morning about nine. Kim called me out of the blue Thursday night and asked me to help her steal something."

I gasped, and instinctively backed from the window, hoping Eric hadn't heard me. But wow. Kim had been more obsessed than I'd imagined if she wanted to involve her brother in theft.

"She told me her fiancé—is it Ernie?" Eric nodded, and Caleb continued, "Kim said Ernie's ex-wife had something of his and wouldn't give it back. Kim wanted to give it to him as a wedding present."

"Did you know she was engaged?"

Caleb snorted. "Except for an e-mail at Christmas every

year or two, I hadn't heard from her since she married her last husband. I seldom heard from her before that."

Eric nodded. "We understood from Ernie Boudreaux that you and your sister weren't close."

"We were closer as kids, but grew apart pretty fast after our parents died in a car accident. Our mother's sister took us in, but she was all about Kim's ambition to win beauty pageants. She couldn't've cared less about me, and neither did Kim." He paused, scowled. "Unless she wanted something from me."

"Then why ask you to help her now?" Eric asked sharply.

"I guess because I'd been in trouble as a juvenile," Caleb blurted out. "I boosted cars, burglarized some houses, lifted jewelry from some sorority girls at a couple of casinos."

Well, well. He sure wasn't holding back. My opinion of him rose, and I stepped closer to the window.

"Is that where you were caught?" Eric probed. "At a casino?"

"I was caught in a house where no one was supposed to be home. I thought I was helping Kim pull a prank on a friend of hers."

"And you took the fall."

He jerked a nod. "Home invasion. I got a light sentence, did my time, and then a friend's parents let me stay with them when I got out."

Eric glanced at the open folder. "Would these be your friend Ray's parents?"

He inclined his head. "Did you meet his grandmother?"

"No. Ms. Nix did."

Caleb's eyes bugged. "Is that the crazy woman who ran out in front of my truck? The one I nearly hit?"

"That's her."

Were Eric's shoulders shaking with silent laughter? They'd better not be.

"Mr. Collier, have you been in legal trouble as an adult?"

He sat board stiff. "If you ran a background on me, you

know I haven't. I straightened myself out, got my education, and got a good job."

"When your sister called, did she mention Ernie Boudreaux? Any trouble between them?"

"I told you when you notified me Kim—" His breath hitched, and he swallowed hard. "Kim had died that she complained they'd been arguing."

"Did she seem to fear for her life?"

A look of cunning flitted across Caleb's expression, like he'd just been handed an out. But then he shook his head.

"She sounded ticked off, not scared, but I didn't trust her calling me like she did." His gaze drifted over Eric's shoulder. "I haven't trusted her since I was a kid."

My detective made a note. "Then why did you come at all?"

He shook his head, not in denial, but as if hindsight had caught up with him. "I had work up this way, and I was curious about what Kim was up to. I kind of hoped I could talk her out of whatever scheme she was cookin' up."

"When you got here Friday morning, what did you do? Call your sister?"

Caleb sighed. "This may sound creepy, but first I found the bed-and-breakfast where she told me she was staying. I wanted to observe her, just to see what she was up to. I figured she'd go shopping sooner or later, so I hung out in the square—mostly in the gazebo— and watched for her."

The courthouse gazebo. Caleb had watched his sister, and Ernie had watched the storm from the same place. Fitting, I supposed.

"She hasn't changed much, in habits or looks, so she was easy to spot. She went to four or five stores, maybe more, then went to that café. An hour or more later, I saw her again. She was with Ernie and that other woman, and they went into the gift store. I waited awhile, then went in myself."

"Weren't you concerned Ms. Thomason would recognize you?"

Caleb shrugged. "If she did, she did, but she hasn't seen me in ten years. I kept this cap on to cover my hair, and wore sunglasses. I stayed for the art thing, but Kim never noticed me."

Gift shop and art thing? Nice to have another perspective, but really?

"When did Ms. Thomason know you were in town? Did you call her?"

"Yeah, after she left the gift shop. I asked her to meet me, but she said she couldn't. She told me she'd call when she saw the opportunity to get Ernie's property back. I started to warn her I wouldn't drop work to come running, but she'd already disconnected."

"Mr. Collier, if you haven't had contact with your sister in years, how is it she had your phone number?"

He smiled, but not with a lick of humor. "Actually, it shocked me she still had it, but I've had the same number since I first got a cell phone."

Eric looked doubtful, but went on. "Let's talk about Saturday and Sunday. Did you see Ms. Thomason either of those days?"

"Saturday afternoon I followed her and Ernie to the gift shop again. I texted her afterward, but she didn't answer. Then she called me Sunday afternoon. I was driving back from checking on a pumper, and happened to be at the edge of town."

"What time was that?"

"Three thirty or so."

I nodded to myself. It didn't take much more than fifteen minutes to drive from one end of Lilyvale to the other if you didn't hit a traffic light. The timing worked.

"She told me to come to the back door of the place she was staying," he went on. "She gave me the door code, and said to hurry."

"What happened then?"

I leaned closer to the window so I wouldn't miss a thing.

Caleb rubbed a hand over his short red hair. "I went upstairs to her room. She told me Ernie's ex-wife had an opal that belonged to him. She wanted me to help search the woman's room."

"Was the room open?"

"No, Kim had the key." He crumpled the soft part of his cap. "She started going through a suitcase. She told me how much she appreciated me and that she'd pay me for my help. I wasn't doing anything but standing by the door. She was talking to me, but she never once looked at me. She was more interested in that opal than her brother, I guess."

He looked painfully bewildered by that memory.

"She didn't find the stone?"

He shook his head. "That made her more agitated. She dumped jars of stuff down the sink, threw clothes around. Kim was single-minded, but I'd never seen her like that. I told her I was out of there."

"You left right away?"

"I didn't look back. She was alive and still tossing the room and cussing last time I saw her."

"What time was that?"

"Four o'clock or so."

"What did you do then, Mr. Collier?"

He fingered his cap. "I went on to Oklahoma for my job."

Liar. I thought surely Eric would call him on it, but he didn't. He made another note.

"All right, just a few more questions. Did you happen to notice any vehicles in particular when you arrived to see your sister?"

"There may have been a red truck parked at the curb. I didn't pay that much attention."

"And when you left the inn?"

"There was definitely a sedan. Late-model Honda, I think. Odd color of blue."

Aha! Ernie's car was a Honda Accord. I hadn't paid attention to it being a two- or four-door, but I remember thinking it looked bluish-purple.

"Did you see anyone else around?"

"An older gentleman walking a German shepherd."

Hmm. I hadn't met a dog or owner of that description, but Caleb's answer was specific enough to be true.

"There's one more point to clarify, Mr. Collier. You said you left for Oklahoma immediately. You didn't. Your truck was seen leaving the alley behind the inn close to five twenty."

Chapter Seventeen

WHAM! NAILED. I HADN'T SEEN THAT COMING, AND neither had Caleb from his reaction. He jerked and slapped his Saints cap on the table. For a long moment I thought he'd ask for an attorney. Instead, his shoulders sagged, and for the first time he looked haunted.

"You went back to see your sister, didn't you?"

"Yes," he admitted raggedly, "but not to kill her. I didn't even go inside. I called her cell, but she didn't answer. There was an Audi in the parking lot, and I thought maybe her fiancé had come back. I got out of there as fast as I could and drove until I got to Antlers."

"Antlers, Oklahoma."

"I stayed overnight in a little motel. The receipt is in my glove box."

Now Eric gave the suspect his laser cop-stare. "If you're lying again, I'll arrest you."

"But I didn't kill her!"

"Maybe you did, maybe you didn't, but by lying you're impeding a murder investigation."

"I'm not lying. I hardly knew Kim anymore, and I didn't trust her, but she was still my sister." He paused, then said softly, "My sister, Detective. That means something to me."

He dashed the back of his hand over his eyes, and I felt the surge of his grief. I also noticed he said "means" instead of "meant." He wasn't used to the idea of her being dead.

Eric tapped the open folder with his pen. "Here's what we're going to do, Mr. Collier. The Inn on the Square is a few blocks from here. I'm going to let you get your overnight gear from your truck. I want that receipt, too, and your keys. I won't impound the truck, but it stays here until I get more answers."

"You need a warrant to search my truck."

Eric arched a brow. "Something you're hiding? Clothes spattered with your sister's blood?"

Caleb blanched. "I'm not hiding anything, but I keep a pistol in the truck. I have a permit."

"Why are you carrying a weapon?"

"Rattlesnakes."

"They hang around oil well pumps?"

"When I do the maintenance, sometimes I can get close to the pump driving the truck. Other times I have to park and walk through high grass."

Eric gave him the silent stare again.

He threw up his hands. "All right fine, never mind the warrant. I'll give you permission to search the damn truck."

"Thank you. I'll walk you to the inn now, and show you to your room."

"I can settle in myself," Caleb said mulishly.

"Ernie Boudreaux and his sister are staying at the inn. I want to head off any problems, but if that doesn't suit you, I can put you in a holding cell at the Hendrix County Sheriff's Office. Your choice."

Caleb picked up his Saints ball cap and crammed it on his head. "Fine."

Kim's brother left the interview room looking defeated,

but I didn't think he'd killed her. In spite of his former thieving ways, his story had a ring of truth.

How interesting that he'd seen the Audi in the parking lot when he'd come back to the inn. Maybe Margot *had* killed Kim. Maybe that's why she'd driven out of the parking lot like a woman possessed.

I'D BEEN INSTRUCTED TO STAY PUT, AND I COMplied, but I plopped into the chair to wait. I pulled out my cell, but left the volume off just in case some of Lilyvale's finest came back before Eric did. To combat the sleepiness brought on by let-down and being in the dark room, I played solitaire on my phone. That helped my drooping eyelids until the door cracked open and my tardy detective stuck his head in.

"Hey, sorry that took so long. Ready to go?"

We exited through the back door, where a picnic table and benches sat in the glow of the security light. I hadn't noticed them when I talked to Eric back here days ago.

"You look exhausted, so I'm not going to read you the riot act about jumping in front of a moving vehicle."

"Thanks," I said dryly.

"What I am doing is driving you home and seeing you upstairs."

"I'm fine," I protested as he grasped my elbow.

"I'm not. When I heard what you'd done tonight, it took years off my life."

"You probably heard an exaggerated version."

"I don't think it was too far off. Keys?" he added, palm open.

I dropped the set that had my apartment and store keys on same ring as my car fob. At ten thirty on a Thursday night, the ride took all of two minutes from door to door, and we didn't speak until I let him in the apartment.

Amber woofed and wagged her whole body as she

bounded to greet us. T.C. wound herself through my legs, then moved on to Eric's.

"Good girls," I praised when I glanced around the space and didn't spot any wreckage. "How about a treat?"

The critters took the nibbles I offered, but were far more interested in attention. Getting it, and giving it. They hopped onto the couch when Eric sat. He patted the cushion beside him.

I sank down slowly, gauging his mood. "I guess you still have to write a report."

"I should go back to the station long enough to make some notes, but I don't think I can type coherent sentences tonight."

"You want something to drink?"

I started to move Amber, but Eric shook his head so I kept her close. Not that I had much in the way of food or drinks in the house, but I felt had to offer. That Southern training. Plus, let's face it, I felt guilty that he had worried about me.

"So what do you think about Caleb's story?" I asked.

"Overall, it's believable. He didn't do himself any favors ducking me for so long, but I think he's genuinely grieving."

"Did he stay away to give himself an alibi?"

Eric snorted. "If he did, it was an epic failure. He doesn't have receipts for the lodging, or food, or gas while he's been in the area. He says he paid in cash for all of that. He only has a receipt for his Sunday night stay over in Antlers."

"Where *did* he stay while he was watching Kim?"

"A chain hotel in Magnolia. I can follow up, see who remembers him. Before tonight, I leaned toward him being the killer. After talking to him, he just doesn't feel right."

"Have you eliminated Margot Vail? Caleb saw the Audi in the parking lot."

"He saw Mr. Boudreaux's car, too. He didn't know it was Ernie's, but he saw it."

"Yes, but he saw the Honda when he left Kim alone and alive. He didn't mention it later."

Eric frowned. "I didn't ask him about that, did I? Damn. That's why I need to go over my notes."

"You can question him about it tomorrow. Heck, you can walk him through what he did and what or who he saw."

"I'd planned to do that anyway."

"Well, you have his truck locked up. He won't be going anywhere tonight."

He scrubbed at his face, then set T.C. aside and rose. "I've got to go."

Amber jumped down and followed Eric. "You'll have more answers tomorrow. You might even hear back from Kim's attorney."

He gave me an odd look.

"You know, about who inherits her estate."

"If it's Caleb, he doesn't act like he knows about it. Oh, by the way, I looked over the inventory. Two diamond rings are listed."

"So if Margot killed Kim, she didn't stick around to search Kim's room for the heirloom." I tilted my head. "Or was that room searched?"

"I'm not commenting."

"Horse hockey."

"Excuse me?"

"You just allowed me to observe your interview. What's the big deal about telling me if Kim and Ernie's room had been searched?"

"Horse hockey, huh?" He gave me a slow, wide grin. "You're sound more and more like the seniors. Is that a Fred phrase?"

I shook my head. "Go home, Detective Shoar."

He opened the door, but stopped and turned. "When this case and your grand opening are over, you and I are having dinner. And not at the Dairy Queen."

I cocked my hip at him. "You're on, big guy."

He ran a finger down my jaw. "Just stay out of trouble, okay?"

I'D ALWAYS BEEN A FAN OF COMFORT FOOD WHEN I needed it. I was fast becoming sold on comfort cuddling. Amber and T.C. sprang into bed with me, but wouldn't settle at the foot of the bed as they had been doing. They burrowed under my summer-weight comforter and snuggled, one on each side, each resting chins and one paw on my stomach.

Okay, I'd have pet hair on my sheets as well as the bed cover. I had a passing thought that I would have to put a stop to them sleeping with me at all, but quickly forgot it as I soaked up their warmth.

I SLEPT LATE THE NEXT MORNING. THE SILVER SIX had not. They were in the workroom when I came down at eight forty to walk the critters, who exploded out the door and down the stairs the second I touched the doorknob. Both animals greeted each senior, but positively danced around Fred and Dab.

"Were we supposed to do something this early?" I asked, and then noticed the murder board open to our last page of notes.

"We want a full report of last night's bust," Maise barked.

"It wasn't a bust. I flagged down the guy Ruth Kreider told us about."

"Rusty, yes," Sherry said.

"And it turned out that he is Kim's brother."

"Caleb Collier, we know," Aster supplied.

"Tell you what, let me walk the pets and I'll fill you in on what I can."

"I do believe we have a better idea," Eleanor said. "We'll go to the café for breakfast."

"But you always have breakfast at home."

"We can't get the latest scoop from Lorna at home."

"Oh. Okay," I agreed, thinking I was off the hook.

"Don't think you're home free, child," Sherry intoned in her stern teacher voice. "If the café isn't filled with diners, we'll grill you right there. Otherwise, we'll get to your story when we get back."

Fred chortled. "Wouldn't wanna be in your shoes, missy. Come on, fur buddies, let's go."

Fred began clomp-clacking his loaded walker to the back door while Dab took the leash from my limp grip, then patted my shoulder. "Later."

The four ladies and I left the men behind, and they all but frog-marched me to the Lilies Café. As soon as I stepped inside, my appetite kicked in and the ambiance took me to another time.

Just like the emporium did. Just like this whole town did.

Then I noticed the silence and the eyes of two dozen people trained on me. Whatever news the grapevine was spreading, apparently these people had heard it.

"There's a table in the back," a harried Lorna said, waving us to a round table by the staircase that ascended to the second-floor inn.

Since the café was packed, I was off the hook for now. We didn't want to be overheard. Plus, if Ernie or Caleb came down to eat while we were here, we couldn't miss seeing them.

Today green cloth napkins with sparkling flatware and green mugs sat on pristine white tablecloths. The single-sheet menus listing breakfast items were wedged between the white sugar packet holder and the salt and pepper shakers.

I was right. The Silver Six had eaten at home. Still they ordered a fruit plate to share. I went for the two-egg cheese omelet because I was going to need the protein fix, and we had coffee all around.

Bushy-beard Clark came out of the kitchen swinging

doors, and snatched a coffee carafe from the warmer. He grunted what I assumed was "Good morning," filled our mugs, then did a refill round at the other tables before striding back to the kitchen.

"Don't say a word about him, child," Sherry advised. "He and Lorna seem to be working things out, and we support her."

I doctored my coffee and sipped as the conversation flowed to the upcoming events of the day. We'd scheduled two presentations, one at eleven, and one at two. The first would feature Colleen Watson, who'd be demonstrating the art of wineglass painting. Fran Givens would do a program on collages with a twist. Then, from four to seven, the big finale to the grand opening with fruit and veggie trays, Ida's pear bread, and of course, cookies and sweet tea. I'd insisted we buy the food trays from the grocery store, and had been happily surprised that the ladies of the Silver Six didn't fight me on the decision.

We did ask Lorna to cater first, but she was swamped with club luncheons.

"I have news," the woman herself said sotto voce as she delivered our meals. "Let me refresh your coffees, and I'll sit with you a minute."

Lorna didn't do gossip. She imparted news.

I'd just put a bite of omelet in my mouth when she pulled up another chair, dropped into her seat, and leaned toward me.

"You need to know," she said in hushed tones so as not to be overheard, "that it's all over town that you stopped a murderer at gun point."

I nearly choked. Sherry handed me a water, and Maise smacked my back hard enough to make my eyes bulge.

"I did no such thing, Lorna," I whispered back. "I don't have a gun, and Caleb Collier isn't a murderer."

"You know that for a fact?"

"Well, no, but he's innocent until proven guilty."

"He certainly must be a person of interest." She paused

to sweep the seniors with her glance. "Detective Shoar escorted him here last night, and came to collect him first thing this morning. Barely gave the man a chance to finish his coffee, never mind his breakfast."

"So he's gone," Aster said. "We were hoping to get a look at him."

"I'm sure you'll have a chance. Unless he's arrested, he'll be back here later."

"Um, Lorna, does Ernie come down for breakfast?"

"He hasn't today. He was with his sister when I took up her tray this morning."

"Did you hear what they said?"

Lorna sniffed. "I don't eavesdrop on my guests."

Sherry patted her friend's hand. "Overhearing isn't the same as eavesdropping."

"And I do believe you have a right to know what's going on in your inn. Especially in light of that woman's death."

Lorna gave a decisive nod. "It isn't like they were scheming. Mr. Boudreaux was all but begging his sister to go to the hospital. He'd asked me about the level of services and care we have here. Well, our facility isn't large, but the doctors can handle a middle-aged woman with a migraine headache."

"I take it Georgine refused?"

"She did, and then he raised his voice to her. He said she was as stubborn as Kim, and he was tired of it."

"That sounds like an oblique threat," Sherry said.

Lorna shrugged. "I'll tell you this. If she gets any weaker, he'll either have to carry her out of here or I'll call the paramedics. As it is, I don't know how the stigma of having a death here will affect business." She paused. "Though I haven't had a single cancellation yet. And the income from their extended stay helps. We have got to come up with events to get more tourists."

"The fall folk art festival will be held in town instead of at the farmhouse," Sherry said.

"That's been approved for sure?"

I opened my mouth, closed it. "Hmm. I don't think we have the official letter yet, but I'll follow up."

"So are you still investigating on Doralee's behalf?"

"I do believe she's in the clear."

"But we're working on the case anyway," Maise said.

"We even created a murder board," Aster boasted.

I groaned. "Ladies, we need to open soon. Lorna, do you have the check?"

"Right here." She pulled it from her apron.

I reached in the back pocket of my jeans for the twenty I'd remembered to stash there this morning. I'd meant to use it for a pastry at Great Buns, but plans changed.

I hoped I could get through the day without being ambushed again.

I'D FILLED THE SILVER SIX IN ON THE HIGHLIGHTS of stopping Caleb, but did not mention the foolhardy flagging down of his truck. I knew they'd piece together the majority of the real story from gossip, and for once that suited me fine.

The wineglass-painting program drew seventeen patrons. I doubted they all drank wine, but we'd mentioned the technique worked on nearly any glassware. Colleen Watson was a woman in her late thirties or early forties, model tall and slim. She wasn't as lively or dramatic as some of our artists. Instead, her voice was calm, her information clear and concise.

She thanked everyone for coming, relayed a bit about her arts and crafts experience, and moved right into instructions for prepping the glass.

"After your glass is squeaky clean, use rubbing alcohol to get off any last oils from your hands, and be sure it dries thoroughly.

"Now then, you can free-hand paint, or you can use a design on paper. Curl the paper, and let it unfurl in the glass, design side out, and there's your template," she said, demonstrating as she talked. "Leave enough space at the bottom of your paper so your design doesn't sit too low in the glass's bowl. Unless that's where you want it."

The audience laughed, and next she emphasized how to wield the paint marker with the warning not to smash the tip of the glass paint markers into the surface.

"You jab, and this is what happens," she said, spearing a marker onto a glass she obviously used to illustrate technique. It was splotched with paint in a rainbow of colors.

"Do you have to paint glass with a marker?" A young mother asked the question. Her sleeping infant nestled against her chest in a sling.

"No, you can use brushes and acrylic paint, but I think markers are easier to control." She flashed a radiant smile. "And I've been doing this awhile. Remember, you can decorate the foot of your glass, too."

As she spoke, she painted, and an adorable lily design in lines and dots emerged. The paint needed to dry for a day, and she usually heat-set her glasses, too, she explained. So instead of donating the one she'd just completed, Colleen gave us a set of four wonderfully different tree-themed wineglasses. Sherry protested she was too generous, but Colleen said she'd bought the glasses at a thrift store. I could see another full class in wineglass painting in our future.

At twelve thirty, we'd finished resetting the chairs for Fran Givens and her collage program. Maise and Aster went home with Dab to take cookies out of the freezer. They'd snag the food trays from the grocery store on the way back and store them in my near-empty fridge.

Shortly after they left on their errands, Ida Bollings came into the store with the aid of her walker.

"I brought the bread early so I can nap before the big doings this afternoon."

"Thank you, Ida," I said even as Fred clomped in from his workroom.

I'd swear he must've been listening for her because he immediately asked her to lunch. He'd removed the tool belt from his own walker, I noticed. He'd even taken some of the tools out of his overall pockets. That was about as dressed up as I'd ever seen Fred.

"I'll drive," she said.

I suppressed a shudder. I'd seen the woman drive. She could qualify for the Indy 500 without much trouble.

"Go get the pear bread, Nixy. There are five loaves in the backseat."

"Goodness," Sherry exclaimed. "That's far too much. You shouldn't have gone to all that trouble."

Ida waved a hand. "Nonsense. If there are leftovers, take them home."

I retrieved the loaves while Ida and Fred wrestled their respective walkers into the cavernous truck of Ida's boat of a blue Buick. Yes, I started to offer my help, but Fred scowled at me before I'd taken two steps toward them.

Doralee and Zach came by just after one. They'd lunched at Lorna's and heard about my single-handed capture.

"Oh, we figured the story was exaggerated," Doralee said with a laugh. "But it's true that Kim's brother has finally made an appearance, right? Does that help your detective's investigation?"

I smiled and gave her the answer I'd mentally rehearsed. "I don't really know, but it can't hurt. Did Lorna mention Georgine to you?"

Doralee gave me a double take. "She didn't say a word. Why?"

"Georgine's apparently suffering from one migraine after another. Lorna's been taking light meals up to her, but says the trays are barely touched."

"Goodness, she was always out of it with one or two doses of her meds. She must be a zombie if she's taking much more, never mind taking it for days on end."

"Lorna did tell me Georgine acted loopy."

"Why on earth doesn't Ernie take her to the hospital?" Doralee fretted.

"I don't believe," Eleanor said, "she wants to go."

"Stubborn woman." Doralee glanced at Zach. "I wonder if I should see her. Maybe she'll listen to me."

Zach shrugged. "From all you've told me about her, she'll shut you out, but it's your call, honey. I'll go over with you if you want."

I tuned out their debate because I spotted Eric striding toward the emporium. Was he coming here, or merely coming this way? A few minutes later I had my answer.

Chapter Eighteen

"HEY, NIXY. LADIES. ZACH. I SAW THE ARTICLE IN THE paper about your big reception this afternoon. Are you ready for it?"

"We're getting there," Sherry said. "I hear Kim's brother finally made it to town."

"He did. Nixy, may I borrow you for a while?"

I glanced at Sherry and Eleanor. "Can you handle things here?"

"Of course we can, and Jasmine will be here soon."

"Detective," Zach said. "Do you know when Doralee and I will be free to leave? We both have commitments next week."

"I appreciate your continued cooperation, Mr. Dalton. You should be able to leave by Sunday morning."

Doralee released her breath in a rush, and Zach nodded his thanks even as he hugged her to his side. Sherry and Eleanor beamed.

"YOU WANT ME TO WHAT?"

I trotted beside Eric because he was a man focused and

forgot to slow his pace for my shorter stride. We'd crossed the street to the sidewalk that ran around the courthouse before he answered.

"I want you to reenact Sunday evening when you brought Doralee to the inn. I don't need you to drive though the sequence, just walk part of it with me."

"But why do you—oh, I get it. This is to compare my account with Caleb's."

"And Mr. Boudreaux's."

"You talked to Ernie again?"

"I did."

"His sister has been laid out flat with migraines for several days."

"He mentioned that when I insisted he come with me this morning."

We'd reached the opposite side of the square. The Lilies Café sat a few doors down, the pharmacy on its far side, the Hendrix County annex building on the corner where we stood. The annex provided extra office space for the various county departments, and a Lilyvale city annex sat behind the county building, just on the other side of the alley.

"All right, Nixy, run me through this with as much detail as you remember."

I closed my eyes to focus in a moment.

"I came out of our alley, down Stanton, took the right to circle around the courthouse." I said, pointing at the route. One couldn't drive straight through on Stanton Drive, not from the direction of the store. "The sky was getting darker and darker, and the wind was gusting some but not any more than when you helped me with the banner."

"Now concentrate on what came next."

"I turned right back onto this side of Stanton. I'd just cleared the stop sign when the truck shot out of the alley. I slammed hard on the brakes. Hard enough to throw Doralee and I against our seatbelts. The animals fell from the backseat to the floorboard."

He asked me to describe the truck again, and I did, sketchy as it was. We continued walking until we reached the stop sign at the next corner.

"The truck blew through this sign and turned left. I was shaking all over from the near T-bone. By the time I drove this half a block, the truck was gone."

We turned right and approached the back entrance of the parking lot. The sidewalk was cracked here and there, weeds growing in the gaps.

"Here I was maybe halfway into the right turn when the Audi's lights flashed in my windshield."

"How did you know the make of the car?"

"The rings on the front. My headlights picked out a blonde driving and a male passenger, but didn't know who they were then. The driver jerked the wheel, missed hitting me, and bumped over the curb as she took off to the right."

"What then?"

"I made sure there weren't any other cars speeding my way," I quipped as we walked into the lot, "and then, I eased up to park next to Ernie's Honda."

"How did you know that was his car?"

"Doralee said it was. It was parked right here where we're standing."

"Is that all?"

"I made sure Amber and T.C. weren't injured, cracked the windows for the animals, and went inside with Doralee."

"Excellent. Okay, you told me when I first questioned you, but remind me what time all this happened."

I sighed. "All I can say with any degree of certainty is that it was right around five thirty. Give or take ten minutes."

"Did you see anyone in the parking lot, or on the streets back here?"

I closed my eyes again and thought back. "No one on foot, and I don't remember any other cars passing before we went inside."

"Good. Now think about when you circled around the

square. Did you notice anything the least bit out of the ordinary? Anything at all? Even a movement from the corner of your eye."

Instinct told me Eric wanted to know if I'd seen any sign of Ernie. I pictured the turn, then passing the gazebo, and driving the short block before swinging into the left turn to double back. I shook my head.

"There were a few pieces of litter blowing in the street, but I've got nothing beyond that."

He shrugged. "If you'd seen anyone, or so much as thought you had, you'd have told me right away. I know that. I trust you."

"So what now? I mean, can you tell me if my account jibes with the others you have?"

"Other than coming from different viewpoints, yes. Although I had a heck of a time getting Mrs. Vail to even admit to being in the parking lot."

"Yeah, she ducked me about the near head-on crash." I strolled at his side, then asked the burning question.

"So are you any closer to an arrest?"

"Close only counts in horseshoes."

"What happened to trusting me?"

"I didn't exactly follow protocol last night when I let you observe, but there's still only so much I can say."

"Point taken. I'll be at the emporium if you need anything else."

I DIDN'T FLOUNCE AWAY. THAT WOULD'VE BEEN childish. However, having Eric share so much with me, seek my input, then shut me down was annoying.

Then again, with any luck whatsoever, I'd never be in a position like this again. Be remotely involved in a crime, that is. Eric and I might have a chance to see if our attraction could grow into something more if our every waking minute wasn't consumed with a case.

I slipped more or less quietly in the emporium's front
door. Jasmine had remembered to take down the chimes, so
our presenter didn't miss a beat.

I eased over behind the counter to stand with the teens
and watch Fran Givens. She was in her early sixties with
hair in a page boy cut that looked more platinum than gray.
As in 1950s bombshell platinum blonde, and she was a ball
of energy in a frame as small as Sherry's five-foot-nothing.
She held a weathered piece of wood, about 8 x 10 inches,
and had an array of fabric scraps, buttons, metal washers,
and a large bottle of glue on the demonstration table.

"Remember, much as you want your weathered scrap
wood to look old, you need to smooth the edges to avoid
getting splinters. Wear your mask whether you're sanding
by hand or using a power tool."

She went on to explain that she didn't generally follow a
pattern.

"I have an image in my head, and I dry-place pieces until
I have the overall effect I want. Naturally, I lay the wood
flat. I've been called a witch, but I sure 'nough can't levitate.
If I could . . ." She glanced pointedly at her chest. "Let's just
say I'd use that power to unsag certain body parts."

The audience burst into laughter, even the women in their
forties who I presumed didn't have that particular aging
problem yet.

Fran went on to glue bits and pieces to the wood until
she'd created what I called a mixed-media wall hanging.
The design was a highly stylized lily. Had our artists decided
together to make lily-themed items, or was it happenstance?
Whatever the case, the result was amazing. Another item
donated to our big round of drawings this afternoon.

After Fran answered questions for nearly twenty minutes,
Sherry gently eased her out. We hustled to fold the chairs
and one demo table, move everything to the workroom, and
get them securely stacked against a wall. Jasmine and I did
lift-and-carry duty while Sherry and Aster, Eleanor, and

Maise took turns dressing the remaining long table with a tablecloth, napkins, and such, and waiting on shoppers who trickled in. Since some were waiting for the reception to start, we held off putting out the food and drinks until right at four.

And then the fun started.

"LOUELLA HEINZ," SHERRY CALLED OUT. "LOUELLA, are you here?"

A slender woman with brunette curls waved her hand and bounced forward to claim her prize. And with that, we gave away the last of the items donated for the drawing.

A few good-natured groans met that announcement, but instead of that being a signal to leave, the crowd lingered. Which was fine since the majority of them were purchasing everything from Lexie Gibson's jewelry, to Sherry's baskets, to Aster's Aromatics products. The small animal statues and some napkin rings Eleanor had whittled were snapped up, and so were the gourds Doralee had placed with us. The work of a dozen more of our artists sold in those three hours. Many who'd agreed to sell with us on consignment were in attendance, and I hoped they were pleased to see their work appreciated. I also hoped they'd be pleased when I sent their checks at the first of the month.

Which wasn't far away.

We'd had an amazing turnout for the reception. In addition to Carter and Kay Gaskin, Grant and Judy Armistead, and Miss Anna, the pharmacist whose last name I'd yet to learn, most of the business owners on the square stopped by. Big George Heath of the hardware store, and the barber, Bog Turner, shot the bull with Fred and Dab, although Duke Richards didn't come. He owned the Dairy Queen, though, and likely couldn't get away.

The Silver Six had enfolded me in their family in April, and I'd been taken into their fold of friends, too. Pauletta

Williamson, who wore squash blossom necklaces, was there along with Marie Dunn. John and Jane Lambert lived near Aunt Sherry and always wore clothes in matching colors. Tonight they were in leaf green. Lorna Tyler came by, and defense attorney Dinah Souse. I'd retained her to defend Sherry in the spring. Luckily, we hadn't needed her services for long.

One surprise was seeing Patricia Ledbetter and Mac Donel together. He was the county tax assessor, and she worked in city hall, but I hadn't heard they were dating. Patricia had her son, Davy, with her. The child was chronically ill, but he seemed healthy and happy enough tonight. Especially cramming a cookie in his mouth.

"Hello, Nixy."

I whirled to find our Hendrix County Library Director standing behind me. Debbie Nicole Samp was a very pretty blonde a few years older than me. Her hair was cut in a breezy style, and she was always wearing low-heeled pumps, denim or light cotton skirts, and scoop neck blouses when I saw her. Which actually wasn't often. Not face to face anyway. We'd had a rough start to our acquaintanceship, and that was putting it nicely.

"Uh, hi, Debbie Nicole," I stammered, shocked that she was here, much less that she'd spoken to me. "How are you?"

"I'm good." Pause. "I haven't seen you since you came in to get your library card."

"Oh, yes. Well, we've been swamped sprucing up the building and getting the emporium ready to open."

She glanced around the store. "It looks wonderful."

"Thank you. Have you had something to eat yet? If you've never had Ida Bollings's pear bread, I recommend it."

"Thanks, I'll look for it." Another pause. "Good to see you, Nixy. Don't be a stranger at the library."

Don't be a stranger? I stared after her as she mingled with our other guests. She'd seemed sincere. Awkward, but sincere. Sherry and the ladies harped about me making friends my age. Maybe Debbie Nicole and I could manage that.

WHEN EVERYONE HAD LEFT EXCEPT DORALEE AND Zach, we sent Jasmine off to get ready for her Friday night date, assuring her we could handle the cleaning up and putting away. While Fred took Amber and T.C. for a walk, the rest of us set the store to rights. In short order, we were finished and ready to open the next day. We'd even swept the floor and run a mop over it to get up any sticky residue. We didn't have food to pack up because the refreshment table had been decimated. Ida's pear bread was one of the first treats to disappear, which made me wish I'd held a few slices back for myself. The stuff was really divine.

We turned off all but the security lights in the store, and retreated to the workroom to perch on the stools we'd used for Doralee's class. T.C. had leaped onto a worktable and was trolling for attention. I bent to scratch Amber's ears, and my hip bumped into the easel. Our flip chart went flying, the pages turning so our notes were exposed.

"What's this?" Doralee asked as she bent to pick up the chart. She eyed it a moment, then turned to us. "Is this part of what you were doing to help clear me?"

"It is," Aster said proudly. "It's our murder board." She said it such relish, I was beginning to worry about her.

"As you can see," Sherry pointed out, "we wrote questions about events and suspects."

"And filled in what we learned," Maise added.

"You don't have me or Zach on here. Did you never suspect us?"

"I do believe Nixy had you on her personal list for a while, but the rest of us believed you were innocent from the start."

"Nixy?" Doralee turned her hazel eyes on me. "You thought I could be involved?"

"Only for a few days. It's nothing personal. Aunt Sherry was a suspect in the murder here in April. So was I."

"We all were," Maise said.

"You never made it to a written-down list, woman, so what are you squawkin' about?"

Zach chuckled and Doralee smiled. "You're right, Fred. So who else is on here?"

I set the chart back on the easel, then hauled Amber into my lap. She was really too big to hold, but she licked my chin, then tucked her head into my neck. I didn't have the heart to put her down.

Doralee stood by the chart, touching a note on the paper with her finger now and then. Then she shook her head. "I can't make heads or tails of this. Who do you think killed Kim?"

I glanced at the Silver Six. Each of them stared back with the unspoken message for me to take the lead.

"I don't know, Doralee. I've thought it was her brother, Caleb, because he owns a truck like the one that almost hit us Sunday when I took you back to the inn."

"And Ernie is a suspect," she said, "because he was angry with Kim and he didn't go straight back to the inn. Or didn't go inside. I remember him saying he was walking around town."

"Yes, but with that storm coming, it seems odd that he stay out in the weather."

She shook her head. "Not really. Remember I told you about Ernie's fiancée dying in a car accident? Well, that was during a storm. Most people would despise storms after that kind of event. Not Ernie. He had a compulsion to be outside in them. I told him the odds would catch up and he'd be struck by lightning someday."

"Huh. Is that something he'd tell Detective Shoar?"

"The storm thing? Probably not. Ernie is a pretty private guy." She ran a hand through her short gold-brown hair. "He's a lot of things, but I can't see him as a killer. I certainly never felt threatened by him, and we had some intense arguments now and then."

She looked at the flip chart, but I could tell she wasn't seeing it. Then her eyes focused and she leaned forward.

"Wait a minute. What about Margot Vail? Was she driving the car that sped out of the parking lot that night?"

"That was her. She even talked to Kim on Saturday."

"Margot willingly spoke to Kim? Why?"

I explained about the heirloom wedding ring. "But if Margot killed Kim, I think she would've searched for the diamond and taken it."

"I don't know. She has people who do everything but chew her food for her."

"And yet, she's here with only her dud of a nephew for company."

"Granted, that is a puzzle. Have you eliminated Georgine?"

I shrugged. "Pretty much. If she was wacked out on migraine drugs, I don't see how she could've done it. Besides, your smock was found out in the country, and she can't drive."

"She can drive," Doralee corrected. "She just doesn't. I'm sure you're right about the migraine pills. I hope she doesn't medicate herself into a coma before this is all over, but that's Ernie's problem, not mine."

"You didn't go see her?"

"I decided to let it be." She looked at her watch, then at Zach. "Honey, are you ready to go? I expect our hosts can use their rest. They've certainly earned it."

She plucked her bag off the worktable. "I just want to thank you all again for being willing to help me. Even if Nixy did have me on the suspect list."

I SHOWERED AND CRAWLED INTO BED, COMPLETELY exhausted.

After five minutes with my eyes closed and my mind racing, I realized I was both tired and wired. I kept thinking I should've asked Doralee something, but what?

When we'd talked about Margot and her precious heirloom, images of the crime scene had flashed on my mental screen. I kept seeing Kim's position on the floor. On her left side, left arm outstretched, her hand limp. The fabulous ring that hadn't looked at all flashy in the end. I thought back. The ring could have been twisted so the diamond wasn't visible. The thing looked so top-heavy, it could've slipped all the way around to her palm, and all I'd really seen was the band, not the stones. I'd had a chunky ring that constantly turned on my finger until I broke down and had it sized.

But Eric confirmed two diamond rings were listed on the inventory. The one Kim had worn, and presumably the Thomason heirloom.

I sighed in the dark, and my pup and cat snuggled closer. Whatever the motive for killing Kim, I had to let go of the rings angle.

Chapter Nineteen

SATURDAY MORNING, I OPENED MY EYES FEELING more refreshed than I'd expected. Especially since I'd dragged the flip chart upstairs, propped it on the couch, and reexamined our old notes. Then I made new notes for another two hours.

Conclusions?

In spite of what Doralee said about Ernie's thing for storms, he was suspect number one on my new list. He could've swiped Doralee's awl—the probable weapon—and he'd have his awl, too. Motive? Kim was driving him nuts with her demand to get the opal, and he struck out in a fit of anger. Last, he had transportation to get the smock out of town.

Caleb Collier came in second place on my hit parade. He'd attended both demonstrations, so he could've taken the awl. Heck, he could have a similar tool in his truck along with his gun. He admitted to having been in the room with Kim. Transportation? Check. Motivation? Could be an inheritance, could be he got angry with his sister. I didn't see the latter as realistic, but with a murder, you never know.

And didn't I sound like an expert? Eric would laugh hard enough to cause internal damage if he heard me say that.

My third slot pegged Margot Vail and/or her nephew Dennis Thomason for the crime. They'd attended Doralee's program, and just because I'd not seen them move from the front doorway didn't mean they hadn't. I still had trouble seeing Margot as an up-close and personal killer, but her motivation was certainly strong. Get the heirloom ring for Dennis and his fiancée, get the family mansion back, and get other bits and pieces of her brother's estate back, too. Motive, means, and transportation.

Georgine was an also-ran compared to the others. However, she had the same access to an awl as Ernie did. She didn't like Kim, but seemed to have accepted her as Ernie's choice. What she didn't have was transportation. And very probably she'd have been too ill and doped up on migraine meds to do much more than go to the bathroom. Of course, she was protective of Ernie. If she thought there was a real chance he'd be arrested, I'd lay odds she'd confess herself.

All in all, not a bad list, but I had no idea who had really done the deed. It would help to know if Eric had heard back from the attorney, but he wasn't likely to tell me if I asked.

With a sigh, I stretched my arms over my head, pushing against the headboard. First T.C. then Amber crawled from beneath the covers, the dog nosing my cheek, the cat greeting me with a loud *mreow* and a stretch that dug her little claws into my sleep shirt.

"All right, okay, I'm up. Breakfast and a walk, girls?"

Since they both leaped from the bed, I took that as a big ole yes.

THE REST OF THE MORNING WAS UNEVENTFUL COMpared to the week—and night—before. We'd given Jasmine the day off, and since business was at a crawl, we tackled some major chores. Even Fred joined us as we took an informal inventory to decide what needed replenishing. Aster's, Sherry's, and Eleanor's stock had nearly sold out, and the same was true of several other artists. In fact, the two small metal art pieces Dab and Fred had made were gone. I put their names on my "call" list so I could remind them later, and I phoned the other crafters on the list to bring more work. A fantastic problem to have.

The activity helped take my mind off the murder, and the Silver Six didn't seem to care about the outcome, other than on an intellectual level. Doralee was in the clear, and that's why we'd been involved in the first place. They hadn't commented that the flip chart was gone, which reminded me I needed to return the easel to Gaskin's next door.

Since all was under control in the store, I went to the workroom, folded the easel legs, and then jumped out of my skin when Fred spoke.

"Returnin' that, I see. Good deal. I need to work, and just seein' that thing reminds me of Maise talkin' about the murder. Medical facts. Ugh."

I chuckled. "She did want to get into the details, didn't she?"

"Sometimes that woman is downright mean."

"But you love her anyway."

He snorted. "Go on with you. And if you have a hankerin' to stop by the bakery, get me a maple donut."

"Maple?"

"You heard me, missy, and sneak it in through the back here."

"You won't feed it to the critters, will you?"

"Nah, they don't cotton to maple. They like plain glazed."

Amber woofed, T.C. *mreowed*, and I rolled my eyes.

I WAS HEADED THE LONG WAY AROUND TO THE ALLEY and the back of the emporium when I saw Eric crossing the street. He waved, and I waited at the corner. He carried a suppressed air of excitement in his step and his eyes.

"You look rested. Did you hear from the attorney? Or the state lab?"

"No, but I'm ready to make an arrest."

I stared. "Today?"

"Justice doesn't take the weekends off."

"Is that needlepointed on a pillow at the station?"

"It's a good thing I like sarcasm in a woman. So what are you doing tonight? I have the okay from Dottie and Donnie to bring the fur buds to the dog park."

In spite of the donut bag in my hand, I planted both fists on my hips. "That is the worst change of subject ever. Who are you arresting?"

"I can't say."

I threw up my hands. "Fine, but if it's Ernie, you need to know something first."

His expression maddeningly impassive, he asked, "What do I need to know?"

"Doralee told us last night that Ernie has a thing for storms."

Eric's brow furrowed. "Is he for or against them?"

"I suppose you could say he's for," I snarked. "His first fiancée died in a car crash in a storm. This was decades ago, but Doralee said he always goes outside when storms are coming."

"You think it would be the other way around."

"Eric, the point is that it looked odd for him to be walking around when that storm was brewing. He doesn't have an alibi, and it's a big factor in your investigation. I get that. But knowing he seeks out bad weather instead of avoiding it partially explains why he didn't go to the inn and up to his room."

"Yes, it could explain why he didn't come running until he heard the sirens and saw the lights flashing behind the inn."

"And?"

"And you never answered my question about tonight. The dog park?"

I growled under my breath. "Did you happen to know you drive me insane sometimes?"

He reached out and squeezed my hand gently. "Ditto. Check your social calendar and I'll call you later."

I DELIVERED FRED'S DONUT, THEN WENT OUTSIDE to phone Doralee. I'd rehearsed what I wanted to say so I wouldn't slip up and breach trust with Eric. Although technically, he hadn't confirmed he'd be arresting Ernie. He'd only said he was ready to arrest someone. *Argh!* My head hurt.

She picked up on the third ring and we made small talk for a minute.

"I have a question for you. I know Georgine is protective of Ernie. I saw that for myself."

"Yes, and?"

"Do you think she'd confess to killing Kim if she thought he was going to be arrested?"

"Do you know something, Nixy?"

"No, but I was playing with notes when I couldn't sleep last night. I got to wondering about this."

"Okay, my answer is yes. Georgine would throw herself in front of a bus to protect Ernie."

"Would he do the same for her?"

"I—"

She broke off. "Doralee, are you still there?"

"I'm here, I'm just considering your question. And yes, I think he would. For much of their lives, they've only had each other."

"Okay, thanks."

"Wait. Are you sure you don't know something new about the case?"

"Not a thing," I responded with a perfectly clear conscience.

Because I didn't know anything new. I only suspected.

* * *

"NIXY, MOVE MY CAR TO THE FRONT OF THE STORE, will you?"

"Sure, but why?"

"I feel terrible about this, but we forgot to bring in the throw pillows we keep outside on the display benches before the reception. Someone spilled tea on them."

"All of them?"

"I don't know about that, but I'm running the whole lot of them to Tommy Lee to be cleaned. Hopefully he can get all the stains out. I don't know what I'll tell the crafters who made those if he can't get them pristine again."

"Worse case, I'll buy them for my apartment," I said, though I had faith that Lang's Cleaners and Tailor could do the job.

Sherry blinked. "But you have throw pillows."

"I can always use more, especially with my new pets. You know, Sherry, I can bundle those up and walk them over. You don't need to drive."

"But I'm going over to the technical school afterward. I'm recruiting students to help with the folk art festival."

"That's months away."

"Time sneaks up on you. And by the way, you need to get that official letter about having the festival in town."

"I'll put it on my list for Monday. Do you have your keys?"

Eleanor reached behind the counter. "Take my set."

I grabbed three large plastic garbage bags, the kind used for yard debris, and moved the Corolla. I only saw small stains on a few pillows, but I tossed them all into the bags. No point in Aunt Sherry making more trips than necessary, and each bag was light enough to be manageable. Of course, Sherry and all the Silver Six were much stronger than they might appear.

I couldn't help but peer across the square at the Lilies

now and then. I was convinced Eric meant to arrest Ernie, and most likely he'd do it at the café. But when? Did he need a warrant? Not that he couldn't get one, even on a Saturday, but maybe he already had one. Bottom line, he could act at any time, and there was still something nagging me that could be important.

ASTER PUT ME IN CHARGE OF REARRANGING THE display benches outside. Three of Sherry's four shallow round baskets held painted wooden balls and blocks of various sizes, a nature photographer's small prints, and old-fashioned clothes pins painted to look like Uncle Sam. We needed to push those. The Fourth of July was a week away. The fourth basket I filled with Aster's lotions and balms. The containers were sealed tight, but maybe some scent would escape and entice people to stop and shop.

Yes, the grand opening had been a success beyond my hopes, but we needed to do a steady business to stay in the black.

I tweaked the group of gourds from another artist, one in northern Arkansas. Her gourds weren't as elaborate as Doralee's, but were beautifully painted, most of them in solid colors.

I gave one gourd a final tweak, and glanced at the café again. No activity other than a few lunch patrons coming and going.

When would Eric make his move?

I TRIED TO HELP MAISE WITH THE BOOKS, I REALLY did. I was too distracted. I kept wandering to the bump-out display window that directly faced the square. I had to pull myself out of this funk.

A customer pushed open the door and set the wind chimes to tingling. She looked up at them, then at me.

"Do you happen to carry a wind chime key chain?"

I smiled at the curly-haired young woman. "We might have one," I said, trying to remember. Had I seen one with the whittled and carved pieces? "Let's look over here."

I guided her to the shelves of animal carvings, both stylized and intricate.

"If you don't mind me saying so, the chimes could get annoying after a while when you're driving."

"Oh, it's not for my keys. It's for my baby carriage. Brittany loves the sound, but regular wind chimes are too large. Even the small ones at the drugstore."

I poked around for a moment and heard a slight bing. I held up a wood chime in a horizontal diamond shape, reminiscent of the diamond in the Arkansas state flag. Four narrow tubes that hung from it rang in a higher pitched than I liked, but my customer was delighted.

"This is perfect. And what is that? A razorback?"

She pointed to the same shelf, and I handed her a carving of lovely detail for a rather unlovely animal.

"I'll take it. My husband will love it!"

"Do you live here?" I said, making casual conversation as I rang up the sale.

"We live in Magnolia. I came over to see some friends, and they told me about your shop, but my husband will be here shortly." She rolled her eyes. "I'm such a ninny sometimes. I dropped my car keys down a drainage grate."

"Is he bringing another set of keys?"

"Oh, he'll bring them, but he has a telescoping stick with a magnet and light on the end. That's the drawback about these car fobs. They can be so expensive to replace, if you can replace them at all. I'll take the baby back home, and he'll fish the keys out if it takes all day." She grinned. "Good thing it's not football season, or I'd never hear the end of this. But the razorback will go a long way to make him happy."

She waved and went outside to wander the square and wait for her husband, and I sat at the stool behind the checkout counter and began aimlessly drawing on the pad we kept there.

My Camry, inherited from my mother, wasn't but a few years old. I still had both fobs, but I needed to dig out the second one. It had to be in one of the yet-to-be-unpacked boxes upstairs. Another reason not to simply take the boxes to a resale shop.

I realized I was sketching a key. Or what looked vaguely like a key. In spite of having a major in fine art, I couldn't draw worth spit. So said one of my teachers. I'd stuck out the program with instructors who helped me reach my goal instead of hindering me. And I found when I didn't have to produce anything recognizable, doodling relaxed me.

I stared at the doodle. Keys. Married couples had keys to each other's cars. The Silver Six had keys to one another's rides. It might be a little odd for a sister to have keys to her brother's car, but not impossible.

What if Georgine had keys to Ernie's car? He'd been parked in the lot behind the inn by around four o'clock, then went walking. If Georgine had roused from her migraine stupor and killed Kim, she'd had the means to dispose of the smock out of town. Maybe this whole migraine thing was a reaction to the stress of killing Kim, or an act to cover up what she'd done. How to prove it, though, unless Eric searched her belongings?

Wouldn't he have already done that? Of course he would, but perhaps not as thoroughly as normal. Georgine was medicated to the gills the day of the murder, and had been ill with migraines since.

The emporium's land line rang, jarring me so much I nearly knocked the cordless unit off the counter. I gathered my wits and answered.

"Handcraft Emporium, how may I help you?"

"Nixy, it's Lorna. Eric came in a few minutes ago to get a code for the back door. His truck and a police cruiser are in the parking lot. I'm not positive, mind you, but it seems to me he's about the arrest someone."

"Do you know who?"

"Nope. Gotta go. I'm going up the inside stairs to see if I can listen at the door."

Chapter Twenty

I SAT STARING BLINDLY AT THE PHONE IN MY HAND. Georgine might have a key to Ernie's car. She might confess everything to save Ernie, but she might not.

I had an idea that just might trick the truth from her.

Or else I was losing my mind.

But my instincts were screaming I was right.

"Aster, Maise, Eleanor," I hollered. "I have to go. Can you cover the shop?"

"Of course," Maise said, "but where's the fire?"

"I'll tell you later," I said, already half out the door.

Good thing I'd worn tennis shoes today. I needed them as I sprinted across the square, around the corner, and into the inn's parking lot.

I took in the scene in one sweeping glance.

Eric had Ernie in handcuffs and grasped by his arm. Office Bryant stood by a patrol car, the back door open.

Caleb Collier stood in the alley, arms at his side, hands balled up in fists. He wore an expression of disbelief and anger on his clean-shaven face.

And Georgine looked like death, not even warmed over. In cotton pajamas, the top buttoned to her chin, she trailed right behind as Eric escorted her brother toward the cruiser.

I didn't understand everything she said through her weeping and waling, but I heard her sob that Ernie didn't kill Kim.

"I did it, I tell you," she sobbed, reaching to grab Eric's arm. He shook her off, but stopped.

"Miss Boudreaux, you need to step away. Right now."

"But I can't let you take him," she blubbered. "He's innocent. I'm the one you want."

"You want to protect your brother, and I understand that, but I don't believe you."

"But it's true," she said, crying harder. "It's true."

Eric spotted me, and tipped his head toward Georgine. I took the hint, and hurried forward, ready to tell him she was telling the truth. But he needed proof right now unless he wanted to arrest Ernie for murder and her for interfering.

"Come on, now, Georgine," I said as I put my arm around her shoulders. "You're just making this worse."

She shook me off, jerking away so sharply that several buttons at her bust line slipped open. Not enough to be indecent, but enough for me to see the last thing I'd expected.

Kim's engagement ring hung on a chain around her neck. The big flashy ring on the same chain I'd noticed on Georgine days ago when they'd all been in Doralee's gourd class.

I didn't react, didn't let on that I'd seen a thing. She fisted the gapping sides of the top in one hand and glared.

I put my arm around her again, and this time I held on. "It will all come out right," I said.

"It won't. It can't."

"You'll see. Detective Shoar," I called, propelling Georgine forward a few steps closer.

He turned. "I'm busy, Nixy."

"I know, but will you let Ernie give his car keys to Georgine so she won't be stranded?" Hint hint.

"That's okay," Ernie said absently. "She has her own set."

Eric got it right away. "What did you say?"

"I said my sister has keys. She doesn't need—" He broke off, a look of horror stealing over his face.

I stepped away from Georgine. "That's how she disposed of the smock. She took your car and drove to the country."

"No, no," Ernie protested, twisting around to look at me. "She had a migraine. She gets her worst migraines in stormy weather. She took her medicine before Kim and I left for that party."

"But you didn't take a full dose, did you, Georgine?" That came out of nowhere, but I went with it. "I don't know how you ended up killing Kim, but you did. And then you waited and hoped that Ernie would come back to the inn and park his car."

"You stop that," Ernie yelled, lunging forward. Eric and Officer Bryant easily restrained him.

I raised a brow, silently asking Eric if he wanted to take over, or if I should go on. He gave me a subtle nod of assent and encouragement.

"Your window looks over the lot. Did you see Ernie park and walk away?"

She shook her head, pulled at her short hair. "The car was there. I knew Ernie would walk in the storm. I don't like them, but he does."

"You knew he was likely to be gone awhile. An hour or more. He probably wouldn't ever know the car was gone."

Georgine gripped the sides of her head, and fell to her knees.

I considered the good black Capris I was wearing for all of two seconds, before I knelt beside her.

"What happened, Georgine?"

"I didn't mean to kill her." She looked up at Ernie, pleading. "You have to believe me. It was an accident."

"What happened?" I asked again, noticing that Officer Bryant now held Ernie's shoulder as he slumped forward as if he'd taken a body blow. Eric unobtrusively moved closer as if he didn't want to spook Georgine or stop the flow of her confession.

"I woke up to Kim screaming and cursing. I didn't know what time it was, everything was so foggy in my head, and I was afraid she was attacking Ernie." She gulped, gasped for breath. "I—I'd stolen Doralee's awl, and I thought I needed a weapon, so I took it with me. I was just going to defend Ernie, I swear."

"But Ernie wasn't there in Doralee's room, was he?"

"No, it was Kim alone, raving and wrecking the room. When she saw me, she screamed ugly names at me, and pushed me down. I got up and started to leave, but she came at me again."

"And that's when you stabbed her."

"Yes," she said hoarsely. "I was afraid and not thinking straight, and I stabbed her in the stomach. There was blood. Not too much but I had some on my hands. I grabbed the first thing close by. It was Doralee's smock. The one she wore in her class."

"You wiped your hands on the smock. Anything else?"

"The awl handle."

"Was Kim still alive then?"

"Yes. She sank down on the floor, but she was shocked that I'd fought back. She begged me to get help, and I was going to. I truly was."

"Why didn't you call 911?"

"I knew Kim would hate me even more. She'd have me thrown in jail, and she'd turn Ernie against me. He's all I have. All I've had for a long time. I couldn't let her hurt us."

"What did you do next?"

"I put the smock in a plastic shopping bag from the drugstore, and hid in my room until I saw Ernie park the car and walk off toward the south end of town."

"And you got out your set of keys, raced down to the car, and drove."

She nodded. "I went up and down side roads until I saw

a big garbage can. It was at the side of the house, but there were no cars in the driveways and no lights on. There should have been lights on. The storm was coming."

"So you dropped your bag in the trash and came back. Your migraine must've been excruciating by then."

"It was. I took a pill and a half, changed into my night clothes, and went to bed." She looked up, first at me, then Eric, then Ernie. "I just meant to defend myself. You have to believe me."

Eric moved forward, but I held up a hand.

"Georgine, you did one more thing before you went to bed. You took the engagement ring Ernie gave Kim. You're wearing it on your chain right now."

She narrowed her eyes, her tone hard. "It was my ring. Ernie should never have had the family diamond reset. Even Doralee said so."

"Where did you get the ring you put on Kim's finger? I know she was wearing one, Georgine. I saw it."

Her expression suddenly shuttered. "My name is Miss Boudreaux. You need to get away from me now."

I did. I dragged myself upright and backed a few steps away.

Eric unlocked the cuffs from Ernie's wrists, and didn't stop him when he strode to embrace his now strangely stoic sister.

"You're better off without her," I overheard.

From the way he shook his head, Eric heard the comment, too.

We all stood in a frozen tableau. Caleb hadn't moved, but looked overwhelmed with grief and confusion. Eric and Officer Bryant gave the siblings another minute before they both pulled Georgine to her feet. Eric spoke the words that formally put her under arrest. He cuffed her, and put her in the squad car.

"You can follow us," he told Ernie. The man looked like he'd aged ten years in the last ten minutes, but he nodded and began walking in the direction of the station before Officer Bryant put his car in gear.

Eric caught Caleb's eye. "You can leave Lilyvale when you're ready, Mr. Collier. Pick up your keys at the station."

"What about Kim's body?"

"The medical examiner in Little Rock has released Ms. Thomason. I can give you information about making arrangements to claim her." He paused. "I am sorry for your loss."

"Thank you."

He turned, punched in his code, and went into the inn.

Eric strode to me, and took my hand. "How did you know and why didn't you come to me?"

"I only had inklings, Eric, and they weren't clear. I didn't put it all together until today. Then Lorna called to say you were over here ready to arrest someone, and it was too late to call."

"What made you think of the dual sets of keys?"

"Mostly the Silver Six. They have keys to one another's vehicles."

"Does Miss Boudreaux really have a diamond ring on her necklace?"

I nodded. "I saw it when her pajama top came partly undone, but I still wonder where the other ring came from. Think you can find out when you interrogate her?"

"If she doesn't immediately lawyer up, maybe." He let go of my hand. "I've got to finish this booking and write a report."

"Yeah, you do. Hope it goes well."

He'd taken three strides toward his truck when he turned to face me again. "Nixy, civilians don't usually solve crimes."

I gave him a wry smile. "Is that a thank-you?"

"It's an 'I'll talk to you later.'"

Chapter Twenty-one

I DON'T KNOW WHERE LORNA HAD BEEN LURKING to see and hear as much as she did, but she passed the news to the Silver Six that not only had Georgine been arrested for the murder in our fair town, but that I'd been to one to get the confession. Which was absolutely not true. I might've guided her to spill her story, but the woman had been so distraught, she'd only needed a little push to come clean.

I should've felt triumph, I supposed. All I felt was drained and sad. If Ernie was all Georgine had, she was all he had now, too. And she'd be in an Arkansas women's prison, if not in a psychiatric facility.

Proving once again that the Lilyvale grapevine thrives, friends began stopping by the store. Since it was only mid-afternoon, there were a lot of friends drifting in and out. Some had to get back to their businesses, others left to finish weekend errands. Dab and Maise pulled the folding chairs out of the workroom to provide some seating for the older crowd. Fred let Amber and T.C. come into the store to comfort me. Aster and Eleanor broke out the tea, coffee, and cookies.

Sherry fussed. "I can't believe we missed all this! Why didn't you tell the girls what was going on before you blew out of here? Why, child, you had no idea what kind of situation you were walking into."

"This isn't like last time, Aunt Sherry. I wasn't in danger. Not with the police right there. Everything is fine."

Amber gave a soft woof at that. T.C. purred in my lap.

Sherry shot me a doubtful look, and she alternated between being a good Southern hostess to our unexpected callers, and fluttering around me.

Meanwhile, I worked to respond cordially to all the inquiries people tossed at me, but the going was occasionally tough. I didn't want to appear to be fueling gossip, especially in case I was called to testify. True, both Eric and Officer Bryant had heard the confession, and that should be enough. I hoped it would be. I really didn't want to face Ernie or Georgine again.

At one point, Judy Armistead bounded into the store and came straight over to wrap me in a hug. Her kindness nearly undid me.

"Girl, what are you? A superhero in disguise? First you capture a suspect, then you put the real killer on the ground. Your exploits are gonna wear me thin."

"I didn't put the killer on the ground," I said, mindful of our listeners. "She sort of folded to her knees all by herself."

"But you did jump in front of that speeding truck."

Sherry gasped, and I grabbed her hand. "I did no such thing. I waved Caleb down."

"What's happening with him now?" Maise asked.

I shrugged. "He's leaving town."

"Well," Aster said, drawling the word into three syllables, "I still say it was kind of him to let Ruth know her former neighbor's pets were alive and in a new home."

I nodded my agreement. Had I ever thanked him for that? Probably not. I put that on my mental to-do list. Eric would give me his contact information now that the case was solved.

"What about Helmet-Hair and the nephew?" Judy asked.

"I suppose they've gone back to Shreveport."

"They had nothing to do with the murder?"

"Nope."

"Bummer. I liked her for crime."

"You've been watching cop shows, haven't you?"

"Of course. I'm not living them like you are. I take my thrills where I find them."

Before I could form a reply, her phone played, and I cracked up when I recognized the tune—the theme song from *Magnum, PI*. She answered, said "Okay, honey" a few times, and disconnected.

"Gotta dash. We made goodies for a birthday party, and I'm doing the delivery. Take care, you hear? And stay out of trouble. You're a new friend I'd like to keep around for a while."

AT FIVE, WE LOCKED THE DOOR. DAB HAD DRIVEN Maise and Aster home to get dinner ready. Before Fred had whisked T.C. and Amber off to the farmhouse, he'd fed them. Eleanor brought their bowls down with scoops of kibble and water for each, and I made a mental note to snag those when I came back. I planned on sleeping in tomorrow, and while I could use the exercise, I didn't want to trot down and back up the stairs as soon as I crawled out of bed.

Eleanor was on the phone back in the kitchenette. I couldn't hear her words, but from the muted rise and fall of her voice, I figured she was heading off more visitors. Bless the woman.

Sherry kept fussing.

"We called Doralee and Zach to be sure they had heard the good news," she said. "Zach phoned Eric to get the okay to leave, so they're packed and ready, but they're coming to have a bite with us first."

"They're leaving tonight?"

"Yes. They'd like to be on the road by seven o'clock, but they want to see you before they go. Please say you'll come to early dinner and spend the night, child," she finished, her voice close to pleading.

I sighed. "I'm in for dinner, Aunt Sherry, but I need to be in my own bed tonight."

"But, Nixy, I hate to think of you being alone."

"I do believe Nixy is right," Eleanor stated firmly, smoothing her hands down her stylish blouse. "She'll be more comfortable in her own space."

Sherry gave Eleanor a sour look for her dissenting opinion, but gave in. "Fine, then. If you're ready, let's go. Remember Zach and Doralee want to be home before dark."

Since it didn't take but a bit over an hour to drive from Lilyvale to Texarkana, and we were smack in the middle of daylight savings time, I didn't think darkness would be a problem. But they had to be beyond eager to get home to their own spaces. Then I recalled Doralee had animals. I'd completely forgotten her mentioning dogs, cats, and a goat. Obviously she'd recruited a friend to care for them, but she must look forward to seeing them. I suddenly realized that I'd feel pangs if I were separated from Amber and T.C. for long, and I'd only known them a week.

SHERRY DIDN'T WIN THE BATTLE OF THE BEDS, BUT she talked me into riding with her and Eleanor instead of taking my own car. "Zach and Doralee can drop you off. It's on their way out of town."

In fact, when I came back downstairs with my purse and phone, Sherry seemed to have let go of her objections to me coming back home to sleep. I didn't question the change in attitude. I was simply happy not to be the least bit on the outs with her.

I should've known something was up.

WE'D BARELY PULLED IN THE GRAVEL DRIVE WHEN Fred told me to go get the prepared plate of food on the kitchen table and take it to Old Lady Gilroy.

"She's itchin' to see you," he said.

I looked over my shoulder toward the tiny home next door. "How do you know?"

"She's been watchin' the house through them binoculars o' hers for the last twenty minutes."

Sure enough, Bernice Gilroy must've been seen me coming because she opened the door and grabbed my arm before I even knocked.

"Get on in here, and put down that plate."

"Yes, ma'am. How are you?"

"Hungry, but enough about me. I hear you took down a killer."

I gaped. "I don't know how you get your gossip, Bernice, but that's an exaggeration."

She peered up at me, head tilted. "Nevertheless, you weathered the storm. You stay out of trouble for a fair while, you hear?"

"Yes, ma'am, but I plan to stay out of this kind of trouble forever."

Bernice snorted. "That will be the day."

I grinned. "Do you need anything while I'm here?"

She eyed the plate of food, and frowned. "Are my neighbors putting me on a diet, or have they turned stingy?"

I shook my head at her outrage. "Neither, but they're having company tonight."

"Humph. Is that handsome detective coming?"

"I doubt it. He's at the station doing police work."

"Booking and grilling the killer. I watch the cop shows. I'm partial to that Mark Harmon. Have I mentioned that?"

"You mentioned *NCIS*."

"Well, that's his program. You bring your detective by sometime, and I'll see how he stacks up to Mark. You can leave now."

Bemused by the visit as usual, I searched my memory of the folks who'd come by the store this afternoon. Mrs. Gilroy had to have a spy who reported Lilyvale news to her, but who? Not a soul came to mind. The question was as puzzling as everything else about the ancient little woman. Someday I'd solve the conundrum.

THE SILVER SIX, ZACH AND DORALEE, AND I GATHered around Sherry's farm table. We were seated close enough to bump elbows some, but no one complained. The atmosphere was festive, and we feasted on a cold collation of sliced and diced fruits, veggies, cold cuts, cheese, and the chicken salad that I adored. I had to learn to make this someday. This, and Maise's fried okra of the gods.

T.C. and Amber weren't under the table trolling for food. Too many feet to dodge. Instead, they'd curled up together under the sideboard. I was sure they'd do their Hoover imitations later.

The conversation centered on Doralee and Zach's plans for the coming week—catching up on work for Zach, and chores and gourds for Doralee. Happy as I was not to have the case at the center of the conversation, it struck me as odd that no one mentioned it at all.

Then I knew why.

The doorbell pealed, and I jumped up to answer it since I was seated closest. Eric stood there, looking fine. He'd changed clothes. Or at least his shirt. Hadn't it been green earlier?

"It's customary to ask people inside," he drawled in that wonderfully low, sexy voice of his.

"Oh, sure. Come on in."

"Bring him in here," Sherry called through the double doorway between the dining room and foyer. "He must be starved."

I cringed. "This may be an official visit, Aunt Sherry."

"Let's call it semiofficial," Eric said. "I *am* starved."

Aster got another set of flatware, a plate, and a glass from the kitchen, and Dab carried in a wicker bar stool. He placed it by my chair at the table, but since I'd finished eating, I gave Eric my seat and took the stool. Everyone passed the platters and bowls closest to them down the table, and Eric took a sample of everything.

"I'm so happy you were able to get away from the station," Sherry said.

"Yes, and I'm glad you caught the killer so we can go home," Doralee added.

"If Nixy hadn't had an inkling that Miss Boudreaux might have a set of keys to her brother's Honda, I'd have the wrong person in jail. That smock disposal was a sticking point for me."

"How did you come up with the two sets of keys?" Aster asked me.

"It hit me that you all have keys to each other's cars. Then a woman in the store today said she'd dropped her key in a storm drain. Her husband was on the way to bring his extra set." I shrugged. "I figured since brother and sister lived together, they might both have a set. And then it all clicked."

Maise smiled. "Good going, Nixy."

"So did Georgine call for a lawyer right away?" Zach asked. "Did Ernie step in to do it?"

"She has an attorney now, but I was able to talk with her first. She wasn't as forthcoming at the station as she was earlier, but she cleared up a few things."

"Like what?" Dab asked.

"She admitted to stealing Ms. Gordon's—"

"Doralee, Detective. Now that you don't have to keep your professional distance, call me by my first name."

Eric dipped his head. "She took Doralee's awl and Eleanor's whittling knife because, and I quote, 'Ernie needed new ones.' She'd shoved both of the tools under the mattress, and put the extra set of keys there, too, when she came back from disposing the smock. If we'd done more than a cursory search of her room, we would have found the whittling tool and keys."

"That's it?" Doralee said. "She took the tools because Ernie needed new ones? She didn't intend to kill Kim?"

"We won't present the case to the deputy district attorney as premeditated murder, no."

"Well, I'm relieved she never meant to frame me, but I've never known Georgine to shoplift. Why start now?"

"Maybe the stress of Ernie remarrying," Zach offered.

"That or having her mind muddled by the migraine medications," Maise said.

Doralee nodded. "Either one is as likely an explanation as anything else. I never did think she was quite right in the head."

"Eric," I began, "what about the diamond ring?"

"Diamond?" everyone but Zach and Fred echoed.

"Are you talking about Margot's ring?" Doralee asked. "I remember you said she wanted Kim to return it."

"It's partly about Margot. I kept thinking how the ring on Kim's body looked different. Not at all the blast of bling I'd seen since I'd met her. I figured the killer might've stolen her ring."

"Miss Boudreaux did steal it. Nixy noticed she had it concealed on a chain under her clothes. Of course, we searched her room again, and we're holding all her property, including the ring."

"But, Eric, you confirmed there were two diamond rings in Kim's effects."

"There still are. Miss Boudreaux put a different ring on the body. Mr. Boudreaux has identified it as the original family ring minus the original diamond. He'd given the old ring to his sister after he married Doralee."

"She had a new stone mounted in the old gold band," Doralee breathed. "I'd forgotten about this, but I suggested she do that very thing when Ernie gave me that monstrosity. I even offered to pay for whatever kind of gem she'd want to use in the mounting. I didn't know she'd followed through on it."

"I must've seen the gold band when I expected to see the shiny platinum one. That's why the ring looked dull to me."

"That and the band had shifted on Ms. Thomason's hand," Eric said. "The diamond was caught between her ring and pinky fingers. I saw it when I had another look at the crime scene photos."

"The entire situation is sad," Sherry said.

"I'm sure Ernie will do all he can to get her as light a sentence as possible." Doralee glanced at her watch. "I hate to leave our hosts with all the dishes, but we should get going."

Aster waved off the comment. "You go. We have many hands to make light work."

Zach turned to me. "Are you staying, Nixy, or can we drop you at your place?"

"I'll take her home," Eric said.

The look he gave me set butterflies fluttering in my middle.

WAGS AND WOOFS MIGHT NOT HAVE BEEN THE MOST romantic of venues, but no one else was there, and it worked for me. Hand in hand, we headed for the same bench we sat on last time while Amber and T.C. entertained themselves. Amber began sniffing for other dogs, then played on the ramps. T.C. got sidetracked chasing a squirrel that shot up to the highest branches of a tree and chattered at her.

I peeked at Eric's expression. He really was handsome, and his depth of character shone in his eyes and his manner. I hoped his restful silence meant no lecturing.

"You did good, Nixy," he said finally.

"Thank you."

"I'm glad you weren't in danger this time."

"I second that, and I feel a 'but' coming."

"But I trust this is the last time you'll be involved in snooping."

I sighed. "I'd be happy if my sleuthing days were over, but you know I can't make that promise. Not with the Silver Six being my family."

"Now I hear a 'but.'"

"But for now I have an emporium to run, and new pets to get chipped."

"And a long overdue dinner date with me."

There were those butterflies again.

They went berserk when he kissed me.

Crafting Tips

Gourd Preparation
and Painting

From Bonnie Eastwood
Hudson, Florida
purplehatsbonnie@yahoo.com

First, establish a work area with good ventilation, and one where you can isolate gourd dust and debris. I have a studio, but a garage will do fine, or work outside.

To clean gourds, I use hot water, abrasive cleaning pads, and elbow grease. Old-fashioned copper or steel scrubbies work great, but may leave metal particles behind. The hot water is partly to soothe my arthritic hands.

While you're scrubbing your gourds, let them talk to you and listen! Not every gourd needs to sit on a surface. They can be mounted on driftwood, suspended on rope, etc., to create wall hangings.

Once it is dry, decide how your gourd needs to be cut. I favor interesting angles, but let your inner artist guide you.

Ready to cut your gourd? Gather your supplies close to

hand. *Remember to wear your mask at all times, especially during the cleaning and cutting processes!*

1. Put on your mask and drill a pilot hole. I use an electric jigsaw to complete the cut.
2. With a spoon, clean out the gourd innards. Gourds are set out after harvesting to cure. When you cleaned your gourd, you may have heard the dry seeds—called cucurbits—rattle inside, but they may be in a ball with the pulp. Whether the inside is papery with loose seeds or the seeds are in a solid ball, scoop and scrape with the spoon.
3. If you want all the fruit and seeds out, soak the gourd in water and a bit of bleach.
4. Sand the top and anywhere else you cut for a finished edge. Wear your mask!

Ready to paint? Anything goes! You can use acrylic or oil paints, stains, paper collage, or any medium that will adhere to the surface. No watercolors, though! Depending on the effect you want, be sure to let each application of paint dry before you layer with new colors and such. Wood burning is another great way to decorate gourds.

When the paint is dry, or you've finished with however you're decorating, "coiling" is a great way to finish the top of your gourd. Yes, beginners can do this! I use pine needles from my yard, but other materials work as long as they can be woven into a circle or oval. Embellish the coil with beads, metal charms, or wood cutouts—painted, stained, or plain. Lately I've been making my own clay leaves to attach to my one-of-a-kind gourds, but you can buy yours. Again, let your creativity shine!

WINEGLASS PAINTING

By Colleen Thompson

WHAT YOU WILL NEED:

*A glass of some kind. Does not necessarily have to be
  a wineglass.*
Alcohol. Rubbing or acetone works best.
Paint markers.
Paper and pencil.

First thing, make sure to clean your glass until it sparkles.
Any streaks of oils from your fingers will hamper your success when you go to paint. After your glass is well washed,
you need to rub over the surface with alcohol. This will help
to ensure no oils from your hands or anything else is left on
the glass. As a side note, the alcohol can be used to touch up
or erase paint on the glass so long as the paint hasn't dried.

Leave your glass to dry and move on to the paper and
pencil. Here you will sketch your piece of work. This paper
can then be rolled up and stuck into the glass to form a kind
of guide for you as you begin to draw. If you have a steady
hand and are skilled in the art of . . . well, art, then go for
the freehand experience.

Before you use the paint markers, which can be bought
at any art store, including Michael's, A.C. Moore, and Hobby
Lobby, there are some rules. Do not—I can't stress this
enough—do not push too hard on the glass with the marker
tip. The markers are designed to slowly release paint as you
glide across the glass. Pressing too hard will make them

bleed, rendering the glass unusable. You can dot your glass, gently and softly, but just be aware of how much pressure you place on the end. The best designs on glass come from lines and dots. These markers cannot fill in, though, like a normal marker on paper. It just won't work and it will leave your design with streaks. If you use acrylic paint and a brush, filling in is much easier, but more time consuming. Instead, use dots.

Let your work dry completely for about twenty-four hours so the paint has time to stick well to the glass. If you want, you may heat set the glass. This step is tricky because if not done right, the glass will shatter or it may even melt. You will need to line a cookie sheet with aluminum foil and turn your oven on to 350 degrees.

DO NOT PREHEAT THE OVEN.

Put the glass on the cookie sheet and into the cold oven. Allow the glass to warm while the oven is heating up because this will lessen the chance of the glass shattering. Leave the glass in the oven for thirty minutes, but turn off the heat after just twenty minutes. Leave the glass in the oven, though, for another ten or so minutes.

Be careful when washing your glass and do not place it in the dishwasher. Hand-wash only.

IDA'S PEAR BREAD

You can freeze it!

1 cup chopped walnuts, toasted
3 cups flour
2¼ teaspoons baking powder
½ teaspoon baking soda
2 teaspoons cinnamon
1 teaspoon salt

3 eggs, slightly beaten
1 large (29-ounce) can pears, drained and finely
* chopped (You may use chopped pears that come in*
* fruit cups.)*
1¾ cups sugar
¾ cup oil
¼ cup milk or pear nectar
2 teaspoons vanilla

Preheat the oven to 350 degrees.

Grease the bottom and halfway up the sides of two 8 x 4 x 2 inch loaf pans.

Toast the walnuts, and add to the flour.

In a large bowl, combine the walnuts, flour, baking powder, baking soda, cinnamon, and salt.

In a medium bowl, combine the eggs, pears, sugar, oil, milk/nectar, and vanilla.

Add the pear mixture to the flour mixture. Stir until combined.

Bake for 55 to 60 minutes. Wrap in foil and store overnight before cutting.

With thanks to the family of our late local Pear Bread Lady, Ida Buckler.

Rest in Peace, Ida.